Revenge is a powerful emotion—especially in affairs of the heart. Broken promises and shattered dreams...love's wrongs always beg to be righted! But vengeance has its price, as each couple in this exciting collection of brand new romances soon discover!

These strongly written love stories will entice and involve you, allowing you to share the passion and the poignancy of four unique, tantalising vendettas, full of dangerous desires and vengeful seductions. These gorgeous heroes and spirited heroines are guaranteed to find their own special happy endings, but will their triumphs be bittersweet? Turn the pages and find out...!

ABOUT THE AUTHORS:

Susan Napier was born on St Valentine's Day, so it's not surprising she has developed an enduring love of romantic stories. She started her writing career as a journalist in Auckland, New Zealand, trying her hand at romantic fiction only after she had married her handsome boss! Numerous books later she still lives with her most enduring hero, two future heroes—her sons!—two cats and a computer. When she's not writing she likes to read and cook, often simultaneously!

Rosalie Ash abandoned her first intended career for marriage, then spent several years as a bilingual personal assistant to the managing director of a leisure group. She now lives in Warwickshire with her husband, and daughters Kate and Abby, and her lifelong enjoyment of writing has led to her career as a novelist. Her interests include languages, travel and research for her books, reading, and visits to the Royal Shakespeare Theatre in nearby Stratford-upon-Avon. Other pleasures include swimming, yoga and country walks.

Natalie Fox was born and brought up in London and has a daughter, two sons and two grandchildren. Her husband, Ian, is a retired advertising executive, and they now live in a tiny Welsh village. Natalie is passionate about her cats, two strays brought back from Spain where she lived for five years, and equally passionate about gardening and writing romance. Natalie says she took up writing because she absolutely *hates* going out to work!

Margaret Mayo was born in the industrial heart of England and now lives with her husband in a pretty Staffordshire village. Once a secretary, she turned her hand to writing after getting an idea for a romantic short story—which turned into a full-scale novel! She enjoys setting her books against various backgrounds, both local and in exotic locations, and she likes to combine her hobby of photography with research for her novels.

Revenge

SUSAN NAPIER

ROSALIE ASH

NATALIE FOX

MARGARET MAYO

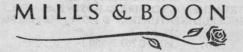

MILLS & BOON

All the characters in this book have no existence outside the imagination of the author, and have no relation whatsoever to anyone bearing the same name or names. They are not even distantly inspired by any individual known or unknown to the author, and all the incidents are pure invention.

MILLS & BOON and the Rose Device
are trademarks of the publisher.
Harlequin Mills & Boon Limited,
Eton House, 18-24 Paradise Road, Richmond, Surrey TW9 1SR
This edition published by arrangement with
Harlequin Enterprises B.V.

REVENGE © Harlequin Enterprises B.V., 1995

VENDETTA © 1995 by Susan Napier
GHOST BRIDE © 1995 by Rosalie Ash
TREACHEROUS DESIRE © 1995 by Natalie Fox
A VENGEFUL INFATUATION © 1995 by Margaret Mayo

ISBN 0 263 79250 1

Set in Times Roman 10 on 12 pt.
31-9508-108012 C1

Printed in Great Britain by
BPC Paperbacks Ltd

CONTENTS

CONTENTS

VENDETTA

BY
SUSAN NAPIER

To my father, Ted Hedge, the Intrepid Traveller

CHAPTER ONE

THE time had come.

Ten years...

For ten years he had looked forward to this moment with a savage anticipation that had blotted out all lesser ambitions. He had forced himself to watch, to wait, to plan, to carry on with the rest of his life as if revenge had not become the pivot of his existence.

Of course, outside the waiting, the plotting, he had gone through all the right motions, maintaining the fiction of Christian forgiveness...smiling, talking, moving, interacting with those around him, accepting their praise for his achievements, cultivating their admiration and envy, consolidating his wealth. But none of it had had any meaning, any reality for him.

The admiration, the envy, the wealth were necessary only as a source of power. The power to see justice done. The power to punish...

He pressed his right hand on the hard, highly polished surface of his desk, watching the faint mist of heat from his skin bloom across the cool, dark surface between his splayed fingers. A heavy gold ring engraved with an entwined briar and snake on the flat shield flashed in the firelight, the only source of light in the coldly elegant room, as he turned his hand over and stared at the bold tracery of life-lines on his palm. They mocked him with their energy. He had had such grand hopes of life until *she* had come along and casually crushed them.

9

But now the long, bitter years of waiting were over. He finally had her exactly where he wanted her... in the palm of his powerful hand. And the timing was perfect. She thought that she was safe. She thought that she had got away with it, that everyone had forgotten her crime. Soon, very soon, she would learn differently. There was no statute of limitations on murder.

He curled his fingers inward to form a brutal fist. All he had to do now was close the trap and watch her futile struggles to free herself. She would probably weep and cry innocence, or bluster and threaten, or, better still, cringe and beg for his entertainment. Then he would strip away her pride and her self-respect and stand witness to the death, one by one, of all her hopes and dreams. It was an image that he treasured in the depths of his embittered soul.

He picked up the squat crystal glass next to his hand and took a long swallow of potent, twelve-year-old Scotch. The raw, smoky bite at the back of his throat was pleasurable, but it was no match for the intoxicating taste of revenge that was flooding his senses. For the first time in a decade, he felt almost whole again.

The time had come...

CHAPTER TWO

VIVIAN took the last two steps in one grateful stride and then paused for breath, forcing herself to look back down the narrow staircase that was chipped out of the rocky face of the cliff.

In spite of the fact it was a cold and blustery day, typical of New Zealand's autumn, sweat was trickling down her torso inside her cream blouse and her palm had felt appallingly slippery on the single, stout wooden rail that had been the only barrier between her and the rock-strewn, sea-green oblivion below.

She shuddered faintly as she watched the two men far below, unloading the cargo from the hold of the squat little ferry-boat.

Reaction hit and Vivian swallowed, her dry mouth suddenly thick with moisture. Her legs felt like jelly and she swayed, fighting the urge to sink weakly to the ground.

She pressed a hand to her abdomen, trying to control the unpleasant churning feeling as she turned away and followed the sharply rising, stony path up through the low, scrubby trees. She had to get a grip on herself before she reached her destination. She smoothed down her neat dark green skirt and adjusted the matching blazer as she went, nervously switching the soft-sided leather satchel from one sweaty hand to the other as she tried to calm herself by projecting a mental aura of professionalism.

She had a reputation to uphold. She was here as a representative of Marvel-Mitchell Realties to close a vital property deal. A lot was depending on her. It wasn't just the money, but the future happiness of people that she loved that was at stake.

It hadn't helped that what she had been told was a forty-minute journey from the north-east coast of the Coromandel Peninsula to the island had actually taken over an hour and a half in very choppy seas. After a rushed three-hour drive from Auckland last evening, and an anxious, wakeful night in an uncomfortable motel bed, her close encounter with the Pacific Ocean had not been pleasant.

Since her destination was the private island of a millionaire, Vivian had naïvely expected a luxury launch or hydrofoil to be her mode of transport, not the ugly old tub that she had been directed to at Port Charles. She had also expected the island to be a lush private sanctuary, with beautiful white-sand beaches and flourishing vegetation, rather than a wind-swept, surf-lashed rock in the middle of nowhere. Although the name should have given her a clue, she thought wryly.

Nowhere. She had thought it quaint; now she realised it had been highly descriptive!

What kind of man would drag someone out all this way to conclude a business deal that would have been better, and more safely handled in a city office? Unfortunately, she thought she knew exactly: a man bent on causing trouble. A machiavellian man who would not be appeased by an easy victory. If she was to thwart any of his aims she would have to play his game first.

Vivian came through a small, wind-mutilated grove of low-growing trees and halted, her mouth falling open in shock.

Across a small ridge, perched on a flat tongue of land at the end of a rocky promontory, was a lighthouse. If she hadn't been so busy hanging miserably over the rail of the boat, wondering whether to cast up her rushed motel breakfast into the sea, she would have seen the tall white tower as they approached the island.

She lifted bleak eyes from the wide concrete base, up, up past the vertical line of four tiny windows to stare at the open balcony just below the diamond-shaped glass panes that housed the light. How many stairs to get to the top of *that*?

Her appalled gaze sank back down again and settled with overpowering relief on the low, white-painted concrete building that adjoined the towering structure. A keeper's cottage.

She got a grip on herself. No need to let your imagination run wild, Vivian. All New Zealand lighthouses were now automated. It might even have been de-commissioned. She had no business with lighthouses. It was the man in the nice, ordinary, *low* building beside it that she had come to see!

The narrow pathway across the short ridge was fenced on both sides with white pickets, offering her at least a notion of security as the wind swept up one side of the steep, rocky face and wrenched at her hair and clothes with berserk glee. She touched each picket with her free hand as she passed, counting to take her mind off what lay at either side, aware that her neat bun was unravelling more with every step.

By the time she reached the stout, weathered timber door, she was resigned to looking like a freak. A quick glance at her reflection in the curtained window beside the door confirmed the worst. Her shoulder-length hair, inclined to be wild and woolly at the best of times, was making the most of its partial freedom in the moisture-laden air, and there was no time to try and torture the tight ginger curls back into businesslike obedience. Hurriedly Vivian pulled out the few remaining pins. Now, instead of resembling a lop-sided hedgehog, she merely looked like a frightened lion.

She took a deep breath, straightened the side-seams of her skirt, and knocked loudly.

After several moments she knocked again, then again. Finally she tried the door-handle and found to her surprise that it opened easily. She tentatively edged across the threshold.

'Hello, is anybody there? Mr Rose? Mr Rose!' The door closed behind her with a weighty clunk, sounding unpleasantly like the door to a cell.

She walked warily down the short narrow hall and into a large room, sparsely furnished in everything except books—walls of them.

A long, well-used, brown leather couch was drawn up in front of a coal-blackened fireplace and there was a big roll-top desk and chair beside a window overlooking the sea. Another small port-hole window among the books showed the smooth white rise of the adjoining lighthouse tower. There were a few rugs on the polished hardwood floor and a large, smooth-sided antique chest that obviously doubled as a coffee-table, but there were no ornaments or plants, paintings or photographs. Nothing that betrayed the excessive wealth of the owner.

Nothing but the books to give the room character...and a rather daunting one at that, thought Vivian, eyeing some of the esoteric titles.

Like the adjacent lighthouse, the house was obviously designed to withstand the constant buffeting of sea-storms, the interior walls made of the same thick, roughcast cement as the outer shell. She wondered nervously whether perhaps it was also designed to endure buffetings from within. The mysterious and formerly benignly eccentric Mr Rose, with whom Marvel-Mitchell Realties had dealt quietly and successfully for years via lawyer, letter and fax, was shaping up to be a chillingly ruthless manipulator. She didn't doubt for one minute that this wait was designed to make her sweat.

Unless he had never intended to turn up at all.

Vivian shivered. She put her briefcase down by the desk and began to pace, trying to burn off her increasing tension. There were no clocks in the room and she checked her watch frequently as ten minutes ticked slowly past. The captain had said the boat would be leaving again in an hour. If Mr Rose hadn't arrived by then she would simply leave.

To pass the time, she re-applied her lipstick and brushed her hair, cursing herself for not tucking extra hairpins into her bag, when suddenly her restless thoughts were drowned out by a loud, rhythmic beating that seemed to vibrate through the walls. Vivian turned towards the window to see a sleek white helicopter descending towards a flat circle of tussock just below the cottage.

She felt her temper fizzle bracingly as the craft settled to rest and the door opened and two men got out, heads ducked low as they battled the whirlwind created by the slowing blades.

Nicholas Rose had a helicopter! Instead of her spending an eternity on a heaving boat, he could have had her *flown* out to the island in minutes! For that matter, he could probably have got to Auckland and back in the time it had taken her to cross the angry patch of water.

She watched as the first passenger, a huge, blond bear of a man in jeans and a sheepskin jacket, stood back and respectfully allowed the man in the dark blue suit to pass him.

Vivian studied the man whom she had travelled all this way to see. Even bowed over, he was tall, and he looked lean and fit, with dark hair and a face that, as he glanced up towards the house, was hard and rugged. He grinned at something that was said behind him and her heart leapt with hope as the grimness dropped away from him and he looked comfortingly sane and civilised. The other one, the beefy blond who shadowed his footsteps with a cat-like alertness, had bodyguard written all over him. They disappeared around the back of the cottage. Vivian was facing the door, her hands clasped nervously behind her, when finally, after another agonised age, it opened.

She bit off a frustrated groan when the jeans-clad figure stepped into the room. Another carefully orchestrated delay, no doubt designed to undermine further her dwindling confidence. Or was the bodyguard here to check her for concealed weapons?

Her eyes darted to his face and the breath caught with a shock in her throat. There was a black patch over his left eye, a thin scar running vertically from his hairline to the top of the concealing inverted triangle and from beneath it down over his high cheekbone to the slanting plane of his cheek. The other eye was light brown, and Vivian's gaze hastily skidded down, afraid he would think she was staring.

His mouth was thin and his face uncompromisingly square and deeply tanned, his thick, straight hair—wheat-gold at the ends and several shades darker at the roots—raked carelessly back from the scarred forehead by fingers and the wind, the shaggy ends brushing the upturned collar of his jacket. Darker gold glinted on the angles of the jutting jaw as his head shifted, revealing at least a day's growth of beard. Even with the eye-patch and the scar he was good-looking, in a reckless, lived-in, don't-give-a-damn kind of way.

Without speaking, he shouldered out of the hip-length jacket and she could see that its bulk had given her a deceptive impression of the man. He wasn't really the behemoth he had first appeared. Although his wine-red roll-necked sweater moulded a fairly impressive pair of shoulders, and was stretched to accommodate a deep chest, his body narrowed to a lean waist and hips that indicated not an ounce of unnecessary fat. His legs were very long, the muscles of his thighs thick enough to strain the faded denim. His hands, as he tossed the discarded jacket effortlessly halfway across the room to land over the back of the couch, were strong and weathered. Big, capable hands. Capable of hurting...or healing, she thought, startled at the unlikely notion that came floating up through her sluggish brain.

He leaned back against the door, snicking it closed with a shift of his weight, bending his knee to brace the sole of a scuffed leather boot on the wood behind him, crossing his arms over his chest. Vivian forced her gaze to rise again, to discover that she wasn't the only person who appeared to be shocked into a momentary trance. The single, brown eye was unblinkingly studying her, seemingly transfixed by the vivid aureole of hair surrounding her tense face.

Another man with conventional ideas about feminine beauty! She knew her own myriad imperfections well enough; she didn't need his startled stare to remind her. As if the scalding brightness of her hair wasn't enough, her green eyes had the garish brilliance of cheap glass, hardly muted by the lenses of her round spectacles, and a mass of ginger freckles almost blotted out her creamy skin.

Vivian's left hand lifted to smooth down the springy ginger mane around her shoulders, and she smiled tentatively at him, flushing when he didn't respond. A small freckled pleat appeared just above the gold wire bridge of her glasses, and she adjusted them unnecessarily on her straight nose, giving him the 'tough' look that she had practised in the motel mirror the previous night.

'Well, well, well...the Marvel-lous Miss Mitchell, I presume?'

His voice was like silk drawn over rough gravel, sarcastically smooth with a rustling hint of hard, underlying crunch.

A voice used to giving orders. To being obeyed. No polite deference or preening arrogance here. Just utter authority.

Vivian clenched her hands behind her back as the unpalatable truth burst upon her.

She would have far preferred to deal with the civilised Suit! A Suit might be persuaded to sacrifice a small victory for an immediate, larger gain.

This man looked too unconventional, too raw-edged, too primitive ever to have heard of the words 'negotiated surrender'. He looked like a man who enjoyed a fight—and had had plenty of them.

Looking defeat in the face, Vivian knew there was no going back. She *had* to try and beat him at his own game. But no one said she had to play it solely by his rules.

CHAPTER THREE

'THE elusive Mr Rose, I presume?' Vivian echoed his mocking drawl, hoping that she sounded a lot more in control of herself than she felt.

There was a small, challenging silence. He inclined his head, still studying her with the arrested fascination of a scientist confronting a new form of life.

Vivian smoothed her hands nervously down the side-seams of her skirt, and to her horror her fingers encountered the crumpled tail of her blouse trailing from beneath the back of her unbuttoned jacket. Somehow it must have worked free on that nerve-racking climb. Trying to maintain her dignity, she continued to meet his dissecting stare coolly, while surreptitiously tucking her blouse back into the waistband of her skirt.

He noticed, of course, and a curious flicker lightened his expression before it settled back into brooding aggression.

'So...do we now blithely proceed from our mutual presumptions, or do we observe strict propriety and introduce ourselves properly?'

His murmur was rife with hidden meanings, and Vivian hesitated, wondering whether she was reading her own guilt into his words.

'Uh—well, I think we know who we are...' She closed her eyes briefly, cursing herself for her faltering of courage at the critical moment.

When she opened them again, he was metaphorically crouched in waiting.

'I think, therefore I am?' he said softly. 'Very profound, my dear, but I'm sure Descartes intended his philosophy to be applied to something more meaningful than social introductions. However, far be it from me to contradict a lady, particularly such a highly qualified one as yourself. So, we have an agreement that I'm Nicholas Rose of Nowhere and you are Miss Mitchell of Marvel-Mitchell Realties. Welcome to my world, Miss Mitchell.'

He kicked himself away from the door and walked swiftly towards her, hand outstretched. Without looking down, she was aware that he limped. She was also aware of the savage pride in the single, glittering eye which effortlessly dominated her attention. It seemed to flame with a strange inner light, until the almond-brown iris was shot with blazing spears of gold as he came to a stop in front of her, closer than was comfortable or courteous, towering over her by at least six inches as he insolently invaded her personal space.

She accepted his proffered hand with a wariness that proved wise when the strength of his grip turned out to be even greater than she had anticipated. His hand wrapped almost completely around hers, trapping it as he extended the moment of contact beyond politeness into the realm of pure intimidation.

The calluses on his palm as he eased the pressure created a friction against her softer skin which felt disturbingly familiar. It was like the faint warning buzz she had experienced when touching a faulty electrical socket. Indeed, the very air around him seemed to crackle and carry a whiff of burning. It was as if there was a huge energy source humming inside him, barely restrained by flesh and blood.

He released her slightly maimed fingers, the gold flecks in his eye glowing with a strange satisfaction as she stayed stubbornly where she was, lifting her firm chin, refusing to be daunted by his superior size and strength, or by the unsettling reciprocal hum in her own bones.

Surprisingly, he was first to disengage from the silent duel, turning away to sling himself down in the chair at the desk, stretching his long legs out in front of him. He didn't offer her a seat, just leaned back and regarded her in a way that seemed indefinably possessive. Vivian's blood tingled in her cheeks and she adjusted her spectacles again.

His thin mouth curved cruelly. 'Shall we proceed to the business in hand, then, Miss Mitchell? I take it you followed all the instructions in the fax?'

She thought of the tense drive down, the nerve-racking hours alone in the motel, the wallowing boat . . . and his helicopter. She set her teeth and nodded.

'Truly a Marvel—an obedient woman,' he punned goadingly, and Vivian's flush deepened with the effort of controlling her temper. 'And, knowing that your company's successful purchase of my land depends on your pandering to my every annoying little whim, of course you followed those instructions *to the letter*, did you not, Miss Mitchell?'

This time she wasn't going to chicken out. She squared her shoulders. 'No. That is, not exactly——'

'Not *exactly*? You do surprise me, Miss Marvel-lous.'

Nerves slipped their leash. 'Will you stop calling me that?'

'Perhaps I should call you Miss Marmalade instead. That would be a more descriptive nickname—your hair being the colour it is... That wouldn't offend you, would it? After all, what's in a name? "That which we call a rose by any other name would smell as sweet"...'

His frivolity was definitely a trap, the quotation from *Romeo and Juliet* containing a baited message that Vivian could not afford to acknowledge without betraying her tiny but infinitely precious advantage.

'As a matter of fact, there's an awful *lot* in a name,' she said, ignoring the lure. 'Mine, for example, is *Vivian* Mitchell——'

Instead of leaping to his feet in justifiable outrage, he rocked his chair on to its back legs with his booted heels, his expression one of veiled malice as he interrupted her confession. 'Vivian. Mmm, yes, you're right,' he mused, in that low, gratingly attractive voice. 'Vivian... It does have a certain aptness to your colouring, a kind of phonetic and visual rhythm to it... razor-sharp edges springing up around singing vowels. I do have your permission to call you Vivian, don't I, Miss Mitchell?'

'Yes, of course,' she bit off, his feigned innocence making her feel like a mouse between the paws of a lion. 'But you requested that *Janna* Mitchell bring you the documents and co-sign the settlement. Unfortunately my sister couldn't come, so I brought them instead. Otherwise, everything is exactly as you asked...'

'She couldn't come?' he asked mildly. 'Why not?'

Having expected a savage explosion of that banked energy, Vivian was once more disconcerted by his apparent serenity.

She moistened her lower lip nervously, unconsciously emphasising its fullness. 'She has flu.'

Janna was also sick with guilt and remorse, and the combination had made her pathetically easy to deceive. As far as her sister or anyone else knew, Vivian's prime motive for taking her place on this trip was her desperate desire to get away from everyone for a while.

'Convenient.'

She winced at the flick of the whip. Not so serene, after all.

'Not for her. Janna hates being ill.' Her younger sister was ambitious. As a newly qualified lawyer, working in Marvel-Mitchell Realties' legal department, she had a rosy future ahead of her, one that Vivian intended to protect.

'Messes up those gorgeous ice-blonde looks, I suppose,' he said, casting a sardonic look at her wild ginger mane.

Vivian froze.

'You knew,' she whispered, feeling momentarily faint. Thank God the masquerade had only been intended to get her inside the door.

'The moment I saw you.'

'But you've never met Janna—or anyone from Marvel-Mitchell,' she said hollowly. 'Until now you've always insisted on dealing through an intermediary——'

'So you decided to be honest, in spite of the fact I might be none the wiser for the deception. I'm impressed. Or was I supposed to be?' he added cynically. 'Are you always so honest, I wonder?'

'I try to be.' Her tartness reproved his cynicism.

'A neat piece of sophistry. You try but you don't necessarily always succeed, mmm?' His voice hardened. 'You can't have been so naïve as to think I wouldn't investigate the people I do business with? I'm not a fool.'

'I never thought you were.' But she had seriously underestimated his thoroughness.

'I'm sure that Marvel, too, conducted its own investigations into my integrity...?'

It was a question rather than a comment, and Vivian answered it as such.

'Other than maintaining a current credit check, Peter felt there was no need, since we've been buying and selling properties on your behalf for several years without any problems,' she replied curtly. 'In spite of never having met you, Peter considers you a trusted ally. So your personal integrity was naturally taken for granted, Mr Rose.' Her green eyes were wide and innocent as she made the final, pointed statement.

'Call me Nick, Vivian.' His reaction was equal bland innocence. 'Of course, one man's integrity is another man's poison. I don't do business with cheats and liars.'

'Very wise,' she agreed distractedly, unnerved by his mention of poison. Was that supposed to be significant?

'Are you patronising me, Miss Mitchell?' he asked silkily, planting his feet back on the floor and leaning his torso threateningly towards her.

She was jolted out of her unsettling ruminations. 'I prefer to think of it as pandering to your every annoying little whim,' she said sweetly.

There was another small, dangerous silence. He seemed to specialise in them.

He rose, unfolding himself to his full height with sinister slowness.

'Brave, aren't you?' he murmured.

The thin, menacing smile and the burning gold splinters in his eye told her it was not a compliment. 'So... Instead of the lawyer I requested, Marvel-Mitchell

Realties sends me a mere receptionist. A suspicious man might take that as an insult...'

'But then, from your investigations you must know I'm not *just* a receptionist,' Vivian defended herself. 'I'm also Peter Marvel's secretary/PA, and for the last eighteen months a full financial partner in the firm. I'm fully authorised to sign cheques and contracts on behalf of Marvel-Mitchell Realties.'

Not that she ever had. Up until now she had been quite happy to be Peter's sleeping partner—well, lightly dozing at any rate. She enjoyed her work and hadn't looked on the investment of her unexpected inheritance in Peter's firm as an excuse to throw her weight around the office, but rather as an investment in their shared future...

Brooding on that sadly faded dream, she didn't notice him moving until a large hand was suddenly in front of her face. For an awful moment she thought his repressed hostility had finally erupted, but instead of the impact of his palm against her cheek, she felt him pull off her spectacles so that his image immediately dissolved into an indistinct blur.

'Oh, please...' She snatched vaguely, but he was too quick for her.

'Salt build-up from all that sea-spray on the boat trip,' he said blandly, retreating out of her reach. She squinted to see him produce a white square from his pocket and carefully rub the lenses with it. 'They need a good clean.'

He held them up to the light and inspected them before breathing on the glass and polishing some more. 'Pretty strong lenses. You must be extremely short-sighted.'

'I am,' she admitted truculently. She could have pointed out with brutal honesty that he had a few glaring imperfections of his own, but she was too soft-hearted for her own good—everyone said so. Even Peter, who was supposed to be madly in love with her, had always been exasperated by her ability to empathise with the opposing point of view in an argument.

'You must be rather helpless without them.'

Was that a hint of gloating in his voice? She squinted harder. 'Not helpless, just short-sighted,' she said flatly.

Unexpectedly he laughed. It was a disturbingly rich sound, unflavoured by bitterness. 'How long have you worn them?'

'Since I was thirteen.'

And never had she been more grateful, for once there were spectacles firmly perched on her nose she found the boys less inclined to stare endlessly at her ever-burgeoning breasts. From a potential sex-pot she had become an egg-head, and even though her marks had been barely average she had managed to cling to the image until the other girls in her class had also started acquiring ogle-worthy figures.

'May I have them back, please?' she asked the blurry male outline, holding out her hand.

There was a pause. All he had to do was clench those strong fingers and the fragile frames would be crushed, leaving her more vulnerable than ever.

'Of course.'

Instead of handing them to her, he replaced them himself, taking his time as he set them straight across the bridge of her nose, his face jumping back into disturbingly sharp focus, a close-up study in concentration as he tucked the ear-pieces carefully into place, his rough finger-pads sliding around on the ultra-sensitive skin behind her ears for long enough to make her shiver.

'Th-thank you,' she said reluctantly, edging back.

He followed her, his fingers still cradling the sides of her skull. 'You have very speaking eyes.' God, she hoped not! She blinked to clear her gaze of all expression and shuddered again at the intensity of his inspection. What was he searching for?

'Are you cold?'

'No.' To her dismay it came out as a breathy squeak.

His hands dropped to her taut shoulders, then lightly drifted down the outsides of her arms to her tense fists.

'You must be, after being out in that draughty old boat,' he contradicted. 'Your hands are as cold as ice and you're trembling. You need some food inside you to warm you up.'

She cleared her throat. 'I assure you, I'm perfectly warm,' she said, pulling her hands away. 'And I'm not hungry.'

'Your stomach still feeling the effects of the trip?' he murmured with annoying perception, his dark brown eyebrows lifted, the one above the eye-patch made raggedly uneven by the indent of the scar. 'It's a mistake to think the ride back will be easier on an empty stomach. You'll feel much better with something inside you.'

Like you? The wayward thought popped into her head and Vivian went scarlet.

He stilled, looking curiously at her bright face and the horrified green eyes that danced away from his in guilty confusion. What in the world was the matter with her?

His eyebrows settled back down and his eyelid drooped, disguising his expression as he took her silence as assent. 'Good, then you'll join me for lunch...'

'Thank you, but the boat leaves again in——' Vivian looked at her watch '—twenty minutes, and I still have to get back down to the wharf——'

'The captain won't leave until he's checked with me first.' He effortlessly cut the ground from under her feet.

'I'm really not hungry——'

'And if I said that I hadn't eaten since lunch yesterday and was far too ravenous to concentrate on anything but feeding my appetite?'

Your appetite for what? thought Vivian as she silently weighed up her options . . . which proved to be extremely limited.

'I'd say *bon appétit*,' she sighed. Maybe he'd be easier to handle on a full stomach.

'On the principle that it's better I take bites out of food than out of you?' he guessed wolfishly, coming a little too close to her earlier, forbidden meanderings.

'Something like that,' she said primly.

'While I arrange something suitably light for you and filling for me, why don't you get those papers out so I can look them over?'

Looking them over was a long way from signing, but Vivian hastened to do as he instructed while he was gone. He had shut the door behind him, and opened it so quietly on his return that she wasn't aware of him until he loomed over her at the desk. The first she knew of him was the hot, predatory breath on the back of her neck.

'You move very quietly——' she began, in breathless protest at his consistent ability to surprise her.

'For a cripple?' he finished with biting swiftness.

'That wasn't what I was going to say!' she protested, sensing that sympathy was the last thing he would ever want from her.

'You were going to use a more diplomatic term, perhaps?' he sneered. 'Disabled? Physically challenged?'

She was suddenly blindly furious with him. How dared he think that she would be so callous, let alone so stupid, as to taunt him, no matter what the provocation!

'You move quietly for such a *big* man is what I was going to say before you rudely interrupted,' she snapped. 'And an over-sensitive one, too, I might add. *I* didn't leap down *your* throat when you drew attention to the fact I was blind as a bat, did I? And I have two supposedly undamaged legs and yet I never seem to be able to co-ordinate them properly. I dreamed of being a ballerina when I was a girl...' She trailed off wistfully, suddenly remembering who it was she was confiding in.

'A ballerina?' He looked at her incredulously, his sceptical eye running over her five-feet-ten frame and the generous curves that rumpled the professional smoothness of her suit.

'It was just a childish thing,' she said dismissively, inexplicably hurt by his barely concealed amusement.

He tilted his head. 'So you dreamed of becoming a perfect secretary instead?'

'I wasn't qualified for much else,' she said coldly. Academically she had been a dud, but she was responsible and willing and got on well with people, her final-year form-teacher had kindly pointed out to her concerned parents, and weren't those things far more important in attaining happiness in the wider world than the mere possession of a brilliant brain?

Of course some people—like Janna and their younger brother, Luke, who was a musical prodigy; and her mother and father, an artist and a mathematician respectively—managed to have it all...good looks included. Not that her family ever consciously made her feel inadequate. Quite the reverse—they sometimes went overboard in their efforts to convince her that she belonged, that she was the much-loved special one of the family. The Chosen One—because she had been adopted as a toddler, and had proved the unexpected catalyst for the rapid arrival of a natural daughter and then a son.

'No other thwarted ambitions?'

'No.' She didn't doubt he would laugh like a drain if she told him that her greatest desire was to be a wife and mother. It was her one outstanding talent: loving people—even when they made it very difficult for her. Sometimes almost impossible.

She looked down at the documents on the desk, concentrating on squaring them off neatly, aware of a nasty blurring of her eyesight that had nothing to do with foggy glasses.

The papers were suddenly snatched out of her fingers. 'This is what you want *me* to sign?'

'Mmm?' Distracted by her thoughts, she took no notice of the faint emphasis. 'Oh, yes.' She pulled herself together, certain that her ugly suspicions were correct and that he was now going to announce dramatically that he had no intention of doing so.

Four months ago, when Nicholas Rose had signed a conditional agreement to sell his Auckland property, his lawyer had cited tax reasons for his client wishing to retain legal title until the end of April. Peter had been happy with the extended settlement date, for it had given him time to chase up the other parcels of land that had been part of the lucrative contract Marvel-Mitchell had entered into with a commercial property development company. Nicholas's property had been the most critical, being a corner lot at the front of the planned shopping mall development, providing the only street access to the larger site. With that in his pocket, Peter had felt free to bid up on one or two other lots, whose owners had demanded much more than current market price.

Then Nicholas Rose had suddenly cancelled his appointment to sign the settlement in Auckland, citing a clause in the conditional agreement that gave the vendor the right to choose the time and place, and Janna had got sick, and Vivian had tried to be helpful and discovered two appalling truths: one, that Nicholas Rose was potentially an implacable enemy, and two, that her cosy dream of love and babies with Peter was shattered beyond redemption.

For long minutes there was no sound but the quiet swish of paper turning, and Vivian's heart thundered in her ears as she waited for her enemy to reveal himself.

'Where do I sign?' He flicked cursorily back through the pages. 'Here? Here? And here?'

'Uh...yes.' He bent and she watched disbelievingly as he uncapped a fountain pen and scrawled his initials in the right places, ending with a full, flourishing signature. The solid gold band on his ring-finger caught her eye as his hand paused, and she stared at the etching of snake and rose, the same crest that she had seen on the letterhead in his lawyer's office.

'Now you.'

She numbly took his place as he stood aside. The shaft of the expensive pen was heavy and smooth, warm from his touch, and she was so nervous that she left a large blob after her name. He blotted it without comment.

'We'll need this properly witnessed, won't we?'

He didn't wait for an answer but went to the door and bellowed for 'Frank'.

The man in the dark suit came in. He gave Vivian a single, hostile, sharply assessing look, then took the proffered pen and co-signed the document with a tight-lipped frown.

'Satisfied?' he asked gratingly as he straightened up, throwing the pen down on to the desk.

'Thank you, Frank.'

Frank grunted.

'Lunch ready?' Nicholas Rose asked, seemingly un-dismayed by his employee's surly air of disapproval.

'In the kitchen. Just as you ordered, *sir*. Just don't expect me to serve it!'

'We'll serve ourselves.' He turned to Vivian, who was watching the by-play with slightly dazed green eyes, still stunned by the inexplicable reprieve. Could she have been wrong about him, after all? 'Frank heats up a mean soup. Frank is my right-hand man, by the way. Frank, this is Vivian.'

Another grunt and a bare acknowledgement.

'I think Vivian has something to give you before you go, Frank.'

'I do?' She looked at them both blankly.

'The money, Vivian,' Nicholas reminded her help-fully. 'If you haven't brought the cash and the bank-cheque, then this contract of sale isn't worth the paper it's written on.'

'Oh!' She blushed. How unprofessional. She was surprised he hadn't asked to see the money earlier. 'Oh, yes, of course. It's right here.'

She unfastened a locked compartment of her satchel, drawing out the thousand-dollar bundle of notes from a cloth bank-bag, and the crisp slip of paper that made up the balance. She was about to put them down on the desk when she hesitated, eyeing the settlement papers still splayed out in front of him, her fears blossoming anew. Her colour drained away as she nibbled her lip.

With a sardonic look, Nicholas Rose silently gathered up the papers and handed them to her. She tucked them hastily into the satchel before she gave him the bundles. She couldn't quite hide her relief at getting rid of the oppressive responsibility and was chagrined when he tossed the money casually to Frank, who stuffed it in his suit pockets and stumped out, muttering something about the pilot.

'This is all very unorthodox,' she said disapprovingly.

'I'm a very unorthodox man.' If that was a warning, it had come far too late to be of any protection. 'Did it make you nervous travelling with such a large sum of cash?'

She thought of her sweaty drive and the almost sleepless night in the motel with a chair propped under the doorknob. 'Very.'

'Poor Vivian, no wonder you look so pale and tense.' He casually brushed her cheek with his thumb and she nearly went through the roof at the bolt of electricity that sizzled her senses.

They looked at each other, startled. His gaze dropped to her soft naked mouth, open in shock, then to the sliver of thickly freckled skin revealed by the modest cleavage of her blouse and the faint suggestion of lace hinted at by the trembling rise and fall of her lush breasts against the cream silk. In that single, brief glance he stripped her naked and possessed her.

'Come into the kitchen,' he said quietly. 'I know just what to give you to relax.'

He ushered her before him and she moved awkwardly, shaken by the most profoundly erotic experience of her life. And yet he had scarcely touched her! She felt confused, fearful and yet achingly alive, aware as never before of the feminine sway of her full hips and the brush of her thighs beneath her skirt. Her spine tingled in delicious terror. Was he stroking her again with that spiky look of hunger? Imagining how she would look moving in front of him without her clothes? She blushed in the dimness of the hall and chastised herself for her dangerous fantasies. Either it was all in her own mind, or Nicholas Rose had decided to set her up for a very personal form of humiliation. He couldn't possibly be genuinely attracted to her, not a man who, despite his physical flaws, possessed a raw magnetism that probably gave him his pick of beautiful women, not a man who showed every sign of being bent on vengeance.

The kitchen was small and compact and clearly the preserve of someone who enjoyed cooking. The benchtop was wooden, slicked with the patina of age, in contrast to the microwave and modern appliances, and in the small dining-alcove was a well-scrubbed kauri table and three chairs. Evidently Nowhere Island was not normally used for business entertaining.

The table was set with rush place-mats and solid silver cutlery, and the steaming bowl of thick, creamy, fragrant soup that was set before her made Vivian's tense stomach-muscles uncoil. There were bread rolls, too, which Nicholas got from the microwave, cursing as he burnt his fingers on the hot crusts.

The relaxant turned out to be a glass of champagne. And not just any old bubbly, but Dom Perignon. Vivian watched as he deftly opened the wickedly expensive bottle over her murmured protests that wine in the middle of the day made her sleepy, and turned his back to pour it into two narrow, cut-crystal flutes he had set on the bench.

Vivian drank some more soup, and when she was handed the chilled flute with a charming flourish accepted it fatalistically. What would be would doubtless be, whether she drank it or not.

'Have you ever tasted Dom Perignon before?' he asked, seating himself again, and this time applying himself to his soup with an appetite that definitely wasn't feigned.

'Why, yes, I have it every morning for breakfast, poured on my cornflakes,' she said drily.

'You must be a lively breakfast companion...albeit a more expensive one than most men could hope to afford,' he said, with a provocative smile that was calculated to distract.

But not you. It was on the tip of her tongue to say it, but she manfully refrained. 'I pay my own way.'

His eyes dropped to her hand, nervously tracing the grain of the table, and the smile was congealed.

'Yes, that's right, you do, don't you. Even to the extent of bank-rolling your fiancé's grand property schemes. I suppose you could say he gained a sleeping partner in more than one sense of the word...'

As she gasped in outrage, he lunged forward and trapped her left hand flat on the table-top, his palm pressing the winking diamond ring painfully into her finger.

'You've been working for him since you left school, haven't you? What took him so long to realise you were the woman of his dreams? It was around about the time you got that little windfall, wasn't it? Did he make it a condition of his proposal that you invest your inheritance in his business, or did you do it all for love?'

'How dare you imply it had anything to do with money?' she said fiercely, fighting the sudden urge to burst into pathetic tears and throw herself on his mercy. 'Peter asked me to marry him before he ever knew about the trust!' The release, on her twenty-third birthday, of funds from a trust set up by her natural parents had been a surprise to everyone, including her adoptive parents, who had refused to accept a cent of it. It was for Vivian to use how she wished, they had said—so she had.

'The wedding's this Saturday isn't it? Your twenty-fifth birthday?'

Her eyes lowered, her hand curling into a white-knuckled fist as she pulled it violently from under his and thrust it down into her lap. His investigations must have been appallingly extensive. How much more did he know? Please God, not enough!

'Yes.'

Her curt response didn't stop his probing as he leaned back again in his chair. 'You must be looking forward to it after such a very long engagement? And only four days to go until death do you part. No wonder you look slightly...emotionally ragged. It's going to be a big church wedding, I understand. I'm amazed you could spare the time to dash down here...or was this a welcome distraction from the bridal jitters?'

Vivian lifted her chin and gave him a look of blazing dislike. At the same time she lifted her champagne glass and took a defiant sip.

He watched her with a thin smile, and suddenly she had had enough of his subtle tormenting. Any moment now she was going to lose her temper and give the game away. Thinking, In for a penny, in for a pound, she closed her eyes and recklessly quaffed the whole lot. It really was glorious, like drinking sunshine, she decided, drenched in a fizzy warmth that seemed to invade every body-cell.

She was still feeling dazzled inside when she re-opened her eyes and found him regarding her with serious consternation.

'You shouldn't knock Dom Perignon back like water!'

Well, she had certainly succeeded in changing the subject! She gave him a smile that was almost as blinding as her hair. 'I thought that was the way you were supposed to drink champagne. It gives such a delicious rush! I think I'll have some more.' She held out her glass.

His jaw tightened. 'One glass is more than sufficient for someone who claims not to drink very much.'

'But I like it. I want another one,' she insisted imperiously. 'A few minutes ago you were trying to ply me with wine, and now you're sitting there like an outraged vicar. More champagne, *garçon*!' she carolled, waving the glass above her head, suddenly feeling marvellously irresponsible. She might as well get thoroughly drunk before she met her fate.

'Vivian, put the glass down before you break it!' he ordered sharply.

'Only if you promise to fill it,' she bargained, crinkling her eyes with delight at her own cunning.

He looked at her silently for a moment, during which her body began to take on a slow lean in the chair. 'All right.'

She chuckled at him. 'You promise?'

'I promise.'

'Cross your heart and hope to die?'

'Vivian——'

'Stick a needle in your eye——!' She broke off the childish chant, putting her free hand to her open mouth, her face blanching under the freckles. 'Oh, God, Nicholas, I'm sorry.'

'The glass, Vivian——'

She was too shocked at her thoughtlessness to register anything but her own remorse. 'Oh, Nicholas, I didn't mean it, I was just being silly. You mustn't think I meant——'

'I know what you didn't mean, Vivian,' he ground out, as she regarded him owlishly from behind her spectacles.

'I would never tease you about your eye,' she whispered wretchedly.

'I know,' he said grimly, lunging to his feet and reaching for her glass just as her limp fingers let it go. It slid past his hand and shattered on the stone-flagged floor into hundreds of glittering shards.

'And now I've smashed your lovely crystal,' she said mournfully, her eyes brimming with more tears at the knowledge of the beauty she had carelessly destroyed. 'You must let me buy you another one.'

'By all means pay for the glass. You've smashed a hell of a lot worse in your time. Perhaps it's time you were made to pay for that, too,' he growled, and caught her just as she toppled off the chair, bumping her cheekbone on the edge of the table.

'Oh!' Her back was arched across his knee, her head drooping over his powerful arm, hands flopping uselessly to the floor. 'You've gone all wavy and soft,' she murmured dizzily.

'Your glasses have fallen off.' His voice came from such a long way away that she had to strain to hear it. Her thoughts seemed to flow stickily through her head, oozing aimlessly like melted honey and slurring off her tongue.

'Why won't my arms move? What's happening to me?'

'Perhaps you're drunk.'

She felt a warm weight slide under her knees and then the whole world went around and she gave a little cry as she seemed to float up towards the heavy-beamed ceiling.

'I don't think so. I never get drunk.' The rocking feeling didn't make her feel sick, as the boat had. She was being carried, she realised muzzily, struggling against the dragging desire to melt into the arms that held her against a hard chest.

'What's happening, where am I going?' she slurred weakly.

'Wherever I care to take you,' came the terse reply. 'Don't you know what you've done, Vivian?'

She had used to know, but somehow the knowledge was now wispily elusive. 'No, what have I done?' she mumbled.

'You've pricked yourself on a thorn, a very dangerous kind of thorn...'

'Poison.' The word floated up through her subconscious without fear. 'Was it poisonous? Am I dying now...?' It was much nicer than she expected, she decided woozily, aware of a strange, shining whiteness all around.

'No, damn it, you're just going to sleep. You're only drugged, not poisoned.'

'Must've been a rose-thorn, then,' she said, having trouble getting her silly tongue around the words. There was a flat, echoing, metallic rhythm coming from somewhere close by, keeping time with the rhythmic rocking that was making her float higher and higher away from reality. Confusing images clouded in her wandering brain. 'Was a rose, wasn' it...tha' caused all th' tr'ble? In B-Beauty an' the Beast...'

'You're getting your fairytales mixed up, Sleeping Beauty.' The bitter steel of his voice cut into her fading consciousness. 'I may be a beast but my name's not Rose—it's Thorne, Nicholas Thorne.' His grip tightened and he shook her until her bewildered green eyes opened, staring fiercely down at her.

'You do remember my name, don't you, Vivian?' he burst out harshly. 'Even if you never saw my face. Nicholas Thorne. The man you almost destroyed ten years ago. The Olympic athlete whose future you smashed to bits with your car?'

She stirred weakly in his arms. 'No...!'

'The man whose wife and son died while you walked away with hardly a scratch,' he went on relentlessly. 'Do you believe in the Bible, Vivian? That justice is an eye for an eye...?'

She rejected the horror of what he was implying, the black eye-patch suddenly dominating her hazy vision. Perhaps he intended that it was the last thing she would ever see! Frantically she tried to bring her hands up to hide her face, to protect her eyes from his avowed revenge, but they, like the rest of her body, refused to respond to orders.

'*No!*' She was falling now, with nothing to save her. He had thrown her from the high place into a pit of horror. She was falling down, down, down and he was falling with her, his breath hot on her face, his unmasked hatred and the formidable weight of his hard body pressing her deep into the soft white oblivion that was waiting to receive them.

'Ssh, I've got you.'

Her body twitched feebly. '*No . . .*'

'Fight it all you like, Vivian, it's too late,' he murmured in her ear, with the cruel tenderness of a murderer for his victim. 'All you're doing is hastening the drug's absorption into your system.' His hand was heavy across her throat, his thumb pressing against the sluggish pulse under her jaw as his voice deepened and roughened. 'You may as well accept that for the next few hours I can do whatever the hell I like with this voluptuous young body and you won't be able to lift a finger to stop me. Would Marvel want you back, I wonder, if he knew that someone else had grazed in these lush pastures?'

Strangely, the lurid threat with its menacingly sexual undertones didn't terrify her as it should have. To be ravished by a man who could make her tingle all over with just a look didn't seem such a bad thing. She was sorry she would miss it. She might even have said as much, for as her eyelids seeped closed for the last time she heard a soft, incredulous laugh.

Her last conscious awareness was of his mouth warm on hers, his tongue sliding intimately into her moist depths, a leisured tasting of her helplessness as large hands began smoothing off her clothes.

And the sound of someone wishing her sweet dreams.

CHAPTER FOUR

WHEN Vivian opened her eyes she was still trapped in the fuzzy white wilderness.

She blinked, and discovered that she was lying in an incredibly soft, warm bed and the whiteness was the curving surface of a wall a few inches from her nose. She reached out to touch the rough plaster surface, using the contact with reality to push herself upright, meaning to peer out of the narrow window which broke the curve of the wall at the end of the bed. Instead she sank back on her heels with a smothered moan as her head swam horribly.

'Poor Vivian. Head thumping like a drum?'

She opened herself mindlessly to the warm sympathy in the sugar-coated voice. 'Umm...' she groaned in inarticulate agreement.

The sugar melted to sickly syrup. 'Hangovers are a bitch, aren't they? I had no idea you were such a reckless drinker. I told you champagne shouldn't be knocked back like water...'

Vivian swung around on her knees and froze, uttering a gasp of shock as she discovered why the bed was so blissfully warm.

'*You*!'

'Who did you expect? The faithful fiancé?'

Nicholas Thorne was sprawled beside her, his solid outline under the covers blocking the only escape-route from the narrow single bed. His tanned shoulders were

dark against the stark white pillows and his chest above
the folded sheet bare, apart from a thick dusting of gold-
flecked body-hair that didn't soften the impact of the
powerful slabs of raw muscle. Even lounging indolently
in bed he managed to exude an aura of barely leashed
strength. His head was propped against the stout slats
of the wooden bed-head and, with his tousled blond hair
and scarred beauty, and a mockingly cynical smile on
his lips, he looked to Vivian like the epitome of sin—a
fallen angel begging for the redemption of a good
woman...

It was a shockingly seductive thought and she
wrenched her eyes away from their forbidden fascination with his body, all too aware that his expression
of sleepy amusement was belied by the tension in the
muscles of his arms innocently resting on top of the bedclothes, ready to thwart any foolish lunge to freedom
across his body. Not that she was in any condition to
make one. She could hardly think, over the riot in her
head. She rubbed a hand across her aching eyes and
gasped, suddenly realising what was so different about
him. He wasn't wearing his eye-patch.

'You have two eyes!' she blurted out.

'Most people do,' he said drily. 'But, in my case, one
is strictly non-functional.' He angled his head so that
she could see the immobility beneath the distorted left
eyelid, the clouded iris.

'H-how did it happen?' she whispered shakily.

'You have to ask?'

She closed her own eyes briefly. 'Yes, it seems I do.
They told me at the time that your injuries weren't
serious——'

'I find that hard to believe.'

Her eyes flew open at his harsh scepticism. 'I was only fifteen! Still a minor as far as the law was concerned—nobody told me very much of anything. The police dealt mostly through my parents——' She broke off, realising the dangers of her impulsive self-defence. 'But you can't blame Mum and Dad for wanting to protect me,' she protested quickly. 'They were just doing what any parents would have done in the circumstances...'

In fact, they had been so anxious that she should not be traumatised by the tragedy that they had shielded her from all publicity surrounding the accident, and most of her concrete information had come from that dreadful night at the hospital where, still in a state of shock, she had been gently questioned by a Police Youth Aid officer. She was told that the pregnant front-seat passenger of the other car, Mrs Barbara Thorne, had been thrown out and killed instantly when it rolled down a steep bank. The driver, Nicholas Thorne, had suffered concussion and leg injuries. His son, who had been belted into a back seat, had also miraculously escaped without life-threatening injury.

The car-load of boisterous teenage party-goers, including fourteen-year-old Janna, that Vivian had been driving home along the gravelled country road had suffered only shock and bruises.

To her relief he didn't pursue the point. Instead he stroked a finger across his scarred lid and said simply, 'Fragments of flying glass. This was slashed to ribbons, although fortunately my sight seemed to have suffered only temporary damage. But an infection set in a few months later. A microscopic sliver of glass had worked its way through to the back of the eye...'

And here she was moaning in self-pity over a mere headache! 'And...your leg?'

'Not as bad as the limp might suggest. I can do pretty well everything on it that I used to.'

'Except run.'

Several days after the tragedy she had overheard part of a low-voiced conversation between her parents in which her father had said it had been a twin celebration for the Thornes that night—Nicholas's twenty-fifth birthday and the announcement that his sprinting had earned him selection to the New Zealand Olympic team.

'Oh, I can still run. Just not like a world-class sprinter,' he said, in a voice as dry as dust.

'I see...' She might as well plough on and remind him of *all* the dreams that meeting her on a rainy road that night had crushed. 'And...you never married again?'

'No.'

The clipped reply said more than all the rest. 'I'm so sorry,' she said, her voice crushed with guilt and compassion.

His expression tightened dangerously, then relaxed as he studied her gravity, the sincerity of the pain-glazed green eyes and tragic freckled nose. His gaze flickered over her kneeling figure, and he smiled with sinister intent that curled her toes.

'How sorry, I wonder?'

'Wh-what do you mean?' She put a hand up to her pounding head, overwhelmed by the impossibility of dealing with his unpredictability in her debilitated state. One moment he seemed charming, almost gentle, the next he was brimming with black-hearted villainy.

Maybe she wasn't even awake yet at all. Maybe this whole ghastly week was just one, ultra-long, insanely bad dream...

'Having trouble concentrating, Vivian?'

'My head...' she muttered, hating herself for showing such weakness in front of him.

'Perhaps you'd like some hair of the dog? Champagne seems to do wonders for your mood. Makes you very... co-operative.'

Vivian stiffened. 'It wasn't the champagne, it was whatever vile stuff you put in it,' she growled raggedly.

'You mean the chloral hydrate?' He met her accusing glare without a flicker of remorse. 'I assure you, it's a very respectable sedative—the drug of choice for a whole generation of spy novels. Hackneyed, perhaps, but very effective: tasteless, odourless, highly soluble and fast-acting. You might feel a little hung-over for a while, but there won't be any lasting physical effects—at least, not from the *drug*...'

She wasn't up to interpreting any cryptic remarks. She was having enough trouble trying to establish the most obvious facts.

'Where am I, anyway?' she croaked, looking around the small, cheese-wedge-shaped room.

'The lighthouse. I'm in the process of having it converted into living-space. In fact, you might say this is the penthouse suite.'

Vivian winced as his words reverberated like a knell of doom inside her fragile skull. She lifted her other hand and massaged her painfully throbbing temples, desperately trying to remember how she had ended up in bed with her worst enemy—a man who ten years ago had accused her of murder and Janna of complicity, in words that had burned the paper on which they were written with their vitriolic spite.

Her fingers pressed harder against the distracting pain as she asked the question that should have been the first thing out of her mouth.

'What are you doing here?'

'If you mean physically, rather than existentially, at the moment I'm just enjoying the view.'

He wasn't referring to the window behind her, Vivian realised, as his gaze slid several points south of her pale face, where it settled with a sultry satisfaction that made her belatedly aware of a growing coolness around her upper body.

She looked down, and gave a mortified shriek as she saw that her chest was as bare as his—more so, since she didn't have a furry pelt to cloak her firm breasts, thrust into lavish prominence by her unconsciously provocative pose. All she had to hide behind were her freckles, which were scant protection from his mocking appraisal. In the split second before Vivian whipped her arms down, she was shamefully aware of a tightening of her pointed nipples that had nothing to do with the invisible caress of chilled air.

Flushed with humiliation, she snatched at the bedclothes, tugging the sheet up to her face as she cringed against the rough wall behind her. Outrage burned away her drug-induced lethargy as her blush mounted. All the time that they had been talking, Nicholas Thorne had *known* that Vivian was unaware of her semi-nudity. While she had been seriously struggling to communicate, he had been encouraging her to flaunt herself like a floozie, savouring the anticipation of her inevitable embarrassment!

She skimmed an exploring hand down under the covers and found to her deep dismay that all she had on were her tiny bikini panties.

'What happened to my clothes?' she demanded furiously, sweeping a blurred look around the room. The bed, a small bedside cabinet and a strange, triangular clothes-horse in the centre of the room appeared to be the only furniture. No closet or clothes, masculine or feminine, appeared in evidence.

'Don't you remember taking them off?' he asked, shifting to fold his arms casually behind his head, his leg brushing her knee under the covers and making her jump.

'No, I do not!' she gritted back fiercely. 'I remember *you* taking them off.'

Her fingers tightened their grip on the sheet, her eyes blazing green fury above the white veil of cotton as it all came rushing back in vivid detail. He had been kissing her, gloating over her helplessness, and it was only because of his insidious drug that she hadn't fought him tooth and claw!

But she wasn't helpless now, she thought grimly. He wanted a run for his money and that was what he was going to get!

After all, that was the reason that she had knowingly walked right into the jaws of his meticulously baited trap.

Her plan was beautifully simple: by presenting Nicholas Thorne with his prime target at point-blank range, she would draw his fire long enough to exhaust or at least appease the machiavellian lust for vengeance that was compelling him to treat anyone and anything that Vivian loved as a pawn to be used against her.

'Did I?' His surprise was patently mocking. 'Goodness, how shocking of me. Are you sure it wasn't just a wishful fantasy?'

'The last person I would want to fantasise about is *you*!' She whipped the sheet down to her chin, raking him with a look of furious contempt. She was prepared to take anything he dished out, as long as he left her family alone. The success of her whole mission hinged on his never finding out that she was a willing self-sacrifice.

'You lured me here under false pretences. You drugged me and took off my clothes!' she hissed at him goadingly.

'Only the ones that were superfluous to requirements,' he replied blandly.

'What in the hell do you mean by that?' She bristled like a spitting ginger kitten, all kinds of wild scenarios exploding through her scandalised imagination.

'What do you think I mean?' He stretched the arms behind his head languidly, expanding the impressive structure of his chest as he murmured tauntingly, 'Are you wondering whether those sexy emerald-green panties are a tribute to my gentlemanly honour...or to my sexual ingenuity?'

Since it happened to be exactly what she was thinking, Vivian reacted furiously. 'In the circumstances, I hardly think the question of *honour* arises,' she said scathingly.

'You may be right,' he stunned her by replying. He came up on one elbow and Vivian reflexively jerked the covers more securely around her.

Unfortunately, her hasty movement tugged the coverings away from the other side of the bed, exposing Nicholas's long, muscled left flank, lean hip and rippling abdomen. The skin was slightly darker on his half-raised leg and thick torso than on his hip, the naked swimsuit line jolting her with the knowledge that, while she might be semi-nude, he was totally naked!

Thankfully his modesty was preserved by a vital fold of sheet, for Vivian's wide-eyed attention lingered for a startled moment before being hurriedly transferred to his face.

'Some parts of me are fortunately still *extremely* functional,' he purred, his undamaged eye glinting with a predatory amusement. 'Especially in the mornings...'

'*Mornings*?' Vivian's hot face swivelled gratefully away from him towards the soft yellow-pink glow at the window. 'But... it's sunset,' she protested in weak confusion. 'It's just getting dark...'

'Actually, it's getting light,' he corrected. 'That window faces east, not west.'

Vivian sucked in a sharp breath as the full implication of what he was saying hit her. She hadn't just lost a mere hour or two. She had already spend half a day and a whole night entirely at his mercy!

'Quite so,' he said softly. 'This is the morning after, Vivian. Which, given the fact that we're in bed together, naturally poses the deeply intriguing question: the morning after *what*?'

Vivian stared at the thin, sardonic curl of his mouth that hinted at depths of degradation she hadn't even considered.

'Oh, my God, what have you done?' she whispered fearfully, her body shivering with the disgraceful echo of a half-remembered thrill.

'More to the point, what *haven't* I done?' he murmured wickedly, pivoting on his elbow in a fluid flow of muscle to retrieve something from the bedside cabinet behind him.

He offered it to her and, when she refused to let go of her flimsy shield of bedclothes, let a cascade of coloured rectangles spill on to the rumpled fabric between them. Her back glued protectively against the wall, Vivian frowned stiffly down, afraid to move, and frustrated that the surface of the bed was just beyond the range of her near-sighted focus.

'Here, perhaps these will help.' He sat up in a flurry of bedclothes, ignoring her automatic cringe as, moments later, he pushed her spectacles on to her wrinkled nose. 'Better?'

It was a hundred times worse! Vivian stared, appalled, at the photographs scattered like indecent confetti over the bed.

'Oh, my *God* . . .!'

'It's a little too late for prayers, Vivian. Your sins have already found you out. Quite graphically, too, wouldn't you say?'

'How . . .? I . . . You——'

He interrupted her incoherent stammering smoothly. 'I would have thought that the *how* was self-evident. There's this clever modern invention called photography, you see . . .'

The sarcastic flourish of his hand made Vivian utter a soundless moan as she saw that what she had myopically mistaken for a clothes-horse was in fact a tripod, topped with a fearfully sophisticated-looking camera, its lens pointing malevolently at the bed.

'And as for the I and you, well—we appear to be pretty brazenly self-evident, too, don't we? Here, for instance . . .'

Vivian's hypnotised gaze followed his pointing finger. 'See the way you're arched across the bed under me, your arms thrown over your head in abandoned pleasure...'

Vivian clamped the blankets rigidly under her arms, freeing her trembling hands to try frantically to push his away as he sorted through the collection and selected another.

'But this one is my own personal favourite, I think. So artistic... so erotic... so expressive. Don't you agree that we make a sensuous contrast of textures and patterns? With your ginger-dappled skin and my deep tan, and the way our bodies seem to flow over and around each other...'

Vivian tuned out his honeyed taunts, transfixed by the searing image suspended from his fingers.

She had seen raunchy advertisements for perfume in glossy women's magazines that were more physically revealing, but it was impossible to be objective now. The couple in this photograph weren't anonymous models posing for public display. That was *her* caught in an attitude of utter abandon, that was *his* nude body aggressively crushing her to the bed. She went hot and cold at the idea that he had somehow tapped into her forbidden desires.

Even as a tiny, clinical voice of reason was pointing out that the alignment of Nicholas's fingers on her hip conveniently covered the precise area where the thin strip of her bikini panties would be, Vivian was shattered by a sickening sense of betrayal. The pictures lied; they depicted an act of violation, not of love!

She tried to grab the photographs out of his hand and, when he laughed jeeringly and held it out of her reach, she fell desperately on the others, tearing them into meticulously tiny pieces, all the while trying to protect her threadbare modesty with the slipping covers.

He laughed again, making no attempt to stop her wild orgy of destruction beyond retaining safe possession of his avowed favourite. 'There are plenty more where those came from, Vivian. It was a very long, exhausting night...'

'I was unconscious,' she panted, rejecting his sly insinuation. 'Nothing happened——' She stopped, stricken. 'My God, you were going to do this to *Janna*?'

'Actually, the original plan was for someone else to play your sister's partner in sin,' he drawled. 'And when they supposedly disappeared together, with the payment for the land, I would send you photos of the lovers and evidence that they had planned the fraud together. You were supposed to come dashing to her defence on the eve of your own wedding, sadly too late to rescue the contract that your company was depending on, but in plenty of time to negotiate the salvage of Janna's personal and professional reputation—at the price of your own, of course...

'Your arriving in Janna's place sabotaged the exquisite complexity of the plan, but I'm nothing if not flexible. As soon as I saw you, I knew I wanted the privilege of handling you to be purely mine...'

She had already guessed much of it, but the callous detachment with which he outlined the bare bones of the plot was chilling.

She gasped, as an even more horrible thought smacked her in the face. 'Who took the photos? Who else was in here, watching us——?' She broke off, shuddering with humiliation at the thought that Frank had been a flint-eyed witness to her degradation...

'I can promise you, Vivian, you weren't seen or touched by anyone but me.' He took a small black wafer of plastic from the table by the bed and pointed it towards the tripod, pressing a button so that she could hear the electronic whirr as the flash momentarily dazzled her eyes. 'Remote control. It's a state-of-the-art instant camera—the photos only take a few minutes to develop.'

He rolled off the bed and Vivian uttered a choking cry, closing her eyes a fraction of a second too late to deny herself a glimpse of taut male buttocks and hard, hair-roughened flanks.

'Prude.' His mockery singed her burning ears. 'Here.'

She peeped warily through her lashes and relaxed a trifle when she saw that he had pulled on his jeans. He was holding out the thin red sweater he had worn the previous day.

He shook it impatiently at her immobility. 'Come on.' He threw it on the bed. 'Put that on.'

'I want *my* clothes,' she said stubbornly, as she watched him apply his eye-patch, raking his thick, blond-streaked hair over the thin band of elastic that held it in place.

'Then want must be your master.' He put his hands on his hips, legs aggressively astride, a bare-chested pirate. 'Or rather, *I* shall—and as your master I'm quite happy for you to remain without clothes indefinitely. In fact, yes, I rather like the idea of keeping you here naked...' He invited her to consider the notion in a dark, seductive voice, watching her defiance waver. 'Nude, you'd be so deliciously vulnerable, so much easier for me to control...'

With a muttered curse, Vivian snatched the sweater and hastily pulled it over her blushing head, contorting herself to arrange it carefully over the top of the bed-clothes before she let them go. Thankfully, the sweater came to mid-thigh, although she still felt horribly exposed as she crabbed to the edge of the bed and swung her feet tentatively to the floor.

'That colour makes you look like a fire-cracker with a lit fuse.'

The faint suggestion of approval confused her. She was acutely conscious of the scent of him clinging to the sweater, mingling with her own, and of the soft brush of the thin fabric against her bare breasts. She licked her lower lip, and then fingered it nervously. It felt fuller than usual.

'What are you going to do—with the photographs, I mean?'

'Why, there's only one honourable thing *to* do with them.'

Hope flared briefly. 'What's that?'

He plucked her hand from her mouth and mockingly kissed the backs of her fingers.

'Have them delivered to the church on Saturday, of course. Your poor fiancé must be given some reason for being left stranded at the altar!'

His tongue flicked against her knuckles, stroking her with a brief sting of moist fire that distracted her from his bombshell. She jerked her hand away, but not before he had caught her wrist and with a savage twist removed Peter's ring from her finger.

'We'll send this bauble along with the pretty pictures, just to make sure he gets the message that he can't have you.'

He tossed it in the air and caught it, flaunting his possession before thrusting it casually into his pocket.

'You can't do that...' Vivian whispered, her first thought of the havoc he could wreak on an already tense situation, that was, if the wedding hadn't already been cancelled. Had Janna and Peter taken her advice seriously and gone ahead with the arrangements, or were they still stubbornly wallowing in joint guilt and remorse?

'Marvel will never marry you now, Vivian. Learn to accept it.'

'No, Peter loves me!' she declared desperately, jumping to her feet. On one level, at least, it was still true. It was because of his deep affection and respect for Vivian that he and Janna had put themselves through such torture over the past few weeks. Vivian hadn't even been able to maintain a righteous fury over the betrayal, for it was obvious that the guilt-stricken pair had suffered agonies trying to ignore and then deny their love, in order not to hurt sweet, gentle, defenceless Vivian.

She had bluntly told them to stop being so nobly self-sacrificing. The practical thing to do would be to forget the huge hassle of calling off the elaborate wedding-arrangements and returning all the presents, and just switch brides. Janna and Peter had looked so appalled that Vivian had burst out laughing. It had been the laughter more than anything that made her realise that perhaps she wasn't as heartbroken as a jilted woman should be.

So, when the first opportunity had presented itself for her to prove that she wasn't the sweet, gentle, defenceless creature everyone was going to feel sorry for, she had grabbed at it defiantly with both hands.

'Marvel's going to take one look at those pictures and know it's all over between you.' Nicholas continued his ruthless attack. 'He'll never be able to forget the sight of you burning in your lover's arms——'

'We're not lovers!' Vivian shrieked. 'Those pictures— they're all fakes. You just... You posed me, like a *mannequin*——'

'Did I really, Vivian?' he taunted softly. 'You were very willing. Don't you remember telling me how I made you feel all soft and hot and buttery inside, and grumbling that it wasn't fair you had to miss out on the thrill of being ravished by a sexy villain...?'

'That was the drug talking, not me! There's a big difference between being barely conscious and being *willing*,' she pointed out with smouldering force. 'And— and, anyway—if I... If we *had* done anything...I'd *know*...'

'How?' He seemed sincerely curious.

She practically melted her spectacles with the glare she gave him. 'I just would, that's all,' she said stubbornly.

'Not if I was *very* skilful and very tender, and you were very, very receptive... Not if you were all soft and buttery inside,' he said, in a satin murmur that slithered over her skin.

'Stop it! I won't listen!' she cried childishly, covering her burning ears with her hands. His eyes dropped to the sharp rise of the hem of his sweater as it flirted against her upper thighs, and she hurriedly lowered her arms. 'No one else will listen to your lies, either. They'll believe *me*...'

'But you won't be there to tell them the truth,' he said smoothly. 'You'll be here with me. You don't think I'm going to let you go so easily, do you?'

'But you have to let me leave eventually.' She tried to sound confident.

'*Eventually*, you may find that you don't *want* to leave...'

His insinuating murmur filled her with alarm. What was he suggesting—that he intended to turn her into some kind of...*sex*-slave, addicted to the forbidden pleasure that he could provide?

'You can't keep me imprisoned here forever...' she protested faintly.

He shrugged. 'Who's keeping you prisoner? You came here of your own free will. In fact, you've already sent a fax to your office saying that everything is fine and that you'll be back with the contract the day before the wedding. So don't think anyone's going to come flying to your rescue.'

That much was true. She had been too secretive, too determined to solve the problem herself.

When she had gone to visit Nicholas Rose's lawyer, to plead that her sister's illness made it impossible for her to deliver the settlement papers personally, as arranged, Vivian had been still reeling from what she had discovered on her visit to Janna's flat.

Then she had bumped into a secretary over-loaded with files, and glimpsed among the scattered papers a letter addressed to Nowhere Island—but to Nicholas Thorne, not Nicholas Rose.

Some fast and furious digging for information had brought answers that had shocked her out of her self-pitying depression and sent her charging off in a spirit of reckless bravado.

Only now was she realising how ill-prepared she was for her mission. Nicholas Thorne had shown no sign so far of being open either to intimidation or to reason.

Vivian swallowed. Damn it, she couldn't afford to let negative feelings undermine the determination that had brought her here!

'Look, I realise that you genuinely feel that you have some justification for hating me, but don't you see that what you're doing is *wrong*. That car crash was an *accident*. The police investigated it thoroughly at the time——'

'Your sister claimed that our car skidded as we came around the corner,' he said neutrally.

'Yes, but Janna wasn't *accusing* you of anything,' Vivian explained eagerly. 'She was just describing what she saw. The police said the skid-marks confirmed that neither of us was speeding...it was just the way the gravel had been shifted by the rain, making the road unstable—an act of God...'

Then she added gently, because she knew the tortuous ways that guilt could haunt the innocent, 'Neither of us was to blame for that night. Not me and not you. We'll never know if we could have prevented it by doing something slightly faster or reacting differently, but being human isn't a *crime*...'

She broke off because he was looking at her extremely oddly. 'You think I blame *myself*?'

She hurriedly changed her tack. 'When I wrote to you back then, I just wanted you to know that I was sorry for the accident...I didn't mean to taunt you with your grief, if that was what you thought. I—I never showed your reply to anyone else. I didn't think you meant those terrible threats. I thought it was just your grief lashing out. I can't believe you've nursed that mistaken grudge all these years. Surely, for the sake of your son, you should have put the tragedy behind you——'

'My *son*?'

The floor suddenly seemed to heave beneath her feet as Vivian realised what his arrested expression could mean. 'I—I know he was injured, and it's all a bit hazy now, but at the hospital I remember the doctor saying he was a very lucky boy to be in the back seat... H-he *is* still alive, isn't he?'

He nodded slowly. 'Very much so.'

'Oh. *Oh*! That's great!' Vivian's eyes were starry with brilliant relief. 'And...in good health?' she asked, with more restrained caution.

'Excellent.'

She beamed at him. 'I'm so glad for you!'

He cocked his head with an ironic smile. 'So am I.'

'It must have been a terrible experience for a child,' she said, her emotions swinging wildly back to deep compassion.

'At fifteen, you were little more than a child yourself.'

She drew herself up to her full height, once more unsettlingly conscious that the top of her head barely reached his unshaven chin. 'I've always been mature for my age.'

'You like children?' he asked inconsequentially.

'Of course I like children,' she said, bewildered.

'Some women don't.'

'Well, I *love* them,' she said firmly. She lifted her chin defiantly. 'Peter thinks I'll make a great mother.'

His eye narrowed. 'From what you know of me, you should be on your knees begging for mercy, not deliberately going out of your way to annoy me,' he warned with silky menace, and she gasped as his big hand suddenly curled around her throat, applying an uncomfortable pressure to draw her towards him until her breasts rested against his chest.

'Take your own advice, Vivian, and forget the past. You're not going home to marry Marvel; you're not going to have his children or share any kind of future with him...'

His hand tightened under her jaw, lifting her up on to her toes, so that she had to clutch at his thick shoulders for balance, her fingers sliding against his smooth skin.

'I'm your future now. I'm the one who controls your destiny.' She gave a little yip as his free hand slipped under the hem of his sweater to splay warmly across her quivering, tautly stretched belly. 'And I'm the one who controls your fertility. The first child you'll ever carry in your womb will be *mine*. The first baby to suckle at your breast will belong to *me*, as you will...'

Vivian trembled in shock at the starkly primitive statement of possession and her equally primitive response. Her lips parted soundlessly as his fingertips skimmed under the lacy band of her panties and pressed gently into the fringes of the downy thicket between her thighs.

'Such a fiery little nest ... Is it as hot and spicy as its colour suggests? I'll bet it is...' She gave a faint whimper that was stifled by the nip of his teeth against her tender lower lip and his purred praise vibrating over her tongue. 'I bet you're hot and spicy all over when you're in sexual heat, peppered with those delicious freckles and salted with the sweat of your arousal. I look forward to dining on your splendour...' His hand moved up to brush briefly across the silky undersides of her heavy breasts, pausing to discover the betraying tightness of her nipples.

He made a deep sound of male gratification and suddenly released her, stepping back to study with ferocious pleasure her swaying body and her dazed look of sensual confusion.

His chest rose and fell rapidly, his body rippling with arrogant satisfaction as he straightened her glasses, which were fogged and slightly askew.

'You do see the exquisite justice of it, don't you, Vivian? An eye for an eye is such a paltry vengeance for a man of my sensual nature. I prefer a much more intimate, pleasurable and *fruitful* form of revenge . . .'

CHAPTER FIVE

'LOST something, Ginger?'

Stomping out of the dilapidated old boat-house, which it had taken her half an hour to break into, Vivian stopped dead.

Yes, my sanity, she wanted to say. She must be mad to allow him to play these games with her; crazier still to be enjoying it.

Nicholas Thorne had threatened her in the most elemental way a man could threaten a woman, and yet it wasn't fear that made her heart race and her stomach churn whenever he was near...

She looked up, squinting against the slanting rays of the setting sun.

He was leaning against the corner of the salt-encrusted wooden building, a familiar, infuriating smile of mockery twisting his narrow mouth, an oilskin jacket flapping open over his grey fisherman's sweater and the usual pair of jeans. Somehow she had difficulty picturing him in a conventional suit, yet he must wear one all the time in his role as ruthless head of a sprawling business empire.

'A boat, perhaps?'

'You have to have one somewhere,' she growled, disturbed as ever by his wicked humour. 'You can't live on an island without owning *some* kind of boat.'

'Feel free to look around,' he replied with another quirk of his lips.

'Thank you, I will,' she said cuttingly.

She was glad she was muffled up in the bulky knitted jumper and her green woollen trousers for around Nicholas she was uncomfortably aware of her body. It was the way he looked at her—complacent, possessive, *knowing* ...

At least she had clothes to cloak her self-consciousness. After staking his nerve-shattering claim on her womb, Nicholas had calmly directed her to her suit, blouse and bra lying crumpled under the bed and led her, clutching them in a bundle, down the iron stairs to the room below, where she had found her empty briefcase and the small suitcase she had left back at the motel at Port Charles. It held only toiletries, her nightdress and a single change of clothes, but it was enough to give her a slight sense of false security.

The sweater she was wearing, however, was his, reluctantly accepted as a necessity if she was to tramp around the island in the blustery weather and not die of exposure. It had amused him to lend it to her, just as it amused him to follow her around so that she couldn't just sneak off and *pretend* to search for an escape, she had *actually* to do it, thoroughly exhausting herself in the process. He was always hovering, offering irritatingly helpful suggestions and teasing her with intriguing little titbits of information about himself that increased her curiosity about him to a dangerous craving.

The more that she found out about him, the more Vivian's compassionate heart whispered that Nicholas was basically a good man whose fixation with brutal revenge was a cry from the wilderness of his frozen emotional landscape. He had found the loss of his beloved wife and unborn child unacceptable, so, in the nature of a competitive man used to winning, he *hadn't* accepted it, and the long years of denial had formed a barrier against natural healing.

In order to save herself, Vivian had realised that she would first have to save him...

'Poor Vivian,' he commiserated. 'Three whole days of scouring every nook and cranny and you still haven't succeeded in finding a way off the island. When are you going to give up?'

'Never!' She pushed past him and began stalking back up the uneven path from the rocky cove.

'Stubborn wench.' He was close on her heels. 'Maybe you should try offering bigger bribes. Frank was quite offended by the low price you put on his loyalty.'

She snorted. His number-one henchman had proved to be predictably incorruptible, but Vivian had known she was expected to go through the motions. She put her nose in the air, and promptly stumbled and teetered on the edge of a sharp, jagged incline.

A powerful arm whipped round her waist, dragging her back against him. Instinctively she reached behind her to clutch at the sides of his coat, her shocked breath rasping in her throat.

'Don't worry, I won't let you go,' he said, wrapping his other arm around her. 'You're safe.'

She felt his face nuzzling into the side of her neck, the stubble of his jaw pleasurably rough against her skin, and for a moment she leaned weakly against him, tempted by his gentleness.

'Safe? That's a laugh! I won't be safe until I get home!'

'Oh, yes, I bet you feel boringly safe with Marvel,' he said mockingly. 'Two years engaged to the man and your dossier says you never stay overnight at his flat.

I'd say that indicates a pretty huge lack of excitement on both sides——'

'Just because I'm not promiscuous it doesn't mean I'm sexless!' she flashed from the depths of her insecurity, deeply resenting his familiarity with the private details of her life.

'I don't think you're sexless, just surprisingly unawakened,' he told her smoothly. 'But I wake you up, don't I? You rise so beautifully to the slightest hint of bait. No wonder you're so gullible—you're tough on the outside and marshmallow within. A delicious bundle of contradictions...'

'*You* can talk,' she said, bristling at the gullible label.

'Oh, do you find me delicious, Vivian? I'm so glad it's mutual.' He smiled archly. 'Would you like another sample?'

'No, thank you!' she lied tightly. That searing, sensuous first kiss in his room had also been his last. His dark threats of sexual domination had made her lightning-swift response to his touch all the more shaming, and yet he hadn't pressed his advantage.

Braced for further brutally expert assaults on her deplorably shaky defences, Vivian had instead been left at the mercy of her own fevered imagination. This subtle form of self-inflicted torture had been refined with an added sadistic twist by Nicholas—she was still forced to share his bed every night.

The first night Vivian had searched everywhere, and been forced to accept that he was telling the truth when he said there were no extra beds. When she had tried to curl up fully-clothed on the couch in the living-room of the keeper's cottage, Nicholas had simply slung her over his shoulder and borne her off to his room in the tower, coolly telling her that she could change into her night-dress in privacy, or he would strip her himself and she could sleep with him naked. She had chosen dignity over humiliation and then lain on her side facing the wall, stiff with mingled rage and agonised apprehension as she felt him get in behind her.

Then—nothing!

He had whispered goodnight, tucked his arm comfortably around her middle, yawned and gone to sleep. She had tried to wriggle out from under his arm, but in sleep he was just as possessive, his hand sinking more securely under her waist, a thick, hair-roughened thigh pushing between her knees to drape over her leg, anchoring her firmly against the bed. Even through her blessedly modest nightgown she could feel the warm shudder of his heartbeat against her back and the firm definition of his manhood pressed against her soft bottom.

Each succeeding night it had taken her longer to fall asleep, and each morning when she woke up in a con-fusion of blushes it was to find that some time in the night she had turned over and mingled with him in a trusting sprawl of limbs.

To her chagrin he accepted her rejection with a careless shrug. 'I came to tell you that Frank almost has dinner ready,' he said. 'And I've already warned you it's not a good idea for you to be stumbling around out here alone when it starts to get dark. Look what nearly happened just now——'

'That was because you were distracting me. Maybe you did it on purpose,' she goaded, inexplicably angry at him for caring. 'Or maybe you'd like to see me go over a cliff, to be killed by an "accident". That would be rough justice for you, wouldn't it?'

In the waning light his features were blurred into softness, his eye deeply shadowed by his fierce brow. 'Do you really think I brought you here to kill you?'

'I... No,' she admitted truthfully. His declared intent had been to cause her maximum mental suffering and she couldn't suffer if she was dead. 'But we both know there are worse things than dying...'

He moved closer. 'Like bearing my child, you mean? Would that really be a fate worse than death, Vivian? To make love with me and create a new life...?'

The wind snatched her breath away. 'You only said that to frighten me,' she choked. 'I know you weren't really serious—— '

'Do you? Just because I haven't mentioned it again?' He captured her gaze with the bold assurance of his glittering brown eye. 'I knew I didn't have to. I knew you were thinking about it every time you looked at me—wondering what it would be like to accept me as your lover. Wondering if I would make love with the same passionate intensity with which I seem able to hate. I was giving you time to get used to the idea. After all, there's no real urgency now that you're here, living, eating, sleeping with me. I've waited this long for you...I can wait a little longer...'

A *little* longer? Heat suffused her body at his arrogant sexual confidence. She fought to cool her instinctive response. How could she feel anything but revulsion at his depraved suggestion?

She shivered. 'Surely you wouldn't use force to—to—— '

'Not force—seduction,' he said smoulderingly. 'We both know that there's been some very volatile physical chemistry brewing between us since the moment we met. Why don't you just accept that we were always fated to become lovers?'

Fate again. Wasn't that the very thing she had come here to defy boldly? Vivian shivered once more.

'You're cold—why didn't you say so?' Nicholas scolded her, shrugging impatiently out of his jacket and wrapping her in the heavy oilskin, tucking her chilled hand firmly through his elbow as he escorted her back along the stony path towards the cottage. 'You should have worn the parka I offered you. No sense in cutting off your nose to spite your face. And if you're going to go storming around in a temper, watch out for the wildlife—they have first priority. Nowhere Island is a wildlife sanctuary and part of a maritime park. All these outlying islands are really the tops of drowned hills, and the eroded volcanic tubes that riddle the shore and sea-floor make very rich habitats for marine life.'

'You sound like an environmental tour-guide,' she said grumpily, trying not to respond to the enthusiasm in his voice.

'I should hope my learning is a little more useful than that,' he said drily as he opened the back door. 'As a marine biologist, I don't approve of environmental tourism.'

'What!'

He pushed her stunned figure over the threshold of the kitchen, where Frank was cursing over a sizzling pan.

'You're a property developer!' she accused, as he whipped his jacket from around her shoulders and hung it on the back of the door.

'I'm also a marine biologist. It *is* possible to do more than one thing with your life, Vivian. One doesn't have to limit oneself to living down to other people's expectations,' he said softly. Was that a dig at her?

He pressed a finger against her jaw, pushing it closed with a slight snap. 'What's the matter, Ginger? Aren't I fitting into your stereotype of a grief-crazed vengeance-seeker?' He stepped away. 'I'm going to have a quick shower before dinner.' The dark gleam of light reflecting off his eye-patch managed to give the startling impression of a wink. 'Feel free to join me if you want to help conserve the tank-water.'

As soon as he was out of the room, Vivian turned to Frank.

'Does he really have a degree in marine biology?'

'Yep. An athletic scholarship in the States.'

She waited but, as usual, further information was not forthcoming.

'You don't talk much, do you?'

'Don't have much to say.'

She would have been offended if she hadn't discovered that he was almost as taciturn in his communications with Nicholas. She hadn't quite worked out Frank's job description yet; he seemed to be a combination of assistant, valet, bodyguard, mechanic—he had already fixed the faulty back-up generator—and chief cook and bottle-washer.

'Where's Nicholas's son?'

He shrugged. 'Ask Nick.'

'He won't tell me. He won't talk about his son at all. Or his wife.' She gave a little huff of frustration. 'How long have you worked for Nicholas? Did you ever meet his wife? Do you know what she was like?'

That brought the hawkish face around, bearing a hard stare.

'Six years. No. Beautiful.'

It took her a moment to realise he had actually replied to all her questions. She sighed. 'I thought she must have been.'

Astonishingly Frank's dour expression broke up in a grin.

'Nothing like you.'

She scowled. 'OK, OK, you don't have to rub it in. She was so perfect he's never met another woman to match up to her.'

'Is that what he told you?' His grin widened and she studied him with suspicious green eyes.

'What's that supposed to mean?'

He shrugged. 'It's your life—you figure it out.'

And, with that irritating observation, he crouched down to open the oven and stir something inside.

Vivian was about to demand a proper answer when her eyes fell on a bulge in the front pocket of the jacket hanging against the door. She remembered the weight of something bumping against the side of her knee with a vaguely familiar chink as Nicholas had hurried her along. His keys! She had searched all over the lighthouse, but there was one place she hadn't been able to look.

She darted silently over and boldly plunged her hand into the pocket. Fisting the key-ring, she just had time to nip back to the other side of the room before Frank closed the oven and turned around.

'Uh, I think I'd better go and change for dinner,' Vivian said uncomfortably, edging out of the door.

Her heart was in her mouth as she crept down the hall. The plumbing in the lighthouse was still incomplete, so Nicholas would be showering in the cottage bathroom and probably had his fresh clothes with him, which meant he wouldn't need to go back to his room before dinner. Even if he did, the locked room was on the fourth landing, and she would have plenty of time to hear him on the stairs and whip up to the next level to fossick innocently in her suitcase.

The locked door hid exactly what she had suspected: an office. A businessman with Nicholas Thorne's autocratic reputation would never trust anyone enough to relinquish control of his business, even temporarily. She pulled the door softly to, and switched on the light.

There was a computer work-station and various unidentifiable pieces of electronic equipment, and a big desk strewn with papers.

Vivian ignored the wall of shelves lined with jars and tubes of dubious-looking specimens, her heart sinking at the sight of the heavy steel combination-safe on the floor.

She went over to the desk. Only the top drawer was locked and she rifled quickly through the others, finding mostly stationery and files of scientific papers and journals. Nothing that might tell her more about Nicholas the *man*. No stray photographs of his wife or son. No photos of any other kind either...

Adrenalin spurted through her veins and her sweaty hands shook as she unlocked the top drawer and sat down on the big swivel chair behind the desk to reach inside.

The first thing she touched was a small medicine bottle, and her fingers tightened around the amber glass as she picked it up and read the typed label: chloral hydrate. Her soft mouth tightened and she pushed the half-full bottle into her trouser pocket, intending to dump the contents at the first opportunity.

Her heart gave a nervous convulsion when she saw what the drug had been sitting on—the settlement contract, signed, witnessed, dated—intact and still viable...

She lifted it out and weighed it in her hands. But no...even if she took it, where could she hide it? The fact that Nicholas hadn't already destroyed it was surely a hopeful sign. As long as it lay here undisturbed, Marvel-Mitchell Realties still had a future.

She put the contract back, her breath fluttering as she slid it to one side and saw her forlorn dis-engagement ring crowning one very distinctive, disturbingly erotic photograph. She tried not to look at the haunting image, afraid to touch it lest she become further victim to her depraved fascination with Nicholas Thorne.

But where were the others Nicholas had taunted her with? The wedding was supposed to be the day after tomorrow. If only she could continue to stave off disaster until the ceremony was over! She didn't want her wedding-present to Peter and Janna to be a bunch of pornographic photographs and a threat of financial ruin. She could just imagine the poor vicar's face if he caught a glimpse of any of those pictures. She would never be able to hold up her head in church again!

However much she longed to believe that her brief presence here had taken the edge off Nicholas's bitterness, had softened and changed him, she didn't dare take the risk of relying on her increasingly biased judgement where he was concerned. Only when Janna and Peter were safely and securely married would Vivian let herself take the gamble of trusting Nicholas, telling him the truth and hoping that he would justify her faith in his basic humanity.

She scrabbled frantically through the drawer, reaching deep into the back where she found something firmly wedged. She pulled it out.

A cellphone. She flicked a switch. A *working* cellphone.

Civilisation was only a single telephone call away.

The alternatives bolted through her brain in the space of a split second. She didn't have to go through with it. She could call Peter—call the cops. She could cause a scandal. Make a great deal of misery for everyone concerned, but save herself.

And perhaps drive Nicholas out of her life forever...

She let the telephone clatter back into the drawer at the same instant that she became aware of another presence in the room.

She hadn't heard him on the stairs and now she saw why. His feet were bare as he crossed the uneven wooden floor, not making a sound. He wore only a white towelling robe and his hair drifted in damp clumps across his brow.

He was breathing hard. And he was angry.

'Careless of me.' Nicholas leant over and slammed the drawer viciously shut, nearly catching her guilty fingers in the process.

'And even more careless of you to be caught.' He locked it and wrenched the keys out with a violent movement. Vivian slid out of the chair and nervously backed away.

'What were you doing, Vivian?' he demanded harshly, stalking her every move. 'Snooping? Or were you frantic to get to a phone so you could warn Lover-boy?'

The back of her thighs hit the computer table and she pulled her scrambled wits together as he halted, his whole body bunched with furious aggression.

'*No*!' His appearance had rendered her split-second decision redundant, but she wanted him to know what it would have been. 'No. I—I didn't even know there was a phone in here. I was just looking for the photos—the other ones you said you had——'

'I also said you were gullible,' he sneered. 'The only photos I had, you tore up—except for my personal favourite, of course...' He wasn't wearing his eye-patch and even his sightless eye seemed to blaze with sparks of angry golden life as he smiled savagely at her bitter chagrin.

'I was thinking of having it blown up and framed before I send it to Marvel,' he taunted. 'It'll have so much more impact that way. Perhaps I should even call him myself, give him a blow-by-blow account of how much pleasure I got from having his chaste bride-to-be *mounted* ...'

She flinched at the crudely insulting *double entendre*. His volcanic rage seemed wildly out of proportion to the condescending amusement, even wry admiration, with which he had greeted her other failed attempts to thwart him.

'OK, OK, so I took the keys because I wanted to steal from you and snoop among your secrets,' she flared, fighting back with her own fortifying anger. 'I thought I might find something I could use to help persuade you to let me go. What's so terrible about that? *You* snooped through *my* life——'

He stiffened, his expression hardening to granite.

'And, tell me—if I suddenly agreed with everything you said? If I handed you your precious settlement contract and said all debts were cancelled—what then? Would you be able to walk away and forget that any of this ever happened? Would you still marry Marvel on Saturday?'

For a heartbeat Vivian ached to be selfish and trust to his sincerity. 'Why don't you let me go, and find out?' she said warily.

She knew instantly that she had made a serious mistake. His jaw tensed and colour stung his cheekbones as if she had delivered him a sharp slap across the face. Oh, God, had the offer been genuine?

'I wouldn't tell anyone, if that's what you mean,' she said quickly, hoping to repair the damage. 'Nobody back home has to know about any of this. It's still not too late——'

'The hell it isn't!' Turning away from her, he jerked his head towards the door and grated, 'Get out!'

Was he ordering her out of the room, or his life? She moved hesitantly past him. 'Nicholas, I——'

He sliced her a sideways glance of fury that stopped the words in her mouth. 'Frank said you were changing for dinner. Don't make a liar out of him.'

Then his voice gentled insidiously. 'And, Vivian...?' Her fingernails bit into her palms as he continued with dangerously caressing menace, 'If I ever catch you here again, you won't find me so lenient. Be very careful how much further you provoke me tonight. I'm in the mood for violence...'

'If I ever catch you here again...' He wasn't sending her away! Vivian was shocked by the turbulence of her relief as she shakily made her way up to the room where she kept her meagre selection of clothes.

Deciding it might be deemed further provocation not to obey his thinly veiled command, she quickly put on a fresh blouse, the cream one she had worn the day of her arrival, and changed her sneakers for her low-heeled shoes. The trousers, she decided with the dregs of defiance, could stay—she could do with their warmth around her woefully trembly knees.

The kitchen had been transformed in her absence. It was no longer a bright, practical workplace; it was a shadowy corner of a private universe, lit only by twin flickering candles set on a table laid for two. A casserole dish sat in the centre, flanked by a bottle of red wine and two glasses. Nicholas, she discovered with an upsurge of her heartbeat, was still wearing his white robe— a spectral white phantom floating at her out of the darkness.

'What happened to the lights?' she asked sharply. 'Where's Frank?'

There was a brief gleam of teeth from the phantom and a movement of his head so that she could see that the dark triangle of his eye-patch was back in place, his vulnerability well-masked. 'I'm conserving generating power,' he said, in a tranquil tone of reason that sent a frisson down her spine. His silky calm was like the eye of a hurricane—she could feel the energy swirling around it. 'And Frank's already eaten. He's in his bedroom. Why? Did you want him for something?'

The innocent enquiry made her seethe. He knew damned well why she wanted a third person present!

Frank was no use as a buffer tucked away in his little concrete bunker down the hall.

It was pure nerves that made her blurt out as she sat down, 'I'm not sleeping with you tonight!'

He sat across from her, leaning his chin on his hand so that his face moved forward into the flickering pool of light, his eye gleaming, a tiny candle-flame dancing like a devil in the hot, black centre. 'What's so different about tonight?'

She was hypnotised by the devil. 'It just is, that's all.'

'Do you mean that you're more aware of me as a man than you were last night?' he murmured.

She didn't think that was possible! 'An *angry* man,' she qualified stiffly.

'I've been angry with you before. Usually you just fling my temper back in my teeth.'

'Usually you behave with more self-control.'

His smile was darkly knowing. 'Maybe it's not *my* lack of control that you're worried about. Don't you trust yourself in bed with me any more, little fire-cracker? Afraid I might have lit your fuse?'

Her soft mouth tightened and he laughed softly, reaching across the table towards her. Vivian stiffened, but he was only removing the lid from the casserole.

'You dish up the food. I'll pour the wine.'

'Oh, but I don't know if I like red wine——'

'You'll like this one. It's a gold-medal winner from a vineyard I part-own in Gisborne,' he said, brushing aside her diffidence as he filled her glass. He poured himself a glass, drank half and refilled it, all in the time it took her to ladle some of the steaming casserole on to their plates.

She waited until she had eaten several mouthfuls of food before she took her first sip. In spite of her determination not to react, she was unable to prevent a murmur of surprised pleasure as the full-bodied flavour exploded against her palate, drenching her senses in its heady bouquet.

'You see, you never know whether you're going to like something until you try it. You need to be more adventurous, Vivian, experiment more...'

She didn't like the strange tension in him...nor the dangerous ease with which he broached the bottle as they both pretended to eat. She noticed he had shaved since their confrontation in his office. It had been necessary for him to shave but not to *dress*? She felt a strange thrill of fear.

'Weren't you afraid?' he said disconcertingly, his deep, hushed tone seeming to weave itself into the darkness. 'The only locked room in Bluebeard's castle... Weren't you afraid of the horrors you might find in there when you stole the key?'

'This isn't a castle and you're not Bluebeard,' she said, resisting the powerful vision he was slyly conjuring out of her imagination. 'You've only ever had one wife,' she said deliberately. 'And I'm certainly in a position to know that you didn't murder her.'

He looked at her broodingly over the rim of his glass. 'Ah, yes, my beloved wife. Frank tells me you're curious about her...' Vivian was suddenly certain that Nicholas was building up towards some kind of critical release of the tension that raged in his face, seethed in his restless eye.

'I'm in the mood for violence...'

She rubbed her damp palms surreptitiously against her thighs and felt the forgotten bulge in her trouser pocket.

The idea sprang into her mind full-blown. Her fingers closed around the glass bottle warmed by her thigh.

'I wouldn't mind a drink of water, please.'

He got up, moving with his usual swiftness and precision, and Vivian knew that in spite of the wine he had consumed he was still dangerously alert. It was only his inhibitions that had been relaxed, and thus the bonds that chained his savage inner demons.

The moment he turned away to the sink, she pulled out the chloral hydrate, wrenched off the lid and tried to shake a few drops into his full wine glass, horrified when the clear liquid came out in a little gush.

She didn't have time to get the bottle capped and back into her pocket, and had to thrust it down on her lap as she accepted her glass of water, feeling the remainder of the drug soak into the fabric over her hip as her heart threshed wildly in her chest.

'You wanted to know about Barbara...'

She watched, her green eyes wide with fascinated horror, as he re-seated himself and took a long swallow of his wine before he spoke again. Oh, God, what madness had possessed her? What if she had given him too much and he died?

'The biggest mistake of my arrogant young life...'

Mistake? Vivian was jolted out of her frantic abstraction.

His mouth twisted at her expression. 'You thought it was the love-match of the century? Mis-match, more like. It was my father's idea. He's an extremely dominating man and I'm his only son, his greatest pride—and his greatest disappointment. We clashed on just about everything. When I came back from university overseas, he was very ill and used some very clever emotional blackmail to pressure me into marriage with his god-daughter. Needless to say, he then miraculously recovered.'

'Then...you fell in love with each other after the marriage?' Vivian said, her thoughts falling into chaos.

'Love was never part of the equation. Like my father, Barbara saw our marriage in terms of status and control. We lived separate lives from the start. She politely endured me in her bed because it was necessary in order to secure her permanent place in the Thorne dynasty— part of her bargain with my father, I gather—and I politely endured for reasons just as selfish, because I wanted nothing to disturb my build-up for the Olympic trials...'

He paused and Vivian held her breath, hoping the fascinating revelations were going to continue.

'Then Barbara told me she was pregnant and I realised just how permanent was the trap my father had planned for me. Except it wasn't—the next day she and the baby were killed...'

He reached for his wine-glass again and Vivian couldn't stop a darting gesture of involuntary protest.

'Oh, no, please don't drink that!' She clumsily tried to knock it out of his hand.

'Why not? Are you afraid I'll pass out on you before I finish baring my soul?' He stopped, his face sharpening as he looked from her stark expression of appalled guilt to his glass, his shrewd brain making the impossible leap in perception.

'My God, is there something wrong with this? *What have you put in my wine?*'

He lunged across the table with a roar, scattering the burning candles, and Vivian's chair crashed over as she jumped to her feet, sending the empty bottle in her lap spinning to the floor.

She didn't wait to see him recognise it. She fled.

She flew down the hall and crashed through the door into the lighthouse in a blind panic, triggering the sensor lights in the stairwell. She was thundering up the stairs before she remembered there were no locks on the doors, nowhere to hide. It was too late now; she could feel the pounding vibration of his mysteriously delayed pursuit through the steel under her flying feet.

He caught her just below the fourth level, not even attempting to stop her but merely gathering her up in his furious momentum, driving her onwards and upwards with the bulldozing threat of his body. Only when they reached the landing of his room did he actually lay a hand on her, catching her right wrist and using their combined speed to swing her away from the stairs and through the doorway, shoving her back against the wall, anchoring her there with the full thrust of his body, slamming his other hand on to the light-switch so that she was exposed to the full glare of his rage.

'How much did you give me?' he snarled, his breath fogging up her glasses, his lips brushing hers in an angry parody of a kiss. 'The whole damn bottle? How *much*, damn you?' He rattled her against the wall.

'I don't know—a little, a teaspoonful, I don't *know*!' she panted desperately. 'I spilled the rest of it, that's why the bottle was empty. I'm sorry, Nicholas, I panicked, you were frightening me...' She was begging now, but she was beyond caring. 'Please, I'm sorry——'

'*Sorry*!' he ground out. He shook his head violently, as if the drug was already beginning to affect him.

'Maybe you should sit down before you fall down,' she said, feeling wretchedly weak herself.

'Maybe I should,' he said thickly. He pulled her away from the wall and dragged her over to the bed, pulling her between his spread legs as he sat down, fumbling in his bath-robe pocket. She felt a cold metallic clasp replace the heat of his hand on her wrist, and looked down just in time to see him snapping the other handcuff around his own wrist.

'My God, what are you doing?' she asked numbly, staring at their shackled limbs. So this was why she had got such a head start on his superior strength and speed. He had gone to get *chains*!

'Making sure you'll be here when I wake up,' he said grimly. '*If* I wake up.'

She shuddered. 'Don't say that! Please, Nicholas, where's the key? You don't need to do this. I promise I'll stay...'

For an answer he fell diagonally back on the bed, throwing his shackled right wrist forcefully out to his side so that she was brought tumbling down on top of him with a soft scream of terror. He pulled off her glasses and tossed them on the floor in a careless gesture that she found paradoxically even more threatening than his violence.

'Nicholas, no...' She struggled to find purchase with her knees against the mattress, conscious that she was straddling him, and the towelling robe was parting over his powerful thighs.

'Nicholas, *yes*!' He pulled her head down, crushing her mouth against his, wrapping his right arm across her back so that her captive arm was forced behind her. He kissed her until she tried to bite him, and then he nudged her face aside with his jaw and sank his teeth into her vulnerable throat. She cried out, struggling weakly as he began to suckle at the bite, murmuring words against her skin that sapped her will and created tiny shocks of pleasure deep in her feminine core. He began to kiss her again, and this time she didn't fight him and the forceful thrust of his tongue gentled to a slow, seductive glide that made her tremble with yearning.

'I may pass out, but not before I've had a taste of you . . . not before you've given me everything I want . . .' His mouth moved to the other side of her throat, nibbling and sucking with tender savagery as his hips and thighs began to undulate beneath her. 'I'm going to devour every lovely inch of you . . . use my lips and teeth and tongue on you in ways that you've never even imagined . . . brand you all over with my mark so that anyone who looks at you will know you've come from my bed . . .'

Vivian knew he was talking about Peter. Briefly surfacing from her passion-drugged state, she tried to arch away, but Nicholas shifted his hand from the back of her neck to the front of her silk blouse, slipping his fingers into the prim neckline and ripping it open with a single downward stroke that scattered the pearl buttons like lustrous tears across his chest.

'Nicholas!'

Her gasp was lost in a spasm of violent sensation as he flicked open the tiny plastic catch between her breasts and allowed them to tumble free of the confining lace. The ginger freckles were stretched over their swollen fullness, the soft pink tips swaying against the hard contours of his chest, contracting instantly into tight points that scraped and caught on his own peaked masculine nipples.

His chest heaved and he uttered a harsh sound, violently tilting his hips to roll her on to her side and then her back, hefting her up against the pillows, rising up and over her on his braced hands. In almost the same motion he loosened the belt of his robe so that it fell open around her, baring the full length of his body to her restless gaze. He was hugely aroused and shuddering with a fierce tension, for all the world as if she had given him an aphrodisiac instead of a sedative.

He looked triumphantly down at the lavish bounty he had exposed, his nostrils flaring as he caught the enticing scent of her body, and recognised the subtle signals of her arousal.

'Yes—*Nicholas*,' he ground out. 'Not Peter, *Nicholas*. Admit it. You couldn't give a damn about him when you're with me!'

He cupped her breast with a possessive movement of his manacled hand, the narrow chain connecting their wrists dragging in a cold caress against the skin of her ribs as he moved deliberately, his fingers contracting and relaxing, his thumb rubbing against the rigid nipple.

He bent his head and his tongue darted out to curl around the tip he was cherishing, dragging it up into his mouth, moistening it with tender care then releasing it to the cool night air.

'You don't love him; you don't want to marry him.' The words were muffled by her flesh. 'You don't want to cling to your safe, unadventurous past...you want the fierce excitement only I can give you...you want this...and this...' He held her pleasure-drenched gaze as his mouth closed over her, slanted softly, sucked lightly, twisted, lifted and lowered again...

'I'm...not...the one who won't let...the past go,' she panted, biting her lip as he repeated the voluptuously unsatisfying action over and over, clenching her chained hand helplessly against her side, groaning with sweet agony as he finally used his teeth and suckled her with the rough urgency that she needed, marking her as he had promised with his erotic brand of possession. Her extravagant response made him explode into action, pushing heavily between her thighs, moving jerkily on her as if the fabric between them didn't exist, as if he was already buried deep inside her, pleasuring them both beyond imagining...

'Say it, Vivian...stop holding yourself back...stop pushing me away.' She was suddenly aware of a settling heaviness in his body as his head sank down on her shoulder. 'Don't let me go down into this damned darkness without a prayer...'

'Stop talking about dying!' she cried frantically, tugging at his hair to try and keep him awake.

'I'm not talking about dying, I'm talking about living. I can't let him get you... Gotta keep you with me,' he said with a blurred illogicality that Vivian knew from experience was the drug tightening its grip on his mind, but she sought to drag him back to her with desperate words of truth.

'Peter won't ever get me because he doesn't *want* me, damn you. Do you hear me, Nicholas Thorne? You were right. I don't love Peter and Peter doesn't love me. He loves my *sister*. It's *Janna* he's going to marry on Saturday, you big, gullible oaf, not me!'

For a moment he remained still, a dead weight, and she thought he had lapsed into unconsciousness, but then he suddenly rolled off her in a tangle of white towelling.

'What did you say?'

The face beside hers on the pillow suddenly looked completely wide awake. But no, his pupil was almost a pinpoint. He was conscious through sheer force of will.

She moistened her lips and nervously tucked her blouse across her breasts one-handed as she said in a husky little voice, 'I cancelled our engagement last week. But not the wedding. You see, I found out Peter and Janna had fallen in love, and, well—they were sort of mired in the inertia of their guilt. They didn't deliberately set out to hurt me, and I realised I hadn't ever really been in love with Peter, not the way that Janna is. So I told her to go ahead and get married in my place and I'd dance at their wedding.'

She smiled to show how bravely she had accepted the crushing blow to her feminine pride, but the smile began to waver under his sombre stare and, to her horror, her eyes began to fill.

'I suppose now you're going to tell me I got what I deserved,' she whispered, and burst into a flood of tears.

But instead of gloating, as she had always dreaded that he would, Nicholas quietly gathered her shuddering body against his warm length and stroked her wild ginger mane, uttering soothing murmurs while she sobbed out all the wretched details against his chest.

It took a long time to expend her storm of stored-up tears, and repeated assurances from Nicholas that he had no interest in wreaking his savage revenge on her damned sister's damned wedding, before Vivian finally hiccupped herself into exhausted sleep. Only then did the man holding her allow his mind and body to go equally lax, finally relinquishing his formidable will to the powerful seduction of the drug in his veins.

CHAPTER SIX

VIVIAN took another frigid slap in the mouth and felt her throat burn with the salty abrasion as she coughed the sea-water out of her lungs.

She sluggishly instructed her head to turn and her arms to rise and fall, rise and fall, in the rhythmic stroke that had won several long-distance ocean swims at the surf-club she had belonged to in her late teens.

The wet-suit that she had taken from among the diving-gear in the lighthouse storeroom was providing her with extra buoyancy and some protection against the cold, but she knew that mental stamina would be her greatest asset in the gruelling swim.

She turned on her side, checking that she was still moving in the right direction, heading towards the uneven lurch against the horizon that Frank had let slip one day was the nearest inhabited island. Thank God the weather was good and the sea not too choppy, but even if there had been a cyclone Vivian wouldn't have cared.

She had woken just before dawn and looked at the man lying next to her in a deep, drugged sleep and acknowledged with a thrill of despair that she was in love with her capricious captor.

In the space of a few days the morals of a lifetime had been swept away. Instead of drawing Nicholas into the sunlight of reason, she had been drawn into the shadows. Something dark in herself was called forth by the darkness in him. She could protest all she liked, but all Nicholas had to do was touch her and she melted. And he knew it.

Last night he had admitted that he had never loved his wife. That called into question everything she had come to believe she knew about him. It made his motive for revenge not one of honest emotional torment, which could be appeased, but of cold-blooded, implacable malice.

The realisation that Nicholas must have uncuffed her before he fell asleep was merely confirmation of her bleak theory that he believed he had won their battle of wills. The empty steel bracelet dangling from his own still-manacled wrist was a mute testament to his confidence in her sexual subjugation.

Protest had exploded in her brain. *No*! She wouldn't let him distort her love into something that she was ashamed of. She had to be out of his reach before he woke up. Before he could touch her again...

Fool, fool, fool, Vivian chanted inside her head, in rhythm to her stroking through the water. To believe that you could play with fire and not be burnt. Fool, fool...

'Little fool! What in the hell do you think you're doing? Of all the ridiculous, theatrical stunts!'

She suddenly realised that the new voice was much deeper than the one in her head and far more insulting, and the loud slapping sound wasn't the rising waves hitting her face; it was the sound of oars striking the water.

Water sheeted down her face from her sopping hair, sticking her eyelashes together and getting in her swollen eyes as she stopped to tread water and was nearly run down by a small aluminium dinghy rowing furiously towards her.

Nicholas was shipping the oars, leaning over the side, yelling, cursing, trying to grab her slippery wet-suited arm.

Vivian swam away, coughing and spluttering as she briefly sank. When she struggled to the surface again, Nicholas was standing silhouetted against the crisp morning sky, the boat rocking dangerously. 'For God's sake, Vivian,' he cried bleakly. 'Where in the hell do you think you're going?'

Still choking on salt-water and shock, Vivian didn't bother to answer; she just pointed in the direction of the distant island.

Nicholas exploded in another series of explicit curses. 'Do you *want* to bloody drown? You can't swim that far! Get in this damned boat *now*!'

For an answer Vivian rolled over and began swimming with renewed energy. Each time she turned her head to breathe, she saw Nicholas pulling on the oars, keeping on a parallel course, his grim mouth opening and shutting on words she couldn't hear through her water-clogged ears.

Gradually Vivian's false burst of strength drained away and the next time that Nicholas veered close she didn't have the energy to pull away.

He leaned over and caught her by the zip-cord trailing from the back of her neck, forcing her to tread water as she clung to the side of the boat, gasping air into her burning lungs. 'That's enough! You've made your point, Vivian,' he said roughly. 'You want me to beg? I will: *please* get into the bloody boat. We'll talk, and then I'll take you anywhere you want me to...'

Her green eyes were enormous in her exhausted face. 'I'm not that gullible any more,' she choked, fighting her pathetic desire to trust him, even now. '*You're* the gullible one. You never fooled me at all. I knew even before I came here who you were!'

He looked thunderstruck. 'You *knew*?'

'That Nicholas Rose was Nicholas Thorne,' she threw into his haggard face. Her frigid lips and tongue shaped the words with increasing difficulty. 'But I came anyway, because I knew that if this was some kind of vicious v-vendetta, then the only way to stop you was to confront you face to face ... so I let you d-drug me ... I only *pretended* to w-want to escape ... Everything you did to me you were only able to d-do because I *chose* to *let* you ... Because I wanted t-time to b-be with you and c-convince you that r-revenge is n-not the way for y-you t-to find p-peace ...'

Her teeth were chattering so much that she could hardly get the last defiant words out, and Nicholas made an abrupt growl and rammed his hands under her arms, hauling her over the gunwale and dumping her into the bottom of the boat.

'Thank you for *letting* me rescue you!' he said sardonically. 'I take it you weren't simply *pretending* this time.'

Vivian suddenly felt blessedly numb all over. Even her bleeding heart was cauterised by the cold. 'Why?' she whispered. 'Why did you b-bother to come and get me?'

'Why in the hell do you think? Because I love you, damn it!' he snarled savagely, not even bothering to look at her as he swivelled his torso to signal with his upraised arm. Automatically following his gaze, a stupefied Vivian saw the blurry image of a white launch that looked as big as an ocean liner foaming down on them.

'Coastguard?' Her mouth seemed to have split from her mind.

'No. Mine. The *Hero*. It's been out doing a marine survey for the last few days. As soon as I found your clothes on the beach, I called her up and used her radar to track you. Ahoy! Derek! Send down that sling, will you?'

She screwed her eyes shut as she was strapped and hauled and bundled, and passed from hand to hand like an unwanted package until she felt the familiar arms taking possession of her again.

Nicholas carried her down a brightly lit companionway and into a spacious white cabin, kicking the door shut before rapidly stripping the over-large wet-suit from her numb body.

His mouth quirked when he saw the emerald-green bra and panties she wore underneath. His smile thawed a tiny slice of heart. Maybe she wasn't hallucinating, after all. Maybe he really had said it.

'My favourites,' he murmured, fingering the saturated lace. 'Underwear that matches your eyes.' And then he peeled them off too, smothering her protests at his rough handling with a thick, blue towel, rubbing her vigorously until she cried out at the pain of the blood returning to the surface of her icy skin.

'Don't be such a baby!' he said, planting a kiss on her blue lips as he finished a strenuous scouring of her hair, which had turned the dripping tails to dark red frizz. 'We have to get you properly thawed out.'

He stripped off his own clothes and walked naked with her to the wide berth, lying down on it and mounding the patterned continental quilt over them both as the boat's powerful engines throttled to full power and the sky began to whip past the brass port-hole above their heads.

'Stop cringing, this is all very scientific. I'm a scientist—I know what I'm talking about,' he said, cuddling her close, warming her with the sensual heat of his body, breast to breast, belly to belly, thigh to thigh. He shuddered and buried his face in her neck. 'Oh, *God*, that feels good.'

Vivian knew what he meant. Tears of exhaustion and confusion trembled on her still-damp lashes.

He lifted his head and kissed them away. 'I'm sorry, Ginger—first things first. If you had bothered to wait for me to wake up this morning, you would have known this already... in fact, you would have known last night if you hadn't sabotaged my good intentions. My name is Nicholas James Thorne... the Second.'

'The Second?' she whispered, bewildered. Was he suggesting they start all over again? A second chance?

'To distinguish me from my father—Nicholas James Thorne the *First*,' he said deliberately.

Her brow wrinkled soggily. 'Your father has the same name as you?'

'No, *I* have the same name as *him*,' he corrected urgently, as if the fine distinction was important. 'Just before I was born he had an illness that rendered him sterile, which was why he was so obsessive about me marrying and perpetuating the name. There are two Nicholas Thornes, Vivian, but only one was driving the car that night—my father.'

Vivian's bleached face stormed with vivid emotion as she realised what he was telling her. 'But, your son——'

His fingers across her mouth hushed her confused protest, and the riot of blood in her veins became a visible tumult that bloomed across her skin. 'I have no son. Your "boy" in the back seat was me. To the doctor who patched me up, a twenty-five-year-old probably *did* seem like a boy—he certainly seemed old to me, although he was probably only in his late fifties.

'After Barbara was killed, my father said it didn't matter that I was crippled, as long as my genes were healthy. We had endless rows about my refusal to marry again. In the end I turned my back on it all—my father, his money, the business I was supposed to take over, the whole concept of Being A Thorne. I didn't realise that after the accident his dream had become a ruthless obsession, and the obsession had developed into a dangerous fixation with you...'

Vivian struggled to sit up, but Nicholas held her down with implacable gentleness. 'Are you saying this was all *his* idea?' she asked hoarsely through her salt-scored throat.

'I had no idea what he was planning,' he said emphatically. 'Not until I paid a long-overdue duty visit last week. As usual, our discussion turned into a furious row. He suddenly started shouting the most ridiculous things...about how it was all your fault his son had turned against him and how he was finally going to make you and Janna pay for murdering his grandson. How he had waited years for just the right moment to get you where he wanted you... He was boasting about how he was going to do it when he had a massive stroke——'

'Oh, God...' Vivian's fist came up to her mouth and Nicholas eased it away, unsurprised by her horrified compassion for the man who had tried to hurt her.

'No, he's not dead, but he's in an extremely bad way,' he said sombrely, wrapping her fist reassuringly in his. His body shifted against hers, enveloping her in a fresh wave of blissful warmth.

'As soon as he was taken to hospital, I scoured his desk and files in case his incredible ravings were true. I found his dossier on you and a load of legal transactions with Marvel-Mitchell, and I got a shock to find it was actually on the verge of happening—and on Nowhere of all places—while I was scheduled to be away in Florida. Here!' His voice hardened and she felt the muscles of his chest tense as if against a blow to the heart. 'On *my* island...the place I used to come to get away from his insidious interference in my life. That was part of his sick delusion, you see,' he added tiredly. 'That he was doing this for *my* sake. So I fired the sleazy hireling who was supposed to do all the dirty work, and flew down here myself to...' He hesitated uneasily.

'To take his place?' she challenged painfully.

He leaned up on one elbow and said ruefully, 'Actually, I came hot-foot to rescue you. To apologise and try to smooth things over and explain about my father's condition——'

'Rescue me? *Apologise*? By *drugging* me and photographing me naked in bed with you and threatening to make me have your *baby*?' Vivian squawked at him incredulously. 'You expect me to believe that was your idea of *smoothing things over*?'

To her fascination he flushed, adjusting his eye-patch in the first unconsciously nervous gesture she had ever seen him make. 'Yes, well, you weren't quite naked. And, anyway, that was partly your fault.'

'*My* fault?'

'I was expecting your sister. I had intended to be very civilised and restrained and then use my power of attorney to sign the settlement contract and wave Janna a grateful goodbye, but I took one look at you and went off like a rocket.' His voice roughened as he began to play with her damp ginger curls. 'I wanted you more than any woman I've wanted in my life. I can't explain it. I just saw you, touched you, and *knew* that we were made for each other, that you felt the same, powerful attraction that I did...

'But I knew from my father's file that you were due to get married in a week, so I didn't have much time. I decided to take some drastic short cuts, use every despicable tool conveniently placed at my disposal, to keep you here and break down your resistance to the notion of breaking up with Marvel. I thought that my pretending to be my father would buy me the time I needed to build on the potent physical chemistry between us. Of course, I didn't realise that you were also doing some bidding for the same reason...' he added slyly.

She placed her hands flat against his bare chest. 'Not quite the same reason,' she teased.

To her surprise he didn't smile. 'Are you trying to let me down lightly?' he asked quietly.

She suddenly realised that she hadn't told him. She traced his tight mouth with her forefinger. 'I woke up this morning horrified to admit I'd fallen in love with you,' she said softly. 'My heart skewered on the sword of an emotional pirate. You can't blame me for choosing the deep blue sea over the devil. You should have been more honest with me from the start...'

'Like you were, you mean,' he said drily, smiling at her rueful acknowledgement. 'It may not seem like it, but I do have *some* sense of honour, you know. I wasn't going to make love to you until you asked, and I wasn't going to ask you to marry me until you'd given Marvel his marching orders.'

'Marry!' He looked amused by her shock, and she recovered quickly. 'I thought you wanted me to be your sex-slave,' she pouted huskily.

'That, too, of course,' he said, lambent flecks of gold sparkling wickedly in his eye at her sensual boldness.

He rolled over on top of her. 'And speaking of slavery...I had to be rescued from a very embarrassing state of captivity myself this morning. Handcuffed to my own bed! I had to drag it over to the door and spend fifteen minutes yelling down the stairwell before Frank heard and came up and jemmied the cuffs open for me. He'll never let me hear the end of it!'

'You should be more careful who you go to bed with,' said Vivian demurely.

His head lowered as his knee brushed between her legs. 'I will be. *Very* careful,' he murmured against her mouth. 'In future I'll only be going to bed with my fire-cracker wife.'

As she slid her arms around his satiny-hard waist and blossomed eagerly for his love, Vivian thought it sounded like a just fate for a retired pirate...

GHOST BRIDE

BY
ROSALIE ASH

CHAPTER ONE

STOP the wedding! The words screamed silently through Beth's brain. She could hardly believe she hadn't shouted them out loud. At the back of the church, hidden behind the early-Norman font, she sat like a statue. Her heart was hammering painfully. Her face was white in its cloudy halo of dark hair, grey eyes huge with fear, her hands cold as ice. The only warmth was Sam's small, solid body wriggling slightly in her arms as she cradled him against her.

A few moments ago she'd slipped into the back of the church, averting her face in case anyone looked round and recognised her. The service had begun. A burning sense of outrage had been fuelling her courage. But the formal trappings of the marriage service, the flower-filled church, the relatives and guests in glossy silk suits and elaborate hats, all these realities were gradually undermining her nerve. A wedding was a wedding. Marriage was marriage. Sacrosanct, somehow. Even if it was Lorna's marriage to Rafael, the greatest outrage of all...

Panic was gripping her now, drying her mouth, dampening her palms. She was so wound up, she could barely focus on the people around her, let alone bring herself to concentrate on the solemn ceremony taking place at the front of the church, a million miles away from where she sat, alone, with Sam in her arms...

She'd come too far to back out, hadn't she? Her presence in the church could be noticed at any moment.

She'd be identified with horror, no doubt. Like the wicked fairy at Sleeping Beauty's christening...

The thought of the tall, black-haired man at the altar made her feel almost faint with nerves. It was over a year since she'd seen Rafael. But even though she couldn't actually see him now, through the massed congregation in front of her, she could guess at the swarthy arrogance of his face, the lidded cynicism of his eyes. Simply visualising the proud set of his head, with the carelessly over-long black hair, the sloping muscle of his shoulders, the supple length of his back in an expensively tailored morning suit, was enough to bring the past bursting back into her mind like a great explosion of pain...

Sam gave a small gurgle, a cross between a hiccup and a laugh. The magenta-hatted woman in the pew in front half turned, and smiled benevolently at the baby's creamy-skinned perfection. Her smile faded a fraction as she took in Beth's tense pallor, emphasised by the stark black of her suit.

Help me, Beth thought in silent desperation. Her throat was so dry now, she felt she was choking. Her heart was hammering, thudding erratically beneath her breastbone. Somebody, help me. I can't do this. But I have to do this...

The vicar, rotund and white-haired, was intoning the time-honoured introductory words of the marriage ceremony. From the distant glimpse she'd caught of Lorna, at the altar with Rafael, her stepsister looked impossibly glamorous—massed blonde curls coiffed into a froth of femininity, trim waist cinched even smaller by the meringue-white wedding-dress. Did she hate Lorna? Until now, she'd felt only resigned dislike, and sometimes even pity. Hate was too fierce an emotion to waste on her stepsister, no matter what their past clash of personality. But now? Hearing that Lorna was staking her claim on Rafael was too much to bear. Yes, right now, she *did* hate her. Almost as much as she hated Rafael for this act of cold betrayal...

But, even so, nothing in her brief, almost twenty years' experience of life had prepared her for today, for the way she was feeling today. Hurt and driven. Torn apart by emotions she didn't understand, couldn't handle...

Distractedly, she stared at a flagstone inlaid with brass, set into the floor of the church. Her thoughts drifted. The flagstone was inscribed with a man's name. The date: 1522. A story went with that stone, and she knew the story well. This was her village church, the church nearest Cobb Barton, the lovely old Cotswold house she'd left in disgrace fifteen months ago. The name on that memorial stone was that of a lord of the manor, infamous for stabbing a priest to death in the parlour of his manor-house after catching him flirting with his wife. By some unimaginable quirk of justice, the lord of the manor had received both a papal and a royal pardon for his act of primitive revenge.

Beth shivered, and hugged Sam tighter. Would anyone pardon *her* for her primitive act of revenge? Because that was what this was, wasn't it? Call it what she liked, fool herself that it was justice or necessity... but it was revenge, basic and simple... Unless she was doing it for Sam...

'...Into which holy estate these two persons present...'

The vicar's speech was approaching the moment when she would have to stand up, if she was going to go through with this. But her knees felt as if they'd disappeared altogether, dissolved into thin air...

'...Therefore if any man can shew any just cause, why they may not lawfully be joined...'

Someone coughed, smothering the next couple of words. A small child in the next pew dropped a hymn book. There was some fidgeting among the congregation...

'...now speak, or else hereafter for ever hold his peace.'

Silence. Short, loaded, accompanied by the rustling of service sheets.

Beth stood up. As if in a dream, or a nightmare, her low heels echoing on the flagged floor, she began to walk slowly down the aisle towards the altar.

Heads were beginning to turn in surprise and dismay, a sea of swivelling faces. The vicar had stopped speaking, but his face was a blur, a pale oval without features. So were all the other faces. Panic was blurring her vision.

There was a noise now, filling the echoing silence, a growing murmur of protest and anger. Feeling as if she were fighting through thick fog, she heard her father's blustering challenge, her stepmother Annabel's warning gasp of anger, Lorna's hissed intake of breath tinged with fury. Abruptly the hazy tableau ahead of her broke from its frozen disbelief into chaotic reaction, like actors on a stage suddenly springing to life.

Her father had pushed his way forward, as if to guard Lorna from the intrusion. It was like a fresh act of betrayal. Even after all this time, her father, her own father, was siding with Lorna. What was it he'd flung at her coldly, the last time they'd spoken? 'You are dead to me now, you might just as well be dead like your mother...'

She'd been disowned, written off, in the cruellest way imaginable, 'like mother, like daughter'. And nothing had changed.

It was the final straw. Tears stung Beth's eyes. The figures surrounding her were just a surreal blur. The only point of focus was the tall, powerful figure which elbowed towards her in surprise, then froze in stunned blankness. Now it seemed as if there were only the two of them, isolated in the midst of the hostile crowd. She blinked and stared at him. Rafael's dark skin, bluish-tinged with five o'clock shadow always around his lower jaw, appeared to flush a shade darker over the high cheekbones, then visibly pale. But the blue gaze held no emotion but disbelief. Rafael was looking at her with blank, stunned incredulity.

'Beth?' Rafael's husky voice sounded bemused. His gaze burned on her now, with mounting emotion, and she shivered again, as if the fire in his eyes held ice rather than heat. 'Beth, what in God's name do you think you are doing...?'

'I thought you should know that this is your son,' she said clearly. Her soft voice carried around the church with a clarity which surprised her.

'My *son*?' His gaze abruptly hardened. He switched that unreadable laser-stare to the child in her arms, then focused back on her white face. '*No es posible...*'

Sam, placidly clutching the lapels of her black jacket, gazed with blissful lack of understanding at the tall dark man towering over him. In contrast to the suppressed ferocity of the adult male, he looked terrifyingly vulnerable in his blue dungarees and tiny quilted blue jacket. But, even at six months old, his eyes were as blue and black-fringed and heart-breaking as his father's...

Rafael's fury was more violent for being tautly suppressed.

'*Dios*, what kind of a joke is this...?'

Beth's heart lurched. The savagery she met in those dark blue eyes was unexpected. But how naïve could she be? Had she imagined he'd take her revenge with a smile and a handshake? This was terrible. A thousand times worse than she'd envisaged. It suddenly struck her that her stunt had backfired. She'd pictured Rafael aghast, embarrassed, even remorseful ... but not icily, furiously accusing...

Lorna was pink-faced, her mouth contorted into such fury that Beth took a step back. She'd had a small, carefully sarcastic speech in her head, but now she found the words stuck in her throat. She opened her mouth and no sound emerged. She tried again.

'It's no joke, Rafael. I thought you should know the truth, *before* you marry my stepsister...'

'Now, hang on a minute...' It was the best man, tall and dark like Rafael, rallying heroically to the bride-groom's cause. Fresh tears blurred her vision, tears of anger and shame, but she blinked them fiercely away, and swung round to retreat as fast as she could.

With the babble of protest and censure ringing unintelligibly in her ears, she plunged back down the aisle. If everything except Rafael's expression had been a blur before, now it was even more so.

The buzz of shocked voices had risen to a crescendo as she fled. Sam, usually sunny-natured and imperturbable, was beginning to whimper as he absorbed the hostility infiltrating his small, secure world.

Fool—stupid, stupid fool, she berated herself silently as she reached the door, pushed blindly into the cool

October air, made as swiftly as her shaky legs would carry her for the four-wheel-drive Range Rover her aunt let her use.

If she'd hurt the people in that small church, struck back at Rafael, at Lorna, at her stepmother, and her own father, she felt a million times more hurt herself. It served her right, she reflected grimly, buckling Sam into his seat in the back, her fingers numb with nerves. Destructive behaviour had a nasty way of rebounding on the perpetrator...

The nightmare had begun, the nightmare of her own making, and now she had the terrifying sense of pursuit, of not being fast enough to escape...

But she managed to fasten Sam's straps, managed to hurl herself into the driving-seat, start the engine, pull away from the parking space in the shadow of the ancient yews, drive without incident away from the church and its stunned, outraged occupants.

Had she half expected Rafael to follow her? Race after her, leave Lorna at the altar? Or, if not Rafael, her father, or stepmother, blocking her escape to demand an explanation? Raking a hand exhaustedly over her face, she concentrated with fierce will-power on driving safely. Sam was too precious to jeopardise his safety because she'd torn her emotions to shreds today...

It was a beautiful day, she noticed with a touch of bitter irony. A low autumn sun was coating the neat Gloucestershire countryside with gold. If only her heart didn't feel like ice. If only this grey cloud would lift from her mind. All she really wanted to do was pull off the road somewhere and give in to the tearing, ragged despair that was shuddering through her. But, with Sam to think about, that was a luxury she couldn't indulge in. She had to get home now, carefully, sensibly. And then she could fall apart...

She pulled on to the M5, and headed south-west. Sam, unbelievably, after all the tension surrounding him, had fallen asleep. She turned on the radio and listened to snatches of a quiz programme. She couldn't concentrate. All she could manage was to function on an elementary level, drive the Range Rover back to Devon without accident, take refuge in the safety and anonymity of her little Exmoor cottage, and regret her wild impulse as passionately as she'd ever regretted anything before in her whole life...

It was mid-afternoon when she halted outside the cottage and stepped stiffly from the driving-seat. Miller's Cottage had never looked more welcoming. Half a mile out of the village, with the wooded beauty of the Quantock Hills rising behind it, and the purple heather of Exmoor to the side, it was her aunt's holiday retreat. For the past ten months it had been home to Beth. And since April, to Sam. Its thick pink cob walls and mossy thatch glowed in the mellow sun.

Beth reached into the car to get Sam. In spite of her anguish, she sent up her regular prayer of thanks for Aunt Jayne. Her mother's sister had appeared in her life at the crucial moment. Beth had been pregnant, working in the kitchens of a restaurant near the Holloway Road in London, and living in a shared, overcrowded fourth floor bed-sit which even the cockroaches had black-listed. She'd bumped into Jayne that Christmas, coming out of Harrods. *Jayne* had been coming out of Harrods, to be exact. Beth had been window-shopping, gazing numbly at the glitter and nostalgia of fir-trees and scarlet bows and glowing golden beads. They'd gone for tea.

Jayne had expertly assessed Beth's condition, and, when Beth had tautly explained her reasons for staying away from home, Jayne had understood. And sympathised. After all, Beth's mother had been Jayne's younger sister. Jayne had known all too well how the land lay in the step-family created by her sister's defection...

Mum had left to live with another man, when Beth was thirteen. Dad had never got over it, thought Beth, her fingers unsteady and abnormally clumsy as she tried to unbuckle Sam's strap without waking him. She supposed she'd always been conscious of how deeply her mother's behaviour had affected all their lives. But abruptly that awareness had been heightened. Dad might have met Annabel and remarried, but he'd never got over Mum's betrayal.

And, to add insult to injury, the desertion for another man had been followed by the tragedy of her mother's death. She'd been killed in a riding accident. Beth had been devastated but, if anything, it had only made her father more bitter. Mum had died, and deprived him of the satisfaction of recrimination or retaliation.

And Beth had been the substitute. Fate had given her the same cloudy dark hair and big grey eyes as her mother. She'd quickly learned that she was an unbearable reminder. She'd shared a love of riding with her mother, and she'd had her own pony, a soft-mouthed little mare called Nutmeg. After Mum had left, the pony had been sold. At the time, that had seemed the meanest act of all. But then Annabel had come into their lives. Annabel, in her mid-thirties, a high-powered businesswoman and already a wealthy widow with a daughter two years older than Beth, had supplied the soothing balm to Dad's ego. Both the new females in Dad's life had been as blonde and curvaceous as Beth and her mother were dark and slim. They had taken pride of place in her father's heart, while Beth, at Annabel's suggestion, had been conveniently despatched to boarding-school.

There'd been personality clashes, of course, before Annabel had played the triumphant boarding-school card. Beth had been confused, lonely and bereft at the loss of her mother. But vague hopes that Lorna would prove a confidante had been dashed. Lorna had resented Beth on sight. The atmosphere at home had grown tense; Annabel had naturally sided with Lorna in any skirmishes, and Dad had just tried to pretend nothing was wrong...

It had been subtle. Petty things. Silly things which would have been bearable if they'd been real sisters and made up between the fights. But it had been an insidious campaign. Clever little lies to diminish her in her father's eyes. And so many spiteful moments, Beth had lost count. Lorna wiped off Beth's videos of *Anne of Green Gables*; borrowed her blue silk shirt and accidentally dropped curry sauce all over it; found Beth's diary and read out her secret crush on a boy at Youth Group to a roomful of friends. If Beth had something she valued, Lorna endeavoured to devalue it. If Beth wore something new, Lorna undermined her confidence with sarcasm and mockery. If Beth had friends, Lorna sought to separate them with the time-honoured 'divide and rule' technique. The crunch came when Annabel bought Lorna a pony, and drove her round to all the county gymkhanas and shows. Beth had been lucky to get to muck out the stable.

So exile to boarding-school had been both a punishment and a blessing. At least she was away from Lorna and Annabel. And at least she got to ride there at weekends. But the uneasy situation had erupted the summer Beth finished boarding-school, and came home to Cobb Barton.

The taxi had dropped her at the end of the drive, and Rafael Mendoza's dark green sports car had been parked outside the house as she walked to the front door. Mrs Parks, the rather haughty housekeeper installed by Annabel, had been supplying him with coffee while he waited to see Lorna...

That had been the start of it, she acknowledged, unclicking Sam's buckle and easing it away from his sleeping form. A chance meeting, thanks, ironically, to Annabel and Lorna. Annabel's PR company had been sponsoring Rafael's polo team and Lorna had met him while working for her mother. But that hadn't seemed to make any difference. One look at a hawkish dark face and smouldering blue eyes, and the fuse was already burning...

Her heart jolted painfully as she leaned closer to Sam, inhaled the warm sweetness of his baby skin, her mind lingering reluctantly on the memory of that first meeting with Rafael. He'd come straight from the polo field. All she could recall was the vision of tough masculinity, in high leather boots and mud-stained white breeches, sprawled nonchalantly on the elegant Regency-striped sofa in the drawing-room, dwarfing his surroundings with his potent personality.

She'd appeared in the doorway, and what an idiotic picture she must have presented. The boarding-school she'd just left had been a strict Catholic convent school for girls, with short white socks, striped green and white summer dresses, straw boaters and even white cotton gloves to be worn with the uniform at all times. She'd rebelliously flung off the gloves and boater on the train, just as she'd dragged her long dark curls from their confining ponytail. She'd intended to change into jeans and shirt in the loo of the train, but realised too late that under the watchful eyes of Sister Ursula she'd packed her own clothes into her suitcase by mistake. So there she'd stood, like something from a 1950s schoolgirls' annual, and watched the lazy grin spread across Rafael Mendoza's dark features...

'Lorna's baby stepsister?' he'd hazarded. '*Encantado, señorita...*'

His voice had been deep and sexily husky. He'd levered himself laconically to his feet, and towered over her in a ripple of muscle and sinew.

'I'm not a baby,' she'd managed, with what she'd hoped passed for a withering smile. 'I'm eighteen, old enough to vote, drive a car, and...'

'And...?' The unholy gleam in his eyes as they had roamed speculatively over the woman's body beneath the schoolgirl's dress had pierced her heart as well as stinging her pride. She should have been furious, she should have felt like slapping his arrogant dark face. This was the incarnation of everything that most horrified the nuns at her convent: the predatory male, with only one basic intention in his mind as he eyed up the vulnerable female...

But there'd been more than taunting chauvinism in his eyes, Beth had felt sure. No man had ever looked at her quite like that before. As if he saw right inside her, inside her heart and inside her head...

She'd wanted to turn and run, and she'd wanted to move closer, as if drawn by a magnet. That same bewildering conflict of reactions had never left her in the hectic weeks that followed, not even after the illicit longing had turned into the hot, dizzy rapture of possession...

Sam was awake, she realised, jolting back to the present. His blue eyes were sleepy as he focused on her face. He gave her a slow, delighted smile, and she smiled back, her heart swelling, her throat taut with emotion. Sam might have been an unwelcome mistake before he was born, he might be the stumbling-block to the Fine Arts degree she'd had lined up at Oxford, but now that he was here she loved him more than she'd thought possible.

'You,' she murmured, her eyes glowing involuntarily as she dropped a kiss on one peachy baby cheek, 'are a very beautiful little boy...'

She was ducking out of the Range Rover, Sam warm and heavy in her arms, when the crunch of gravel behind her made her turn quickly with a faint smile, expecting to see her aunt's round humorous face, and youthful chestnut bob. The smile faded to blank dismay, and then froze in terror.

The car blocking her in wasn't her Aunt Jayne's small town run-about, it was a sleek black Ferrari. And stepping out, striding rangily towards her, still wearing his grey morning suit, was Rafael Mendoza, looking like a warrior from his favourite polo field, like a man with savage retribution on his mind...

CHAPTER TWO

'How did you find me?' Her demand sounded too shaky to be convincingly aggressive. She was so shocked that she hardly knew what she was saying.

'I followed you,' Rafael said tersely. 'It was not too difficult.' His eyes were narrowed, shuttering his emotions, furious slits of dark sapphire.

'Where's Lorna?' She was shaking, she registered dimly. So hard that she was in danger of dropping Sam.

'Let's go inside,' he ordered softly, ignoring her question. 'We have to talk.'

Standing her ground, withstanding the onslaught of his powerful personality, was like a physical effort. But she was shaking her head decisively.

'We have nothing to talk about——' she began. She regretted the words instantly. With a long stride, Rafael closed the distance between them. Grasping her shoulders, he dug strong fingers into her upper arms with such force that she gasped in pain.

'Just open your front door, and we'll go inside,' he insisted. The softness in his husky voice was sending tremors of panic shivering down her spine. It was ominously soft. Rafael wasn't just angry, he was possessed by a controlled, white-hot fury which was terrifying.

'Rafe.' For Sam's sake she managed a more reasonable, compromising note. 'You're hurting me. And there's no way I'm inviting you into the cottage until you calm down...'

'Calm down?' The echo was savagely sardonic. 'You reappear after all this time, you walk into church and—and sabotage my wedding. And you ask me to calm down?'

For some reason his words cut her deeply, hurt so much that tears stung the backs of her eyes. What had she expected him to say? *To hell with Lorna and my marriage, let's talk about you and Sam and the past and how everything went wrong...* She hadn't *really* expected that reaction, had she?

Of course she hadn't. This had been revenge. Simple, sweet revenge. Except that revenge wasn't sweet at all. It was sour, bitter, left an acrid taste in her throat...

'Let's go inside, Beth.'

With a shudder, she found herself released. Sam wriggled restlessly against her breasts. Catching her breath, she fumbled for the key, tried to fit it into the lock, jammed it, dropped the bunch of keys on to the paved path at her feet.

With a muttered curse, Rafael retrieved it. He thrust the key into the lock and shouldered his way into the low-beamed hall, held the door open for her with a bleak travesty of courtesy. In the small, square sitting-room, she sat Sam down on the rust and cream rug and tried not to show how overwhelmed she felt by Rafael's large, potent presence in the room. She bent to light the fire, clicked on a peach-shaded table-lamp. She finally looked over her shoulder to see that Rafael had squatted down on muscular haunches, and was gazing at Sam with the air of a scientist making some earth-shattering discovery after a lifetime's research. Sam was gazing back, with that solemn, wide-eyed concentration that babies bestowed on strangers they found fascinating.

'*My* son?' Rafael's voice was cool, quietly threatening. A Spanish inquisitor. 'How do I know that the adolescent *William* is not the father?'

He pronounced William's name like an insult. The accusation was so absurd that she would have laughed if she hadn't felt so angry.

She said scornfully, 'Does he look like another man's child?'

He straightened at last, scooping Sam's small form up with him. He studied Sam's features for a while longer, his expression unreadable.

'No,' he conceded softly, 'he does not.'

Beth waited for Sam to cry, but instead he gurgled happily. Her heart squeezed in her chest. Abruptly, she sat down on one of the navy blue and peach floral chairs, and watched the tall dark man and the tiny dark child with mounting unease.

'How old is he?' Rafael slanted that narrow blue gaze at her.

'Six months.'

'What have you called him?'

The matter-of-fact question made her throat tighten. It was like being interrogated by a cool stranger.

'Samuel. Sam, for short.'

'And what surname have you given him? Mendoza?'

A hot tinge of colour crept into her face. Rafael's cool arrogance had faded in her memory until now.

'Haversham,' she amended coldly. 'But your name is on the birth certificate.'

He slowly sat down, lowering the child to the floor again. Father and son regarded each other in grave silence for what seemed an eternity. She felt as if she were part of a frozen tableau, looking on, witnessing this strange, wordless communication between the two.

Rafael leaned slightly forward, with his arms rested on his spread knees, hands hanging loosely between. She couldn't take her eyes off him. The grey morning suit, its crisp formality dishevelled by a loosened collar and a crooked bow tie, might have looked out of place on another man, but on Rafe's lean, hard body it looked almost indecently good. She found her eyes drawn to the dark plane of his chest beneath the fine white shirt. She found herself involuntarily remembering the steel of his body against hers, possessing, exciting, crushing her with exquisite strength, arousing her to pleasure so strong it was more like pain...

When he raised lidded blue eyes to Beth, he probed her hot face with a disturbing intensity. Her throat was too dry to allow her to speak. She swallowed jerkily, and ran her tongue quickly over dry lips.

'I'd have good reason to suspect you of lying,' he said softly, 'since you jumped from my bed straight into William's...'

'I did *not*...' She stopped, conscious of having let herself be goaded into indiscretion.

'So you lied about that?' She shivered under the narrowed concentration of his gaze.

'What I did after I—after we broke up is my business,' she defended herself stiffly. 'But do you really think I would lie about something like this?'

He gave a slow shrug. 'In the circumstances, anything is possible. But I would find it hard to believe that even you could halt a wedding to pass off another man's child as my own. Also——' he cast another burning glance over the small replica of himself sitting on the floor at his feet '—William, as I recall, had reddish-blond hair and a fair complexion. Whereas Sam——'

'Looks like you.'

Rafael's gaze took on a glint of wry humour.

'Quite possibly. So perhaps, this time, you are telling the truth.'

'I'm gratified by your faith in my character!'

'You conceived our child,' he confirmed at last. The deep voice grated with suppressed anger. 'You said nothing. You disappeared from my life to join your friend William, with *my* son growing inside you...'

'Sam is my son too,' she cut in huskily. 'He's far more mine than yours!'

'Because I was not allowed to know of his existence?' The scathing glint in his eyes made her flinch slightly, but she held his gaze.

'Rafe, that was only because——'

'You disappeared to Italy to join your teenage boyfriend. You then chose the moment of my wedding to Lorna to reappear and reveal my son's existence?' he persisted brutally. 'And then you were running away again? To hide? To keep my son from me?'

The heat in her face felt like fire now. Slowly she stood up, even though her knees were like jelly.

'Don't try to pretend you cared.' She picked her words carefully. 'You never did. It was just to—to get back at Lorna. Wasn't it? The way you began that affair with me.'

'Is that why you came to the wedding today?' he cut in icily. 'To right your imagined wrongs, Beth? An eye for an eye?'

'Yes,' she agreed finally. 'Yes, it was.'

There was a frigid silence.

'You thought you would use the existence of our son to wreck my wedding-day,' he mused at last. There was biting irony in his tone. 'Or was it more *Lorna's* wedding-day you wished to sabotage?'

Something about the analytical line of his questioning made her go hot and cold.

'I don't want to discuss this,' she said quietly. She was trying to hide the shake in her voice. 'I'd like you to leave. You must have plenty of people wondering where you are...'

She met the hard gaze across the room, and her heart plummeted almost down to her stomach.

'You would like me to leave?' he rasped. 'I do not choose to leave. I choose to stay.' The supreme arrogance of the Latin male gleamed resolutely from his set features, his steady regard across the cottage sitting-room.

'*Stay*?' Panic was creeping in now. He couldn't be serious, could he? 'What do you mean, stay? You can't stay here...'

The blue gaze narrowed. 'You say this is our son? What better place for me to get to know him? I have missed the first six months of his life through no choice of my own. Just because his mother is self-centred and pathetically immature does not affect my feelings towards my own child.'

His insult made her breath catch in her throat.

'Rafael, please go,' she managed stiltedly. Her blood was pounding round her veins in a crazy dance of anger. But she felt vulnerable. Cornered and vulnerable. As if he read her thoughts, he gave a slight, humourless smile.

'You thought you could wreak havoc today, then escape the consequences?'

'I'd have thought it was the other way round,' she threw back shakily. 'You've escaped the consequences for too long. That's why I came today!'

'The consequences?' His cool echo was derisive. 'The consequences of what, precisely?'

'Of *using* me!' She balled her fists furiously at her sides. This wasn't supposed to be happening. This wasn't how she'd planned her retaliation at all. She'd planned to strike back then disappear, and stay out of reach for as long as it took for the dust to settle again...

'I did not use you.' Rafael's words were carefully clipped. He sounded as if he was talking to someone who didn't understand the language.

'Of course you used me. You used me to get back at Lorna, because she'd kicked you out of her life and you were furious with her!'

Rafael's face was mask-like. When he finally spoke, he was bitterly ironic.

'Of course. How remiss of me to forget the way it was between us, Beth.'

With a ripple of hard muscle, he stretched back on the sofa and flexed his arms to link his fingers behind his head. He projected a lazily relaxed air. His whole attitude fuelled her temper unbearably.

'But I cannot be seen to neglect my responsibilities now, can I?' he added softly. 'Back into my life comes my little infatuated convent girl, with my baby son in her arms. Make no mistake—this time, *cara*, I can see clearly where my duty lies.'

His patronising arrogance made her whole body rigid with resentment. She longed to fly at him and punch the mocking smile from his face. Sam distracted her. He'd recently been dabbling in the complicated art of crawling.

He was now on all fours, rocking backwards and forwards near the stone hearth with such comical concentration that she blinked away her anger and went to pick him up. He gave a squirm of protest. Rafael watched with wry amusement.

'What was he doing?'

'Trying to work out which hand and knee go first to achieve forward transmission,' she explained shortly.

Rafael grinned. 'Then why did you interrupt him?'

'Because he was in danger of pitching himself head first into the hearth. Kindly don't question my ability to take care of my baby!'

Their eyes locked, stormy indignant grey with mocking smoky blue.

'Our baby,' he supplied tauntingly. '*My* son, as you were careful to inform the entire congregation in church.'

'Forget it,' she snapped. 'I didn't do it because I wanted you back in my life! I didn't imagine you'd follow me back here. And I don't want your interference, or your—your patronising sense of duty! I don't want anything from you!'

'Except to know that I have not married your stepsister Lorna?'

She opened her mouth to retort just as Sam grabbed a handful of her hair and tugged gleefully. She winced with an involuntary yelp.

'That hurts,' she advised the child solemnly, disentangling the small hand from her dark curls, adding flatly, 'It's time for Sam's tea...'

To her chagrin, Rafael followed her into the kitchen, and leaned casually against the tiled worktop as she strapped Sam into his high-chair, prepared boiled egg and toast fingers, and supervised the extremely messy process of getting him to eat.

The gaze narrowed on her as she moved around the kitchen made her prickle with tension from head to toe.

'Do you take care of him by yourself? With no one to help you?' The cool probe made her swing round cautiously.

'Quite a lot of the time I'm here alone. But Aunt Jayne comes most weekends and helps. That's when I get some work done...'

'Aunt Jayne?' Rafael's expression was blank.

'My mother's older sister. Of course, you wouldn't have heard of her. My father likes to pretend that my mother and anything connected with her never existed. Including me...'

'Including you? Your father pretends you no longer exist?'

'He informed me when I came back from Italy that I was dead to him,' she said tautly. She turned away. She didn't want to talk about her family. Sometimes she thought the only way she survived being a member of her family was to pretend *they* didn't exist.

'That would explain a great deal.' Rafael's tone was drily thoughtful. 'I was aware that your father was angry at your behaviour, Beth, but I did not know he had pronounced you dead in his eyes. Annabel and Lorna advised everyone that to mention your name to your father was to risk imminent apoplexy, heart-attack or stroke. It is as well, then, that the appearance of his daughter's ghost in church today triggered no such adverse reaction.'

A sharp twinge of guilt tightened her stomach. She flicked a wary glance at Rafael. She felt almost mes-

merised by the scathing intensity of his gaze. She hadn't
thought of her father's reaction. She hadn't considered
him at all, except with the usual bitter sense of betrayal
which went with his image. She pictured him now. He
was a grey-haired, ruddy-faced, genial-looking man, but
his glow of health was deceptive. He was a workaholic,
a partner in a big City firm of accountants, and he'd
had a warning heart-attack several years ago. But she
hadn't thought of that. She hadn't thought of anything,
except the intolerable news that Rafael was to marry
Lorna, and the burning urgency of her need to lash out,
strike a blow for justice, to hurt Lorna and Rafael as
much as they'd hurt her.

Shame engulfed her now. She lowered her eyes.

'What do you do for money?' The interrogation was
merciless. 'Are you dependent on your Aunt Jayne?'

'Not for much longer, if I can help it.' She felt her
face warming with angry embarrassment. 'I run my own
business.'

'With a baby to look after?'

'It's a craft business. I work in whatever spare time I
have. As I said, Aunt Jayne helps out most weekends...'

'And you're saying you'll make enough money to
support yourself and Sam, independently?'

'Well...' Her stomach sank. *Was* she going to achieve
that goal? The uncertainty of the future could be ignored most of the time—she was too busy to think about
it—but now it loomed in a frightening way...

Sam broke the tension by grabbing his half-eaten
boiled egg in both hands and pulverising the shell with
a gurgle of glee. She bent to field three rejected toast
soldiers from the quarry-tiles.

'Does he always have such appalling manners?' Rafael's voice held a laughing note which caught her off guard.

'I'm doing my best!' The shortness of her retort brought a deeper gleam to the blue eyes scanning her face.

'Hey! That was meant to be a joke, Beth. Where is your sense of humour?'

She tried to swing away to hide the sudden sting of tears. Rafael caught her in mid-swing. His fingers closed round the slender muscle of her upper arm, through the sleeve of her black suit jacket. Even through the fine wool, his touch stabbed through her precarious defences.

'Leave me alone...' It was half-shout, half-sob. The hard fingers tightened on her arm, and she was jerked against him. The breath left her lungs in a rush. Body-contact with Rafael had always felt like getting burned. Fifteen months ago, it had been a welcome fire, irresistible, totally engulfing. Today it felt dangerous, destructive. She tensed furiously against the inevitable heat but it was useless. The flames leaped. Anger and resentment, fear and desire tangled together in uncontrollable measures.

'Relax, Beth...' The deep voice held a mixture of anger and mockery, and, buried beneath them, a thicker trace of emotion she tried to block from her ears. Victory? Arrogant knowledge? She lifted her head to protest, and he kissed the words back into her mouth.

She shuddered, her heart thudding maniacally against her ribs. She was trapped in his arms, and his lips were wickedly hard and insistent. It was more like a punishment than a pleasure, but pleasure was there, creeping in unwelcome shivers of response along her nerve-ends, uncoiling like a treacherous snake in her stomach.

'Stop it...' Her husky whisper was breathed against his lips as he drew briefly away from her.

'It was good between us,' he murmured, ignoring her shaky demand. His eyes had darkened. The pupils were dilated, almost obliterating the brilliant blue of the irises. The thickening in his voice drew an answering shudder from her. His body-heat branded her through their clothes. 'Wasn't it?' His wide mouth twisted wryly as he watched the colour surge and recede in her face. 'Why did you run away from me, Beth?'

She struggled from his grasp, and stepped back quickly. Her legs felt weak.

'Did you think I'd hang around to have more humiliation heaped on me?'

'I made love to you,' he countered quietly, a darker glint in his eyes. 'And here——' he gestured drily towards Sam, who was busy smearing eggshell and runny yellow yolk in a swirly pattern all over the white tray of his high-chair '—sits the perfect result of that union. In what way did I humiliate you?'

'You are just...*totally* amoral, aren't you?' she burst out. 'You take what you want, when you want it. And you haven't even got the conscience to see when you've caused other people pain along the way! I thought I hated you, Rafael, but I think I just despise you! You're not worth hating!'

Rafael's face tightened. The gleam of emotion in his eyes was so dangerously explosive that she swallowed on a suddenly dry throat.

'So I am not worth hating?' His challenge held ominous softness. 'Then why go to such lengths to destroy my wedding-day? Only hatred could fuel such an act, Beth.'

'All right, so I hate *and* despise you!' she spat, trembling with emotion. 'Satisfied?'

The angle of his dark eyebrows suggested grim amusement. Already she was appalled at her idiotic outburst. It could only be because her nerves were already stretched to fraying point that she'd allowed herself to be provoked to such unwise declarations.

'Satisfied?' he was drawling quietly. 'Hardly. The only satisfaction I can foresee is the ability to safeguard the future of a son whose existence I have only just discovered. And rest assured, Beth, now I have finally been given the chance, that is a responsibility I intend to take very seriously indeed.'

CHAPTER THREE

THE telephone started to ring. It broke the taut silence. In acute apprehension, Beth stared at it, where it hung on the wall by the back door. Had Rafael told Lorna where he could be contacted? He had a car phone, she felt sure. He could have rung Lorna, at some pre-arranged venue, as he pulled into the drive at the cottage. Told her the address. But he wouldn't have known Aunt Jayne's surname, so the telephone number wouldn't be easily discovered, would it...?

'Is this a new way of answering the telephone? Thought-wave transference?' Rafael's taunting voice cut through her guiltily racing thoughts.

Furious with herself, she strode across to lift the receiver, her throat unpleasantly dry. Aunt Jayne's voice allayed her fears, and her spirits rose a fraction at the thought of rescue at hand. Then her heart fell as she listened to the information being relayed. Aunt Jayne couldn't come down to the cottage this weekend. She'd somehow managed to contract chicken-pox, she informed Beth, and she'd be confined to her London flat for at least two weeks. 'At *my* age,' her aunt added cheerfully. 'Maybe it's proof that I'm young at heart!'

'You're definitely that,' Beth smiled, an image of her aunt's round, lively face floating into her mind. 'Look, are you sure you'll be all right? Shall I drive up with Sam and look after you?'

'Don't you *dare*! What if Sam caught it?'

Beth's assurances that Sam would be too young to be badly affected found no favour. It was left that Jayne would ring when she was feeling better, and meanwhile her housekeeper in London would do all that was required.

Replacing the receiver, Beth met Rafael's enquiring gaze.

'Your aunt is ill?'

She briefly explained. His frown deepened.

'You were prepared to risk Sam's health to go and stay there?' he queried bluntly.

'Babies and children contract chicken-pox as a matter of course,' she informed him coldly. 'Don't look at me as if I was proposing a visit to a leper colony!'

'I would have thought the welfare of the child came first,' Rafael countered, equally coldly.

She felt electrified with rage.

'How *dare* you suggest I'm not a good mother?'

'You are very young to cope all alone.' His voice held no warmth, even a hint of hard distaste. 'My son would be better off within a stable family unit.'

'What are you suggesting?' Her hot fury turned to an icy dread inside her. 'That you and *Lorna* have him?'

There was a fraught silence.

'What do you think?' When he spoke at last, the hard gaze had narrowed on her flushed face. His expression was unreadable.

She could hardly breathe. The idea of losing Sam was so bleakly unthinkable that it rose like a black cloud of pain inside her.

'I think . . . that nothing you suggested would surprise me.' She spoke slowly, controlling herself with extreme care, but the bitterness crept through, so much so that she could barely force the words out. 'But forget it, Rafael. There is no court of law in this country that would hand over my son to you.'

With a jerky movement, he raked his hand through his thick dark hair. His face was suddenly weary as he stared at her across the small figure in the high-chair.

'*Basta*. Enough. We will discuss this when we are both calmer.'

He turned on his heel and moved towards the door.

'Where are you going?'

'To get my suitcase from the car.'

Heat surged into her face. She held her breath for a few seconds, fighting her temper and losing the battle.

'You are *not* staying here! Do you hear me...?'

'You forfeited any say in the matter when you gatecrashed my wedding and made your dramatic announcement,' he retorted flatly. His glance over his shoulder before he disappeared was so coolly derisive that she had to stop herself from grabbing the nearest missile to throw at him.

Beth kneeled by the bath, watching Sam's small fingers carefully fitting a floating blue plastic sailor into a red boat bobbing in the bubbles. He succeeded at last, and rewarded himself by inserting his thumb in his mouth. He sucked quietly as he watched the craft sail precariously towards the taps. It was warm, steamy and fragrant in the pine-furnished bathroom. With its white suite, cork floor and green checked curtains, it was very much cottage-style, simple and homely. It felt even more of a cosy oasis because an autumn storm had blown up outside. Rain was lashing down off the moor, and a gale was rattling against the small windows of the cottage.

She could hear it moaning under the back door downstairs.

Lifting the sponge, she gently squeezed soapy water over Sam's small shoulders as he splashed the water to propel the boat. The boat capsized, ditching its occupant into the foam. Sam gave a delighted gurgle of laughter and launched himself forward to retrieve it. Laughing at his antics, in spite of the turmoil in her heart, she caught him quickly before he disappeared beneath the surface.

Sam displayed a fearlessness bordering on recklessness. Wasn't that how Rafael Mendoza was always being described? The wild, unpredictable hero of the polo field. Darling of the crowds. But Rafael wasn't reckless, or impulsive, she amended truthfully. She was the impulsive one. Which was no doubt why she was in this unenviable situation right now. Rafael, on the other hand, might be daring but he was probably level-headed at the same time. In daily life, he thought things through with cold-blooded rationality. No reckless risks or impulses there. Just measured calculation... On the polo field, he was prone to taking risks, but they were calculated risks which often won the match. He was a formidable adversary...

Beth shuddered, her heart clenching. Like father, like son? Could this sweet but impressively determined little baby one day turn against her, to pursue some ruthless, mercenary goal? Was there any of herself in Sam? Glancing in the mirror over the bath, she saw her soft cloud of dark hair, the preoccupied grey eyes. She'd discarded the black suit for dark green leggings and a long, loose, off-the-shoulder charcoal-grey jumper. She could see smudges of fatigue under her eyes. Her skin was very pale, taut over the high cheekbones and determined chin. Her neck and collarbones looked very slender and vulnerable at the wide neck of the jumper. Maybe Sam had a look of her sometimes. But usually, when she looked at him, all she could see was Rafael . . .

Above the noise of the wind and rain outside, and the excited splashing in the bath, she didn't hear Rafael come in. When he spoke behind her, she jumped nervously.

'I'm sorry,' he murmured, not sounding it. 'Did I startle you?'

'Please don't creep up on me like that,' she snapped, spreading a big white towel on her knees and bending to lift Sam out of the bath. She glanced up as she wrapped the warm, wriggling little body in the towel. Then she stiffened in alarm.

The formal grey morning suit had been discarded. Rafael had changed into faded blue Levi 501s. The rough, time-honoured fabric moulded the powerful thigh muscles and lean narrow hips, cupped the male bulge at his groin with such overt sexuality that she felt the breath seep from her lungs. Above the waistband of the Levis he was naked. The dark torso was lean and hard, the shoulders wide and athletically sloping. A sprinkle of black hair shaded the ridge between impressive pectorals, arrowing down the muscled ripple of his abdomen and disappearing from sight. Hurriedly dragging her eyes back up again, she met his derisive stare.

'I was hoping to take a bath myself,' he murmured, unperturbed. 'If you stick around you can wash my back.'

'Nothing like an uninvited guest making himself at home at high speed.' She shot him a frosty smile. She hated the way he could make her blush like a schoolgirl again. She was far from being that, now. She might be only nineteen—painfully young, as Aunt Jayne was fond of saying—but the last fifteen months seemed more like five years. 'And how come you conveniently had a suitcase full of clothes in your car?'

Before she'd finished asking, she realised the idiocy of the question, and the obvious answer. The dark glint in his eyes held grim irony, plus a flicker of some other emotion. Was it secret amusement? Could he really find this situation funny? The pause lengthened for several seconds before he finally said, 'Maybe I was planning on taking a holiday following my wedding? I believe it's called a honeymoon.'

The colour swept up her neck, suffused her entire face. As if for the first time, the enormity of what she'd done today hit her with full force. Along with full knowledge of her stupidity. Who had she thought she was hurting? What had she imagined this melodramatic revenge would accomplish?

But there was Sam, she reasoned bleakly. Hadn't she owed it to Sam? That was hypocrisy, though. Sam might deserve to know his father. But that hadn't been her motivation. She'd wanted to revenge herself on Rafael, and Lorna. And the whole thing had backfired. Because, most of all, she'd brought more pain on herself. She didn't want to think about Rafael with Lorna. She didn't want vivid pictorial images of their wedding-night, their honeymoon, invading her mind like this. It hurt too much. Everything about this fiasco hurt too much. It hurt like a physical attack, like a vicious punch to the kidneys...

Sam had begun to cry, straining in her arms as her tension seeped into him. She'd closed her eyes, and was hugging Sam as if she were drowning, and he was her only lifeline... She opened them to find Rafael bending down to take the baby from her, lifting his small son into his arms. He cradled him there with such raw tenderness that her heart jolted in despair. She stared at the sight they made—the tall muscular man, the vulnerable baby. Tears threatened. She blinked them fiercely away.

'I hope you realise you could have wrecked my social life, as well as my love-life?' he murmured, lifting Sam higher and watching that heart-catching baby laugh take over from the tears. 'The county set, plus a few notable polo-playing royals, were due to be at the reception today.'

He sounded deadpan. It was impossible to tell if he found such a dire social gaffe amusing or abysmal.

'Well, I'm so sorry...' The sarcastic words were torn from her. The tears welled infuriatingly. She caught a ragged breath, and dashed her fingers over her cheeks.

'Is there plenty more hot water?' His curt query made her jerk a blank glance at him. She was scrubbing her eyes and nose with a pink tissue grabbed from the box on the shelf.

'What? Yes...'

'Then get in the bath yourself. You're obviously exhausted. I'll put Sam to bed.'

'*You*?' The disbelief in her voice drew a wry grin.

'If you show me where to find nappies, leave the rest to me.'

'You wouldn't have a clue...'

'My sister Marietta is a feminist.' He gave a fleeting grin, taking the white towel from her knees and draping it round Sam. 'She is a high-powered lawyer, and has a nanny to care for her small children. But, whenever I visit her and her husband and family in Buenos Aires, I am forced to practise ''New Man'' techniques on my nephew and nieces. For my own good, she says.'

'New Man? You?' she echoed, even more disbelieving. The tears, at least, had dried, in the process of assimilating Rafael's extraordinary statement.

'The accomplishment is sporadic,' he admitted. The gleam of genuine humour in his eyes shook her with its impact. 'But the skills remain. Now, where are the nappies?'

She led the way into Sam's small nursery bedroom, and found herself stiltedly explaining procedures.

'*Bueno*. I understand. Now go.' He spun her, with surprising gentleness, towards the door, lying Sam down on the changing-mat on a wide pine table near his cot. 'Relax in the bath. I shall endeavour to fasten my baby son's nappy before natural disaster strikes...'

As if prompted by the prophetic words, the baby chose this moment to respond happily to the call of nature. The miniature fountain found Rafael's bare chest with unerring aim.

'*Dios*! Too late...' Rafael's expression, as he dried himself with a handful of tissues and made a dive for the baby-powder, was almost comical in its dismay.

She hesitated at the door. The scene in the nursery was so unexpected, Rafael's intimate involvement with Sam so alien to expectations, that she was deeply shaken. A sudden, gripping fear took hold and wouldn't fade.

'Rafe...you won't—you wouldn't...try to take him...?'

The amusement died. He slowly lifted his head to gaze at her, his face taut. His dark hair had fallen forward in a thick tousled wedge above his eyes. For a fleeting second, she imagined he looked almost as vulnerable as she felt.

'Spirit him away while you relax in the bath?' he mocked harshly. 'You do despise me, don't you, Beth?'

She caught her breath and turned away, going out and closing the door quietly behind her.

She wasn't quite sure how, but somehow his response infuriated and reassured her at the same time. At least, she trusted him sufficiently to strip off her clothes in the privacy of the bathroom, and take the bath he had suggested. The sheer luxury of having time for a long, hot soak proved more irresistible than she'd have thought possible.

She wound her dark curls into a wobbly topknot, added more hot water and some sweet almond-scented bath-foam, closed her eyes, and wallowed. She firmly closed her mind to images of herself and Rafael, in the dangerous, impulsive, deliriously happy beginning. It didn't work. No amount of positive concentration on the present moment, the soothing warmth of the bath, the uplifting aroma of the foam—nothing worked. It all came swooping back, like silent torture...

That summer day, at Cobb Barton. It had all begun with such irresistible certainty, which was crazy, really, when she thought about it. Rafael had been waiting at the house to have a bitter row with Lorna over some local golf pro she'd got involved with behind his back. Then she, Beth, had arrived home before Lorna did, and a curious chemistry had begun to work. She couldn't have said what it was. She'd been very wary during that brief chat they'd had. She'd sensed the magnetic pull, and shrunk from it. He was waiting for Lorna. He was

Lorna's property. To poach a boyfriend of her step-sister's would have been unthinkable.

Tossing and turning in bed that night, she had managed to convince herself that the only reason for the attraction she'd felt was the fact that he was a person who evidently shared her own liking for horses. On top of that, he was a polo player, the kind of rider she revered above all others. It was just a touch of hero-worship, not a desperate, melting desire to let him kiss her...

But, the following morning, Lorna had pettishly declared at breakfast that Rafael Mendoza was the biggest jerk living, and that their relationship was finished. Beth's private reaction had been confusion, tinged with disbelief. Lorna had finished with Rafael? Or was it more the other way round? Whichever, she had resolved to stay well clear of him, if she happened to meet him again. He had mesmerised her, and that feeling frightened her...

She'd reckoned without Annabel's unwitting interference.

Anxious to keep her well occupied, and therefore out of the house as much as possible during the holidays, her stepmother insisted she have a holiday job. Dad, mindful of Beth's liking for horses, accordingly fixed her up with a job as a stable-girl. Within forty-eight hours of coming home, she found herself employed in the stableyard of Rafael Mendoza's gracious seventeenth-century house near Stow. On the second night, one of his best ponies developed colic. She stayed up all night, walking the animal round the stable as the vet prescribed. Rafael, his dark face taut with anxiety, returned again and again to the stable. By morning the horse was out of danger, and she and Rafael had a rapport which developed far, far deeper than that first, electrifying shiver of desire...

She should have seen the danger. But then it was too late. She was in too deep. Rafael shrugged off her protests about what Lorna might think if she knew. As far as he was concerned, his relationship with Lorna was finished. He'd been waiting to speak to her that day at Cobb Barton to tell her that it was finished. She'd apparently made clumsy attempts to make him jealous by parading other boyfriends at his polo matches, and he'd given her free rein to go ahead and date whomever she chose. So what harm could there be in Lorna finding out about them?

'Don't say anything for the moment. Lorna and I— well, we've never exactly been...best friends,' she had confessed ruefully, curled against him on the wide green hammock-swing in the twilight of his summer garden. There were bats flitting high overhead. A strong scent of honeysuckle and roses. The world had shrunk to this enchanted moment, this shivery excitement, this shy terror of what she might do if Rafael's amused restraint should crack under the sexual pressure building up between them...

'Relax, *cara*,' he murmured, with a wicked grin. 'Lorna is safely occupied with her golf pro. She'll find out soon enough.'

And so it had gone on. Trips around the sleepy Cotswold villages to dinner in luxurious little country hotels. Flights round the county in the helicopter he used, part of an international hire fleet he owned, which catered for wealthy businessmen who wanted to beat traffic jams. Visits to watch him play polo, where the sight of his powerful figure made her feel boneless with longing...

She had the feeling Rafael knew her secret confusion. He certainly knew that she was totally inexperienced. Her lack of composure the first time he had kissed her triggered his husky laugh, but the darker gleam in his eyes spoke volumes. He desired her. He was playing games with her. She was being used. She was just too naïve to realise it...

In the end, one of the stable-girls, who was also a friend of Lorna's, told Lorna what was going on. The scene at Cobb Barton was explosive. All the bitterness of the years came to a head. Lorna poured scorn on the relationship. Rafael had told her all about it, she'd said. It was simply a ploy of his, to make Lorna jealous and mend their broken affair.

Hurt and rebellious, Beth went to see Rafael. She confronted him with Lorna's claims. There was a furious row. Her stubborn accusations seemed to enrage him, and any restraint or amusement vanished. They made love—or rather Rafael took her virginity, dragging her to his big blue and white bedroom which overlooked the walled garden next to the stables, and branding her for life with his lips and hands and body...

The next day she was working in the stables, and saw Lorna and Rafael together. They were in Rafael's car, locked in an intimate embrace. She could still remember the sickening thump of her heart against her ribs. The rank taste of disillusion in her throat. The hollow pit opening in her stomach. So it was true. He *was* still in love with Lorna. His interlude with Beth had been a diversion. And yet he'd done what he'd done the night before. He'd taken advantage, forced her to show her

precious emotions, driven her to the edge of commitment and then thrown her over to the rocks below...
He was as callous as that...

Lorna, Beth decided numbly, was welcome to him.
They were clearly made for each other. She was too
shocked and angry to think beyond this knee-jerk reaction. Years of needing to defend herself from the pain
of rejection had equipped her with a very efficient
mechanism for protecting herself. Escape was essential.
She had to get away. And she had to save face, hide her
hurt pride.

She'd spent several past summers in Italy with
Charlotte, a friend from the convent whose family owned
a holiday villa on Lake Como. There'd even been a
childish flirtation with William, Charlotte's brother,
which had ended up as a firm friendship instead. That
night she rang Charlotte, who commiserated loyally and
came up with a master-plan to rescue Beth from
humiliation.

And so it was that, early the next morning, she disappeared from Cobb Barton bound for Italy, leaving
letters for her father and for Rafe informing them that
she was spending the rest of the summer with her
'boyfriend' William, sharing the family's summer villa
near Lake Como.

The triumph of this plan carried her through the next
few days, as she was welcomed into Charlotte's family
and gently teased by William for the deception. It even
carried her through the ordeal of a visit from Rafe. He
followed her out to Italy, his pride presumably stung by
her letter. In it, with Charlotte's connivance, she'd informed him that she'd only wanted to sleep with him

for experience—that, being eight years her senior, he was really far too old, far too old-fashioned for her...

He found her, as luck would have it, on the lakeside beach with William, laughing and talking while she rubbed Factor Twelve on William's fair, freckled skin to protect him from the hot Italian sun. The look of hard anger on Rafe's face was still etched into her memory. She clung on to her proud composure, but it was the most difficult thing she'd ever done, when she just wanted to drop the bottle of sun-lotion and run to him... But one minute he was standing there, at the top of the beach, motionless in black jeans, black collarless shirt, black sunglasses, the next he was gone. Fifteen minutes later, Charlotte had come to tell her that Rafe had walked back up to the villa, got into his hired car, and driven off without a word.

It was a week before her numbed emotions revived sufficiently for tears. Four more weeks before she realised that queasy mornings, tender breasts and a sudden odd distaste for coffee were clues that she was pregnant, that she was going to have Rafe's baby.

She left Italy, reluctant to burden Charlotte and her family any further with her personal problems. She went back to England, begged an overnight stay with another schoolfriend in London, and rang her father. Any hopes of a shoulder to lean on rapidly disappeared. He was disgusted by her behaviour, he told her coldly. But then, what could he expect? he hissed down the phone. She was her mother's daughter—plunging into liaisons with two men, one after another, then growing bored and abandoning both. He didn't want to know her any more. And, with his scathing indictment of her character, telling him she was pregnant was out of the question. She was on her own...

There was a knock on the bathroom door. Beth's eyes flew open, past abruptly surrendering to present. She'd almost fallen asleep in the bath. The water had cooled; the bubbles had subsided.

'Beth? Are you all right in there?' Was it her imagination that Rafael's voice sounded huskily concerned?

'Hang on...' she called faintly. She began to stand up.

After another brief knock, the handle of the door turned. Beth froze in alarm. The bolt was insecure, she knew. Had she shot it properly? As she stared at the offending lock, it slipped its wobbly catch. The door swung open. Adrenalin leaped through her. She nearly fell out of the bath in her haste to take cover. Rafael, his dark face impassive, stood there in the doorway, two glasses of white wine cradled in one hand. He wore a loose denim shirt, open like a jacket, over the denim jeans.

'I was concerned you might have fallen asleep.'

Shocked indignation made the towel slip from her fingers. It dropped into the bath-water.

'What do you think you're doing?' she spat, fishing furiously in the water. The sodden towel weighed a ton. She struggled to pin it over her nakedness, stinging with embarrassment and mounting anger. 'Get *out* of here!'

'Sorry. But we're playing mummies and daddies, aren't we? The least I can do is stay to pass you another towel,' he countered smoothly.

He swept a gaze from her head to her feet, lingering on the full, high globes of her breasts, the slope of her stomach, the long, slender curve of her thighs. His eyes held glinting amusement. Her temper overtook her.

She grabbed both wine-glasses from his outstretched hand, and threw the contents violently in his face. There was hardly a pause between the satisfaction of retaliation, and being hauled from the bath and slammed hard into Rafael's arms.

'I've been doing some thinking,' he drawled softly, raking both hands down the wet curve of her spine to the smoothly rounded jut of her buttocks, and sending earth-tremors of reaction shivering through her. 'As I recall from our past relationship, the only way to get through your prickly defences was full-on physical. Talk or action. I tossed a coin——' he grinned unforgivably as he lowered his mouth to her furiously compressed lips '—and guess what? Action won...'

CHAPTER FOUR

'THAT'S all you understand!' she gasped, snatching air into her lungs as he released her a fraction. 'Physical aggression! Flexing your muscles to get your point across...'

'Hush, *cara*.' His murmur was implacable. 'You'll wake Sam.' Snatching a towel from the rail, he wrapped it round her shivering body and lifted her, to her wriggling outrage, into his arms. The short journey to her bedroom was over in seconds. Plonked unceremoniously on the bed, she fought to bury herself in the towel and push Rafael away, accomplishing neither.

'If you think dis—discovering Sam's existence entitles you to just—just pick up where we left off...'

'But I did not *discover* my son's existence,' he grated, ruthlessly pinning her kicking legs to the duvet. 'My son's existence was hidden from me. Until it could be used by you, revealed with maximum effect by you, for your ultimate reprisal...'

His hard fingers stroked possessively along the tense length of her thigh, moulded upwards to trace the swell of her breast. Heat prickled her skin. This was hard to believe. She couldn't be this gullible again. Rafael couldn't have the power to arouse her after his past treatment of her, after his casual games. But his fingers against her breast were almost irresistibly arousing. When the seeking palm shifted, and brushed her nipple, she sucked in her breath. Her nipple pointed and peaked

147

under his touch, a small pink nub of desire. She was outraged and ashamed, acutely embarrassed and aching with longing.

'Rafe, stop it...'

'Why should I?' The deep voice was mocking, but thicker with desire. Fear trickled down her spine. Rafe wanted her. This wasn't just a teasing game. The darkening of his eyes, the mounting insistence of his hands, told her he was intent on seducing her. This was madness. Rafe wasn't making love to her, he was using sex as a means of humiliation, of his own kind of subtle punishment. She hated him. Anger and desire clashed and spiralled into more heat. A sheen of perspiration broke out all over her body. Her breathing was shallow and laboured. She tightened her fists and thumped at his chest.

'Maybe it's your—your macho South American traditions!' she spat shakily, rigid with denial as he moved his hand to the other breast and rotated his fingers skilfully over the tightening nipple. 'Maybe that's what makes you feel entitled to treat women like this...'

'Do not resort to insults against my race and upbringing, *cara*,' he taunted darkly. 'It will not work. I have no insecurities on either count. Tonight should have been my wedding-night. Remember? A night of sexual satisfaction which I have been deprived of. No matter. You must act as substitute...'

'*Rafe*!' She could hardly believe her ears. But even as he stopped taunting verbally, he intensified the physical assault. Talking stopped as he forced her words back into her throat, his tongue delving and fencing with potent demand. She struggled ferociously, every last ounce of strength gathered up to kick, scratch and punch.

With a husky laugh, he moved to cover her, immobilising her limbs. She was pinned beneath him. The rough denim of his jeans chafed her thighs. The smooth steel of his chest crushed her breasts.

She heard herself groan. She closed her eyes tightly to hide her thoughts. Because, despite his brazen macho-act, the past magic had crept back. The hard weight of his body imprisoned her against the duvet, but the feel of him unlocked something inside her, something buried inside her for the last year and a quarter.

Angrily, blindly, she shuddered and wrapped her arms round his back, and half sobbed his name.

'I was right,' he whispered roughly, rolling away a couple of inches, tossing away his shirt with controlled impatience, thrusting a determined hand down to unzip his Levis. 'You do want this, as much as I do...'

She was shaking. The physical fight had drained from her. But she had some pride left.

'No! I don't want this! Stop now,' she warned jerkily, 'and I'll forget you tried to force yourself on me...'

'Stop now?' It was a derisive echo, in that sex-thickened rasp which sent her up in shameful flames. 'No way, lady. You're hot, burning for this...'

'You really are the——' she cast about unsuccessfully for apt insults '—the most conceited, the coarsest...'

'No. I'm a gentleman. I'm doing you a favour, sweetheart...'

She jerked her hand up angrily to slap his face. He deflected her, caught her arm, gathered both her wrists into one strong hand and wrenched her arms above her head. For a burning few seconds, she lay there in a red blur of rage while he surveyed his spoils, raking that devastating blue gaze from her straight slender feet up the smooth curve of her legs, lingering outrageously on the tender swell of her hips, the glossy junction of dark curls, the soft quiver of her stomach, to the unbelievably swollen ache of her breasts.

'Believe me or not,' he grated softly, 'but I have never forgotten the way your body feels next to mine...'

He dropped his mouth to one hot, tingling nipple, and she went blank. The sensations magnified. She didn't want to, but she arched her body, unable to stop herself from offering her breasts to the exquisite relief of his lips and tongue. Where did anger stop and desire take over? How could she block out the humiliation of being a substitute for Lorna?

Half sobbing, she lost herself in the purely physical. Rafe's lovemaking was consuming, lifting her expertly, level on level, until she was squirming, writhing, saying his name again and again, not knowing if it was pain or pleasure or both sending her crazy and mindless.

'Do you want this, Beth?' A rasped murmur, warm in her ear. 'Do you want me to stop now? Or go on?'

'You know how I feel...' She could hardly speak. Her tongue wouldn't obey her brain. It was as if she were drugged; she was shivering with sensations. The snakes of sexual need uncoiled and reared inside her.

'I want to hear you tell me, *cara*.' He was remorseless, sliding hard fingers powerfully along her inner thighs, forcing them apart. 'I want you to beg me...'

Her eyes flew open. Rafe's narrowed blue gaze blazed down at her. His harsh face was carved in tension. Sweat glistened on his brow, gleamed on his shoulders.

Beth's eyes filled with tears, dark pools of grey in her white face. She felt pinned, vulnerable, raw with need and longing.

'I'll never beg you.' Her whisper was fierce and broken. 'I just wanted you to love me, Rafe. That's all. That's what you couldn't do...'

'*Dios*!' His low groan was wrenched from him. He jerked himself away from her, subsiding on the bed with a muttered obscenity. 'Love? What do you know about love? What did you imagine there was between us?'

She started to shiver. It was hard to believe he'd stopped. It was what she wanted, wasn't it? For him to stop what he was doing? But she ached, still. Inside. Ached and burned.

'I'm not sure.' Her voice came out as a shaky whisper. She hardly recognised it. 'I was too childish to think straight.'

'So I seduced a child?' The question held a wry bitterness.

'You know how old I was.'

'Eighteen...' He was silent again. She raised a shuttered look at his face. It was carved in cold cynicism. 'Old enough to vote, drive a car, and...' he drawled softly.

He remembered that first exchange, when she'd walked in wearing her school uniform? Fumbling for the towel, she pulled it around herself, winding it firmly in place. If only she felt stronger. More like hitting him, fighting her corner. But his ruthless sexual tactics had left her feeling debilitated. If he could have devised the most suitable punishment of all, for her invasion of his wedding today, then this would be it. This arrogant display of sexual dominance. This demonstration of how much he could make her want him...

Anger came to her rescue again. Determinedly, she wriggled off the bed and grabbed her bath-robe from

the back of her bedroom door. Glimpsing herself in the
pine dressing-table mirror, she inwardly winced. The
topknot she'd fixed for her bath had come loose. Her
hair tumbled in wild disarray. She looked like a small,
white-faced witch. Impatiently, she turned to face him,
tying the belt of the soft green towelling tightly round
her waist.

'And?' she taunted, her voice brittle. 'Old enough to
be *used* by the first self-serving womaniser who came
along?'

Rafe had pulled his Levis back on. He was lying on
the bed, his hands behind his head, ankles crossed,
watching her expressionlessly.

'I am beginning to wonder,' he mused bitterly, half to
himself, 'if this is worth the effort.'

'I'm sure it's not!' she flared. Misery closed round her
without warning. She was hurting so much inside that
she felt as if one of those snakes had bitten her. 'If you
think I'll ever forgive you . . .'

As she stared at him he levered himself off the bed
and bent to retrieve his shirt. His actions were deliberate, his air preoccupied. He looked as if he was ex-
ercising careful control, and thinking fast at the same
time.

'I'm sorry. I should not have lost control just now . . .'

'That's the way you usually operate, isn't it?'

His dark face hardened.

'Only with you.' The admission was wry. 'This is crazy.
Today has hit me like a missile. I am making a mess of
what may be the most important thing in my life so far.
We have to talk,' he added flatly. He swivelled towards
the door, thrusting his hand through his tousled black
hair. 'What do you do for eating around here?'

'How do you mean?' Beth widened her eyes in mocking disbelief. 'I cook food, and Sam and I eat it.'

'I meant restaurants...' A fresh thought occurred to him, his dark brows drawing together in a slight frown. 'Shouldn't a child of six months old be breast-fed?'

She gritted her teeth in a parody of a smile.

'For your information, I breast-fed Sam until he was four months old. At that stage I made the decision to wean him. You've seen for yourself that he's happy and healthy. Do you have any more interfering comments to make?'

'OK. Cool down. I'm interested. I'm still in shock. Did you think I would not be interested in the up-bringing of my own son? Who do you use for baby-sitting?' The clipped question held no more expression than the last.

'I don't go out.'

'Never?' The quizzical disbelief made her hesitate.

'Aunt Jayne sometimes sits for me, if there's a craft fair or something. If I'm really desperate, there's a girl in the village who comes in.'

'Is she reliable? This girl?'

'Would I leave Sam with her if she wasn't?'

'Telephone her. We're going out to dinner. I assume there is somewhere locally that cooks and serves food?'

She fought her reactions. It was on the tip of her tongue to tell him to go to hell. She didn't want to go anywhere with him. But the thought of another argument made her feel exhausted. The thought of eating in was too intimate to contemplate. And the prospect of escaping the claustrophobic sexual tension in the cottage opened up in front of her like a lifeline.

With a stiff shrug, she pushed past him and went down to telephone.

'You mentioned a craft fair. What exactly do you do? What kind of craft?' Rafe leaned across the table to pour more wine into her glass. They'd come to the local pub, leaving the sleeping Sam in the capable hands of Alison. She was a red-haired fifteen-year-old from a nearby farm, who lugged with her a huge rucksack of GCSE work, and welcomed the peace from her numerous siblings to study.

'I paint things.'

'Landscapes? Portraits?'

She shook her head. 'No, I paint *things*. Chairs, chests of drawers—I do decorative patterns on them, flowers or birds or whatever the client likes.'

He regarded her levelly. 'Sounds innovative.'

'Oh, it is.'

'Do you enjoy it?'

She took a sip of wine. The small dining-room of the Rose and Crown was unpretentious, but with its ancient Elizabethan beams, and polished brasses reflecting the flickering log fire, its atmosphere was soothing. An aroma of grilling fillet steak filtered out of the kitchens. In spite of everything, Beth felt her mouth watering.

'I enjoy it a surprising amount,' she admitted expressionlessly.

'It's very different from your original career plans.' Rafe's voice was cool. 'How did you get into it?'

'I bought an old cupboard for Sam's room, from a junk shop. I cleaned it up, stained it dark green, then painted teddy bears on it to make Sam smile. A woman from the village, who cleans the cottage once a week for

Aunt Jayne, saw it. She told her niece, who had two-year-old twins, who told everyone at the village play-group, who told their friends and relatives... It just grew from there.'

'Don't you long to fulfil your potential? Get your university degree?'

She stared at him across the dark oak table. The apprehension she'd felt earlier was back. Was he subtly trying to undermine her right to look after Sam? A shiver of fear clenched her stomach. If only she'd seen this danger ahead. If only she'd realised that he might follow her back to Devon. But it simply hadn't occurred to her. Even with the mayhem she'd triggered with her announcement in the church, the thought of him actually abandoning the church, Lorna, the other guests, the whole wedding, to leap in his Ferrari and chase her... It was unbelievable...

'I'm happy being Sam's mother,' she said flatly.

'You are only nineteen, Beth.' He spoke almost gently. Her suspicions grew. God, he was so arrogant, he was capable of anything.

'If you're trying to suggest I'm too young to care for my own baby, forget it! Plenty of nineteen-year-olds cope, when they have to. I love Sam. I'm happy to build my world around him. He's worth any sacrifice to me...'

The kindling warmth in Rafe's eyes made her heart squeeze unexpectedly. She stared at him in growing confusion. In the quiet confines of the country pub, he'd been attracting a bit of covert attention from the landlady, and one or two females eating at near by tables with their male escorts. She decided she could see why. They probably thought he was a film actor—someone famous and glamorous they couldn't quite put a name to. He'd stayed in the Levis and denim shirt, and added a designer-loose black jacket. His thick black hair was clean and shiny, falling in a casually over-long style past his collar. The blue denim turned his eyes a mesmerising cobalt-blue. Quite simply, he looked so sexy that she could feel her own limbs jellifying as she sat there hating him.

'I'm not criticising,' he said quietly. 'Maybe I'm trying to handle my own guilt. *Dios*, if I had not lost my reason that night...'

A slight flush surged and faded in her cheeks. She toyed with the stem of her glass.

'Sam wouldn't be here? Don't talk as if you—you *forced* me into anything,' she whispered tensely. 'You know damn well it was a two-way thing...'

'No. You were a virgin. What happened between us was instigated by me. I should have known better.' He spoke with clipped distaste, as if he found the recollection unpleasant. Her heart contracted again. Did he regret it all so much? Even the part that was supposed to give him pleasure?

'Quite. Not much of a partner, I admit.'

He flicked his eyes up to her hot face. His expression was bleak. She couldn't remember ever seeing him look so bleak.

'Is that what you think I meant?' The bitterness had intensified.

She couldn't drag her eyes away from his. The sudden silence seemed to radiate around them, until she felt as if she was marooned alone with Rafael, with no one else around.

'You tell me.' It was a brittle, trivial reply. It was all she could find to say.

'I meant that... Hell's teeth, I cannot forgive myself for taking advantage of you, at a time when——'

'Here we are!' Emerging from the kitchen, the chef, beady eyes agog with interest, laid plates of fillet steak, chipped potatoes and salad before them with a flourish. Too late, Beth realised that village tongues would be freshly wagging. Letting Rafe bring her here had been a mistake, if she valued her privacy. Sid was landlord-cum-chef, and gossip was the breath of life to him.

The silence resumed after Sid's departure. Beth became vaguely aware of a wider silence, encompassing the tables near them as well as herself and Rafe. Were their neighbours eavesdropping on their low-voiced conversation?

'At a time when you were supposed to be seeing Lorna?' she supplied coolly. 'Quite.'

'No!' He spoke through stiffly clenched lips. 'At a time when you were most vulnerable... *Dios*, Beth, don't pretend you don't know the effect you have on me! Or do you imagine I fall rabidly on every female I meet?'

She fell silent. What he was saying didn't seem to fit with anything else. It didn't make any sense. Her mind whirring in confusion, she fiddled with the neck of the charcoal-grey sweater. It had a habit of slipping off her shoulder. Winding one legging-clad leg around the other beneath the table, she resolutely picked up her knife and fork and attacked the steak.

'If you are trying to tell me,' she ventured at last, keeping her voice very calm, 'that you find me totally irresistible, please don't insult my intelligence. Today you were about to marry my stepsister Lorna. True or false?'

His gaze was like blue ice, glinting across the table.

'Do I need to answer that?'

She quelled her irritation at the goading reply.

'True,' she supplied shortly, her tone cuttingly sweet. 'I was there, remember?'

'Quite so. How could I forget?'

She glared at him, her temper rising.

'Well, then. How—how *fickle* can you get?'

He shrugged. 'Fifteen months ago,' he drawled softly, 'when you left your cryptic little letter about this adolescent William, and I came to see you at the address in Italy, you demonstrated to me how *fickle* you could be, with your new lover!'

She lowered her lashes to hide her expression, unwilling to let him see how much the past still hurt.

'And that letter you left for me,' he persisted. 'Would you not describe that as *fickle*?' His deep voice held a husky anger. 'You told me how you and William loved each other. How you had allowed me to make love to you purely for experience. How I was too old for you. Too "old-fashioned", I think was the phrase you used.'

'I was surprised you bothered coming to Italy at all, after what happened!'

'What happened was that I refuted a number of wild accusations, and then I took you to bed with me,' he said carefully, picking his words. 'Within twenty-four hours you had disappeared to Italy——'

'Rafe, there's no point going over it all,' she said, her voice low with suppressed anger. 'There's that hackneyed phrase that says actions speak louder than words. You used me to get back at Lorna. Don't deny it, because I'm not stupid!'

'You are clearly determined to think the worst of me.' Rafe spoke with cold mockery. He put down his knife and fork and gazed levelly at her white, tense face. 'So I find myself tempted to think the worst of you. If your claims are to be believed, you used *me*, as a brief diversion before being reunited with the pallid William.'

'William and I... That is, my relationship with William... That was just an invention...' She bit her lip, too angry to think straight. How had he managed to back her into this particular verbal corner?

Rafe had gone very still. He had that motionless but watchful air about him, the one that made her think of a large cat assessing its prey.

'Was it, now?' he said quietly. 'So why should I not suspect everything you tell me is an invention?'

She felt hot all over. She didn't care for her own sake, she realised abruptly, but she did care for Sam's sake. It was terribly important for Sam to know that his father acknowledged his existence...

'If you mean Sam, you can *see* he's your son, for heaven's sake! You can take blood tests, paternity tests, if you'd feel happier. But he's so like you it hurts to look at him sometimes...'

'Thank you.' Rafe's voice was ironic. There was another pause, longer and more unsettling than the previous one.

'You need not worry,' he said at last. 'I believe he is my son. And his existence changes everything...' He had leaned back in his seat, his expression arrogantly decisive. 'Whatever drove you to do what you did, the facts are now clear. You have neither the financial nor the emotional resources to bring up Sam alone. Today, I was at the altar with the wrong stepsister. I propose to rectify the mistake as soon as a registrar can be available.'

CHAPTER FIVE

'YOU'RE insane...' Faced with such breathtaking arrogance, Beth felt numb.

Rafael was shaking his head decisively.

'No. *You* were insane, to think you could do what you did today and then run and hide again, avoid the consequences, continue to lead the life of irresponsibility you have led up till now——'

'I don't have to listen to this...' Blindly, she got up, dropped her crumpled napkin on to her plate. She was causing a scene, she realised dimly. The eavesdroppers in the small dining-room could hardly hide their avid enjoyment. Trembling, she started to march towards the door. The landlord appeared from the kitchen, his face comical in dismay.

'Everything all right for you?' His doubtful tone made her wince. Poor Sid, he'd think his meal hadn't been up to the mark. From the depths of her self-control, she mustered a reassuring smile.

'It was fine. Delicious. I—I have to dash back, though. I—I forgot to tell the baby-sitter something...'

'Don't you fret.' Sid was visibly relieved. A twinkle had come into his eyes. 'The little one'll be all right...'

She couldn't wait to escape. She left Rafael settling the bill, with Sid beginning to ask nonchalantly probing questions about his identity, and dived into the gale outside. They'd driven down to the village, but it wasn't far to walk. The rain had stopped now, but the wind

160

hadn't. It whipped her hair into tangles, almost took her breath away. The savage weather suited her mood. The clinical way Rafe had stated his intentions. As if she had no choice in it. As if she'd even contemplate marriage to him, in the circumstances . . .

She stormed up the hill, her breathing ragged. When the black Ferrari overtook her, she wasn't in the least surprised to see Rafe jump out and grab her.

'Let go of me. I want to walk . . .'

'And I want to make sure you don't vanish again,' he said grimly, propelling her rigid body into the car. 'No more games, Beth . . .'

The injustice of this last statement hit her like a physical blow. No more games? She wasn't the one who'd been playing games! Did he think being pregnant, alone, having a baby to care for, did he think that was a game? What would he know? she argued silently, in fierce inner turmoil. He was about as sensitive as a pneumatic drill. Just like her father . . .

She sat in fulminating silence as the short drive was completed. Rafael swung the Ferrari into the cottage gates with controlled precision, and cut the engine. Taut as a reed, she went through the motions of paying Alison, checking that she was happy to walk the short distance home alone, dashing up to look at a peacefully sleeping Sam, all the time her brain seething with desperate ideas of how to get Rafe out of her cottage, out of her life, to stop this pain and anger and outrage from getting worse and worse the longer she spent in his company . . .

'Would you like some coffee?' For some unknown reason, Rafael's casually reasonable offer as she came back downstairs was the last straw.

'You're unbelievable,' she breathed, shaking with fury. 'You act as if you already *live* here! I want you to go away and leave me alone, and you think that because Sam is in his cot upstairs you have the right to force yourself on me...!'

Rafe had sprawled himself in one of the chairs, in the flickering firelight of the sitting-room. With the curtains drawn, and the wind rattling around outside, it looked deceptively cosy and peaceful. But the air almost crackled with tension. Rafe's mood was hard to decipher. Long denim-clad legs were stretched out, crossed nonchalantly at the ankles. The swathe of black hair on his forehead shadowed his eyes. His face looked hollow, almost gaunt. She couldn't tell what he was thinking.

'Beth, listen...' He spoke softly.

'No! You listen!' The turmoil inside her erupted. 'You accuse *me* of playing games? Your whole life is a game! You—you play around with Lorna, then deliberately start something with me to make her jealous. When you get caught, you take what you want from me just for—for the fun of it, then you're back with her the very next day! And now—now you think you can just forget about Lorna, on the very day you were seconds from marrying her? You think *I* could forget about her? You think because of Sam you can just—just get a licence, wave a magic wand, make everything all right? You're totally out of your mind!'

Rafe expelled a long breath. His eyes were harder.

'What did you expect to happen today? What did you think would happen in church after your bombshell? Maybe you thought we'd all exchange surprised glances, roll our eyes, shrug and get on with the ceremony?'

'No, of course I didn't...'

'Then, what?' He was implacable. His features were steel-hard as he scanned her face. 'What did you do it for, Beth?'

She stared at him. Her throat felt dry. She wet her lips with her tongue. She felt hypnotised by the cold fire in his eyes.

'I told you before. Revenge,' she whispered determinedly. 'I wanted to hurt you.'

There was a freezing silence. The shutters which clamped down over Rafe's expression were like a physical mask.

'To hurt me? But you had already succeeded, beyond your wildest dreams,' he murmured with acid distaste. 'With your immature grasp of life, your twisted, suspicious outlook, and your cruel little deceptions...'

Something seemed to shrink inside her.

'If you hate me so much,' she managed through stiff lips, 'how can you even think of marriage?'

'*Dios*!' The flash of white-hot fury in his eyes made her step back. He uncoiled from the chair like a bullet from a gun. The potent force of his fury was terrifying. He looked overpoweringly large, male and threatening, but his voice was deep with passion. 'You think I hate you? What did I ever do to make you think that?'

Her recoil was instinctive, but too slow. He caught her by the upper arms, dragging her towards him. A flame shot through her, half pain, half agonised longing.

'Rafe, stop it...'

He shook her slightly, his eyes fierce.

'Tell me. What form did this hatred take? In the way I sought your company? In the way I chose to spend time with you? In the way I could not stop myself from touching you? From making love to you? Even though I knew it was wrong?'

'You *used* me! Maybe that's not hatred—just contempt. Lorna once said that you have a—a general contempt for all women.' She managed the challenge through clenched teeth. She was shaking so much that she could hardly stand. His words, the savage emotion in his voice... It was like verbal whipping.

'Contempt is what you have shown towards me,' he snapped. Twisting round, he forced her back against the closed door, trapping her there with his body. 'Today was the final straw...'

His body was hot. Hard and hot. Slammed against unyielding oak planks, she could not escape him. He crushed closer, slid a hand to cup the nape of her neck. His fingers tangled painfully in her hair, and her head was jerked back. She gasped, and he dropped a cruelly hard kiss on her parted lips, his tongue thrusting inside her mouth, devouring her breath and her arguments, driving everything but physical sensation from her mind. His violent anger burned like a blow-torch.

'Rafe...' She snatched her mouth away for a second, tasting blood on her lip. 'You're hurting me...'

'Isn't that what this is about?' Ferociously he pushed the charcoal-grey sweater from her shoulder, dragged it violently down. The sweet curve of her breast was exposed, the creamy skin flushed pink from the pressure and heat of his body. He tugged the jumper further. The peaked rosy nipple sprang into sight, pointed with stubborn arousal. Raking his fingers down, he caught the nipple in his thumb and forefinger, rolled it hard until she gasped with desire, jolting as if an electric shock ran through her. 'You hurt me, I hurt you? Revenge and retribution? Isn't that the game we are playing?'

The sob jerked from her. 'Rafe, no... that's not how this should be... Oh, God, please...'

With a shudder, he dropped his mouth to her breast, suckled there with savage tenderness. Helplessly, she let her fingers move to rake into the thickness of his hair. The texture was clean, coarse and silky at the same time. Something swelled and broke inside her. Her anger exploded into a sensual awakening, long suppressed.

'Rafe... Don't—don't hate me, please...' She heard herself breathe the words, fighting for air, drowning in desire. His short laugh was bitter. The sweater was thrust upwards, ripped off and thrown to the floor. Her breasts felt so swollen that the merest touch sent cramps of lust to the aching base of her stomach. He pushed his knee between her melting thighs, and heat surged into her pelvis.

'*Dios*, if you knew how I have felt all these months...' His hoarse groan tingled through her, like a rough caress. His groin was powerfully hard against her softness, the outline of his arousal thrusting explicitly beneath the denim of his jeans.

'Rafe...' She was dying with wanting him, all rational thought gone, all pride suspended. 'I need you... I want you to——'

Their eyes met and held. Midnight-blue clashed with wide, dilated grey.

'To what?' He jerked her harder against the door, raking impatient hands down her back, scooping the stretchy leggings down so that her buttocks and thighs were exposed. She could hardly stand. 'To what, Beth?'

'To—to make love to me...' She shuddered the words on a ragged out-breath. She couldn't breathe. Her breasts rose and fell jerkily as she snatched for air.

'Yes? But this time you do not have to beg me, *cara*, this time I have to have you...' There was brutal mockery in him. But beneath it his voice shuddered with raw need. The glimpse of vulnerability engulfed her in molten heat. White-faced, trembling like a leaf in a tempest, she felt the bruising invasion of his knuckles between her upper thighs, the testing stroke of his fingers in the slick hot centre of her, and then there was no time, no time to draw breath or retract or regret or resist. Passion flared, wildly out of control. Frantic, frenzied, urgent, so urgent that she heard her own voice like a stranger's voice, sobbing his name, and felt herself cling to him, wrap herself round his hard frame as he thrust her roughly against the oak door and slammed into her like a man possessed...

'Beth...' The tortured groan was ripped from him. 'Beth, oh, my God, *Beth*...'

'Don't stop... Don't stop...' She buried her head against his bunched shoulder, dug her fingernails into his back, and screamed a silent scream of pure ecstasy as her body spiralled into spasm after spasm of release...

It was over. Like a refugee from a war-zone, she let herself be lifted into his arms and carried to the sofa. Pride was already creeping back, but Rafe held her on his lap, stopping her from struggling.

'Keep still,' he ordered softly. His voice was throaty, still thick with emotion. With a possessive hand, he crushed her head tightly against the hair-coarsened muscle of his chest.

With a shiver, she closed her eyes. She breathed in the scent of his skin. He smelled glorious. Clean, tangy, rampantly male. The brief urge to fight seeped away again.

'I'm too exhausted to argue,' she muttered. There was a lot, everything in fact, to sort out. But not now. Not with her body sending such conflicting messages to her emotions and her intellect. Not with every atom and cell of her body feeling as if it had been marinated in champagne...

'At least we have proved one thing,' he murmured finally. He shifted slightly beneath her weight, and she shivered at the movement of his body. The taut, silky texture of his skin was unbearably sensuous with its ripple of hard muscle underneath. He'd shed his jacket and shirt, but in the fierce impatience of their lovemaking his denims had stayed on. She'd retrieved her sweater. With her bare knees curled up beneath its long loose hem, and her face hidden in the cloud of her hair, she felt cocooned, temporarily safe.

'That we can communicate on a basic animal level?' she suggested, her voice muffled.

His arms tightened round her. 'That as a married couple we will at least still be physically compatible.'

'We're not going to be a married couple. And anyway, it's the same thing.'

'Beth...' He probed a finger down to seek her chin, levering her face up for a grimly ironic inspection. 'Why do you do that?'

'Do what?'

'See the worst. Reduce things to their bleakest level.'

She frowned slightly, blinking under the challenge of his gaze.

'Do I?'

'You have a jaundiced view of life,' he confirmed quietly.

'I do not. I love my baby son, I have a satisfying job doing my furniture-painting——'

'A jaundiced view of adult relationships.'

'If I have——' She stopped, conscious that she was struggling for an honest answer. 'Maybe that's only because of how my life has turned out?'

'I assume you mean since you met me?' His voice was harder. 'But your reactions were already defensive, weren't they? From the first moment we met?'

She wriggled free of his arms, and sat up. One look at him, naked to the waist, tousled and golden and sleekly devastating, made her wish she'd kept her eyes averted.

'Of course...' She shrugged stiffly, avoiding that narrowed stare. 'How was I expected to react? I came home for the holidays and found this—this macho Latin polo player, years older than me, lolling around in the sitting-room waiting for my stepsister Lorna! Was I supposed to fling myself at you and declare instant infatuation?'

There was a fleeting gleam of humour in his eyes.

'The dilemma worked both ways,' he pointed out drily. 'And I am only eight years older than you. Do not make me sound like an elderly uncle.'

She couldn't help herself; a smile caught at the corners of her mouth.

'You are an uncle, though. To your sister's children?'

'True.'

'And, compared with nineteen, twenty-seven sounds pretty elderly to me!'

The brief laughter flared and died. She gathered herself together sharply. What was she thinking of? How could she risk relaxing with him?

'Anyway, you're probably right. I am defensive. And I was defensive before you appeared on the scene, so don't think you can take all the credit. My father is the kind of person who puts people on the defensive. And as for Annabel and Lorna——'

She stopped abruptly. The wry tilt of his eyebrow made the colour seep into her cheeks.

'Go on—as for Annabel and Lorna?'

She shook her head, anger returning.

'I can't talk about this to you!' she said flatly, starting to get up. Rafe grabbed her round the waist, hauled her back down again.

'I can handle talking about Annabel and Lorna,' he said coolly. 'I don't owe any allegiance to them.'

She wondered if she'd heard correctly.

'You were about to *marry* Lorna today.' She spoke with caustic emphasis. 'Annabel was about to become your mother-in-law! If you don't call that allegiance, you're even more of a callous bastard than I thought!'

'Annabel's PR company sponsors my polo team,' he said evenly. 'Maybe Lorna and I were cementing more of a useful business relationship than a loving partnership?'

'*What*?' She jerked her head to stare at him. The expression in his eyes was blankly amused. She fought to control her breathing. His cavalier attitude to the family he'd almost married into today, his cool dismissal of Lorna... He was even more self-centred, shallow, utterly ruthless, than she'd imagined...

'Is that supposed to make me see you in a better light, Rafe?' she managed, choosing her words with elaborate care. 'Knowing that you were marrying Lorna for such cynical...materialistic motives?'

'Not necessarily. I appreciate that my character is blackened permanently in your eyes, *cara mía*.'

'Of all the mercenary, cold-blooded...'

'Perhaps we share this jaundiced view of adult relationships.' There was a wicked gleam in his eyes, even as he kept his voice expressionless. She was rigid with distaste, straining to escape from him. He'd closed his fingers around her wrist, trapping her on his knee, when she would have jumped to her feet and put a decent space between them. 'Don't you agree with me that marriage for any other reason than financial gain or practical advantage is a high-risk enterprise?'

'You'd get no money or practical advantage if you married me!'

'No.' There was a pause before he added, 'Unless you call supplying a father-figure for my son a practical advantage?'

The silence which followed seemed to elongate, until it formed a taut, bitter gulf.

She swallowed on a sudden lump in her throat.

'So it's money or duty?' The words were jerked out. 'There has to be an ulterior motive for marriage?' She could hardly believe she was having this conversation with him.

'No child should be raised by one parent when there are two in existence.'

'Fine, in theory,' she agreed. She kept her tone icily polite. Her heart felt so tight that it was as if an iron band had clamped around it. The warmth from Rafe's body was sending unwelcome shivers of response where her bare thighs were pinned to the rough denim of his lap. 'But if you think the poisoned atmosphere of a—a loveless marriage would benefit Sam, or satisfy me, you're wrong.'

'But it would not be a loveless marriage,' he teased softly. Panic shot through her as he pulled her back against his chest, sought her lips again, his kiss devouring and knowing as he ran his fingers relentlessly beneath the hem of her jumper. 'And I think our marriage would satisfy you very well, my sweet Beth... No woman makes love the way you just made love without caring, just a little, for the man involved...'

CHAPTER SIX

BETH lay in the bath the next morning, swishing bubbles around with her toes, agitated beyond belief. The gale had blown itself out. Autumn sunshine shone through the window, turned the oak ceiling-beams to rich copper. But inside herself, in her thoughts and emotions, a rough storm was raging. Memories of last night lingered in her brain. Last night she'd been stupid. Stupid and weak. She was furious with her own weakness. What had possessed her to give in to him like that? Not just that swift, ferocious coupling in the sitting-room, but again, when he'd carried her victoriously up to bed, and yet again, during the night, when she'd woken to find herself cradled in strong male arms.

The pain of remembering how he'd made love to her then, how he'd pulled her tenderly into his arms, how he'd traced new erotic pathways of desire with lips and hands until she'd shuddered with wild hunger and abandoned all reserves... The pain was so acute that she tensed under the warm water, rigid with denial from her toes to her shoulders. 'My greatest regret was taking your virginity in anger,' he'd whispered raggedly, his lips against the soft dark mass of her hair. 'That I had no chance to show you tenderness, before other lovers took my place...'

'There's been no one else...' Overwhelmed by this emotional and physical onslaught, she'd confessed it with husky honesty. He'd pulled back a fraction, stared deep into her eyes, his own eyes burning.

'Not even William?'

She'd shaken her head, her eyes locked with his, her throat so full she could hardly speak.

'I told you, William was just a smoke-screen,' she'd whispered. 'A defence...because you hurt me so much...'

'I didn't mean to hurt you. How did I hurt you, Beth?'

'I saw you and Lorna. The day after we made love. You were kissing...in the car.' She'd tried to struggle free then, to sit up, but he'd pinned her down under the covers.

'Lorna set that up,' he'd murmured despairingly, 'to stir trouble. She kissed me, knowing you were watching. I swear I did not kiss her, Beth...'

She'd stared up at him, at the shadowy hollow of his eyes in the darkness, and felt the hopelessness of the past descend on her with bitter-sweet pain. She could never trust him, because today he'd been on the brink of marrying Lorna. That was fact. The rest was wishful thinking. But she still couldn't fight this deep, throbbing need he awakened inside her. No other man had ever managed to set her on fire like this...

'Just kiss *me*, now...' she'd heard herself whisper, wrapping her arms blindly around him. And his thick groan, his abrupt eruption of fierce passion, had swept over her, submerged her in the dark swirl of sensuality that flowed on and on into the night...

But sanity had returned with daylight. And even if he had insisted she stay in bed, even if he had got up with Sam, demonstrated this touching fatherly ability to care for his baby son, wasn't it just typical male conceit? she seethed inwardly. Assuming that he could do everything better than she could? Just as he seemed to be assuming that the physical attraction between them somehow equalled the kind of caring love which marriages were made of. Rafe might think she had no pride. But could he honestly think she'd marry him? Maybe next he'd suggest she borrowed Lorna's wedding-dress as a practical solution to an unfortunate little mix-up?

Down in the hall, the telephone was ringing, she registered. Automatically, she scrambled out of the bath, grabbed her towelling robe from the back of the door, and hurried on to the landing. Rafe had answered it. It was probably Aunt Jayne. What would she make of hearing Rafe's deep, attractively accented voice on the end of the line? She'd never told her aunt who Sam's father was. More habitual self-defence, she supposed. The less people knew, the less opportunity they might have to use their knowledge to hurt her in some way. When Aunt Jayne had casually mentioned Lorna's forthcoming marriage, she'd had no inkling of the hornets' nest she was stirring up in so doing...

Now Beth felt a twinge of guilt. She'd been so tangled up in this present emotional situation with Rafe that she hadn't rung, as she'd intended to last night, to see how her aunt was feeling...

She hovered, making damp footprints on the tan carpet, expecting Rafe to call her. He didn't. Instead, she realised that a low-voiced conversation was taking place downstairs. A one-sided conversation, of course. Rafe's voice was terse. She heard her name mentioned, but it was impossible to tell who he was talking to. Lorna? It had to be Lorna, didn't it? Lorna had somehow found out where she was, where Rafe was, and no doubt she was now ringing, with some degree of justification, to enquire where her errant bridegroom had vanished to...

Why, in God's name, was she creeping around like this, on her own landing? Impatiently, she ran downstairs. She heard him say abruptly, 'One o'clock. See you there...' The click of the receiver told her he'd replaced it just as she appeared.

'Good morning.' His calm greeting made her even angrier.

'I heard the telephone,' she managed lightly. She wanted to scream, but that would only make things worse. Staring at him made things worse, too. He'd had a quick shower, and pulled on denims and a loose navy blue sweater. He hadn't shaved yet. But even with the tousled black hair, the barbaric smudge of beard-growth, he was so achingly good-looking that she hated him for it.

'We have to talk, Beth.'

'Talking is the thing we're least good at,' she quipped, with a calm she was far from feeling. Glancing past him, she saw Sam and went, smiling, to greet him. Safely strapped into his high-chair, with a bowl of Weetabix in front of him, he was wearing a clean T-shirt and dungarees, but no bib. There was Weetabix everywhere. Gleefully, he stepped up the spoon-smacking routine as he spotted her.

'Thanks for giving Sam his breakfast...'

'I am afraid things have not gone quite as I planned.' Rafe's tone was dry.

'I'm sure you've done your best,' she retorted equably, finding a bib in the drawer. Sam began squirming crossly in his chair as she began an unpopular clean-up routine.

'Who was on the telephone?' She avoided Rafe's eyes, concentrating on her task.

She stiffened as Rafe put out his hand, took hold of her arm.

'Why are we talking to each other like strangers,' he probed softly, 'after the things we did and said last night?'

She shivered, even as a wave of heat swamped her.

'That wasn't real, it was just——'

His fingers tightened, digging in through the towelling robe.

'Not real? We made love all night, and you say it was not real?' The quietness in his voice was more threatening than anger.

'I don't deny that—that I find you physically very—very attractive.' Her own voice was unsteady. 'But, in reality, we *are* strangers. It's just that there's a—a sexual chemistry or something...'

'Our son is real,' he murmured, his voice hardening.

'Oh, yes.' She reached to stroke the baby's wispy dark curls, but her eyes were bitter on Rafe. 'Sam is very real. Are you going to tell me who that was on the phone? Or should I just guess? It was Lorna, wasn't it? Tracking down her missing husband-to-be? What did you say to her? "I *was* going to marry you, but due to *practical* considerations I've proposed to someone else twelve hours later. Hope you're not too *miffed*."'

'Don't be so bitter.' He gave her a slight shake, then released her abruptly. 'It doesn't suit you.'

'You'd better get going, hadn't you? If you're going to be back in Gloucestershire for one o'clock? That was when you said you'd meet her, wasn't it?'

'As usual, you already have your own version of the truth neatly worked out.' His clipped dismissal made her inwardly wince. Pausing at the door, he swung round, adding softly, 'There is one thing I have to ask. Last night I used no protection, Beth. Is there a possibility that you could have conceived again?'

She wanted to cry. Instead she glared at him, in hot indignation.

'You really do think I'm stupid, don't you?'

'You said there'd been no one else,' he pointed out, huskily impatient. 'That is why I have been wondering.'

'I think the common phrase is once bitten, twice shy,' she informed him, her fists clenched in her pockets. 'So, since I had Sam, I've been taking the pill. Just in case. Satisfied?'

A slight twitch at the corner of his mouth was the only visible reaction. But he nodded slowly.

'I have to go out, Beth. I have to meet someone. But I will be back.'

'Please don't bother!'

When the door had closed with elaborate care, and she was left standing in the middle of the kitchen staring at it, and the pain gnawed at her insides like a knife, she wondered what had possessed her to fling that last bitterly proud statement at him . . .

He hadn't even bothered to say goodbye, she reflected, a couple of hours later. He'd just gone, slammed the front door behind him. She'd heard the Ferrari's throaty growl, a spit of gravel, then the sound of the engine retreating into the distance. Left in the cottage, cuddling Sam as if he were a shield, she'd longed to release her tension in a storm of weeping. But she'd felt too choked.

And besides, hadn't she cried enough over Rafe Mendoza? Wept enough tears to last a lifetime? She was past caring now. And the repercussions from Lorna, and her father, and Annabel... She was past caring about those, too. Let them do their worst. The worst was that Rafe could somehow try to take Sam away from her. But she'd fight him to the end on that...

Alison had come to look after Sam while she delivered a chest of drawers to a client, forty minutes' drive away. Dressed casually in soft black boots, denim jeans, green checked shirt and grey waistcoat, her hair vigorously brushed and tumbling loose down her shoulders, she steered the Range Rover cautiously along the narrow, high-banked Exmoor lanes. The sun shone brilliantly. All looked well with the outside world. She couldn't decide which emotion she felt more strongly—frustration at Rafe's autocratic behaviour, or relief at escaping the claustrophobic tension of the past twenty-four hours. Both, she told herself silently. The desolate feeling at Rafe's absence, the persistent tug of memory after last night's flood of passion, these were treacherous stabs of weakness which she strove to ignore...

Besides, she found herself thinking, he hadn't taken all his possessions with him. So, despite her sharp advice, he planned to come back...

She caught a glimpse of her handiwork in the rearview mirror. The customer had supplied the old stripped pine chest, and left the decoration up to her. She'd painted clumps of primroses at each corner, and along the tops of the drawers. It looked good. She felt pleased with her efforts. She was making a small profit now, instead of merely breaking even. But, even so, she had to be honest. This wasn't a major money-earner. It probably never would be. It required too much time and energy for too little return. What sort of security could she offer Sam? She couldn't expect Aunt Jayne to help out indefinitely. That abrupt, bleak vision of the future opened before her again as she drove. She felt a sick apprehension spreading in her stomach.

What was it Rafe had said? She had neither the financial nor the emotional resources to bring up Sam alone. She chewed her lip distractedly as she drove. That wasn't true. She had the emotional resources, if love and patience and total commitment were all that were needed. But lone parenthood was a long, lonely haul which didn't get any easier, she knew. And money was definitely a scant commodity in her life...

Sam needed a father. Her pride was the only thing stopping Sam from having one. A father, and a future in which Rafael Mendoza's plentiful supply of money could buy him the best of everything. Was she irresponsible? Rafe had said so. But then, who was he to judge? Had he really been marrying Lorna to cement a business relationship? That casual claim still echoed in her head, and she found it difficult to believe.

Yet it somehow made more sense of his peremptory offer of marriage to herself. She had no idea why he was so cynical, but Rafe didn't believe in marriage for love, from what he'd said. He needed solid, practical reasons to tie the knot. Maybe he believed in sex as a substitute for love? But he wasn't too worried about loyalty. Presumably discovering an illegitimate son took precedence over a useful connection with a polo sponsor?

And now he'd gone to meet Lorna, gone to talk over the last twenty-four hours' interruption in their wedding-plans... She couldn't even guess at the outcome of such a meeting. Fear and anger vied for place in her heart. She blinked away tears, hardly aware of the dazzle of golden gorse and purple heather as she came out on to the autumn glory of the moor. She was at the mercy of Rafe's cynical whim. She felt as if he'd cornered her. And, worse still, it was all her own fault. For giving in to the temptation to vent her bitter feelings at his wedding, for giving herself away, drawing attention to herself, when she could simply have carried on the way she was... Worst of all, last night she'd admitted that her relationship with William had been a sham, a defence against her infatuation with Rafe. How could she have left herself so vulnerable and exposed?

The cottage was very quiet when she let herself in later on. Walking expectantly through the downstairs rooms, she called hello, found no one. No sign of Sam or Alison. Maybe she'd taken him out for a walk in his pram, in the sunshine. Retreating to the kitchen, she was about to fill the kettle to make a cup of tea when she spotted the note on the scrubbed wooden table, secured under the teabag jar. It was a folded slip of lined, school exercise-book paper.

Mr Mendoza came to collect Sam, so I thought I might as well go back home. Half-term next week so I'll be free if you want me. Alison.

Beth sat down, mainly because her legs were suddenly shaking so much that she was afraid she'd fall over. 'Mr Mendoza came to collect Sam.' She read the words several times, and began to feel physically sick. Rafe had taken Sam? He'd come back here, while she was out, and just *taken* him?

Her heart thudded faster against her ribs. He'd decided to end this pointless wrangling, she realised numbly. He'd humiliated her by demonstrating his sexual power over her. He'd driven her to confessing how much she'd cared about him in the past. He'd made a perfunctory offer of marriage which she'd declined. Now he'd opted for Plan A, and guaranteed polo sponsorship, but he'd taken Sam, the perfect accessory for a trouble-free, instant family with Lorna... Was this Rafe's revenge on her? For daring to upstage his wedding? As human beings went, she reflected fiercely, Rafael Mendoza had definitely crawled out from the bottom of the heap...

Tears were pouring down her face. Dashing a hand furiously over her eyes, she stood up, blundered clumsily for the telephone. The number of Cobb Barton rang for so long that she thought no one was in. When Annabel's voice eventually answered, she'd been about to hang up.

'Is Rafe there?' She blurted out the words without prevarication.

'Is that Beth?' Annabel sounded different, somehow. Not friendly. But flat, oddly vulnerable, her voice lacking its usual poised edge. But Beth was too stressed to query it. The very sound of her stepmother's voice brought back all her old defences, made her curl up inside with misery and resentment.

'Yes, it's Beth. Is he there?'

There was a loaded pause before the answer came.

'No, I'm afraid not.' Her stepmother's tone had hardened to distinctly sarcastic. 'Frankly, I can't think why he would be! I gathered he was with you.'

'Is Lorna there?'

'No. Beth, I don't know what the devil you thought you were doing in church yesterday, but your father is——'

Beth caught her breath shakily, and slammed down the receiver. Annabel's lecture was the last thing she had time for now. Lorna wasn't there. She was with Rafe. Lorna and Rafe and Sam, together somewhere, playing happy families... She decided she knew how a tigress might feel when a cub was stolen. She could kill someone...

Shuddering with suppressed emotion, she dialled another number. When the call was answered, she heard herself informing the local police station that her baby had been snatched by his natural father...

CHAPTER SEVEN

THE policeman who came round was young, calm and sympathetic. They drank tea by the fire while Beth described Rafe and Sam, gave a shaky account of the situation, and tried very hard to suppress hysteria. Being without Sam felt like a nightmare. As if someone had cut off her arm. She wanted to scream and sob and kick the walls, but all she was doing was politely answering questions, while the policeman laboriously wrote down her answers on an official-looking clipboard.

It was nearly dusk when a car engine sounded outside, and it was the policeman who stood up to see who it was. Glancing out of the sitting-room window, he shot a wry look back at Beth, where she sat stiffly controlled in the armchair by the fire.

'A man and a child in a black Ferrari have just driven up. From the description you've given me,' he said cautiously, 'could this be runaway father and son, safely back home?'

Her heart gave a tremendous thump. Dizzy with shock, Beth jumped up. Relief and fury welled in equal measure. She half expected to see Lorna, arm in arm with Rafe, but he was alone, except for Sam. And there was consternation in his eyes as he saw the police car.

'What is it?' He frowned intently at Beth's white, taut face. 'What has happened, Beth? Is everything all right?'

'Where have you *been*?' she flung at him passionately, holding out her arms to take Sam. Hugging her son tightly, she closed her eyes, then glared accusingly at Rafe. 'How *dare* you take my baby to meet Lorna?' Her legs felt so weak that she sat down hard on the sofa. Sam's soft baby skin smelled so sweet and familiar that gratitude at getting him back almost overcame her intense fury.

'Beth——'

'I thought you'd kidnapped him,' she whispered.

Observing the scene with deadpan concentration, the policeman cleared his throat and opened his mouth to speak, but Rafe cut in abruptly.

'I merely took my son out for a drive. There was no need for concern. Beth and I will sort this out,' he said flatly. 'Don't worry. There is no question of anything illegal.'

'Miss Haversham?'

'It's all right,' she conceded, her voice strangled. She shook her head as the young constable hovered determinedly. 'Really, it's all right. I'm—I'm very sorry I bothered you...'

When they were alone, Rafe came to sit down heavily beside her on the sofa. His eyes were dark with an expression she couldn't identify.

'You called the *police*? You truly thought me capable of kidnapping Sam?'

'What was I supposed to think? I came back, found him gone, found Alison's note. And I knew you'd gone to meet Lorna——'

'No. You did not know that. You assumed that. Just as you assumed that the telephone call this morning was from Lorna.' His voice grated with anger, but his tone was ominously patient. 'The trouble with you is that you make too many false assumptions. You then act on impulse. You are governed by emotions. You lack logic.'

The scathingly arrogant verdict made her stiffen in fresh outrage.

'At least I have some emotions! Which is more than can be said for you!' she hissed. 'So... who *were* you talking to?' She twisted to see his expression. It didn't tell her much. His face was shuttered.

'Your father.'

She stared at him. 'My father? My *father* rang the cottage?'

'I rang him. He rang back.'

'But why...?'

'To sort things out.' Rafe cursed softly at her aghast expression. 'To arrange to meet. Your father has come down to the West Country. He is staying at a hotel on Exmoor. That is where I went this morning. And, when I had visited a garage and had a child-seat fitted in the Ferrari, I came back to get Sam. You were not here, so I took him to see his grandfather. Do you really want to stay estranged from your family forever? Is that fair to Sam? To deprive him of his birthright, of his blood relatives?'

'You're so... arrogant! I can hardly believe this...' She was so furious that she could hardly focus on Rafe's dark face, hardly string coherent words together. 'How— how *dare* you interfere like this? You have no right to interfere in my life——'

'I have every right.' His tone was harder. But there was a husky, compelling note in his voice. It made her skin prickle with sudden awareness. 'I have a vested interest.'

She sucked in her breath. Sam, lying in her arms, had fallen sound asleep, she realised suddenly, despite all the tension surrounding him. Over-sensitivity obviously wasn't going to be his handicap in life. Very gently, she eased off his small red jacket, then stood up and carried him upstairs, placed him carefully in his cot. When she came out, she met Rafe on the landing. They faced each other like wary opponents in a boxing-match.

'Rafe, I think you'd better leave——'

'If you were worried this afternoon, I apologise,' he said quietly, ignoring her challenge. His gaze held hers, against her will. 'If Alison did not make it clear in her note to you, she must have assumed you knew why I was taking Sam.'

She was desperately weary, she realised. The trauma of the afternoon was beginning to catch up with her. Raking an unsteady hand through her hair, she pushed past him and went downstairs. She needed a cup of coffee. Or maybe something stronger. When she got to the kitchen, and realised that Rafe had calmly followed her, she swung on him in frustration, staring at him properly for the first time since his return. He was wearing the denim jeans and shirt, and the loose black jacket he'd worn for their meal at the pub. And now there was a heat in his eyes, a heat that burned right through her cool defences, right through to the tight ball of anger in her heart.

She felt herself shiver and melt inside, and furiously clamped down on the stupid reaction. Don't let him get to you, she ordered herself fiercely. He might look wonderful, he might have hypnotic eyes and a personality to match, but he's cold, calculating, amoral, totally heartless . . .

'I'm amazed my father is even speaking to you,' she managed unevenly, 'after you left Lorna standing in the church! And he'll certainly never forgive *me* for wrecking his beloved Lorna's day. Not to mention Annabel's elaborate arrangements...'

'You are his daughter.' Rafe's eyes were sardonic on her flushed face. He put a hand on her shoulder, and she tried not to flinch. 'Your father cares about you.'

'My father,' she countered quietly, 'does not care about me. All he cares about is commuting to London to his nice, safe accountancy business, and commuting back to Gloucestershire again to his beautiful second wife. He has never forgiven me for reminding him of my mother. After she left him, and then was killed, he punished me with indifference all through my teens. And when I came back from Italy and telephoned him from London, when I really needed him to—to stand by me, he disowned me. He informed me that I was fickle and shallow, just like my mother——'

'He told me.' Rafe's voice was equally quiet, with a wry edge of bitter humour. 'He couldn't forgive you—firstly for abandoning me——'

'Abandoning you?' she cut in incredulously. 'What about you and Lorna?'

Rafe continued as if she hadn't interrupted.

'And then apparently abandoning William, after claiming in your letter that it was a serious relationship. But he had no idea you were pregnant. He's regretted the way he treated you ever since. He's been through his own kind of hell, Beth. Just as I have...'

'Rafe——'

'He's not proud of the way he's behaved. He's sorry. He wants to make it up to you. And, as I said, I have a vested interest in glueing together the shattered family of my baby son.'

'Very heroic. But you're wasting your time.' She kept her voice low. She had to stay cool, stay in control of herself. As a means of self-defence, it could prove far more effective than losing her temper. 'My father could have come to see me. One of Aunt Jayne's conditions for helping me was that my father must be told that I was all right. She's been in contact with him all this time. That's how she knew about your marriage to Lorna.'

'Your aunt Jayne did not tell him about Sam. Nor would she give him your precise address. She respected your desire for privacy and independence. But at least your father knew that you were safe——'

'Rafe, listen, last time I spoke to my father, do you know what he said to me? He—he told me that as far as he was concerned he never wanted to hear my name again, that I was dead to him...' She blinked away tears, glaring defiantly at Rafe's intent face.

'I know. But now you have returned from the dead. Be generous. Forgive him, Beth.' Rafe's gaze held a glint of bleak humour.

She shook her head.

'He took Lorna's side in that row over you, fifteen months ago...'

'I suspect your father found it hard to accept the existence of a relationship between us. *Dios*, you'd just come home from the convent, in your short white socks. He said that even though I was only eight years your senior, you were much too young for me. I convinced him otherwise. And then your behaviour in Italy made me think that perhaps he had been right...'

She was hardly listening to Rafe. The past injustices were too hot in her mind.

'Didn't you see the way he leapt to Lorna's defence in the church yesterday? How come he's holding out this—this belated olive-branch to me today? It doesn't make sense! When I wrecked his beloved stepdaughter's wedding——'

'Not quite.'

In the midst of her anger, she froze.

'What do you mean?'

'I mean that you did not quite wreck the wedding.'

She could hardly believe she'd heard him correctly. Then understanding dawned. Just as she'd suspected, he'd withdrawn his rash offer to marry the mother of his son. He was appeasing his conscience instead by attempting a reconciliation between father and daughter...

'So...you've set another date already? Congratulations.' She could hardly form the words, her lips were so stiff. Avoiding his eyes, she began to turn away.

His fingers closed on her arm. He jerked her back to face him. His eyes were very hard and bright as he locked his gaze with hers.

'There was no need for another date. After your interesting little scene in the church, the wedding went ahead, almost as planned,' he informed her expressionlessly.

She blinked at him in mounting horror. What was he trying to tell her? That he was *already* married to Lorna? If so, how could he have dared suggest that Beth marry him? How could he have made love to her last night? She felt sick, suddenly. Rafe wasn't just amoral, arrogant, self-centred, he was a monster...

'I don't understand... Rafe!' she burst out, frustratedly. 'Would you mind spelling out in words of less than four syllables what is going on?'

The glitter in his eyes was wickedly ruthless humour, she realised, her anger increasing.

'I regret that your dramatic revenge backfired a little, *cara*. When I said that the wedding went ahead as planned, that is not quite true. It went ahead in an atmosphere of bemused surprise, and without the presence of the best man.'

She stared at him blankly. Then her jaw dropped. She almost felt the colour drain from her face.

'Oh, no. Oh, no... Are you telling me that you were the *best man*?' Her voice rose at the end of the sentence, into a husky wail of horror.

'Absolutely.' His face was deadpan. 'Lorna is now happily married and enjoying her honeymoon with a fellow member of my polo team by the name of Patricio Fernandez.'

'Oh, you—you...' She covered her face with her hands, almost shaking with anger and mounting humiliation. Reaching blindly for the table-edge, she supported herself. Shock was making her feel as if she might lose her balance.

'Rafe, why didn't you *say* something?' she managed furiously.

'It was time to teach you a lesson. Who told you that Lorna was marrying me?'

She bit her lip, fresh waves of embarrassment descending on her. Aunt Jayne had told her about the wedding. But what exactly had been said? Had Rafe's name actually been mentioned? She couldn't swear to it. The more she thought about it, Aunt Jayne might

have spoken of a 'South American polo player and friend
of the family' and her own imagination could have supplied the bridegroom's name...

'I must have misunderstood what Aunt Jayne told me,'
she began stiffly, clinging on to the shreds of her
composure.

'Even so, when you got to the church,' he probed drily,
'could you not see who was at the altar beside Lorna?'

Her face was scarlet under Rafe's wickedly amused
gaze.

'I was in a slightly... hysterical state...' The confession was wrenched from her. She cast her mind back
desperately, trying to recall the moment of her arrival,
the furtive glimpse she'd snatched of the ceremony taking
place at the front of the church, her preoccupation with
her own shattered emotions. She'd been so nervous that
she'd probably have had trouble recognising her own reflection. 'It was all a bit of a blur,' she finished up in
shaky defiance, 'but now I think about it, the best man—
that is, the man I thought was the best man—was *very*
similar to you in height and colouring...'

'Nowhere as good-looking,' Rafe taunted remorse-
lessly. 'Has it occurred to you that getting your eyes
tested might be a sensible course of action?'

She glared at him with growing indignation.

'But... you were so convincing. Even down to your
suitcase full of clothes for your honeymoon...'

'I was supposed to be driving the happy couple to
Heathrow, then spending the weekend with friends in
Surrey.'

'You've actually been *enjoying* this, haven't you? How
could you play along with my mistake, all this time? Of
all the cruel, heartless, sadistic...'

'You deserved every minute of it, you suspicious, conniving, vengeful little witch...'

She lunged a blow at him which he neatly fenced, and found herself caught up against him. She was half sobbing, half laughing. The laughter abruptly died.

'Tell me one thing,' he grated, locking eyes with hers in a gaze which seemed to burn right into her soul. 'Why would I marry your stepsister Lorna, when it is you I love? You I have *always* loved? Whether or not you choose to believe me this time, Beth, I love you, and only you. Marry me. Stay with me. I need you. If you want revenge, all you have to do is walk away from me now. You have the power to hurt me beyond your wildest dreams, *cara*. Believe me. It is the truth.'

She gazed at him breathlessly, struggling with her memories, dazed with confusion.

'I can't—I can't take it in...' she whispered raggedly, examining the taut lines of his face, seeing a nerve jumping in his cheek, the tension in his eyes as he waited. All she had to do was believe him, she realised. Believe that he'd cared about her, all this time. Believing seemed like the hardest step she'd ever contemplated taking.

'I want you to be my wife, Beth. Even if it were not for Sam, I would still want you.'

'Really...?' she breathed hoarsely. But her eyes were shining.

'Do I have to kneel at your feet to convince you?' There was such raw emotion in his voice that she lifted a hand to touch his face.

'If you love me, then nothing else matters. I think I could forgive everyone everything—Lorna, my father, the whole world...'

With a low curse, he crushed her closer into his arms, pinned her there, his heart thudding roughly next to her own. She linked her arms round his neck, slid her fingers into the thick black hair at his nape. Abruptly, nothing else mattered but letting her feelings show. She wanted to get close to him. She wanted it so badly that she was faint with longing. She wriggled fiercely against the warmth of his chest, pushed her hands inside his jacket, couldn't get close enough. He gave a muffled groan, scooped her up with muscular ease and carried her into the sitting-room, where he flattened her along the length of the sofa, crushing her there with the disturbing heat of his body.

'Kiss me...' she managed weakly.

'Is that all you can say?' His soft tease was breathed against her parted lips. 'Is that all you want?'

'No!' She couldn't keep track of the emotions seething through her. 'I want you, in every way, as my husband, my lover, the father of my child...'

'And do you love me?'

'I hate you for tricking me, for making even more of a fool of me than I'd already made of myself...'

'Do you love me?' His breath was hot, his mouth tantalising hers. His body was hot, hard with wanting her, pressed against her own.

'Yes...*yes*! What do you think? Why do you think I was so frantic...so jealous when I thought you were marrying Lorna?'

'Then say it...'

'I love you... I love you... Oh, God, Rafe, I do love you...'

Feverish need took over from teasing. For the first time in her life, she found herself with the confidence to initiate their lovemaking impatiently, pulling his mouth down to hers, raking her nails down his back, wrenching his shirt from his trousers. Rafe's reaction was reassuringly forceful. Deserting the sofa for the floor, he relieved her of her waistcoat, checked blouse and jeans, and discarded his own clothes with a reckless urgency which catapulted a shirt-button into the corner of the dusk-filled room . . .

In contrast to the antiquity of his church, the vicar of Cobb Barton displayed a refreshingly modern, understanding approach to the complex family situation outlined to him. He married them, at a quiet, simple service, a few weeks later. Charlotte was delighted to be Beth's bridesmaid. Her father gave her away. Lorna and Annabel were conspicuously absent, having apparently failed to see the funny side to Beth's dramatic interruption of Lorna's wedding. Beth, on the other hand, had managed to see the joke. She and Rafe had laughed about it so much that she hardly dared picture the scene any more in case another bout of giggles welled up . . .

'I hope Sam will be all right with Aunt Jayne . . .' The reception, at an exclusive Cotswold country-house hotel, was in full swing downstairs, relieved of any awkwardness by the presence of Rafe's polo team, drily amused to be attending Rafe's second 'wedding' in the space of a month.

She shot her new husband an anxious look in the haven of the luxurious room they'd been assigned as a changing-room.

'He is welcome to come on our honeymoon,' Rafe grinned. He came up behind her as she stood in front of the mirror, struggling with the zip of her dress. He unzipped the ethereal ivory silk chiffon, slipped it sensuously from her shoulders. 'But, apart from the heat of Bermuda, and the length of the flight, Aunt Jayne adores him, and your father adores him, and he'll be spoiled out of all recognition when we get back, my darling little bride.'

'I know...'

He dropped a light, arousing row of kisses along the slope of her neck, and drew her back against him. He'd stripped off his shirt. The heat of his body burned her like a naked flame.

'Rafe...' She gave a small gasp as he slid his fingers down to her breasts, freeing them from their flimsy covering, then moved slowly lower to caress her slender thighs above her stocking-tops.

'Do you have any idea how sexy you look in that outfit?' His husky tease made her move her eyes to the mirror. She bit her lip at the sight of wanton abandon she presented, in lace basque, suspenders, and high-heeled cream shoes. Her cheeks were flushed, her eyes bright. Her dark hair was beginning to tumble out of its carefully pinned style...

'I don't look much like a respectable married woman,' she conceded dubiously. 'It's your fault. We're supposed to be changing to go and catch a plane, not starting a post-wedding orgy.'

'I have to reassure myself that you are flesh and blood.' He was devouring her with his eyes. 'When you walked down the aisle in church, I could hardly believe you were real. My beautiful little ghost bride...'

'*Ghost* bride?'

'I'm very glad you're alive again in your father's eyes.' His grin was unrepentant. 'But, as the months went by,

I had almost resigned myself to you being dead to me, too...'

'Feel me,' she whispered. 'I'm real flesh and blood and I love you so very much...' Her eyes were brilliant with love. She took his hand and cupped it around one swollen breast, shivering as he caressed its tight, hot peak, then she turned urgently in his arms, splaying her own hands on the thudding width of his chest, exploring him inch by wonderful inch. She shimmered with golden fire as he groaned, and raked his fingers down her body to her taut thighs, found the slick heat between. 'And if you don't make wild hectic love to me right now, I'm going up in flames...'

'As you wish, Señora Mendoza...' The solemn set of his face was belied by the glint of laughter in his eyes. She dissolved in the heat of his arms, helpless in the great wash of erotic sensation which followed.

'Doesn't it feel weird,' she teased huskily, lying exhausted in his arms, 'making love to a ghost?'

'Out of this world,' he agreed, poker-faced. But he kissed her laughter back into her throat with all the worldly love and desire he possessed.

TREACHEROUS
DESIRE

BY
NATALIE FOX

CHAPTER ONE

'SO WHAT exactly have you got against him?' Melanie Hyams reasoned. 'Apart from the obvious,' she added knowingly.

Sarah, palms down on the desk, faced her editor-in-chief unblinkingly. 'Apart from the obvious, just about everything. He's arrogance personified with a mega-sized ego. He's unscrupulous, a deceiver of hearts and——'

'And the best lover you ever had,' Melanie interjected.

'The *only* one,' Sarah corrected hotly. 'And that was one too many. No, Mel, I'm not going to do an interview with him, not even if you quadruple my salary.'

'No chance,' Melanie grinned, and then gave a shrug of her well-tailored shoulders. 'Sorry, darling, being jilted by Matt Constantine does not make you exempt, or even qualify you for preferential treatment——'

'You're my cousin, for pity's sake!' Sarah howled.

Melanie shook her head. 'And nepotism won't work either.'

'Perhaps my resignation, then,' Sarah threatened scathingly, her blue eyes narrowed to give emphasis to her threat. Oh, yes, she would resign. If Mel insisted on her going through with this interview with Matt Constantine, she would.

'Hot-headed you might be, Sarah, honey, air-headed you are not. You have a good career here, and besides, my father wouldn't hear of you leaving.'

'Now who's screaming nepotism?'

'My privilege,' Melanie drawled, getting up from her desk and coming round to Sarah. 'My being the daughter of the owner of this magazine has definite advantages, and you having once been jilted by Constantine has definite advantages too, if only you'd look at it in a different light. You're halfway to getting the scoop of the decade if you did but realise it.'

'Mel, Matt and I are history,' Sarah tried to insist.

How could she convince her cousin that the last person he would want to be interviewed by was the one woman in his glittering life who had turned him down? Matt hadn't been the jilter, but the reverse. It had been easier to explain their split that way to her family, because it shut everyone up. She'd made out she was the injured party so that sympathy came her way instead of probing questions that she hadn't been able to face at the time. It had all been too painful.

'And Matt Constantine is hot news *now*,' Melanie argued. 'This will be a scoop for us. The only interview before this massive take-over he's going for next month. Don't you see, because you were lovers once and because you know him so very intimately you are the ideal person to cover it?'

'I'm the *last* person to cover it, Mel,' Sarah fought back. 'Even if I agreed to take him on, he wouldn't let me over the threshold of his life a second time.'

'Oh, no?' Melanie breathed mysteriously and, fluttering her very black lashes, she hit Sarah with a knowing look that rocked her.

'Wh—what exactly are you trying to say, Mel?' Sarah croaked. She didn't like that look, not one bit.

Melanie took her time, as if she was weighing up what to tell her. Eventually she shrugged and said, 'I haven't been completely honest with you, Sarah, because I thought I'd give you the chance to do it willingly but, seeing as you are putting up a fight against it, the truth will out. Matt Constantine offered us this chance of an exclusive interview on one condition. You did it.'

Sarah's heart thumped. He couldn't have, not after what she had done—walked out on him after that ghastly row. She stared helplessly at her cousin and then shook her head.

'I can't, Mel, I just can't,' she pleaded.

Melanie held her gaze for an eternity and then landed a bombshell on her.

'You have to do it, Sarah. He asked for you and he added that if you didn't agree he'd offer himself to our rivals and give them such a hot story we might as well rename the mag *Goodbye* and shut down our printing presses now.'

Stunned, Sarah slumped down into the nearest chair, her head spinning. Oh, how could he make a threat like that, how could he?

Melanie leaned back against her desk and, not taking her eyes off her cousin, folded her arms across her chest.

'So, you see, you have no choice, Sarah. You must do it.'

She nodded, feverishly rubbing her forehead. Mel was right, she had no choice but to do it. The threat was too disturbing to be overlooked. She owed so much to her uncle Josh. Her parents had been sent to a diplomatic post in South America when she had been in the middle of her O levels, so she had moved in with him and Mel and her uncle had seen her through university and offered her a job on the magazine at the end of it. She couldn't let him down.

Sarah cleared her throat before saying in a small voice, 'No, I haven't a choice. So, when and where?'

'Good girl,' Melanie murmured, and went back around the desk and sat down. She shuffled papers on her desk and said, 'He wants you this weekend and said you would know where.'

Sarah's heart floundered then. Yes, she knew where and, because of the location, she knew that Matt could only have revenge in mind. It all became clear now. For one crazy second she had toyed with the idea that he might want a reconciliation, but because of the location she knew that thought was hopeless. He would be tidying up his life before making the biggest take-over of his career—a group of holding companies that would sweep him into Europe with a vengeance. And he would want that take-over to go smoothly, and it might not if the world knew what she had done.

Shakily she stood up and straightened her silk jacket down over her pencil-narrow skirt.

'For the record, Mel,' she said firmly, 'I'm putting my feelings aside and doing this for you and your father because I know Matt well enough to know he'll carry out that threat.' She took a deep breath. 'So you want a story. Well, you'll get one and——'

'A good one,' Melanie warned. 'This mag doesn't publish rubbish. Not that squeaky-clean Matt Constantine has anything untoward in his life to consider, unless you know otherwise.' She paused and waited for Sarah to say something.

Sarah smiled and gave nothing away. Matt was clever, too clever to get caught out in anything that wasn't on the level. But he had bent the rules once, and Sarah knew that this was what all this was about.

'All I want is a little insight into his personal life,' Melanie went on. 'You know—pets, hobbies, ambitions and, of course, if he has any marriage plans for the future.'

Sarah winced painfully. Melanie sighed.

'Darling, I'm sorry,' she breathed sympathetically. 'But you should be over this by now. A year is a long time, long enough to get over a broken love-affair. You were ill-suited anyway; you admitted that. Far too young and inexperienced for him. He was far too sophisticated for you and he did the right thing by letting you go, for both your sakes. You know this could all work to your advantage, meeting up with him again.'

'Oh, yes? How do you see that? Laying a few ghosts, perchance?' Sarah snapped bitterly. She strode to the door and opened it, and by then had cooled down. She turned to her cousin and gave her a weak smile. 'You could be right. I might set eyes on him again and wonder what I ever saw in him in the first place.'

She slammed the door after her and leaned back against the corridor wall and closed her eyes. And I just might die of a broken heart for all that was lost. Oh, how she had loved him. Oh, how she still did, but Matt had been far too much for her to cope with. Older and wiser with a life behind him, whereas she had had no track record of experiences to learn from. Out of university and into the harsh world of the media and that was about it.

But they had fallen in love, in spite of their differences, and it had looked so good and promising, but then their differences had become painfully obvious when he had become involved with the lovely Marion and then mysteriously taken over her husband's company, shocking everyone in the commercial world.

'A conspiracy? Sarah, don't be ridiculous!' he had protested. 'First I'm supposed to be having an affair with Marion, and now this childish nonsense!'

They had arranged to meet at his country retreat in Cumbria that weekend. Sarah had arrived first, armed with the financial papers she had taken to reading to try and get on Matt's wavelength. He had arrived late and was tired, and she had known she ought to wait but she just couldn't.

'You're always with Marion these days, Matt. She phones all the time, her husband has dropped out of the scene and now this.' She had waved the paper at him. 'You've taken over Edwin Stimson's company and everyone is surprised by it, everyone but me. It doesn't surprise me one bit after all the time you spend together.'

'Sarah, you don't know what you are talking about. You know nothing about business——'

'I know what I know!' She had burst into tears then because it was all so hopeless. And because he hadn't tried to comfort her she had stormed from the room.

She had tried again later, after he had changed and relaxed with a drink. Again he had denied an affair and again he had denied any sort of conspiracy with Marion to get Edwin's company and, because he had clammed up after that and told her once again that he had no wish to discuss his business life with her, Sarah had known the gulf widening between them was un-bridgeable and she had left.

Some would have stayed, she mused, as she headed back to her office. But it had all been too much for her. Matt had been too much for her. Her pride had won over her heart, though her idiotic heart still bled for him and the loss. Love was a useless pastime. She'd never fall again, that was for sure.

'Oh, and who are you?' she asked the tall, straight-backed man with silvery hair who answered the door at Wentworth House. Sarah was stiff and tired and nervous after her long drive up to Cumbria. Why Mr Successful didn't live in Knightsbridge like all the other Mr Successfuls, she didn't know, though she did really. Matt enjoyed his privacy, loved his rural retreat, and she had shared it with him once and loved it equally. Now it looked cold and forbidding.

'Mr Constantine's butler, miss, and who might you be?'

'Sarah Martin,' she told him tightly, not appreciating being held up outside on a windy porch with flurries of snow pestering the back of her neck. But then, she supposed he was following orders, to make her feel uncomfortable and out of place, the first stage in Matt's revenge scheme of things.

'Ah, yes, you're expected. Your bags, miss?'

Sarah stepped inside the warm, welcoming hallway. 'No bags. I stopped on the way and booked into a hotel for the night. I'll only be here for a couple of hours.'

'As you wish, miss.'

The door closed behind her and she looked around, familiarising herself once again with the surroundings. How cruel of him to insist she came here. The first place they had made love so passionately and declared their love, though his declaration must have been a blatant lie.

And then she saw him, at the top of the stairs and not alone.

Her heart bleeped. She had thought he might look different after a year but he didn't. Dark, handsome, tall, broad—it was all still there. The charisma, the potent sexuality, even the arrogance she had fought against once, only to realise that it had been part of the attraction in the first place. An arrogant man was a confident man, a successful man, a fascinating man. Why did women fight it so?

The woman with him on the gallery landing above wasn't fighting it. She looked as dewy-eyed as Sarah once had. Poor soul, Sarah thought, as the lovely brunette linked her arm in his and started down the curving stairway, with him smiling at her as if they were doing a coffee ad.

Sarah cleared her throat, but she knew it wasn't necessary. He knew she was there. This was all part of the game.

'Sarah, how lovely,' he said, and took the last steps as if he was actually pleased to see her. He had the audacity to touch her shoulders, to peck at her frozen cheek, to look as if he was greeting an old, dear friend. A show for his lady friend or a punishment for her? Neither mattered, so speculation was a waste of time. She had hardened her heart on the long drive here.

'Sarah, this is Penny, a dear neighbour.' He swung round to the butler as the two women eyed each other, neither smiling. 'Gordon, would you see Mrs Connaught to her car, and then bring coffee to the sitting-room and remind Mary that we'll be dining at nine?' To Penny, the dear neighbour, he directed, 'We'll talk more about this next weekend, Penny. Best regards to Felix.' He kissed the air at the side of the brunette's face then without another word he took Sarah's arm and guided her to the door of the drawing-room, and before she knew it she was almost thrust into the room and the door was slammed behind them both.

To her discomfort Sarah realised she was shaking, but hardly knew why. Since being landed with this job she had convinced herself she wouldn't allow herself to be affected by it. But now she was here, she was. She watched him cross to the fire, his legs strong and powerful under navy corduroy jeans, his back broad and muscular under a denim shirt. She'd always loved him this way, the casual Matt Constantine, but then, the elegant, sophisticated Matt had always turned her on too. She had to face it: she had loved him which way and however.

She slid out of her cashmere coat and flung it down across the back of a chair by the door, while he prodded at the coal fire with a heavy brass poker.

'We'd better start right away if you have guests coming for dinner.' She fumbled in her bag for pad and pen and a small portable recorder. When she looked up he was watching her with broody black eyes.

'The dinner is for us, sweetheart. You didn't really think I'd get you this far up country without offering you my hospitality for the evening?'

Sarah returned his gaze with open hostility. 'I'm not dining with you, Matt. My work will be long done by then and I'll be off. You might as well know from the start that I'm not happy about this arrangement and——'

'I'm not asking you to be happy, Sarah,' he interjected. 'You forfeited that little luxury when you walked out on me. I'll see you in hell before you see happiness again.'

So, she had been right. She was here to be punished. Well, he could be as vitriolic as he liked but he couldn't hurt her any more than he already had done in the past. She stood stiff as a ramrod and braced herself for whatever he might throw at her. There was a long, long pause as they eyed each other, because of their past both unwavering in the eye contact.

'You'd better come and warm yourself. You look half frozen.'

Her heart hammered as she took those steps towards the welcome warmth of the fire. Concern she didn't need from him; that was more dangerous than anything.

'You've cut your hair,' he remarked, as she plopped down on a dark green club chair by the fire.

Her hand went instinctively to the red-gold bob she wore now. She'd had it done this way because he had loved her hair when it had flowed halfway down her back. She'd also changed her dress sense, too. Now she wore designer suits, because he had loved her in her gypsy-style flowing silks. Everything he had supposedly loved about her, she had rearranged.

'You've changed,' he said quietly.

She looked up at him towering over her. 'You haven't. Still pushing for other men's wives,' she spiked back at him meaningfully. Penny was very obviously married to a Felix, but not ideally so by the look of the way she had clung on to Matt's arm as they had come down the stairs. 'So what was a *dear neighbour* doing upstairs, anyway? No, let me guess. She's a plumber and your pipes need lagging!'

'Antique dealer, actually,' he told her flintily. 'And, though it's none of your business, she's conducting a local charity auction and I was showing her a Regency chair she might be interested in.' He smiled, not pleasantly. 'And your interest in the *dear neighbour* says a lot,' he drawled.

First mistake, she thought heatedly, letting him know his betrayal still hurt. She floundered for a cutting retort to throw back at him, but she knew it would only make matters worse. Mercifully the door clicked open and Gordon came in with the coffee. It gave her time to glance at her watch. Six o'clock. She'd give him two hours for the interview and then she would be free. There was absolutely no way she was staying to dine with him. She wasn't going to play into his hands any more than she could help.

Gordon retreated graciously and Matt poured the coffee and handed her a cup. He sat down across from her and watched her again. It made her feel vulnerable and uncomfortable. Once she had loved it, thinking his heart must be toying with loving thoughts for her; now she hated it because it threw her.

'What's the idea of the butler?' she asked, thinking it might lead her into the interview. The interview. What a farce. She knew his hobbies and his ambitions, and as for pets, other men's wives—oh, yes, that would make great copy. Mr Respectable, without a supposed blemish on his character, had a penchant for out-of-bounds women. Trouble was, who would believe it? Somehow Matt had put himself on a pedestal, out of reach of lowly things such as gossip. The media saw him as a fascinating saint of the business world. No scandal, no affairs. Something quite rare these days.

'I decided my privacy wasn't quite so important after you left me,' he told her coldly. 'Gordon was hired to take the place of a wife. You know the sort of thing—general household duties——'

Sarah let out a snort of cynical laughter. 'Keeps your bed warm too, does he?'

She thought he would explode at that bare-faced insult, but he surprised her by keeping his cool.

'According to you, other men's wives keep my bed warm, and you should know from past experience where my sexual preferences lie.'

Didn't she just? Sarah drank her coffee and then put her empty cup down on a side table and reached for her pad.

'OK, shall we stop this goading each other and get down to business?'

'And what business is that?'

She flicked her eyes up to look at him. 'You know, the interview. My time is precious, Matt, and pleasant as all this reminiscing is, it is a costly waste of time for us both. You're quite a busy man these days, company-crunching to your heart's content. Well, there was life for me too after we split up and this is it: work.'

'This is whatever I want it to be, Sarah, sweetheart. You get your interview when I choose, not when it slots into your schedule.'

She stared at him bleakly, hating him for doing this to her, kicking her feelings around as if they were of as little importance as autumn leaves on the ground.

She clasped her hands tightly on her lap. 'OK, I'll wait till the mood takes you, but if it doesn't happen in the next half-hour you can forget it.' She leaned back in the chair, rested her head against the dark green velour, and closed her eyes. This would show him she couldn't be messed with.

His mouth on hers was hot and powerful, flinging her backwards in time, a painful reminder of the searing heat of their past passion. She couldn't succumb to it, though her senses screamed submission. Her heart was too hard to allow him in a second time. She was able to fight it quite easily, because she knew why he was doing it.

He drew back and her eyes flickered open; he was leaning on the arms of the chair, his face only inches from hers. His breath was pulse-racingly warm on her skin, his scent another painful reminder of a loss. He was looking down at her with an expression she didn't understand.

'What was the point of that?' she murmured painfully, her heart hammering with the after-effect of that surprising kiss.

He smiled thinly. 'I just wondered if there was a little of the Sarah I once knew left. You come up here bristling with hostility and sweeping away any good intentions I had for the weekend.'

He straightened up and moved to the coffee-tray and poured himself more coffee. He held the silver pot up to her and she declined with a shake of her head.

Good intentions? Who was he kidding? He must think her still the doe-eyed kid who had once hung on his every word. No, there was nothing left of the Sarah he had once known. Thank goodness.

'Matt,' she said softly and sensibly. The change of tone made him look at her quizzically. 'Don't let's make this any more difficult than it already is. You insisted on me doing this interview and I'm here, and isn't that enough?' She tried to keep the pleading out of her eyes because she didn't want him to see just how easily he could hurt her.

He settled down on a sofa across the fireplace from her and gave her a long slow smile. 'It'll never be enough, Sarah,' he murmured darkly.

Her spine chilled. So what more did he want? To hurt her, that was obvious, but what deeper form was it going to take?

'Let's get on with this interview, Matt. You've made your intentions quite clear enough and I'm submissive. I'll write whatever you like. I'll paint the picture exactly as you want to appear to your adoring public.'

'Why exactly did you come, Sarah?'

The question took her aback for a few seconds. It was obvious. To save her uncle's magazine. She didn't doubt for a minute that Matt would carry out that threat if she hadn't complied. But she wasn't going to let on that she had taken the threat seriously.

'It's my job,' she told him. 'Nothing more, nothing less. Now, can we get on?'

He stretched his long legs lazily and then got up. 'Tomorrow will do. I have some calls to make before dinner. I'll have Gordon show you your room.'

'Hold on!' Sarah cried, on her feet immediately, her pad and pen sliding to the carpet at her feet. 'I won't be here tomorrow!'

A lazy smile crinkled the sides of his mouth. His eyes were dark and teasing. Cat and mouse, Sarah thought despondently.

'Sweetheart, if I wish you on the moon tomorrow, you'll fly.'

'Matt, don't do this!' she wailed. She wouldn't be able to bear it. He couldn't insist on her staying and they both knew it. He was just trying to undermine her till she didn't know which way to turn.

'Don't do what?'

'Don't play dumb, for one thing,' she stormed back. 'I'm not dining here tonight. I'm not staying the night and I'm doing this interview this evening and not tomorrow. Got it?'

He said nothing, simply smiled at her as if he knew the secrets of the world but wasn't letting on. And then he did something that really mystified her. He crossed to the door, lifted the phone from a small mahogany table next to it, bent down and took the jack-plug from the wall and, with one last glance at her, tucked the phone under his arm and left the room.

In disbelief Sarah glared at the back of the door. So he had calls to make and he obviously didn't want her listening in on the extension but, for heaven's sake, why would she do a thing like that? She had no interest in him any more. Ah, but she was here to do a magazine profile on him, and if those calls were strictly confidential...

She slumped back down into the chair and stared at the glowing coals of the fire. She wouldn't do that, eavesdrop, though she had once before and made the mistake of admitting it to him, but it had been unintentional. She hadn't meant to hear what she had. But he wasn't going to risk it. So he didn't trust her and she didn't trust him, and what on earth was she doing here?

It was a question she asked herself fifteen minutes later. Her temper was hanging on by a thread as she glanced at her watch.

She got up, jammed her pad and the recorder back into her bag and gathered up her coat from the chair by the door. This was ridiculous. The interview could take a flyer for all she cared. She wasn't going to hang around any longer waiting for him to appear when it pleased him.

'You're joking!' she cried to the door as she twisted the heavy brass knob in vain. This wasn't happening, surely? She was locked in!

'Matt!' she screamed, rattling the knob and only just holding back from kicking at the door. 'Matt, open this door before I scream the house down!'

Nothing. Not a sound came from the hallway beyond.

'You rat,' she breathed to herself. Now she understood why he had taken the phone with him. He was keeping her a prisoner here, and knew that once she had realised it she would phone for help; he *knew* it.

She flew across the room to the windows and flung back the heavy brocade drapes. To her horror, heavy snowflakes were flinging themselves at the window-panes and piling up on the ledges. She heard a car engine ticking over and, rubbing the glass, she peered through and then cried out, 'Gordon! Gordon!'

Surely he must hear her cries? The butler was loading up the boot with hold-alls and a suitcase, and then helping a woman into the passenger seat. Oh, no, they were driving away! Sarah shouted as hard as she could and thumped her palms against the toughened security glass of the windows. But nobody heard.

Crying with frustration, Sarah hammered and hammered at the windows till the tail-lights of the car disappeared in the blizzard, and then she hammered some more just for the devilment of it.

'Oh, Matt Constantine!' she shouted furiously. 'You are going to pay for this!'

Wiping the tears from her cheeks with the backs of her hands, she took her portable tape recorder from her bag and switched it on, after clearing her throat. She spoke clearly, giving the date and the time of day, and then she went on.

'I am being kept prisoner here at Wentworth House by Matt Constantine. I'm locked in with no means of making contact with the outside world. The staff have left. I fear we are alone in the house. There is a blizzard raging outside. He intends to punish me. I intend to keep a faithful record of all that happens.' Before switching off, she added lethally and determinedly, 'And I intend to use that information, Matt Constantine, because two can play at the revenge game.' She poked her tongue out and crossed her eyes at the back of the door, feeling ridiculously childish but nonetheless wishing he could see how little she cared for his silly games.

She switched on the television, settled down in the chair by the fire, and vowed to make as little of this as possible when he came to let her out. She really didn't care if he kept her locked up all winter. The longer, the bigger the story. World scoop? She had it, here in the palm of her hand. Was this kidnapping or was it holding a person against their will, and when were they both the same thing? Whatever it was, it was a criminal offence, she felt sure, and Matt was guilty. He'd live to wish he'd never started this.

CHAPTER TWO

By NINE o'clock Sarah had been through the anger and boredom barrier and was hard up against worried. She was hungry too, and the fire was going down and there wasn't any more coal to put on it. The blizzard was still raging outside, and already snow was creeping so high up the window-ledges that she could scarcely see out.

Supposing Matt had had an accident and was unable to release her? How would she get help for him if he was lying somewhere injured? Huh, why should she worry about him when he hadn't even checked to see if *she* was all right?

She jumped as she heard him at the door, but coiled tighter on the sofa and made out that she was asleep. She yawned and stretched when she thought the time was appropriate.

'Oh, I must have dropped off,' she said sleepily, and swung her long legs over the side of the sofa.

'Good. I hope you slept well enough, because you're in for a long night. Champagne?' He put two fluted glasses down on the table beside her and filled the glasses to brimming point.

'Champagne! What are we celebrating, your fifth birthday?'

He laughed thinly.

She took the champagne he offered her, but vowed not to drink too much of it. She'd be on her way back to the hotel shortly. He'd left the sitting-room door wide open and, when the time was right, she'd make a bolt for it. Of course, it would cut short the exposé on him she planned, but she had enough to make a good story: In fierce blizzard, plucky girl reporter escapes the clutches of mad Matt Constantine and lives to tell the tale.

'Here's to the long night you are going to have to endure, though it's up to you whether you make it endurance or indulgence.' He held his glass up to her for a fraction of a second and then drank. Sarah sipped.

'Meaning?'

'Two people of the opposite sex marooned in Cumbrian hideaway during a snowstorm. Hearts running wild and free, passions clamouring for release, result—the obvious,' he stated confidently.

'How about, crazed tycoon finally loses his marbles, believing that his ex-lover is gullible enough to plop into bed with him for old times' sake?'

He grinned, wickedly. 'Doesn't have to be for old times' sake, Sarah, dearest. Could be a new voyage of discovery. Neither of us is the person we were a year ago.'

She gave him a wan smile. 'I'm older and wiser, not so you.'

'I'm older and more embittered.'

'I'd noticed.'

'More champagne?' He stood over her, waving the bottle temptingly in front of her.

'I would need it if I took your innuendoes seriously, Matt,' she told him. 'But I don't, you see. I'm not sleeping with you, drunk or otherwise.'

'You weren't so choosy once,' he fired back, a cruel reminder of the one time, a hilarious time, in this very house, when they had gone over the top, drunk too much, laughed and fooled around and made wild passionate love in that glorious four-poster bed upstairs. She held his eyes as he defied her to say one word against that time, then he turned away from her and gave his attention to the fire.

Her eyes couldn't help misting with tears as she watched him pick up the Victorian coal-scuttle and leave the room. She had been so in love then, and had honestly believed him to feel the same way. He had acted as if he had, loving her with such intensity, such depth of passion that it had ruined her for any other relationship in her life. When you had tasted perfection, second best wasn't a consideration.

The mist from her eyes cleared, and suddenly she was on alert and knew what she had to do. She had to go, and now, because if he stabbed at her emotions the way he just had she'd never make it through the night.

Quickly she picked up her bag and slid into her coat, only stopping to whisper hurriedly into the recorder: the time, and how she was making her escape, right through the sitting-room door and out of the front door to her car.

The biting cold hit her lungs, catching at her breath and nearly choking her. It hadn't been this cold when she had arrived. Mercifully the blizzard had eased but there were inches of snow on her car. She swiped at the thick, glistening layer on her windscreen with her bag and then tried to open the driver's door. It was frozen solid. It took her precious seconds to get it open and slide behind the wheel, teeth chattering with nerves and the cold.

'Oh, no,' she breathed fearfully. The car wouldn't start; it just wouldn't start. Strewth, what was that awful whining sound coming from under the bonnet?

Suddenly the door was wrenched open and she was hauled out of the seat and her high heels skidded on the snow. She was falling, and then was swung up into Matt's arms and he was carrying her back into the house.

'You idiot!' he stormed, dropping her in the hallway so suddenly that she only just kept her balance. The heel of one of her shoes gave under her and she kicked them off furiously.

'I'm an idiot, am I? I'd call myself a heroine——'

'For trying to escape!'

'Aha, you admit it, then,' she cried triumphantly. 'You *are* trying to keep me a prisoner here!'

'There was no doubt of that in my mind. Trying and succeeding too.'

'And I know why!' she blurted furiously. 'For—for revenge . . . to punish me——'

'To protect you,' he insisted, equally furiously, eyes threatening her against arguing with that.

Seeing that she hadn't a clue what he was getting at, she did question it, heatedly. 'To protect me from what? If I need any protection it's *from* you, not *by* you.'

He gave her a chilling look. 'You always were wildly impetuous, naïve, and getting the wrong end of the stick. Once I found it endearing; now, a year later, it palls. Get your coat off and get inside in the warmth.'

Oh, it was useless. Sarah remembered her shoulder-bag. She'd flung it into the back of the car. It was obvious she was going nowhere tonight but she needed her recorder, because all of this torture she wanted to note.

She stepped back into her damp shoes. 'I need my handbag out of the car.'

Her submission eased his temper. 'I'll get it, and your overnight bag. Is it in the boot?'

'It's at the hotel. I booked in on the way here, and I'll get my shoulder-bag, if you don't mind.'

'Suit yourself.' He shrugged and turned away in the direction of the kitchen and, without looking back at her, said, 'And don't get any foolish ideas of trying to start your car again. It won't.'

She scowled at his retreating back and, hugging her coat to her, braved the elements again and skidded to the car, brushing snowflakes from her face. Just one more try. She turned the ignition and there was that awful sound again and she knew it was hopeless.

When she shivered her way back into the house he was waiting for her, leaning on the oak panelling, arms folded, wearing an expression of derision.

'You don't give up, do you?'

'I thought it worth another try,' she told him defiantly, chin jutting. 'At least give me credit for not being a simpering little useless female.'

'Oh, yes, you have spirit—pity you haven't the common sense for it to get you anywhere. Your radiator is frozen solid, Sarah. Ever heard of anti-freeze? Well, it's this pretty blue fluid you put into your radiator to prevent such a thing happening. Very silly of you to have got this far into the winter without it. Some people learn the hard way.'

She stared at him bleakly, feeling incredibly stupid. Anti-freeze. It had been the last thing on her mind.

'How long before it thaws?' she whispered.

'Long enough.'

Sarah clenched her fists at her sides. He was loving all this, making her feel a fool.

'Long enough for you to work your revenge on me, eh? So you locked me in for my protection, did you? Some protection.'

He looked at her stonily, a look of sufferance. 'You've just proved it, sweetheart. You need protecting from yourself. You drive all the way up here without a thought for the weather. Did you bother to get a weather forecast before setting out?'

'Of course not!'

He sighed. 'Of course not, because you haven't the sense you were born with. The forecast is below freezing temperatures, snow, ice and fog. If I hadn't locked you in this evening——'

'So you did lock me in!'

He shrugged again. 'I've never denied it. You seem to be the one finding difficulty in accepting it.'

'And so I should. I'm outraged by it.'

'Well, outrage as much as you like, Sarah, but I remind you I did it for your own good. I know you, you see, and I was right in thinking you wouldn't have changed in a year. A little bit of emotional discomfort and you are off. You would have sped out of here without a thought for the weather. If I hadn't locked you in, you'd have made your escape and by now would be stranded on some snowbound road, perishing with cold and panicking——'

'I'm a perfectly competent driver, thank you very much!'

'So competent you didn't give a thought to the weather or to making sure your car was roadworthy enough for a long winter journey.' He glared at her angrily for her stupidity. 'Sarah, get your coat off and get upstairs and into a hot bath before I throw you back outside.' He turned away and headed for the kitchen again.

'Well, I'd rather brave a Siberian storm with a yeti than stay here to be gibed at constantly!' she shouted after him.

'Yetis come from Tibet, not Siberia,' he threw back over his shoulder.

'Oh, they would, wouldn't they!'

Furiously she ran upstairs to the bathroom, inwardly cursing for being stupid enough to forget anti-freeze. She had dashed out of London with just one thought occupying her mind: how she was going to feel when she came face to face with him after a year apart. It proved one thing, she supposed: she hadn't matured very much in the last year. So he was saving her from herself, was he? A clever cover for the real reason he had locked her in—to punish her. The weather had just been a convenient coincidence, though she wouldn't have put it past him to do a snow dance outside on the lawn to ensure such a thing happened.

She soaked for a long time in the bath, not worried about him joining her because this time she had locked *him* out, wondering what his intentions were for the night. Seduction for punishment, maybe? He had, after all, lost little time in kissing her. She could think of no more painful revenge than that: drugging her with his sensuality till she succumbed and loved him, and then he would roll away from her and show her the door. Was he really capable of such cruelty? Once she would have been ashamed by such thoughts; now she just thought it a distinct possibility.

'I have no clothes,' she told him later, finding him in the kitchen gazing worriedly at a casserole he had just pulled out of the oven.

'It's never bothered you before,' he said absently, not even bothering to turn to look at her.

She leaned on the side of the door with his bathrobe wrapped tightly around her, not liking herself very much for allowing the smell of him from his robe to spin her head on a voyage of bitter sweet nostalgia.

'This is different,' she murmured.

'Yes, it's different.' He glanced quickly across to her, let his dark eyes flick over her, wrapped seductively in his towelling robe, and then studied the casserole again and added, 'But not surprising. You always were very forward in coming forward.'

She blushed hotly at the reminder. Often she had led the way, not that Matt had needed leading, but she had loved him so deeply and passionately that at times she hadn't been able to contain herself. He'd loved her for it at the time—her spontaneity, her lack of inhibitions with him. He'd loved the way she playfully tore at his clothes in her eagerness to be one with him. He had loved her gaucheness. At least, he had said he had.

'I'm not coming on to you, Matt,' she said softly. 'I really haven't any clothes with me.'

He turned his head to look at her then. 'Odd, that.'

She widened her eyes. 'What's so odd about it?'

'Surely you expected to be put up for the night?'

She lowered her lashes. 'I told you. I booked into a hotel, and before you ask why I think it's obvious. Once we had a relationship, now we haven't. I didn't think for a minute you would want me under the same roof as you. In fact, when it comes down to it, I don't know why I'm here at all.'

'No, you wouldn't, would you? It's all way above your head, isn't it?' His tone dripped sarcasm.

'OK, so I know.' Yes, she knew, revenge. 'Do you want me to say it, so humiliating me even more?'

'Even more? I don't see that I've even reached the perimeters of humiliation yet.' He peered at the casserole again. 'I think this has gone beyond the realms of edibility.'

'And you've gone beyond the realms of *credibility*,' Sarah said scathingly, crossing the kitchen to gaze down at the casserole with him. 'It's just dried up a bit, like you. What happened to your faithful retainers tonight? At the thought of being stranded here in the snow with their wild master, did they abandon the sinking ship?'

'They've left for the sunny Caribbean. Gordon and Mary are married. Mary said this would be ready for our dinner at nine, but it's way past that now.'

'So I suppose it's all my fault the dinner is spoiled?' she retaliated, heart drooping at the realisation that the staff wouldn't be here in the morning to rescue her.

'I wasn't the one soaking in the bath for forty-five minutes.'

'I needed it,' she retorted. 'And that casserole needs to be binned. It's irretrievable.'

He looked up at her and held her eyes. She thought for a second he was going to reach for her, but he didn't.

'And is our love irretrievable, Sarah?' he said softly.

Her heart leapt at the thought that this was the reason he had manipulated her here. A reconciliation? Her heart steeled again. If she thought for a minute the question was a genuine one, she could make an attempt at answering it. But she knew he could never really have loved her in the first place, so what was there to retrieve?

Lowering her eyes, she went to turn away but he didn't allow it. He caught her wrist, and his fingers around her soft flesh were a challenge to her senses. She looked up at him and saw that unfathomable look in his dark eyes again.

'I thought it was possible, Sarah. When I first decided to ask you here, I thought you might have grown up and realised what a mistake you had made in walking out on me. You haven't grown up but you have changed drastically, and I'm beginning to think I loved a myth of my own imagination.'

Her heart twisted with pain at that, and the only defence was attack. 'If I ever thought you'd loved me enough in the first place I'd be more than willing to give that some serious thought,' she told him coldly. 'Don't take me for a fool, Matt. I know why I'm here. I don't doubt for a minute that you want this profile done on you—after all, better the devil you know than the one you don't. Another reporter might delve just a bit too deeply for your liking. You could have got me here for several reasons, but one of them wasn't to try and resurrect a past love, Matt.'

His eyes darkened and his grip on her wrist tightened threateningly. 'Once you were open and trusting, now you see nothing but revenge. You've got yourself into a sorry state since we parted——'

'You have a short memory, Matt. I walked out on you because I saw something in you I didn't like. And that is the reason you've brought me here, because of that mistake you made with Marion and that suspicious take-over. Now you want me to do this profile so you can somehow smooth it over with me, somehow persuade me that it wasn't the way I saw it... and while you're doing that, why not wreak revenge on me for having the strength to walk out on you?'

'And how do you think this supposed revenge will take form, Sarah?' he bit out angrily. 'Me seducing you back into my bed and hoping you'll fall so madly in love with me again that you'll put this supposed mistake of mine behind you and write a glowing holier-than-thou profile on me? Well, let me tell you something. To do that I would have to *want* you in my bed, and at this precise moment I'd rather run barefoot up the Pennines in a loincloth!'

He thrust her wrist away from him and, giving her the same disagreeable look he had given the spoiled casserole, stormed out of the room.

Sarah hugged herself tightly, listening to him thudding up the stairs and slamming doors one after the other, as if one wasn't enough to assuage his anger.

And why was he so angry, if all she had said was true? He should have just shrugged his arrogant great shoulders and agreed.

In pathetic confusion she started moving around the kitchen. Was their love irretrievable? Hers had never gone anywhere to be retrieved from. It had always been with her—reluctantly, but nevertheless deep inside her. But he had posed the question as if he really had loved her and was wondering if it was worth trying for a second time.

'No way,' she breathed into the fridge. 'I'm here for revenge—nothing more, nothing less.'

Omelettes and salad and some French fried potatoes? They had to eat. It was going to be a long night.

She went through to the sitting-room just before she was about to put the omelette in the pan. She'd heard him come down ages ago. He was sitting by the blazing coal fire going through some papers. He looked intent and serious and her heart tightened at the thought of all the work he must be snowed under with so close to the take-over. Don't go soft, she resolved. But wasn't it too late? She'd cooked him a meal, after all.

'I'm just about to put some omelettes on—actually only one, a big one we can split. Do you want yours in here or will you join me in the kitchen?'

He looked up at her. 'You make me so bloody mad, Sarah,' he said quietly.

She nodded. 'I heard.' She shrugged. 'Boys will be boys. Kitchen or here?'

'Here. Together. It's cosier. Remember?'

How could she ever forget those cosy evenings, coiled in front of that very fire, stuffing pizzas and sipping wine. When she had first met him at a London cocktail party she had never thought of him as a pizza man. So elegant and sophisticated and arrogant, he had looked as if he had only ever dined on oysters and fine Scotch beef. But she had soon found out that he wasn't the man she had thought, and finding out had been delicious, and then the finding out had gone a stage too far when she had discovered the real man, the cheating man. It had all soured after that.

She carried the tray through, wishing she had dressed in her creased suit after her bath. This damned dressing-gown of his kept flapping open. She set the tray down on a table and tightened the gown around her waist. He'd poured more champagne, which was a bit flat now and not out of place next to her flat omelette.

'Your cooking hasn't improved,' he told her, forking it gingerly.

'Be grateful I didn't slice and fry up the casserole. I put it out for the birds. Wouldn't be surprised if it polished off the whole blue-tit species.'

'What are you trying to say, that Mary is a lousy cook?'

'The proof *wasn't* in the eating.'

He smiled and tasted her omelette. 'Tastes better than it looks.'

'Two up on Mary's burnt offering, then. Is she always that bad, and why do you put up with it if she is?'

'Gordon is indispensable and she's his wife and needed the work, and I'm not often here, anyway.'

This was the Matt she had fallen in love with. The kind, caring man under the façade of a cool businessman. She supposed that was why the discovery had hit her so badly, because she had thought him incapable of it. But the evidence had been overwhelming and, though he had denied it, he had never fully explained.

They ate in silence and finished off the champagne, and Sarah wished with all her heart that they were a year back in time and planning their wedding, as they had been doing just before the Stimson episode had reared its ugly head. Sarah had tried to understand his work; Matt had said it didn't matter, but she had thought it important. The trouble had been that it was way over her head and made her feel insecure. Then had come the take-over of Edwin's huge electrical corporation by Matt Constantine, shocking everyone in the commercial world. Though Matt and Edwin had been friends for years, they had been business rivals too. Matt had tried unsuccessfully before to buy him out, then suddenly he was in control. Sarah had seen it as some sort of conspiracy between the two of them, him and Marion, because they had been seeing so much of each other and Edwin hadn't been around.

'Do you still see Marion?' Sarah asked. She had nothing to lose by asking. Her pride was still around, but a little dulled with time.

Matt didn't answer straight away but stood up to put his empty plate on the tray on the table. He came and stood at the back of her chair and reached over her for her plate.

'I never did ask you what got to you most, the thought of me making love to Marion or the fact that you thought I had used her to cheat her husband.'

'I don't know,' she admitted. She heard him piling the plates together and stared into the fire. She felt him behind her again, leaning on the back of the chair, waiting for her to say more. 'They both hurt; combined, they were a lethal dose. I loved you so much I *might* have forgiven you a brief encounter with an attractive older woman. I mean, people do these days, don't they?'

'Do they?' he murmured into her hair on the top of her head.

'People say they do. We did an article a while back, a survey: Would you forgive your partner a one-night stand? The majority said they would.'

'I wouldn't,' he breathed. 'Never. I wouldn't even consider forgiveness. You can't possibly love your lover and indulge in wild passion with another. It's unforgivable.'

'But you expected it of me.'

'I don't remember.'

'You don't want to, Matt.' She sighed deeply. 'You didn't even want to believe that I knew all about you and Marion. You denied it, true, but facing such an accusation men usually do. It's instinct——'

He laughed. 'But you didn't want to believe it, did you? It went much deeper than that for you at the time. I wonder if, faced with it now, you would feel the same way. It appears your thinking has become more liberal since working on a magazine that faces emotional problems in a nineties-thinking way.'

She tried to turn her head to look up at him, but suddenly his hands went to her neck and then slid down under the robe to massage her shoulders tenderly. The feeling was delicious but she couldn't let herself sink and really enjoy the experience. She had to hold on to her senses.

'So,' he went on, 'keeping that article in mind, would you forgive me now, believing I had been having an affair with Marion?'

Oh, what a difficult question. Sarah took a stab at it.

'Before reading that article of Melanie's I was adamant that I couldn't forgive you, but it brought up a few relevant points. Why ruin a life for the sake of a one-night stand? If the couple could work it out and find trust again, it would be best put behind them and, hopefully, the relationship would be stronger for being able to come to terms with it in a rational manner.'

'And who were these people laying bare their souls?' he asked.

'Oh, the usual. Upwardly mobile sorts who thought they were being very trendy and free-thinking in their opinions.'

'Hardly the sort you were able to identify with a year ago,' he told her cynically. 'Then you were a little innocent and let your immature emotions rule your judgement.'

She wasn't about to let that thought get to her—confirmation that she had been out of his league at the time.

'Anyway, you and Marion were more than a one-night stand!'

His fingers dug deeper and she knew she had got to him with that gibe.

'So, with this new-wave thinking in mind, suppose I tell you I did make love to Marion. Do you forgive me?'

She stiffened her shoulders under his fingers, not comfortable with the way this conversation was going. 'Faced with it now, no, because there were other things too, and——'

'Now, come on. You're backtracking.'

'There was more to it, Matt,' she insisted. 'You used her to get what you wanted from her husband, his company.'

'So, bedding Marion was all right, bedding her for her husband's company wasn't. You did right to walk away from me, Sarah. Before I did the walking.'

'Oh, for heaven's sake, Matt,' she cried, and stood up, pulling the robe tightly round her and swivelling to face him. 'You're twisting everything to suit yourself.'

'And you twisted everything to suit yourself a year ago. So, twelve months on, Sarah, what have you learned about yourself?' He stepped round the chair to her and Sarah backed away, but short of backing into the fire she could go no further.

'I—I've...'

'I don't think you've learnt a thing,' he said levelly. 'In fact, I think you are as confused about how you feel about me now as you were then.'

Suddenly he lifted his hand and tugged at the belt at her waist, so unobtrusively she scarcely felt it. Because of the size and weight of the robe it fell heavily into folds and scarcely exposed her heated skin to the eye. He didn't need to look, though, he knew every inch of her and there were certainly no more inches than when last he had touched her.

And then touch her he did. A searing caress that instantly flamed fire to her nerve-endings. His hand was just inside the robe, just by her breast, almost avoiding her breast to smooth the skin down her side.

'So, are you confused, Sarah?' he whispered, holding her gaze, intently studying her, trying to read the fire in her eyes.

She stayed mute because it was the only way. What could she say when he knew his touch fired her so, and always had done? He must be able to feel the reaction of her skin, just as he always had.

'Let me unravel that confusion,' he said thickly.

His fingers on her breast caused her eyelids to flicker in such a dead give-away that she might as well have moaned out her submission. Softly, softly, his fingertips circled her erect nipple, shooting delicious sensation down to the backs of her knees. She was in such danger then, feeling herself falling into his trap of revenge and not being able to stop herself. He meant to hurt her and would succeed if she wasn't stronger. Could she break away now, at this very delicious second? Could she?

CHAPTER THREE

TENDERLY his mouth closed over hers and his hand kept up the delicious caressing of her breast, small squeezing touches that alerted every sexual pulse in her body.

She wanted. She needed. She ached. She still loved him and it was all so hopeless because, though he was putting up a pretence of wanting her, it was only a punishment.

But he did want, surely? Quite badly too it seemed, as he thrust his other hand around her waist and pulled her so powerfully against him that she felt his need. He ground against her, the blatant sexuality of it spinning her head with the delights it promised. But sex was one thing, love another. Sex was pushing him now, spurred on by his need to hurt her emotionally. Love filled her heart, though. She wished it could be hate...but she wasn't strong enough for hate.

'So, you still want me,' he murmured thickly as he grazed his feverish mouth down her throat.

'And—and that is what you want, isn't it?' she whispered hoarsely. She lifted her hands and held his shoulders, tried to force him away but he was too strong for her. 'To know you have that power over me and then to crush me when it suits you, to punish me for walking out on you.'

'I'll tell you something, Sarah, something you have obviously been blind to this last year. That year was my revenge, my punishment to you for not having trust in

235

me. I thought you would suffer so much that you would beg me to take you back.'

In horror she tried to speak but it was impossible. His grip on her tightened and she was so hard against him that she could hardly breathe.

'But, sweetheart, you have some heart to crack. Your body is easy to break down. I could take you now, here, on the floor. A few more physical reminders of a passion that was almost beyond control a year back, and you would crumble willingly before me.'

To prove his point he ran a hand across her stomach, a featherlight touch that forced shivers of ecstasy down her spine. Then he ran the back of his hand provocatively over the triangle of silky fair hair that was the only barrier between his flesh and the most sensitive of hers.

'Oh, no!' she cried out, and let her head drop forward against his shoulder. She bit her lip, fought for control of her senses as he cupped her erotically and then tenderly opened her like a flower with the tip of his finger.

She nearly lost control, nearly lost her mind. Strength came from somewhere and she twisted away from him, hating him then for exposing her weakness. She grasped at the robe and hugged it to her, and her blue eyes were wide and misted with agony as she looked up at him.

'You're cruel!' she cried heatedly. 'So damn cruel to do that to me.'

He smiled benignly. 'I promise you it's hurting me more than you.'

'Physically, yes, maybe, but you are too hard and cruel to let any of what we've been through get to your very soul.'

He gripped her arms tightly above her elbows. Even with the thick covering of towelling, she could feel the force and the anger behind it.

'It's my heart and very soul that spurred me to get you here, Sarah,' he grated fiercely. 'This, the here and now, isn't the revenge you think it is. This is the last attempt to make you see sense, see that we can't live without each other.'

Her head spun, not with hope and joy but with dismay that he should admit such a thing.

'Yes, but now is the very essence of it all, isn't it? The point in your life where you can't afford to take any chances. Just one snippet of scandal could affect your credibility for this take-over looming, and you daren't risk it. Go on, then, Matt, do what you have to. Make love to me tonight. Prove the point that I still love you, and even ask me to marry you again, because me beside you as your wife is far safer than me apart from you!'

He let her go then, almost thrusting her away from him as if she was contaminated. His eyes were furiously black, so terrifying that she shrank further into his thick robe.

'You can do nothing to my reputation, Sarah, because I have nothing to hide. But what you are doing to yourself is sickening. What exactly are you punishing yourself for—the mistake you made by leaving me? Is this what is powering your revenge on yourself? Self-punishment for making a wrong decision?'

A small splutter of laughter came from her lips. She wasn't punishing herself, *he* was punishing her.

'You're trying to blame me for what happened,' she accused bitterly. 'You feel such guilt for what you did with Marion Stimson that you are turning it on me, blaming me!'

He lowered his head and raked a hand through his dark hair. 'This gets worse,' he flung at the hearth. Then he raised his eyes to catch hers again.

'If you remember, at the time the accusation disgusted me. I couldn't believe you could be so naïve as to see it that way. It was beneath me to discuss it further. You shocked me. It truly shook my faith in human nature that you should think such a thing of me after all we had been to each other.'

Guilt flooded her for that, but she refused to let it get to her. 'The evidence was overwhelming,' she argued bitterly. 'Even down to corny old lipstick on the collar!'

He laughed then, so caustically that the shock of it curled her spine, and then the words that followed nearly crumbled her.

'And who was to say that was Marion's lipstick?'

Tears spurted to her eyes with shocked horror, and the only words that could come to her lips were, 'You rat!' She flung herself out of reach of him then, turned and headed for the door. How could he? How could he make it so much worse than it already was?

She tore upstairs, blindly, wondering where she could hide herself away. She was trapped in his house, was definitely here for the night, but where could she curl up and cry the night out? She flung open doors. His room, out of bounds; the second bedroom, freezing and unwelcoming; the third, the fourth. In the fourth, the room they had planned as a nursery, a fire blazed in the old Victorian grate. Tears streaming down her face, she forced herself over the threshold, slammed the door after her, dropped to her knees on the rug in front of the fire and cried till she thought her heart would break. More misery, more revenge... This room of all rooms. This room, he had planned for her to sleep in. It didn't bear thinking about.

Other women? Not just Marion—other women? He couldn't have, he wouldn't have?

With one last sob of anguish she raised her tear-stained face and stared bleakly into the fire. What had she done to herself? Tortured herself so much over the year that she was half crazed with it. Try to be rational, she reasoned with herself. Think about everything he has said and done since you arrived. Oh, yes, he had said cruel things, wound her up, kissed her, tempted her with his tantalising caresses. He had also said that the year apart had been his revenge on her, not now. Now he wanted to prove to her that they couldn't live without each other.

She hadn't lived this last year, she had existed, and now she had a lifetime of existing without him, because even now he couldn't explain away his closeness with Marion. To say he had been hurt beyond measure by her distrust was just a cover-up.

She heard the door open softly behind her and she refused to look round. Her hand came to her face and rubbed at the last remaining tear.

Matt crossed the room and sat in the chair by the fire.

'I lit the fire in here in the last hope that you might see sense. Remember what we planned?'

His voice was hoarse with emotion and she was suddenly overwhelmed with a desire to fling herself in his arms and beg for his forgiveness. In confusion at such a thought, she turned to look at him.

'Yes, I remember,' she said faintly. 'Then our relationship was good and pure, and then you spoiled it all. I didn't know how greedy you were for power, so greedy you did what you did without a thought for me. You didn't fight for me because your pride was hurt; you couldn't fight because it was all true!'

'If I was such a beast, I wouldn't have thought twice about what you thought. I would have been conceited enough to think I could have got away with it. I *was* hurt, Sarah, so badly it stunned the fight from me. I thought that if you believed that of me you couldn't have truly loved me.'

Sarah couldn't help a sneer marring her face. 'And yet you got me here under false pretences, pretending——'

'Pretending what? That I needed this profile on me, to publicise and emphasise what a good chap I am, worthy of heading the biggest consortium of companies in Europe? I already know all that, Sarah. I don't have to fight to show my worth to anyone but you, because you are the only person that matters to me.'

'Stop it!' she suddenly cried, covering her face to shield herself from his accusing glare.

'Stop what? Making you feel guilty for what you have believed all this time?'

And then she knew that there was a hell of a lot of truth in that flat statement. Slowly she let her hands slide from her face. She stared desperately at the fire, willing it to give her answers, but the contented glow just added to her misery. Yes, she had guilt inside her, had buried it under the guise of fury and betrayal. Had she made more of this than there was to cover that feeling of insecurity she had suffered?

'I'm so confused,' she murmured at last.

'You were very confused a year ago, Sarah,' he said quietly. 'At the time I didn't understand, but at least I've tried to make sense of it since. I don't think you were ready for marriage. I don't think you were mature enough for a deeper commitment. Try and unravel that confusion now, Sarah, for both our sakes.'

She *had* been worried about those differences between them. Not at first, but then her insecurity had got a hold on her and she hadn't been able to reason it all out. She supposed it had all gone to prove that she wasn't ready for marriage. She had loved him, but somehow that hadn't been enough. She had been afraid. It was so confusing.

'I—I can't,' she admitted weakly. 'It's too hard to unravel.'

'Do you still love me?'

Didn't he know that she did? Was this another of his tortures? To get her to admit it and then stab her with the truth that he *had* been involved with Marion, so crushing her forever?

'I still love you, Sarah,' he added emotionally. 'I've never stopped and I never will.'

There was a long pause as she tried so hard to digest that. The past, their past, spun her reasoning till she felt sick and dizzy with it. She was here now, crumpled on his floor in the room they had planned for their children, and not knowing if she was coming or going. He loved her. Once she had never doubted it, but then she had, and it had all spiralled out of control. Could she believe him now?

'Come to bed with me, Sarah,' he suggested softly and oh, so temptingly. 'Now, before giving it any more

thought, just come with me to my bed and let me prove
just how deeply I care for you.'

She shook her head, unable to speak, to say yes or
no. Her body burned for him; even now in her deep
distress it burned with need. If he reached down and
touched her...

His hand came down and touched the top of her head,
tentatively at first, and then he started to smooth her
silky hair—long, languid strokes of temptation. Her hand
clamped over his and she drew it down to the heat of
her cheek and pressed it hard against her, and squeezed
her eyes tightly. It was the one small submission he
needed.

Slowly he raised her to her feet and gathered her into
his arms and held her tightly against him.

It wasn't the answer, she knew, but she wanted his
comfort. She wanted it to be all right, she wanted to be
blinded to the past and have what he was offering now.
His love and need, his passion.

'I love you, Sarah, darling,' he murmured. 'If we love
now, it will make it all right.'

And it might not, she wanted to cry, but here in his
arms she couldn't think straight. Nothing was real when
he held her this way and their need was so apparent.

His hands slid down to her trembling hands and he
squeezed them tightly, offering reassurance. She sensed
he was looking down at her but she was incapable of
looking up at him. He had said so much that confused
her. That he loved her, for one thing. She wanted to
believe, and she forced it on herself because it was so
much better than thinking of revenge. And perhaps he
was right: making love might open up their hearts and
that might make it all come clear.

He let go of one hand to lift his and tip her chin so that she was forced to meet his gaze. His eyes were dark and she read no treachery in them, just a need that reflected her own desperate need to bring their emotions to a head.

'Not here,' he murmured. 'In our bed.'

She didn't argue, simply allowed him to take over. He led her out of the disturbing room where the fire glowed softly and, holding her hand, he took her to his room and closed the door gently behind them. She could barely bring herself to look across the room to that wonderful four-poster bed where they had shared so much laughter and happiness.

'I—I can't,' she uttered, but deep inside her she knew it was hopeless to argue. He must have known this from the very start, that she would be overwhelmed by all the reminders of their past affair. Yes, he was cruel, but maybe this was the only way it could be. Cruel to be kind. He was risking his very future by bringing her here, but maybe he knew her better than she knew herself.

'Yes, you can,' he murmured, brushing his warm lips across her throat, holding her so tenderly. 'No punishment, Sarah. No thoughts of revenge. No thoughts of anything but our loving.'

He slid the robe from her shoulders and she lowered her head with shame, not able to look at him. And then he *made* her look at him, lifted her chin and gazed deep into her eyes, forcing her to keep the contact with his own intense look of desire.

'Neither of us would be able to do this if there wasn't hope, my darling. We are going to make love, because at the moment it is a barrier that needs to be broken down between us. Once I'm moving inside you, you will know the answer to everything. You will know that there has never been another woman in my life since we met. Now let me touch you, let me show you.'

His hands dropped to her naked breasts and she was lost. He cupped them, and she closed her eyes as white-hot sensation blazed down her body, making her tremble under his caress. His movements were rhythmic, circles of silk and fire, losing her in another world.

Her arms were weightless as she lifted them to circle his neck, and then his mouth was crushing hers and there was no going back, only forward into that erotic world of their own. His lips parted hers and the kiss was one of fire, scorching their desire till it was almost a physical pain. They clung to each other, Sarah naked and vulnerable, Matt disadvantaged by his clothes. He groaned in frustration as she ran her hands down him, only to find the barrier of his shirt against her fingers. He lifted her and carried her to the bed and she watched, mesmerised, as he shed his clothes, letting them fall in a heap on the floor.

She clung fearfully to him when he came down to her, hungrily ravishing her face and neck with kisses of fire. So rampant was the heat of their desire that Sarah had no will to think beyond the pleasure and the joy of holding him to her at last. No thought but one of desire, no questions or answers, nothing but indulgence and need.

A new voyage of discovery, he had said, and now she understood. They had known each other's needs so well before, and yet it was all different now. A year away from each other had heightened the intensity till they were dazed by the power of feeling between them. She was more wanton under his exploration, pressing herself against his strokes, mouthing her passion silently across his heated skin. She wanted more than ever, wanted to be under his skin, not just touching it. She wanted him inside her, deep inside her, to thrust into her and take the pain away, but he held back and fear struck her for a paralysing second, and then she remembered how it had been. How he had held back, wisely, so that when it happened it was more exquisitely erotic.

He towered over her at last and she gazed up at him, hot and dazed and longing, and she saw the same in his dark, fiery eyes, the passion, the tension and the anticipation. She saw his love, too, and her heart brimmed with hope and she clutched at his shoulders, drawing him down into her.

She cried when at last he thrust into her, smoothly and fluidly, deeper and deeper till he moaned and closed his eyes and shuddered hard against her. She cried with the depth of love she felt for him and the intensity of her passion as he moved inside her, plunging her into that surreal world of flame and fire. Everything around her dimmed and then shone and blazed and the feeling inside her grew and grew and brought her to the very edge of insanity. His breathing was ragged and uneven against her, his thighs hot on hers, and then his mouth closed possessively over hers to stem the cry from her lips as he moved faster and faster. She knew ecstasy then, as passion burst inside her. Together they came, writhing and pressing against each other, a tangle of moist limbs entwined, pulsing and pulsing till there was only strength for soft movement left. Down and down they sank, into a velvety cloak of darkness which wrapped around them as they lay achingly in each other's arms.

They lay forever wrapped together, holding each other, levelling their breathing till a silence enveloped them. No sound but softening heartbeats.

Later, when the cool night air chilled their bodies, Matt moved and Sarah steeled herself, life coming back to her limbs and her mind and panicking her.

'It's all right,' Matt murmured, and she bit her lip as he unwound himself from her and got up.

It wasn't all right. This was it, the final humiliation, the final revenge of rejection. She felt the soft down of a cover snuggle around her and she turned her head into the pillow to stifle a sob of anguish, and then relief flooded her as he slid in beside her and gathered her into his arms under the duvet and held her close.

She let go then, let the momentary tension seep out of her. She was desperate for sleep but fought it because she wanted to think, but it was all hopeless. Matt was with her, holding her as if he would never let her go, and for the moment that was all she could hope for.

Sarah awoke in the small hours of the morning, hot and needing the bathroom. Matt was in the same position as when they had fallen asleep, his arms wrapped around her, one leg flung possessively across hers. His breathing was deep and regular and she knew she could easily move away from him without disturbing him. She slid out of bed and felt for her robe, pulled it around her and went out of the room. The bright light of the bathroom brought her fully awake and she stared at herself in the gilt-framed mirror over the washbasin.

She had done that very thing long ago, after the first time they had made love. Now she saw a very different person. Then she had been delirious with happiness, and now? Now she looked gaunt and feverish, spots of high colour on her pale cheeks, put there by shame, not happiness. She lowered her head and couldn't look any more because she didn't like how she looked. He'd said it would be all right but it wasn't. She had allowed that to happen, had been weak enough to let it happen, and it had done no good. She loved him, of course, that could never change, but then, nor had their circumstances. Marion still hung over them, threateningly.

She noticed her bag down on the floor where she had left it when she had come up to bathe. She took the small recorder from it and her fingers were trembling as she re-wound the tape, turned down the volume and held it to her ear.

Heart thudding nervously, she listened to what she had recorded earlier. Her voice was furious and intense and thick with revenge to counter his. What on earth had happened to them? She sounded like someone she didn't know and didn't want to.

Sitting on the edge of the bath, she held the recorder in her hands. She couldn't analyse why she felt this knotting inside her. They had made love and she was in love and he said he loved her, and yet the insecurity was still inside her. Perhaps if she...

She pressed the record button and spoke in a whisper. She spoke of her love for him and how she felt at that very moment, frightened and insecure, even now doubting his love, and yet not wanting to doubt it because it was so negative and love should be positive. She started to speak of their lovemaking and then her whispers faltered, because to speak of it felt like a disloyalty, a confidence somehow broken, but she steeled herself against such thinking. This was for her ears only, after all, and it might help to be able to refer back to it some time, some time when she could think more rationally.

Later, she crept back into bed and he reached for her sleepily, and then not so sleepily as the warmth of her body against his aroused him.

'I thought you might have fled once again,' he murmured softly against her breast.

She held his head, ran her fingers through his hair. So she wasn't the only one feeling the uncertainty. It hurt her that he should feel it too. She brushed kisses across the top of his head and murmured back, 'There's nowhere to run to any more.'

'So long as you remember that we've a chance of making it.'

She thought she detected an undertone to that, but it was quickly forgotten as he moved urgently against her. His passion would always put trivialities to the back of her mind. She acknowledged his passion with her own, and once again they lost themselves in a world of heady sensation, till a snow-brightened dawn clawed into the room.

CHAPTER FOUR

SARAH woke alone in the blinding brightness of the day and was disappointed. It would have been so much easier if she had awoken wrapped in his arms. She lay there for a while, dreading getting up and facing him in this awful brightness. She strained her ears for any sound of movement but heard nothing but the stillness of blanketing snow.

Matt came into the room with coffee. 'More snow,' he told her. He was dressed warmly in black cords and a thick black wool sweater and there was a smudge of coal on the back of his hand. It wasn't him, shovelling coal to keep the house warm. It made her wonder just how well she knew him after all.

'Which means I can't leave,' she uttered hopelessly as she struggled to sit up, tucking the duvet round her breasts for warmth and propriety. Though propriety shouldn't have been a consideration after the night, sadly it was.

He noticed, she knew, because his eyes darkened momentarily. But he said nothing, only, 'You're not going anywhere, Sarah. Not till we wade through the confusion of your mind.'

She took the coffee-mug and sipped at it gratefully. He sat on the bed and drank his, too, watching her and no doubt waiting for her to say what a big mistake the night had been, because that was what he was thinking, otherwise he wouldn't have mentioned the confusion of her mind.

'I can't even begin to start to unravel it,' she told him honestly.

He gave her a small smile. 'It's essential you do because, if you don't, we haven't a chance.'

'You said it would be all right, that if we made love it would make it all right.'

'It helped. Surely you agree to that?'

She clutched the mug with two hands and stared into the murky coffee. 'It only proved that in bed we are compatible,' she whispered.

He laughed. 'Compatible, eh? I thought it proved one helluva lot more than that.'

She looked up, painfully. 'It's nothing to laugh at, Matt.'

The smile drained from his lips. 'You're right, but the tragic truth is that once sex was fun for us.'

'Was that the key word—sex?'

He sighed. 'No, the key word was fun.'

'Well, fun isn't funny any more. That went out of my life when I realised what you were up to with Marion.' Oh, she wished she could forget all that, but she couldn't.

'What you *thought* I was up to with Marion,' he corrected.

She sighed helplessly. 'I thought I had come to terms with it,' she murmured. 'You know, this weekend is the nearest I have come to accepting it.'

'The nearest?' he declared. 'Can't you do better than that?'

She shifted uncomfortably under the duvet. She hadn't believed last night, it had all still been hanging over her, but need and desire had swayed her and she wasn't very proud of that. She confessed it.

'Matt, what happened last night didn't happen because I suddenly believed you. I'm not proud of that, I promise you, but it just goes to show the depth of my feelings for you. I put it all aside because I wanted you so much.'

He put his mug down on the bedside table and raked a hand through his tousled hair. 'And yet a year ago you couldn't even bring yourself to do that. I thought you had changed, but it obviously isn't for the better.'

She shrugged hopelessly and finished her coffee.

He reached out and took the empty mug from her fingers and cradled it in his own. 'I have my own theory on the whole messy business. You *were* looking for an excuse not to commit yourself totally to a married life with me. Marion was that excuse.'

'I know, you said that and you could be right, but at the time I only saw it the way it was—a reality. You and Marion—a reality.'

'It was what you wanted to believe.'

'It was what I *did* believe. The evidence was overwhelming, Matt,' she reasoned. 'You were always with her—well, when you weren't with me, that is. Edwin faded out of the way and she was always there. Phoning you, long, long conversations on the phone. I overheard some of them. I told you that, especially that one when you promised to stand by her. Remember?'

'How could I forget?' he uttered ruefully. 'I should have known then that you were immature and——'

'Immature again!' she cried, suddenly wishing she wasn't in this great bed, naked and unable to flounce out of the room in a temper. Dear God, the very thought of running again was an immature thought. Even now she was finding it hard to face anything with maturity—like last night, for instance. 'Was I so immature?' she bleated painfully, knowing full well she had been, and very probably still was.

He put the mug down on the table and took her hand in his and, without looking at her, started to speak. 'When I first met you at that cocktail party in London you were like a breath of spring air into my life.' He looked up at her then and gazed deep into her wide blue eyes. 'Fresh and just a little gauche, so very different from all the sophisticated women I usually met in my working life. I loved you because of your uncomplicatedness. You'd just started with your uncle's magazine and at first I thought you would never make it a success because you were far too innocent. The media is a hard business and you hadn't that toughened mind. You saw only good, when the world was always looking for the dark side of everything.'

Sarah smiled then, albeit ruefully. How very true. She had learnt though, quickly, under Melanie's watchful eye. Yes, the magazine had opened her eyes, so far that she had seen the truth when confronted with it, the truth that Matt Constantine wasn't what he had appeared at first, the good, kind, caring man under the façade of a tough, arrogant businessman.

'I want to get up,' she suddenly said, and kicked at the duvet.

He held her wrist tightly, not allowing her to move out of the confines of the bed.

'You see? I am right and nothing has changed. You fled at the first sigh of emotional discomfort when you thought I was having an affair with Marion, and you are still wanting to flee when a few home truths are being laid bare before you. I gave you that year to grow up and straighten yourself out, but it was a hopeless waste of time.'

'You let me go because I caught you out, Matt,' she argued. 'And you can't let me go now because I'm a danger to you.'

He let go of her hand then and got up from the side of the bed. He reached down and lifted his robe from the floor and flung it down on the duvet.

'I'm wasting my time and yours,' he bit out angrily and, gathering up the dirty coffee-mugs, went to the door.

'Now who's running?' she spiked at his receding back. He turned and gave her a dark look. 'Not running, sweetheart, just giving up on a bad job. You weren't ready for a deep commitment a year ago and nothing has changed. You're not ready for one now. You're no danger to me and you never were. I missed you enough to want you back in my life for reasons of the heart, not because I needed to shut you up for what you think you know. But it's all beyond you, and I lament the loss of your innocence because it was what I loved so very much about you in the first place.'

With that, he closed the door after him and Sarah got to her knees and flung a pillow at the back of the door, and then threw herself face down on the duvet and conceded that she was no match for him and never had been.

'Oh, God,' she moaned, sitting up and clutching another pillow to her chest tightly. That was it. The real reason for her leaving him. Marion had just been an excuse because she was terrified of the difference between them. From her mind she dredged up the past.

His overwhelming courtship, intense and passionate, an education in life for her. Yes, she had been innocent, and at the first sign of emotional discomfort she had let it all go and run, unable to face it.

Suddenly she needed air and space to think. She wanted to go out and trudge through the snow, to clear her head somehow. But she had no clothes or suitable shoes. She found sweaters in his wardrobe and threw one on, found track-suit trousers of his and pulled them on and tightened the cord around her narrow waist. Socks she found in a drawer.

Matt was in the kitchen unloading the dishwasher when she went down, and looked at her curiously as she stood before him, his clothes hanging ridiculously sloppily on her petite frame, his socks flapping at her toes.

'Do Gordon and Mary live in?' she asked.

He frowned. 'You know the house isn't big enough for staff to live in.'

'But I saw Gordon leaving with suitcases.'

'They live in the village but stayed here the night before leaving for the airport. It's nearer the motorway. What's this got to do with anything?'

She wriggled her toes in his oversized socks. 'I wondered if Mary had some boots I could borrow. I want to go out in the snow.'

He looked at her as if she was crazy. 'Don't be absurd, you can't go out in this.'

She glanced out of the window. Though there had been fresh snow in the night, it had stopped snowing now. It was bright and crisp and very inviting. 'I want fresh air because I need to think,' she told him in a small voice.

He shook his dark head, not understanding. 'Go into the sitting-room and sit by an open window, then. You are not going out in this,' he told her determinedly. He turned back to the dishwasher.

Sarah bit her lip and went to stand next to him. 'Matt, I *need* to go out,' she pleaded. 'I want to walk and think and I can't do it in here, surrounded by all the reminders of the fun we used to have here. I don't want anything to sway my reasoning. You have made some very relevant points this weekend and none of them sits happily with me at the moment. You've made me feel bad about myself. You've laid open so many conflicting emotions that my head is spinning with them. I want space and——'

He shrugged helplessly. 'OK. OK. Space you shall have, but I insist on coming with you.'

'No!' she cried, and raked her hand through her golden hair. 'That's the whole point. I want to be on my own. I know what will happen if you come: you'll try to reason again and I need to do that for myself. I'm the only one to help myself.'

He held her fiercely determined gaze before turning away to the back porch off the kitchen.

'There's some boots here Mary uses, and an old anorak and gloves. Keep to the grounds and don't venture far——'

'I'm not a child!' she objected hotly.

He thrust the anorak at her, his eyes flaming with anger held back. He said through tight lips, 'That is exactly what you are, Sarah.'

He left her to it, and Sarah closed her eyes in sufferance for a few stinging seconds and then dressed quickly for the outdoors.

Icy air caught her breath, but she soon acclimatised and crunched through the snow, across the lawns that separated the house from the informal gardens and the copse. Oh, how she loved this place, their secret retreat from London and the fast lane of his life. Here Matt Constantine was himself. Here was the place he shed his business persona and became her equal.

Her equal. He didn't have to be equal; no couple needed to be equals to be happy and she should have realised that a long time ago. He was so right. He had loved her because they were different, whereas she had seen it as trouble for the future. Marion and that wretched take-over of her husband's company had been the focus for her uncertainty. But he hadn't helped by not explaining it fully to her, so he was partly to blame. Even now, she was none the wiser; even after this whole traumatic weekend he had not even begun to explain just why he and Marion had been so close, and she knew that was the root of it all.

He expected me to understand, or at the very least to give him the benefit of the doubt, she mused, and I wasn't mature enough to give it a try. She had struggled so hard to match his sophistication, but had been incapable of it. It hadn't mattered at first, they had been so in love it hadn't mattered, but then it had started to go wrong for her. She had lacked confidence, and the only reason for that had been her immaturity. There had been no one before him and he had overwhelmed her. But was she ready to try again? To put it behind her and so prove she had grown up?

She stopped just before the copse, where the young trees were bowed down with the weight of the snow. Beyond the fringe of copse the taller, mature oaks and beeches stood tall and strong and unbent by the ravages of the blizzard. Older and wiser, and not to be cowed by the storm. She smiled, seeing the symbolism of her thoughts, and, brushing the hair from her flushed, weather-cold cheeks with the back of her gloved hands, she started to work in the snow.

'I might have known,' she heard behind her and, swinging round, face flushed with effort, gloves caked with pellets of snow, she saw Matt standing watching her, muffled in a puffy ski-jacket with a thick scarf wrapped round his neck and his hands plunged into the pockets of his cords.

Because of the deep snow she hadn't heard him approach. She wished she had, because it would have given her time to think of an explanation for her efforts. She was tongue-tied for a few seconds, her throat dry and lips pale, and then she pulled herself together and held her head up high.

'So what do you think of it?' She stepped back to give him a clear look at the snowman she had laboured over, for how long she couldn't begin to imagine. It had totally occupied her mind and her strength.

'I think it's wonderful,' he murmured, and smiled.

She turned back to it, gathered a ball of snow and slapped it on to the head of the snowman and worked it in. 'It's symbolic,' she told him.

'Really? I'm not sure I understand.'

'You said you might have known, so you do understand. This is what children do, not grown-ups.'

'Some do. Parents do for their children.'

'Well, I'm not a parent so I must still be a child. The child you still think I am.'

He crunched closer. 'So where does the symbolism come in?'

She loaded more snow on to the snowman's head and patted it and, without looking at him, gathered up more snow, almost feverishly.

'Doing this is a rite, an act representing repressed conflict.'

He laughed. 'That's too deep for me.'

'It shouldn't be.' She shrugged. 'It should be as plain as the nose on his face.'

'He hasn't got one.'

'Easily remedied,' she said, eyes searching around. She hadn't even begun to get through the inches of snow to the bare ground beneath, so there was nothing she could use.

'Try this,' he volunteered, taking half a packet of mints from his pocket and holding it out to her.

Sarah took it and pushed it into the face of the snowman.

'Still doesn't help,' he said.

She faced him, eyes very slightly moist. 'It's my childhood, Matt,' she said quietly, trying desperately to avoid emotion in her voice, 'my immaturity. The last thing I will ever do as the child you think I am.'

He looked at her for a long, painful second. 'Dear God,' he breathed and went to reach for her, but she stepped back, nearly overbalancing in the disturbed snow at her feet.

'No, don't,' she breathed quickly. 'Don't touch me or try to say anything, not yet. I want to try and explain. I didn't know what I was doing when I started it, building a snowman at my age.' She tried to smile, though it was hard when the air was so bitingly cold and her heart was aching so painfully. 'How old am I now? Twenty-one? I was nearly twenty when I first met you. I hadn't begun my life and then you were my life. You were right, Matt. I wasn't mature and yet you loved me, and because you did it gave me confidence and I thought it would be all right. Then all that confidence went when I started to see the differences between us. I tried to understand your work, and you said it didn't matter and I felt that it should, and then Marion. I didn't have the wherewithal to handle it or try to look at it the way you expected of me. You expected too much of me, Matt. You really did.'

His expression looked pained. 'Yes, you're right. I did. It was wrong of me,' he admitted.

'But—but I don't blame you, not now. I think I understand. I think I understand that you expected me to love you without having to explain your reasons for doing what you did, and you expect me to love you now and I do, Matt. I do love you. You made me come here, hoping that I would have learnt something in the year away from you, and I have, but...'

'But it's still not enough,' he murmured reproachfully.

She made a decision then. It would have to be enough, because if it wasn't she would lose him forever.

'It is enough, Matt. While I was building him——' she nodded to the snowman '—I was thinking of our differences, you being so successful in a world I know nothing about. And I was battling with thoughts of us being equals and decided that it didn't matter. You wouldn't have built this snowman with me because it's a childish thing to do, so I decided to do it on my own and bury the part of me that wanted to do it, my immaturity.'

'Oh, my darling,' he breathed. 'You have got it all so twisted.'

'I haven't, Matt. It's why I took it all so badly, the Marion thing. Emotional discomfort, you said, and you were right. I hadn't the experience of life to come to terms with it, but you had the experience to make it look as if it never happened.'

'It never happened, Sarah. There was no affair and no miscarriage of justice when I took over Edwin's company. It was legitimate. I told you that, and you must have known I wouldn't do anything like that, anyway.'

'I *should* have known, and you were right when you said you didn't have to fight me over it because it was beneath you. You see, if I hadn't been troubled by those thoughts of our differences I could have handled it all more maturely. But it just brought me up with a sharp jolt. I've never told you this before, Matt, but you overwhelmed me with your attentions. The all-powerful Matt Constantine falling in love with the nobody Sarah Martin. I felt as if I was being swept along by a tidal wave.'

'So coming up against Marion was like being thrown on the rocks of reality.'

She lowered her head and kicked at the hard-packed snow at her feet. 'Yes,' she admitted, 'and she was my out from a relationship I felt I couldn't handle any more. I was so afraid for us. If I had married you and then we had drawn apart it would have been so much worse. Divorce. I couldn't——'

'Divorce?' he said, and shook his head in disbelief. 'No, darling, you weren't ready for marriage if you had already got us in the divorce courts.'

She tried to laugh because he was smiling now. How stupid and illogical and negative she had been.

'And what about now?' he asked seriously. 'Do you think you are mature enough to handle it now?'

Her heart was pained with the effort of trying to think if she could. What she couldn't tell him was that Marion was still a part of her uncertainty, simply because he had never given her an adequate explanation for what exactly had gone on a year ago. And she couldn't ask because the very question would be an admission that she hadn't come to terms with it, in spite of what she was saying to him.

She nodded at last. Funny, but she *did* believe that they hadn't had an affair, and she had known last night, because her heart would never have allowed her to love him so completely if there had been doubt. But there was still a doubt of sorts and one she was still battling to push hard down out of reach. Still he hadn't explained why they had been so deeply embroiled with each other. Maybe it was something she would never know, because surely he would have told her by now, even just to clear the matter up once and for all. He was reticent about it. She didn't understand that, but if she was to get any happiness out of her life maybe she would have to live with it.

'I want to try again, Matt,' she told him, stepping towards him. She smiled. 'I'm not fighting or pleading with you for it because I don't feel I have to. You've given me the chance and I've taken it and done a lot of soul-searching, and here I am. Very grown up and reformed and——'

He held his hands up in mock defence, then he stepped towards her and gathered her into his arms. His warm lips on hers revitalised her and all doubts were swept aside as the kiss deepened. It was going to be all right— no, better than all right. It was going to be just perfect.

They drew apart at last, and Matt tipped her chin to look into her misty blue eyes.

'I'm worried about these differences of ours, you know.' But the laughter in his eyes made him look as if he wasn't worried at all.

'Oh, yes,' she laughed up at him. 'What are you going to do about them?' Though for the life of her she couldn't see any on the horizon in this moment of her glowing happiness.

'I think they are a figment of your imagination.'

'They are not!' she protested with humour in her eyes. 'Not in a month of Sundays would you dream of building a snowman!'

He laughed and held her ever tighter. 'Perhaps not, but you've started one and the poor old devil is standing there stark naked and freezing to death, and I can't bear to see him with only a nose.'

'Matt!' she laughed in puzzlement.

He stepped back from her and unwound his scarf. 'This might help,' he said, and wound it round the snowman's neck. 'Now all he needs is eyes and a mouth and coat-buttons, of course.' He grabbed her hand and pulled her laughing into the copse. 'We're sure to find some nuts here if we kick around.'

'Nuts!' She screamed with laughter, floundering in the snow after him. 'You won't have to look far—just peer in the mirror when we get back and you'll see one!'

Later they returned to the house, half frozen, sopping wet and yet glowing with happiness.

Sarah shivered in a kitchen chair as Matt pulled Mary's boots off her frozen feet and massaged them to bring the life back into them.

'Oh, Matt,' she moaned, 'I wish I had some clothes with me.'

'I don't,' he told her meaningfully.

She laughed, and they both stood up and she wrapped her arms round his neck. 'I've missed you,' she told him softly as his arms came round her to bind them together.

'And I've missed you, and never again are we going to be apart. It's going to be as if this last year had never happened.'

Sarah shivered in his embrace and he kissed her deeply and warmed her through and through, and when they finally drew apart he said thickly, 'I'll go up and run us a bath and you make the hot chocolate and bring it up.'

'Sounds divine,' she murmured happily.

He smiled down at her, more relaxed than she had ever seen him before. 'And then we have some decisions to make about our future. I'd rather like us to be married before this wretched take-over business next month. I don't think I could face it without you at my side, Mrs Constantine.'

She couldn't help it, she really couldn't, this irritating little spike of uncertainty stabbing at the base of her spine. It pricked at her conscience, a painful reminder that there was still a very small doubt masking her happiness.

'So soon,' she uttered weakly, as she turned away from him so that he wouldn't see that uncertainty in her eyes. She took milk from the fridge as he moved away to gather up their boots and their hastily discarded jackets to deposit the whole soggy mess in the back porch.

'I think it would make good copy for this interview you are supposed to be doing on me.' He slid his arm round her waist as she stood at the cooker pouring milk into a pan. He lowered his mouth to nuzzle the back of her neck and whisper in her ear. 'A beautiful conclusion: and they lived happily ever after.'

She forced a grin to suddenly white lips. 'You'll never make a reporter.'

He leaned round to peck her cheek. 'I already have,' he retorted meaningfully, and left her to go upstairs to run the bath.

She tried so very hard to push it down into the pit of her unconsciousness, but it was impossible. He wanted to marry her *before* the take-over. Such haste was almost indecent, as if he really had forgotten their year apart. The trouble was that she still couldn't forget the reason that had spurred that year apart. Not her immaturity, that was all dealt with now, but the Marion episode still hadn't been dealt with, even though she had tried. He had never explained and that was the basis of her unease.

She hated herself for those doubts and the awful thoughts that were now spinning around in her head. Married, he'd be on safe ground. Married to the only woman, apart from Marion, of course, who knew about that strange buy-out of Stimson's, he would be on rock-solid ground and——

The milk bubbled over, burnt and spoiled, and brought Sarah down to earth with a bump. She refused to think this way. She would cast it from her, shed it from her heart. She loved Matt deeply, and when you loved someone that hard there should be no room for doubt. Except that there had been doubt a year ago, and now it was still floundering around on the perimeters of her heart.

But no, this had to stop. Matt loved her and only wanted to marry her in haste because they had already wasted a year of their lives. She was still slightly paranoid about it all because it had been such a deep part of her life for so long. It was history to him and so therefore not important.

Well, it's not important to me either, she told herself stoically as she refilled the pan with fresh milk. We love each other and that is all that is important. It really is.

CHAPTER FIVE

'AREN'T you supposed to get chilblains if you plunge freezing cold feet into hot water?' Sarah asked as she kicked open the bathroom door, her hands occupied with grasping two mugs of steaming hot chocolate. 'Matt? Where are you?'

She put the mugs down on the edge of the bath. It was full of frothy hot water but Matt wasn't in it. She remembered the phone ringing while she had been making the chocolate, and supposed he was still on it. She went out on the landing and hung over the gallery rail to listen for his voice below, and heard the murmur of it coming from his study next to the sitting-room. She smiled and went back into the bathroom.

She was still soaking in the deliciously fragrant water ten minutes later, alone.

'You'd better get used to this,' she mumbled out loud, 'sharing his precious time with the rest of Europe.'

She supposed he would be madly busy for the next few weeks, and yet he wanted to be married almost immediately. She sank further down under the bath-foam and felt an overwhelming excitement tingle through her. He wanted her by his side to make it easier for him. He loved her so much that he couldn't face it alone. Matt needed her and she was here for him and her heart was filled with such love that she thought she would burst with it.

Ten minutes later the bath-water was cooling and Matt hadn't appeared. Sarah hauled herself out of the bath and dried herself. She'd go and make lunch.

The clothes she had come in were hanging over the Victorian towel-rail in the corner of the bathroom and, rather than rummage through his clothes again, she put them on and went downstairs in her stockinged feet.

'Matt!' she called. 'The bath's gone cold and...'

She found him in the sitting-room and stopped dead in her tracks in the doorway. A fire glowed warmly in the grate but there was no warmth in his stiffened stance as he stood by the fire, one elbow leaning on the oak mantel, staring into the red coals. In his other hand he held a whisky-glass, ominously empty. He looked as if he had received bad news.

'Darling!' she breathed worriedly, and stepped towards him. She prayed nothing had gone wrong with this take-over bid. She knew from old how much his work meant to him.

He looked up at her, eyes black, mouth thinned. 'How dare you?' he grated murderously.

She stopped at the other side of the mantelpiece, her heart seizing and such a deep chill running down her spine that she thought it might not support the weight of her body.

'Matt, what's wrong?' Her voice was barely a whisper, because she had seen him in anger before, seen him fraught before, but she had never seen him murderous before. Her eyes were wide with shock.

'And you have the audacity to look at me with that contrived innocence,' he breathed harshly. 'Those damned great innocent blue eyes looking at me as if bloody butter wouldn't melt in your mouth.'

Sarah almost physically reeled under the onslaught of such harshness.

Contemptuously his eyes raked her up and down. 'You're dressed and ready to leave and the pity is you can't.'

'Matt!' she protested, her heart thudding desperately. 'Whatever is the matter?'

He turned away from her, about to refill his glass, then thought better of it and swung to face her again.

'What the devil was this weekend all about, Sarah? I can't believe you capable of this—this treachery.'

Anger suddenly surged inside her. What an earth had she done? She clenched her fists at her sides to give her strength. 'I'm not a mind-reader, you know. If you don't tell me what all this is about, how do you expect me to defend myself? Though what I'm supposed to have done escapes me!'

He snatched up her portable recorder from the sofa. She hadn't seen it lying there because she hadn't been looking for it.

'This,' he accused her, waving it in the air. 'This is the only reason you came, isn't it? To get your revenge on me. For Marion. For Stimson's——'

'No, Matt!' she cried. Oh, no, he must have played it back. She reached for it angrily but he held it just out of reach, triumphantly, as if he had won some trophy. It infuriated Sarah even more. 'It's part of my job, and don't forget that was why I came—to do an interview. At your request, let me remind you. No, not at your request,' she blazed on. 'Blackmail got me here. You threatened to ruin the magazine if I didn't——'

'What the devil are you talking about?'

The look of shocked disbelief on his white face temporarily rocked her reasoning. She had completely taken him aback with the accusation. Oh, no, had Melanie made up that story to get her here, knowing she wouldn't refuse if the family livelihood was threatened? Oh, it didn't bear thinking about.

'You—you threatened...' she started uncertainly.

'Threatened?' he roared, and Sarah flinched. 'I've never made a threat in my life. I approached Melanie because I saw it as the only way of getting you back. That year was agonising without you and...' He couldn't bear to look at her. He threw the recorder back down to the sofa, angrily. 'That isn't an issue any more because it is patently obvious why you came.' He pointed at the recorder and then glared at her. 'Your damned revenge. Kiss and tell. My God, it would have made quite a story, wouldn't it? It would have ruined me, Sarah, totally destroying my credibility.'

'Oh, no,' Sarah cried. 'I'm not taking that, Matt Constantine. You're quite capable of ruining your own credibility, you don't need any help from me and—and how dare you go rummaging in my handbag?' she accused bitterly. 'That's a disgusting thing to do.'

His eyes narrowed, as if he couldn't believe she thought that a problem. 'Is that the best you can come up with? Some petty little female illogical response to cover up something that is far more sinister and damaging.'

'Don't you know a woman's handbag is deeply personal and——?'

He couldn't take any more. He turned and poured himself another drink, and then crossed to the window as if he couldn't bear to share her air-space a second longer. He stood glaring out of the window, shoulders stiff.

It gave Sarah time to think and try to compose herself. It was obvious he had played back the tape and heard what she had said. She remembered the first part, when she had been trying for her first escape. It must have sounded awful to him, but she had thought he was holding her a prisoner. And the rest—he must have thought she was going to publish the whole damn lot in a horrendous kiss-and-tell splurge. But surely he couldn't think that of her, not after all that had happened this weekend?

So what had spurred him to delve into her bag in the first place? He couldn't truly love her to have done that. It was an action of mistrust. She had to know.

Her voice was low as she said, 'I'm sorry to keep on about it, but it's important to me. Why did you do it, go into my handbag that——?'

He turned quickly, so she knew he was still furious. It helped somehow, making her stronger and more determined not to be cowed.

'OK!' she cried, shrugging her shoulders. 'Another thing beneath you to discuss. It bodes ill for our future, doesn't it? If I can't ask you a question and get a civil answer because you think it's beneath you to answer it. At this rate, I'll be too terrified to ask you what you want for your dinner in case it offends your sensibilities!' Oh, no, what was she saying, implying they had a future together after all this?

'Would you believe I dropped the soap in your open bag?' he said stonily.

'Huh! If it wasn't so serious it would be laughable,' she cut back.

He stepped towards her, but not close enough to share her air-space once again. 'I can scarcely believe I'm repeating myself here, but it's true,' he told her scathingly. 'I dropped the wretched soap in your bag and when I went to retrieve it I saw your recorder. Now listen to this, because I promise you it is the very last soft thing I will ever say to you. I was going to leave a message on it for you, something like how much I loved you, something like how happy I was we were going to be married——'

'Matt, don't,' she breathed faintly. Oh, he was making her feel so bad.

He stepped closer to her then, towered over her, tall and angry and very embittered. 'I pressed the wrong button, heard your pathetic little voice threatening to expose me.'

'No, Matt. I wouldn't have done it,' she protested. 'I—I was so angry with you for locking me in, really mad. I thought you had got me here to punish me. I went a little crazy. I wanted to hurt you as I thought you were trying to do to me.'

'So you plotted your revenge,' he bit back, 'and how low can you get?'

'And your revenge wasn't lowly, I suppose?' she raged in defence. 'Yours was an *honourable* revenge, was it?'

'Revenge is a figment of your imagination, Sarah.'

'Oh, go take a jump at yourself!'

She couldn't take any more. He was being totally unreasonable. She swung away from him and he didn't stop her. She flew out of the room and had nowhere to go but the kitchen. Her legs were shaking so much that she would never make it upstairs, and what was upstairs anyway but misery? His bedroom with his loving bed, the little room that was to have been a nursery...

She got to the kitchen, clung to the edge of the sink and burst out crying. She cried till she could cry no more. She had thought it was all over and everything was resolved and was going to be all right. She had reasoned out her past fears and come to terms with them. She had pressed down the last remaining doubts about Marion and dealt with them in an adult way, and now it had all crashed around her because of that stupid, stupid recording.

She rubbed at her face with a kitchen towel, crumpled it fiercely and tossed it in the bin. He wouldn't listen to reason, had made no attempt to understand why she had done what she had. If he truly loved her he would have done. He would have heard her out, calmly, and then they would have talked it through...

'Oh, no,' she moaned, biting her lower lip in dismay. This was history repeating itself. A year ago she hadn't given him a chance, just stormed her suspicions at him and, when he hadn't given her an explanation that had satisfied her, she had fled out of his life. And still he hadn't given her a proper explanation, and she had thought it wouldn't matter, but this brought it all back to her. It very much *did* matter!

Determinedly she made coffee, forcing herself to do it without crying again. She had to show him she had grown up, and besides, it was time he did too. Fancy actually believing she would kiss and tell?

'You amaze me,' she thrust at him, placing the tray of coffee on a side table next to the sofa he was sitting on, working through a pile of paperwork.

'What amazes you?' he asked indifferently.

He had certainly calmed down while she had been making the coffee. He was all Mr Efficiency now. Back to work, clinically and unemotionally, while she had been crying her heart out over the kitchen sink.

'You, working. You have the capability to shed your emotions at the drop of a hat. Says a lot for the depth of those supposed emotions.'

'And yours are something else, are they? Yours, I suppose, are as fragile as a cobweb. More like a black widow's cobweb. Kiss and then kill!'

Steadily she poured the coffee. She wasn't going to lose her cool; no, she wasn't. She was going to be so maddeningly mature about all this that he would wish he'd never plundered her heart and her handbag.

She handed him his coffee and he took it, and she thought that was something, at least. She sat down in the opposite chair; to sit next to him would be too pushy.

'Matt, listen to me, because I have a lot to say. I want to draw some comparisons here.'

'You will be wasting my time, Sarah. Decisions have been made——'

'Your decisions, not mine. For the moment yours don't matter, mine do. I've taken a lot from you this weekend and most of it made sense. You were right about so many things, but very wrong about one thing.'

'Is it really in my interests to ask what?' His tone was one of boredom.

Stay cool, Sarah warned herself. She sipped her coffee and the caffeine tingled through her, giving her the nerve she needed.

'I love you, Matt,' she told him bravely, praying he wouldn't throw it back in her face. It would crumble her if he did. 'I believe you love me, and because of our love we have to sort all this out.'

'Sarah, it's gone beyond redemption. To do what you did——'

'I want to explain about that, if you'll give me the chance. The very least you can do is pay attention and listen.' Her voice had risen and she hadn't wanted it to, and she could see by his strained expression that he was struggling to hold down his temper too. She put her coffee-cup down and pushed her hair from her face. She got up and started to pace the rug in front of the fire.

'I would never have done anything with that tape, Matt. Whatever you might have done to me—revenge, punishment, rejection—I would never have done anything with it, not after what we have been through this weekend.'

He let out what sounded like a small growl of disbelief. 'But at first you had every intention——'

'I was mad with you! Surely you can understand that? You locked me in, you were hurtful to me at first, gibing at me at every opportunity. The fact that you insisted on me coming was punishment enough, and then when I got here that neighbour woman was here and it made me jealous, and I thought that was part of your plan too. I didn't think I would be able to suffer it. I'd only brought the recorder because it's part of my work, and then you locked me in and I saw Gordon leaving and I panicked, thinking you were plotting revenge, and I wanted to hurt you back. But surely you realised I couldn't when you heard the rest of it, how much I loved you and how I——'

He stood up jerkily. 'What are you talking about, the rest of it?'

She stared at him. 'D-didn't you hear all of it?'

'I heard enough!'

She knew then that he hadn't heard the half of it. 'Where is it?'

He nodded to the sofa where he had thrown it. At least he hadn't locked it away in his desk. If he had, it would have shown complete distrust in her. 'Listen,' she said, holding it out to him.

He looked at it bleakly. She let it run through the whole tape. The beginning, when she had threatened revenge, then the other bit, when she had tried for her escape, and then the last part. Her tremulous voice whispered her love for him, how she had felt when they were making love, how she had felt after, her vulnerability, her insecurity. There was a long silence when it had finished. Sarah had watched him all the time it had been running, but not with hope in her heart. She could tell by his expression that he was thinking it was all getting worse.

'I heard the beginning of the last part earlier,' he told her coldly. He stood in front of her, eyes so cold and ungiving that she felt a new fear thread through her. 'But I snapped it off in disgust before it finished, and if you think your vulnerability and your insecurity make any difference to my heart at this moment you are badly mistaken. In fact, Sarah, it makes it a damn sight worse!'

She blinked her wide blue eyes with shock, and then she steeled herself, and with ferocity tore at the back of the recorder. She wrenched the tape out, waved it at him and then tossed it to the back of the fire.

'There!' she cried triumphantly. 'That will prove I have no intention of using it, and for your information I haven't a copy secreted about my person, and further for your information I did that for my sake as well as yours. I made that recording for myself, Matt, because my feelings were so hopelessly muddled I wanted to refer back to it at a calmer moment. Well, it's quite obvious now that there isn't going to be a calmer moment. You won't allow it, and besides, it would pain me beyond measure ever to hear it again!'

She might as well be trying to reason with a brick wall. His eyes blazed furiously. 'After our night of love, you thought you might *forget* it?'

She stepped back from him, but he reached for her and grasped her wrist and pulled her towards him. He lowered his voice so drastically it made her shake inside.

'It was the most important night of our lives, Sarah. I thought you would have realised that and——'

'It *was* the most important night of my life,' she whispered hoarsely, her throat so tight she could hardly get the words out. 'And it was also the most emotional, because it showed me just how much I needed you. I'd made a mess of our past and couldn't talk to you about it, and the damned silly machine was therapy in a way. Oh, it was a mistake. I know that now.' She wrenched her wrist from him, rubbed it and stepped away from him.

She looked at him finally and met his hardened gaze, and knew he couldn't accept her feeble excuses.

'It's over, isn't it?' She gave him no space to answer because she knew the answer. She shrugged. 'Then I have nothing more to lose by telling you something else.' She took a deep breath. 'While I was making the coffee I was thinking that your reaction to that tape was the same as my reaction a year ago when I thought you were having an affair with Marion.'

: 'Not that again,' he breathed, and raked his fingers through his hair.

'Yes, that again, Matt.'

'It's entirely different.'

'The only difference is that I've explained my reasons for what I did, truly and honestly. I made a mistake in making those recordings and have admitted it, but you never have explained why you were seeing so much of Marion. The worst thing about all of this is that a year ago I couldn't accept it, and today, yes, today I convinced myself I could. You gave us both a second chance and I convinced myself that I loved you enough to put it behind me, but when you accused me of treachery just now it brought it all up again. You believed I was capable of betrayal, just as I believed you were capable of betrayal a year ago. Can't you see the danger of that in a relationship? We have mistrust between us, and that is all wrong.'

'And you think I have failed you by not telling you all about my involvement with Marion?'

He wasn't angry any more and neither was she. They seemed to have burned anger out. It left Sarah feeling weak and disorientated. She rubbed her muddled forehead.

'I don't know,' she admitted. 'I seem to have lived with it so long I've probably blown it up out of all proportion. I was jealous of the time you spent with her, and I suppose, in spite of claiming my maturity now, I still am jealous. Maybe I haven't grown up at all.'

She saw his shoulders sag hopelessly, as if he couldn't fight her any more. It gave her hope, but she clung to it with reserve.

'Yes, you have,' he told her tenderly. He lifted his hand and gently brushed the red-gold hair from her pale face. 'Now you have the maturity to try and work it out. You've made some very relevant points, some very mature points that put me to shame.'

Her eyes widened. 'I—I don't understand.'

'Marriage is an enormous commitment, Sarah. A lifetime commitment. I was prepared to make it a year ago because I've had a longer run at life and knew it was right for me. But you, you were afraid of failure because of your inexperience. I didn't know that at the time, and let you go far too easily. It's only now I realise the damage I did by not telling you everything about Marion. I'd hoped a simple denial of your accusations would have been enough for you at the time, because anything more was out of my hands. I made a promise, you see, to Marion and Edwin.' He sighed. 'I realise now I should have broken that confidence and told you it all, but it wasn't the root of the problem, was it?'

A promise? He'd made a promise to Marion and Edwin? She lowered her head and shook it. 'No, just an excuse because I was so afraid of failure with you.' She raised her wide eyes to look at him. 'Matt,' she breathed, 'I'm not going to let it get to me. I promise you——'

'You shouldn't make promises you can't keep. It will always be between us.'

'No, Matt. It won't. If you made a promise and kept to it, then I can keep one too. I won't mention it again.'

He shook his dark head. 'You won't be able to help it, my darling. One hiccup in our marriage and you'll bring it up again, and understandably so.' He took a deep breath. 'I'm breaking a confidence now because I can't bear to lose you again.' He drew her into his arms.

He held her head against his shoulder and smoothed a hand down over her silky hair. 'Just after we met, Marion came to me for help. She and Edwin had just received the devastating news that Edwin was suffering from cancer——'

'Oh, no!' Sarah gasped. She drew back from him then, her eyes wide with shock. Matt grasped her shoulders to steady her.

'Listen to me—you must. He knew he hadn't long, and he was working himself into the ground to secure a future for Marion when the time came. Marion tried to convince him to ease up but she couldn't do it on her own. She asked for my help and I promised it. They are both old friends and it was the least I could do. I convinced Edwin to let go of the company, to me.'

'Oh, Matt,' she whispered, her whole body stiff with shock. Tears filled her eyes, for Marion and Edwin and for Matt. She'd drawn this out of him and she shouldn't have done. She should have left it to rest. Shame flooded her. She forced words to her dry lips. 'And—and you promised to stand by her . . . if—if anything happened to Edwin?' she croaked desperately.

'It was the very least I could do. They both made me promise not to divulge Edwin's condition. They just wanted to go away and be together and not have people offering sympathy.' He smiled ruefully. 'And the lipstick on the collar——'

'Oh, Matt, don't!' Sarah breathed painfully, tears spilling from her brimming eyes. 'I can't bear it. All those times you must have had to comfort her, all those times I thought . . .'

'Don't, Sarah. Don't feel bad about it,' he told her tenderly. 'Edwin's in remission and he and Marion are enjoying a quiet life in Florida.'

She pulled out of his arms then and covered her face with her hands. She cried because she couldn't help it. She should be feeling better but she wasn't. He went to put his arms around her again but she recoiled, guilt swamping her. She wanted to get away because she couldn't face him.

'Sarah!' he called, as she fled from the room.

Blindly she ran to the kitchen. She needed air. She pulled on Mary's boots and anorak and flew out of the back door.

The chill air cooled her face and brought her up sharply. Her eyes were dry now and she blinked against the whiteness of the snow and a brilliant sun that had the audacity to shine down on her. Miserably she trudged through the snow, hunched and pinched, hating herself. She didn't deserve his love; she didn't deserve him. She had forced that out of him and she shouldn't have done. He had broken a promise so as not to lose her a second time which meant . . . It meant that he loved her so very much.

She reached the snowman and glared at him, and he glared back.

'You helped me this morning, for all the good it did me,' she ranted at him. 'You think you know so much but you don't know the half of it. I'm an idiot, a blind idiot and I *haven't* grown up.'

She bent down and with her bare hands she gathered up a ball of snow and hurled it at his head.

'There, what do you think of that, then?' she cried.

'I think that is a terrible thing to do to a helpless snowman.'

She swung round and Matt was standing behind her, rolling a snowball ominously in his hands.

Oh, she loved him, so, so much. Could he ever forgive her? Could she ever forgive herself? She held his eyes for a long, long time, willing him to forgive her, willing him to love her as much as she loved him.

'No, Matt!' she suddenly cried, and ducked, but it was too late. The snowball hit her shoulder, exploding into a thousand snowflakes and showering her face and neck.

'Oh, you!' she cried. 'Just you wait!' She scooped more snow, balled it, hurled it. Missed.

'Rotten shot!' He laughed. 'I love you,' he shouted.

'That won't help you now!' She hurled another snowball at him as he made advances towards her through the deep snow. This time she hit him in the middle of his chest. 'Shot!' she cried, and then she was holding her palms up defensively as he got closer and closer, laughing and yet...

She turned and started to stumble through the snow, laughing and trying to get away from him.

He lunged at her and brought her down and she screamed and tried to roll away, but he had her pinned under him with the weight of his body, and then she was clinging to him, laughing and crying.

'Oh, I love you too, Matt Constantine, and you had better hurry up and marry me before I revert back to my childhood again.'

'Revert back to it! You've never left it!' His mouth pressed hard on hers, a kiss so ardent and deep and positive that she felt all guilt wash out of her. Only love was left, a love she wasn't going to mess with in the future.

'Can you forgive me?' she mouthed against him, as he broke away from her for breath.

'Can you forgive *me*?' he breathed heatedly against her, leaning up to brush snow from her face and hair.

'I've nothing to forgive you for.'

'And I've nothing to forgive you for, so let's call it quits.' He kissed her again and told her he loved her again and then...

'Matt!' she cried, laughing. 'Not in front of a snowman!'

He laughed and drew his hand out from under her blouse, and hauled her to her feet, and she fell into his arms again and they held each other so tightly.

'Promise me you'll always discuss your insecurities with me when we are married,' he growled in her ear.

'When we are married I won't have any,' she told him, lifting her hands to smooth down the sides of his face. 'I love you, Matt, and always have and always will, and you waited for me and I'm so happy you did.'

'It was an agonising wait, darling,' he told her, and kissed the tip of her cold little nose. 'And now you are going to make it up to me because you owe me. I'm going to take you back to the house and throw you in a warm bath and——'

'And join me this time,' she warned, eyes glittering with mischief.

He nodded and smiled, and then looked worried for a second. 'Unless, of course, I find another recorder lying about.'

She grinned up at him. 'If you ever go in my hand-bag again...'

'If you ever kiss and tell...'

'Oh, but I must, Matt,' she interrupted, trying to look serious but not doing very well. 'It's a world scoop, and you want the world to know we are going to be married, don't you?'

'I can't wait.' He slid an arm round her shoulders and together they trudged through the snow, back to the warmth of the hideaway they loved so much. 'But perhaps I ought to censor it,' he added.

'Coward,' she laughed.

'I'm thinking of the children's future. It wouldn't do for them to know what their parents got up to in their youth.'

'Oh, I'll tell them anyway—it will be an education for them,' Sarah laughed. She stopped at the back porch and turned Matt towards the snowman, way down by the copse. 'And I'll build them snowmen while you are making more millions——'

'You'll do nothing of the sort,' he protested. '*We'll* build them snowmen. Why should you have all the fun?'

She stretched up and kissed him passionately on the lips, and then she looked into his dark eyes. 'You know something? You're nothing but a big kid.'

He tilted her chin as a flurry of fresh snow whirled around her head. 'It takes one to know one,' he teased, and captured her mouth again in a long lingering kiss of love. Then he drew back and looked up. 'Looks like more snow. You know what that means?'

'Yes,' she murmured hungrily, and slid her arms under his jacket. 'I hope it never stops and keeps us here for a year.'

'A year of making up for lost time, and then another year, and another.'

'Forever, Matt,' she breathed happily.

'Forever,' he agreed, and swept her up into his arms and carried her inside, kicking the door shut and the world out.

A VENGEFUL
INFATUATION

BY
MARGARET MAYO

CHAPTER ONE

TANNICE'S spine turned to ice. It had been many years since she had last seen Benedict Ryal but he had not changed. He still looked the same ruthless, cold-hearted, unfeeling monster who had broken her heart and turned her life upside down all those years ago.

She was the one who had changed; she was no longer a weak, pliable girl who had fallen in love with a man who had taken her and used her and then declared that his first love was making money and she had no part in it.

To give him his due he was still a handsome devil, but she was immune now to his charm and she looked at him dispassionately. Black hair was expertly cut, not too short, not too long, the merest hint of silver glinting now at his temples. He was tall, broad as he had always been, powerfully muscled, and had dark mysterious eyes which could easily reduce a girl to jelly, as she knew to her detriment.

He had the long, loping stride of a feral animal, and many heads turned as he crossed the room. Their eyes met and, to her amazement, to her chagrin, to her disbelief, he gave no sign of recognition.

Eleven years was a long time; she had been just another girl, supposed Tannice bitterly—probably one of many he had used and discarded along his ambitious road to wealth and power.

As she had prepared for this meeting earlier, nervous tension had knotted Tannice's stomach, but not because she had been expecting to see this man—far from it. It was Simon Foxton, development manager for the Keene Hotel Group, with whom she had an appointment.

For twelve months now, ever since her father had died, she had refused to see Simon Foxton, even to discuss the possibility of selling. However, with bookings down by over fifty per cent, and even the restaurant not doing as well as it should, she was getting close to being given little choice.

Her great-grandfather had opened The Grange during Queen Victoria's reign and, although there had been inevitable changes over the years, it was still warmly traditional and essentially a family-run hotel—except that there was only herself running it, her brother showing absolutely no interest.

In Tannice's own mind KHG had been the cause of her father's death. With the onset of the vendetta against him when he had steadfastly refused to sell, Maurice Muir's health had declined. Vendetta was perhaps too strong a word, Tannice realised, but it had verged on that. They had received threats that they would be put out of business if they did not co-operate, and in the end it had all been too much for her father.

As she had slipped on the jacket to her formal navy suit, Tannice had brooded over the meeting that lay ahead. She had no proof, but she felt certain that KHG were also responsible for the decline in trade. It was a more subtle approach than the one they had used against her father, but there was no other reason for business to go down; it had to be their doing.

KHG built ultra-modern hotels, entirely anonymous places, each room an identical copy of its neighbour, and the thought that they wanted to turn her cosy, individual little place into part of such a package made her blood boil.

The company had already bought up adjacent properties—she was the only one standing in the way of their development—and her bank manager was urging her to sell while she still had a certain amount of bargaining power. Tannice, however, was determined not to, not while she had breath in her body to fight.

Having taken one final glance at herself in the mirror she had nodded, pleased with her appearance. The navy suit was crisp and businesslike, her yellow blouse unfussy, even her golden hair was cut short, wedge-shaped at the back and with the merest hint of a fringe to soften her face. Shampooed every day, it needed no more than the stroke of a brush to keep it in its almost severe style—and this evening she definitely wanted to project a power image.

Her face was carefully made up, her sloe-shaped blue eyes subtly defined, the merest hint of blusher emphasising her high cheekbones, a soft coral lipstick outlining her lips. Not too much, not too little. She had not wanted Simon Foxton to think that she was trying to impress him.

Having decided that home ground was better, she had arranged to meet him downstairs in the hotel lounge, and it was exactly eight o'clock as she entered the oak-panelled room with its subtle lighting and warm red carpet.

She had never actually met Simon Foxton but she had no doubt in her mind that the red-haired young man just seating himself in the corner was he. He had a sharp face and a wiry body, and looked as sly as he had sounded over the telephone. Tannice instantly knew it wasn't going to be an easy meeting.

Her head was held high as she walked across the room, confidence in every step. She smiled and held out her hand. 'Mr Foxton?'

He had not seen her approach and immediately stood up again. 'Miss Muir.' He turned on the full charm of a surprisingly attractive smile and his handshake was firm and a little longer than necessary.

Was that the way he hoped to do business? mused Tannice as she sat; if so, he was in for a big shock. He was younger than herself, probably about twenty-four, and obviously ambitious or he wouldn't have reached the position he was in today.

'Can I get you a drink?' he asked.

She shook her head. 'Not yet. Business first, I think.'

'We may have to wait a little while,' he said, hesitating slightly. 'The—er—head of the company has decided to sit in on this meeting.'

'He doesn't think you're capable of handling it?' Tannice allowed her fine brows to rise, fairly confident that her implication would anger him.

He did not disappoint her; pale blue eyes looked across indignantly. 'Not at all—he simply likes to keep abreast of what is going on in his vast business empire. It's an honour, actually.'

She did not believe him; he was clearly uneasy though he was doing his very best not to show it. 'Then I will have a drink,' she said, catching the eye of one of her staff who was hovering nearby. He immediately came to her side.

'Good evening, Miss Muir, sir,' he acknowledged.

'My usual drink, Paul,' she said, with a warm, friendly smile, 'and whatever Mr Foxton wants.'

Mr Foxton clearly did not like the fact that she was taking charge, and his wiry ginger brows pulled into a close frown as he ordered a gin and tonic.

'Paul has been with us for many years,' she said, 'as have most of my staff. They are very loyal.'

'Then perhaps they will consider working for us when our new hotel is built?' he asked. 'I think personal recommendations are always best, don't you?'

The smarmy tone of his voice infuriated Tannice and she looked at him coldly. 'Because I have agreed to this meeting, Mr Foxton, it does not mean to say that I am finally willing to sell. It depends on many factors.'

'But of course,' he said with a reassuring flash of his white teeth. 'Please, do not think that I am assuming it is all cut and dried. You are a very astute business woman, I am aware of that. There is much we have to discuss.'

'A great deal,' she agreed.

Their drinks arrived and she sipped her Martini. 'What time is your—employer arriving?'

'He said he would try to make it for eight,' answered her companion, 'but he is a very busy man.'

'Do you need his approval for this deal?'

Pale eyes were condemning, as though he felt she was trying to put him down; even so, he still smiled. 'Most definitely not. I have full power. He's merely showing interest. He will not interfere in anything I do or say.'

Tannice nodded. 'It is good he has confidence in his staff; I like that. I myself am very much of the same mould.' But nothing had prepared her for the fact that the man in question was Benedict Ryal.

Simon Foxton introduced them. 'Miss Muir, Benedict Ryal. Mr. Ryal, Miss Muir.'

Benedict held out his hand and there was still no indication that he remembered her, merely a smile of appreciation for a beautiful woman. His eyes were boldly appraising. She had changed her hair colour and its style more than once since their last meeting, and she was a much more assured person. It could be the reason he did not recognise her, but somehow she did not think so. He was merely the sort of man who went through women like a hot knife through butter.

As she put her hand into his, Tannice experienced the strength and the warmth that had once excited her but now left her cold; she felt nothing except fresh anger over the way he had treated her.

He was a louse, the world's worst swine, and—the thought hit her like a blow from a sledge-hammer—also instrumental, however indirectly, in her father's death. If it was company policy to harass people until they sold, then the injunction had to come from him. All the more reason for her to hate him now.

'Mr Foxton told me you were joining us,' she said as he sat. 'Is there any particular reason why we're—honoured with your presence?'

Her slight hesitation caused him to frown; it was gone immediately. 'You're a very direct person, Miss Muir.' His eyes met hers, deliberately provoking.

'I think you have to be in business,' she said abruptly. 'I don't believe in pussy-footing around.'

'Admirable qualities.' Once again his eyes grazed over her.

Tannice's chin lifted fractionally and she tried to forget that she had once been his lover, which was difficult when he was sitting so close, still exuding that same highly sensual, intensely charismatic quality that had attracted her to him in the first place. 'You haven't answered my question,' she reminded him coolly.

'I occasionally sit in on business meetings,' he admitted. 'I like to keep in touch.'

She glanced at Simon Foxton, and he looked cool and calm and not at all concerned by the fact that Benedict Ryal would be listening to the proposition he intended putting to her, although she knew, from his earlier attitude, that beneath the surface he was worried—and who wouldn't be with a man like Benedict Ryal breathing down his neck?

'A drink, Mr Ryal?' she asked, but he was already beckoning to Paul. This was very definitely a man who liked to take charge. Her mind drifted back over the years to when she was just seventeen and Benedict Ryal had been her whole world.

They had met at a friend's birthday party and at twenty-four he had been the oldest there. 'I intend becoming a millionaire by the time I am thirty,' he had announced confidently, and Tannice had been terribly impressed.

He had seemed to her like a man of the world even then, already operating his own business, having bought several properties very cheaply and selling at a tremendous profit after he had renovated them. His father was a master builder and it was from him that Benedict had learned his trade.

'I have always had a flair for making money,' Benedict told her matter-of-factly. 'I used to sell anything I could get my hands on, even my own toys once I'd outgrown them. I'd wash cars or mow lawns, anything to earn a few pounds, which I'd either save or use to buy something else which I could sell at a profit. I ran quite a lucrative business when I was at school.' He had never gone to college or university, relying on his instinctive entrepreneurial skills instead.

Tannice was hooked. He was magic, he was different, and she fell instantly and deeply—and irrevocably, she thought at the time—in love.

She had unfortunately been like a clinging vine, too young and inexperienced to hide her feelings, wanting to see him every night of the week, throwing a tantrum when he declared that he had other more important things to do. She began to think he did not care for her, until the day he saw her out with her cousin and immediately jumped to the conclusion that she was two-timing him.

'Who was that guy I saw you with last night?' he asked brusquely when she met him the next evening. 'What's going on?'

About to explain that it was her cousin from London come to spend a few days with the family, she was stopped dead in her tracks when he added, 'How many other guys have you been seeing behind my back?'

'Is that how much you trust me?' she asked indignantly. 'Don't you know how much I love you?'

'I know what I saw,' he said tersely.

'And you jumped to conclusions.'

'What other explanation can there possibly be?' he rasped. 'You tell me, Tannice. I'm waiting.'

She shrugged and lifted her chin defensively. 'Maybe I did go out with someone else.' He didn't deserve the truth if he could not trust her, but it pleased her that he was jealous. It could mean only one thing. 'And is it any wonder, considering the way you're always coming up with excuses for not seeing me?'

But she had never thought that denying him the truth would end their relationship. She was entirely devastated when he announced a day or two later that making money was more important to him than making love. 'I've decided that there is no place in my life at the moment for a woman,' he told her brutally. And no matter how much Tannice sobbed and begged and pleaded, he would not change his mind.

She was in no doubt that he was using the excuse of seeing her with another man to end their relationship, and it hurt to think that he had never truly loved her, that he had merely been temporarily excited by her pretty face and good body, and that now the initial surge of desire had gone he had no further use for her. He would probably never think about her again!

She, on the other hand, was heart-broken for months and lost so much weight that her family and friends were desperately worried. When her mother died ten months later, her father declared that running the hotel alone was too much for him. Would she consider coming into the business? Before that she had always insisted that she wasn't interested, that she wanted to be an artist.

It had been a psychological ploy on her father's part, she realised later—he had been perfectly capable of running the place himself—but it had worked. Her love for Benedict Ryal slowly turned to hatred, and although she occasionally still thought about him it was not with any feelings of pleasure.

Running the hotel became her whole life—there had never been another man, at least no one serious—and now that she knew who was trying to take her over she was even more determined not to sell. She would become penniless first. It would do Benedict good to discover that there were some things in life his money could not buy.

'Perhaps you'd like to look at these figures, Miss Muir,' asked Simon. 'I think you will agree that we're making you a very fair offer.'

She took the sheets of paper but, although her eyes were on them, it was Benedict Ryal who was at the forefront of Tannice's mind. If she was honest with herself, she was piqued because of his lack of recognition; it hurt to think that she had made so little impact on him.

She discussed with Simon Foxton various details of his offer, conscious that Benedict was watching her all the time. He was even more charismatic than he had been eleven years ago, success and maturity sitting well on his shoulders, and if she had been meeting him for the first time she would have undoubtedly felt a strong attraction. As it was, the hatred that had simmered subconsciously over the years began to well up and it was all she could do to keep the hostility from her eyes.

Two drinks later, Simon asked if she had come to a decision. His pale eyes were sharp upon hers, with nothing like the dynamism of Benedict's, or the magnetism, or the chemistry. He was a cold individual who was more intent on going places than on human relationships—a bit like Benedict had been when she had first met him, though there the comparison ended.

It took all Tannice's will-power to concentrate on the younger man and ignore Benedict, but somehow she managed it. 'I would never make a decision so easily,' she said.

'But you are interested?' He leaned eagerly towards her.

She pushed the sheaf of papers across the table and her eyes were cool on his. 'I suggest you go back and rethink your figures. Your offer is an insult.'

He sat back in his chair and looked at her in disbelief. 'What are you expecting, Miss Muir? I thought it a very fair offer—in the circumstances.'

'What circumstances?' she asked icily.

Benedict was listening closely to their interchange, his eyes narrowed, but other than that no expression at all on his handsome face.

The younger man lifted his shoulders. 'The value of your hotel is not what it was.'

'Why do you say that?'

'It is not as sought after. I think the days of quaint little hotels are numbered.'

'Really?' She turned her attention to Benedict. 'And is that your considered opinion too, Mr Ryal?' Her beautiful deep blue eyes were brilliant.

'The demand for such places in the middle of a busy metropolis is definitely limited,' Ryal answered thoughtfully. 'Your establishment would most certainly benefit from sitting in the heart of the country, and if you accept Simon's offer then you'll be able to——'

'I do not want to move,' cut in Tannice viciously, 'and it may interest you to know that The Grange *was* once surrounded by open countryside. It is not my fault that the area has been developed.'

'I'm not suggesting that it is,' he said, and although his tone was deceptively mild a muscle jerked in his jaw, giving away the fact that he was controlling an inner anger. He obviously did not like the fact that they were getting nowhere with her. 'But times change,' he went on, 'and you should be prepared to move with them.'

Tannice threw him a damning look. 'Maybe if I'd been approached differently, if my father had been approached differently, I might; but as things stand I have made up my mind on this matter and nothing either you or Mr Foxton say will make me change it.'

Simon looked horrified that she was daring to talk to this powerful man in such a manner, but he was as determined as Benedict to make her sell. 'It has come to my notice that your bookings are down,' he said. 'Surely, Miss Muir, that in itself is a perfect indication that your days here are numbered? People are looking for places such as ours with theatres and nightclubs within easy reach, with an all-night service, cable TV, everything geared towards the modern pace of life. You have to agree that you really are out of the running.'

He sounded so patronising that Tannice could have spat in his eye. Her chin came up. 'We have many guests who return year after year because they prefer the homely atmosphere.'

'But they are in the minority,' he retorted confidently. 'You cannot make a living out of nostalgia. My advice would be to sell while you have something worth selling.'

'In other words, your bid is going to go down and down in line with my trade?'

His eyes flickered. 'I will naturally give my offer some further consideration, though I am making no promises. It is already more than generous. And now I think we have taken up enough of your time.' He glanced at Benedict. 'Are you ready to leave, sir?'

Benedict's lips twisted. 'You go ahead, Simon. I wish to talk to Miss Muir.'

Simon frowned, Tannice frowned, but Benedict looked eminently relaxed all of a sudden. 'Nothing to do with business, Simon. I'm not treading on your toes.'

With reluctance the younger man rose and shook Tannice's hand. 'I'll be in touch.' And to Benedict, 'Goodnight, sir.'

'Goodnight, Simon.'

The moment the younger man was out of sight Benedict said softly, 'I'd like to take you out for a meal—for old times' sake.'

Tannice gasped. 'So you do remember me?' And her stupid heart skipped a couple of beats.

'How could I ever forget?' he asked, a cynical smile playing about his lips.

CHAPTER TWO

TANNICE stared at Benedict in shocked bewilderment. 'Why the devil didn't you say anything earlier?'

'Why didn't you?' His deep voice sounded amused.

'Because, if you must know,' she said coolly, her composure regained, 'I thought you'd completely forgotten me and I didn't want to embarrass you.'

He laughed, though it held no real humour. 'Embarrass me? I think you were the one who was feeling disconcerted, Tannice.'

'Why should that be?' she asked haughtily.

'What woman doesn't like to be remembered, especially by her first lover?' There was a deliberate taunting tone to his voice.

'You're a swine,' she grated, blue eyes flashing, 'and I have no wish to spend any more time with you.' She pushed herself furiously to her feet. 'Goodnight, *Mr* Ryal.'

Tannice's wrist was caught in a vice-like grip. 'Sit down,' growled Benedict, 'before you make an exhibition of yourself.'

'If anyone's making an exhibition, it's you,' she hissed savagely.

'All I want is a quiet meal somewhere,' he said, 'for old times' sake.'

'There are no old times I care to remember,' she told him, her eyes cold and condemning on his.

Benedict frowned harshly, as though this was something he had not expected. 'You've changed, Tannice. You were never like that, you——'

'I am older *and* wiser,' she cut in, 'as are we both. Nothing stands still.'

'Nevertheless, I'd like to spend some time with you,' he insisted, 'and if you refuse to let me take you elsewhere then we'll eat here.' He caught the eye of her head waiter and beckoned him across. 'Could you find a table for Miss Muir and myself, please?'

'Certainly, sir,' came the pleasant reply.

In no time at all they were seated in her favourite spot by the window, with a view over her herb and rose-garden—which would soon be no more if Simon Foxton had his way. The thought brought a nasty taste to her mouth.

'I really don't see the point in any of this,' she told Benedict testily.

'Relax, Tannice.' It was evident he was deriving a perverted form of pleasure out of the situation. 'Forget the reason I'm here, forget you're the proprietor of this establishment—we're just old friends about to enjoy a meal together.'

'Old friends?' she echoed tartly. 'Friends like you I can do without.' She picked up the leather-bound menu that had been placed in front of her and pretended to study it. Tannice knew the menu upside down, inside out and back to front, but it gave her something to do while she placed her thoughts in order.

There was no doubt that he was still a handsome devil, and most women would fall at his feet like ninepins, but he no longer had the power to stir her feelings; hatred was her uppermost emotion, and the last thing she wanted was to share a meal. How she had let herself be engineered into this situation she did not know. It was a weakness from her past, it had nothing to do with the mature, confident woman she had become. And it was time she did something about it.

She lifted her chin and looked at him coldly, startled to find him watching her, dark eyes narrowed and assessing and entirely unreadable. 'I'm sorry, Benedict, this is a mistake.' She slapped the menu down on the table. 'I do not want to eat with you. I do not, in fact, ever want to see you again. Please do me a favour and leave.'

A frown lashed his brows together, her attitude clearly angering him. 'Such hostility,' he declared, 'simply because we cannot come to an agreement about your hotel.'

'That has nothing to do with it,' she shot back. 'I am sure you know very well what I am talking about.'

Dark eyes widened. 'You're not still holding it against me after all these years because I ended our relationship? Is that really it? You insist you've grown up, that you've changed, and yet you still bear a grudge. It doesn't sound like a very grown-up attitude to me. Or——' and his tone dropped an octave '—could it be that you're—still in love with me?'

Tannice's eyes flashed fire. 'Don't be ridiculous. I hate your guts, if you want to know the truth, but I have no wish to discuss our past relationship. It's over and done with as far as I'm concerned.'

'Then we'll talk about the present,' he said pleasantly. 'Or even what has happened to you in the years between. No ring on your finger, I see. Is there a current boyfriend? Or have you given all that up to concentrate on running this hotel? What has happened to your parents? Have they retired? There is so much to talk about, Tannice. How can you dismiss me?'

'It's very simple,' she declared haughtily. 'We have both forged new lives for ourselves.'

'And because of that we cannot sit down together and have a reasonable conversation. Is that what you are saying?'

It sounded petty, and yet why should she talk to this man when she did not want to? He had hurt her brutally, he had devastated her; why should she be civil and pretend there was nothing wrong? He had been out of her life for eleven years, and she wanted it to stay that way. 'I am saying that I would *prefer* not to talk to you,' she said quietly. 'However, if you insist, there is not much I can do about it.'

He looked at her long and hard. 'Whatever harsh thoughts you are harbouring,' he said eventually, 'I don't think our affair would have lasted. We were too young, too inexperienced to know our own minds.'

'What makes you say that?' At twenty-four he had already been well versed in the opposite sex. Or was this his way of saying that she had been too young and innocent for him?

'I was too intent on making money to devote my full attention to you,' he said. 'However——' a disarming smile softened the harsh contours of his face '—that has now all changed.'

Surely he wasn't hinting that he wanted to take her out again? Tannice was horrified. What a massive male ego he must have if he thought she would agree to such a preposterous suggestion.

'Is there a man in your life at the moment?' he asked.

'No,' she admitted reluctantly.

He leaned slightly towards her, his voice a low growl. 'Then maybe we could get together?'

Tannice glared. 'There is the little matter of feelings—perhaps you've forgotten that?' Out of the corner of her eye she could see Nick, her head waiter, watching them curiously, and she knew that it was imperative she maintain her dignity. She had no wish for her staff to see her exchanging harsh words with this man.

Benedict linked his fingers together and rested his elbows on the table, supporting his chin as he looked at her with a glint of amusement in his eyes. 'What is it that you're saying?'

'Simply that all I feel for you now is hatred. You dismissed me so casually—how can you expect me to feel anything else?'

'There is none of that free love left?' he queried, his eyes hooded and unreadable.

Free love! Was that how he had seen it? 'I never really loved you,' she told him loftily. 'It was infatuation, infatuation for someone older, someone different from the norm. That's all it was. I came to my senses as soon as you were no longer on the scene. In fact, I wondered how I could have been so stupid.'

Muscles clenched in his jaw. 'I'm sorry to hear that, Tannice.' And there was a cutting edge to his tone.

She ignored it, questioning coldly, 'Are you? Somehow I don't think so. I never meant anything to you, did I? You amused yourself at my expense because I had a stupid crush on you.'

'Is that what you think I was doing?' No expression now on his handsome face, but his jaw was still hard.

'Tell me otherwise.'

'I somehow don't think it would make any difference, whatever I say,' he retorted grimly. 'I suggest we order. The pork fillet in pepper sauce sounds good. Do you recommend it?'

'I can recommend everything on the menu,' she answered, equally cool and distant. It looked as though she had no choice but to accept that they were spending the rest of the evening together.

The way he took control was what she had liked about him in the beginning. Now it irked her beyond measure, especially when he signalled to Nick with the merest movement of his head that they were ready to place their order. She had attained a high degree of independence and did not like Benedict Ryal taking over—especially in her own restaurant.

Unwilling to talk about herself or their past relationship, Tannice questioned him during their meal about his success in business, and discovered that apart from his hotel group he also had interests in many of the related industries such as catering and tableware, enabling him to equip and run his establishments extremely profitably.

But inevitably the conversation turned back to themselves. 'I cannot understand why someone as beautiful as you has not been snapped up,' he said.

His dark, powerful eyes were more intent than they had ever been. In fact they were distinctly unnerving. He would have made a good QC, she thought; nothing escaped him. Under that penetrating gaze no one would dare speak anything but the truth.

'When my mother died I helped my father with the hotel, and when he died twelve months ago——' she could not keep the accusation out of her voice '—I took over the running of it altogether. Therefore I haven't had time for relationships.'

He pursed his lips. 'It's a pity I never met your parents. You never even told me that they ran a hotel.'

Tannice shrugged. 'It seemed of no consequence, and in any case I don't think they would have approved of you.' Tannice had never taken Benedict home. Seven years' difference in their ages was nothing now, but when she was seventeen, and a very young seventeen at that—and Benedict a very old twenty-four—her parents would have done their utmost to discourage a relationship, she felt sure.

Attending art college at the time, she had lodged with a friend, coming home only at infrequent weekends, and had, therefore, been able to keep Benedict a secret. A beautiful, magical secret she had thought then; now she was filled with nothing but bitterness.

A frown carved his brow, and he paused with his fork halfway to his mouth. 'Wouldn't have approved? Why do you say that?'

'Because I was their protected, innocent, only daughter,' she told him, 'born quite late in their lives. You were too much of a man of the world, even then.'

'Is that what drew you to me?'

She shrugged. 'It was part of your attraction.' Under that piercing gaze she was compelled to tell the truth.

'Shall I tell you what attracted me to you?'

Tannice felt her heart pound unaccountably, and she put her knife and fork down on the plate. 'If you wish.'

'Your mouth,' he announced. 'It's incredible, and it's infinitely kissable.' And he set his cutlery down too.

She felt surprise. She had always thought her mouth too wide, her lips too full; she could see nothing nice about it. She looked at him sharply.

'Has no man ever told you that before?'

'No,' she admitted with a faint shake of her head.

'But there have been other men in your life?'

'Naturally.' Not for anything would she tell him that they had been few and far between, that most men were interested in her because of the hotel, seeing it as a meal-ticket for life. She was in fact disillusioned with the whole male race in general.

He leaned across the table and to her amazement touched his fingertips to her mouth. 'Then they must have been blind.'

Tannice jerked away. 'Don't do that. Don't touch me.' She had discovered a treacherous weakness and, although she knew that it had nothing to do with the love she had once felt, that it was nothing more than a perhaps not unexpected chemical reaction, she had to dismiss it straight away. She could not, would not, drift back into any sort of relationship with him.

Benedict's lips pursed, his well-marked brows rose, and behind his eyes she saw a flicker of what looked like anger—or it could have been disappointment. 'I'm sorry you feel like that,' he said quietly.

'Surely you don't find it surprising, in the circumstances?' she asked, her tone cool.

'Perhaps I shouldn't,' he agreed.

'Did you know that you would find me here today?' Tannice's question was abrupt as a suspicion formed in her mind. 'Is that why you decided to join Simon Foxton?'

His dark eyes met hers. 'I knew, Tannice.'

Unease stirred her stomach. He had sought her out deliberately, perhaps with the intention of rekindling their love-affair. She found it hard to believe, and if he really thought she would agree he was going to be one disappointed man.

'But, as I said earlier, it is not uncommon for me to sit in on such meetings. Simon Foxton was scheduled for a visit—overdue, in fact.'

'He reminds me of you,' she said bluntly.

Benedict frowned instantly. 'Me?' And she could see that she had confused him.

'Yes, you when you were a young man, channelling your energy and resources in one direction only—to the top—at the expense of those near and dear to you.'

His eyes narrowed. 'You're talking about yourself, of course?'

Tannice shrugged. 'There could have been others, I don't know.'

'And you really think I was like Simon?'

She nodded emphatically. 'Simon doesn't care who he hurts so long as he gets what he wants.'

'And he's hurting you?' Benedict's tone was suddenly sharp.

'Yes, and he hurt my father also.' And because of it he died, she added silently and bitterly. 'Was he trained by you, Benedict? Are his methods a direct result of what you taught him?'

For several long seconds he held her gaze, then said quietly, 'I do not discuss my employees' working methods.'

'Because you know damn well it's the truth,' she retorted strongly. 'Perhaps I ought to let you know that you've a fight on your hands. I have no intention of selling—ever. And if it's spoiling your little scheme, then I'm glad.'

Again he looked at her with that disconcertingly direct way of his. 'Is this some form of revenge, Tannice?' And there was ice in his voice; a muscle jerked in his jaw.

She shook her head and looked at him haughtily. 'I wish it was, it's what you deserve, but unfortunately I didn't know that you were head of KHG.'

'The Grange has been in your family for many years, is that not so, founded by your great-grandfather?'

She inclined her head.

'Therefore your reluctance to give it up is understandable.'

'It's not only that,' she told him vehemently. 'It's the methods your company uses. My father was distinctly harassed, and if you hadn't been here Simon Foxton wouldn't have been so polite to me either.'

'What makes you say that?' he asked sharply.

'It's not the first time I've had dealings with him— though it is the first time we've come face to face. I do not like the man, Benedict.'

'And yet you say he and I are alike—or were alike, when I was his age. You must have changed your way of thinking very dramatically.'

'Indeed I have,' she told him tightly.

'And would you say that I have changed?'

She allowed herself a faint smile. 'It's difficult to make a judgement. You're more mature, obviously, and you have the trappings of wealth and success, but personality-wise I don't know, and I have no wish to find out.'

He looked at her long and hard before finally saying tightly, 'I see,' and after a pause, 'Would you like dessert?'

Tannice shook her head. 'No, thanks.'

'Coffee, then.' And a finger went up to summon a waiter.

His fingers were long, square at the tips and well manicured—as they had been in the past; it was one of the things she had liked about him. Strong hands, hands that had explored her body and turned her insides to jelly. She felt a faint, familiar quiver, banished instantly, but real enough to horrify her. Goodness, what was happening to her hatred?

'What sort of figure were you thinking of?'

Tannice frowned as she dragged her suddenly tortured mind back. 'I'm sorry. What are you talking about?'

'For the hotel.'

Her chin came up. 'I thought Simon was in charge of all that?'

He shrugged. 'He is. It's friendly interest, nothing more.'

Tannice did not believe him. It occurred to her that the whole of tonight could be a set-up. He and Simon had got together. They probably knew she would reject their offer, and he thought he would work on her and find out what her lowest price would be. She loathed him more than ever in that moment.

'I bet it is,' she snapped. 'If you must know, this place is priceless as far as I am concerned. You can offer any amount of your precious millions and I will refuse. By the way, did you make it by the time you were thirty?'

It was his turn to look puzzled.

'Become a millionaire,' she enlightened.

'Ah, that,' he said. 'Do you know, it suddenly didn't seem very important.'

'But you are a millionaire?' she asked, not believing him for one moment.

'Yes,' he said slowly, 'I guess I am; though it's all paper money. Will you change your mind and let me take you out some time?'

'I see no point,' Tannice returned crisply as she poured cream into her coffee. 'If you haven't got the message, I'll make it clear to you right here and now. Whatever we once had going for us is over. I have no feelings for you whatsoever. I do not wish to see you again. I do not wish you to contact me again. I want you to stay right out of my life.'

'It's nice to feel wanted,' he growled, with an attempt at humour, but she could see the glint of steel in his eyes.

He had obviously never been rejected before. She had no doubt that he only had to lift a finger for girls to come running—as she had herself in the old days. They probably chased him whether he wanted it or not, and it went against the grain to be told so bluntly that he had lost his charm.

She sipped her coffee and watched him over the rim of her cup. He drank his black and unsweetened, and his eyes were on her also. 'So this is it, Tannice?'

She nodded.

'There's no chance you'll change your mind?'

She set her cup down. 'Not one, and as we've now finished I see no point in lingering.' She got to her feet and he rose again. 'I would like to say it's been nice seeing you again, Benedict, but it hasn't. There are too many bitter memories.' She held out her hand. 'Goodbye.'

She had never seen his eyes quite so murderously hard, except perhaps on the occasion he had accused her of two-timing him; and when he took her hand it was in a bone-crushing grip. She guessed he was hurting her intentionally.

But when he used the action to pull her close to him, when his mouth claimed hers in a kiss that was deliberately insulting, when his arms tightened around her, she felt raw colour flood her cheeks, and a covert glance around the room revealed that every single member of her staff was watching.

'You swine,' she gritted through her teeth. 'Let me go at once.'

'Only when you promise to see me again.'

'Never,' she hissed.

'Then we will stay here for ever.' And once more his mouth came down on hers.

CHAPTER THREE

TANNICE did not want to fight Benedict in front of her employees, but neither did she want to agree to his request. How, though, could she extricate herself with her dignity intact?

'I'm waiting,' he muttered against her mouth.

Her mind flitted this way and that, seeking a solution, and suddenly it came to her. She would get her own back on Benedict! He would learn that he could not hurt her so thoughtlessly and cruelly and expect to get away with it. And he—the thought was even more pleasing—had unwittingly put the idea into her mind.

Benedict had mentioned revenge. Yes, revenge would be sweetness itself. All the torture and torment he had put her through, all the heartache and suffering, would be well and truly avenged by the time she had finished with him. She relaxed her body and smiled at him. 'Very well, Benedict, you win.'

He looked at her sharply and questioningly.

'I'll come out with you,' she said. 'And don't look so surprised. I know when I'm beaten.' And all too soon he would know it too!

His smile was tinged with triumph as he let her go. 'I'm glad you've come to your senses.'

'You didn't give me much choice,' she retorted acidly.

Still he smiled. 'One way and another it's been a remarkable evening. I'm sorry it's come to such an abrupt end.'

Tannice wasn't; she couldn't wait to get rid of him.

315

'I'll be in touch, Tannice,' he said, taking her hand and pressing his lips to the back of it. 'I'm really looking forward to renewing our—er—friendship.'

She looked around after he had gone, and her staff quickly turned their heads and got on with their work. With her chin held high, Tannice left the room. What had just happened was an unprecedented scene in her life as proprietor of this hotel, and one that would cause a lot of tongues to wag for a long time to come. She only hoped that it did not undermine her authority.

She had always been treated with due respect and deference, despite her age, probably because they had all worked for her father before her, and she wanted it to continue that way. She would do all in her power to prevent any further such embarrassing situations.

Back in her attic suite she took off her jacket, let out a long, disturbed sigh, and flopped on the settee. She felt sapped of energy, as wrung out as a wet dish-cloth— and all because of a man named Benedict Ryal.

What fates had caused their paths to cross again? Had it truly been his plan all along to ask her out? Was that the reason he had joined Simon Foxton? Or was it purely and simply because of the hotel? Of one thing only was she sure—and the thought brought a bittersweet smile to her lips—he had no idea why she had suddenly capitulated.

It would be difficult, she knew, letting him think that she was once more interested in him. It would hurt her immeasurably to pretend emotions she did not feel— emotions he himself had killed stone dead—but it would be worth it in the end.

Her smile widened as she visualised his capitulation. She tasted the sweetness of success as she pictured him declaring his love for her, and gave a hollow laugh as she saw herself throwing it back in his face, as she left him as totally devastated as he had left her. She wanted to break this man, she wanted to destroy him completely.

Eventually Tannice pushed herself up and got ready for bed, already aware of the fact that sleep might prove elusive. If, when she had prepared for her meeting with Simon Foxton, she'd had any inkling that Benedict Ryal would turn up she would have cancelled. Time is a great healer, everyone said, and as the months and years went by it had proved to be the case, but no one had said anything about old wounds reopening.

The hurt and the bitterness had resurrected themselves a hundredfold. She could feel again the intense, physical pain of his rejection—and all because he had wanted to pursue his career!

It made her question why he had bothered with her in the first place. Why he had let her think that he returned her love. Why he had let their relationship go on for as long as it had. Of only one thing was she sure now—this man was most certainly going to get his comeuppance.

Several days went by before Tannice heard from Benedict; she had almost begun to think that he had changed his mind, that he had accepted she wasn't interested, and her relief had been enormous. The telephone call came early on Sunday morning, before she had even got out of bed. 'Tannice, I'm taking you out for the day. I'll be round in an hour.' And that was it. The line went dead.

Hadn't it occurred to him that she might have other plans? she asked herself, full of indignation. That she might have already arranged to go out? Or that she might be short-staffed and needed in the hotel? Didn't he care that he could be upsetting her arrangements? Nevertheless, her heart quickened at the thought that here was a perfect opportunity to spin the first strands of her web.

It was a warm, summer day, a beautiful day in fact, perfect for going to the coast. She wondered whether that was what he had in mind? Or was something more sophisticated his line?

It occurred to her that she did not know Benedict Ryal's tastes any more. He had never been particularly the sort to enjoy a picnic on a rug with the wind blowing through his hair. It would be a waste of time, as far as he was concerned; time could be spent far more profitably. She was amazed, looking back, that he had ever found time for her.

Half a grapefruit and a slice of wholemeal toast was her breakfast, a quick shower afterwards, and then she dressed with care in a blue silk two-piece that perfectly matched the colour of her eyes. Tannice knew she had to look good if her plan was to succeed, and a quiver of excitement ran through her. She was ready well within the hour and Benedict was early.

How he knew there was a back entrance to her apartment, reached by an outside wrought-iron spiral staircase, she did not know, but he turned up there exactly fifty-five minutes later.

No one, but no one ever used this entrance except herself, and Tannice was extremely annoyed as she opened the door. 'Please do me the courtesy of entering through the hotel in future,' she said tightly, all thoughts of being nice to him gone.

Benedict was not in the least perturbed. 'So there is going to be a next time?' he asked, a touch of wry humour curling his lips. 'I thought your sudden capitulation the other night was merely to escape the interested eyes of your staff. I was actually trying to be discreet, coming this way.'

Tannice's sloe-shaped eyes flashed her disdain and she refused to be goaded. 'Where are we going?' She already had her bag slung over her shoulder and had no intention of inviting him in.

'There's no hurry,' he said, his lips quirking, fully aware of her dilemma.

She eyed him stonily. 'Be ready in an hour, you said, and I'm ready.' She stepped out on to the metal grid and closed the door securely behind her, preceding Benedict down the iron staircase.

It was not until she reached the bottom that she saw the car—a beautiful, gleaming, fully restored 1922 Sunbeam sitting in all its elegant glory in the courtyard.

'We're going in this?' Tannice was unable to hide her surprise.

'You don't like it?'

'I love it,' she confessed. 'It's just that it's so unexpected.' Her father had been interested in vintage cars, though he had never owned one. He would have loved to see this standing here in his own back yard.

Benedict opened the door for her and she stepped on to the running board before seating herself on the rich leather upholstery. It was not as comfortable as a modern car but it had an exciting feel, transporting her back to another age. She felt that they ought to be dressed in twenties clothes.

Pleasure in the car had completely worn away her anger, and when he started the engine and they rolled slowly out of the yard she was grinning all over her face.

'You look seventeen again,' he commented appreciatively.

In that moment, Benedict looking at her with

the same heart-melting expression she remembered so vividly from years ago, it was as though the time in between had never been. She was riding high with the man she loved and——

Tannice pulled her thoughts up with a jolt. The man she loved! Not any more. He had taken her heart and then cruelly stamped on it. He had discarded her with no more compunction than he would feel for a spent match. She was out of her mind even to let such a thought take form.

But she had a role to play and, carefully fixing a smile on her lips, she said demurely, 'Thank you, kind sir.'

'It's my pleasure.'

Expecting a fairly long run out in his car, Tannice was startled when he passed between the open gates of an old mansion house just a couple of miles the other side of her home town of Guildford.

She looked at him expectantly.

His answering smile told her nothing.

A little further on, round a sweep in the drive, she was again taken by surprise, for on the lawn in front of the hall sat, not one, but more than two dozen vintage cars: Rolls Royces, Bentleys, Bugattis. A very impressive array. It was obviously a gathering of some sort, and groups of people stood around drinking champagne and nibbling canapés.

'What's this all about?' she asked.

'Our local classic car club's annual get-together,' he answered with some satisfaction. 'I only bought this beauty a couple of years ago. She compares well, don't you think?'

They all looked good to her, all restored to their original condition, all loved and looked after by their owners as if they were new-born babies. How her father would have liked to be here today. The thought caused her smile to fade. She could not help remembering that Benedict's firm was instrumental in her father's death.

'Is something wrong?' he asked, frowning as he saw the shadow cross her face.

She shrugged. 'My father loved old cars.'

'Did he own one?'

'No,' she confessed, 'but it was his ambition.'

'I'm sorry,' said Benedict.

Tannice wondered if he truly was.

'Come, let me introduce you to Janet and Trevor Oliver, very close friends of mine.'

The couple were much older than Benedict, probably in their early fifties, extremely friendly and very interested to learn that she was an ex-girlfriend.

'I have never known Benedict take up with an old girlfriend,' said Janet in her well-modulated tones. 'Usually when he says goodbye he means it.'

Tannice glanced at Benedict and surprised a thoughtful look on his face—it was gone instantly, turned into an easy smile. 'I have to confess that Tannice made a lasting impression on me,' he said.

'And did Benedict make a lasting impression on you?' Janet asked Tannice.

'But of course,' she answered blithely. 'He's impossible to forget.'

Janet laughed. 'You can say that again. He's quite a man, is our Benedict. If I were twenty years younger I'd be after him myself. Trevor and I cannot understand why he has never married. Although——' looking archly at Tannice '—maybe it has suddenly become clear.'

About to refute emphatically the veiled suggestion, Tannice had second thoughts. 'I think it's a little early for that; Benedict and I only met again the other day.' She slanted him a mischievous smile. 'It's been eleven years, Janet, there's nothing between us any more.' But she let the suggestion hang in the air that there could be if he was willing.

And Janet picked up on it happily. 'Maybe there will be something—soon. Have a glass of champagne, my darling, and let me introduce you to a few more of Benedict's friends.'

But Benedict himself had other ideas. 'I refuse to let you monopolise Tannice,' he said firmly. 'She came with me and she's staying with me. See you later, you two.'

As the morning progressed, Tannice gained the impression that she was being shown off. Why, she did not know, but Benedict seemed to be taking much pleasure in introducing her as an old flame. Maybe they all thought the same as Janet, that there had to be something in it. And maybe he knew that was what they were thinking.

Lunch on the lawn began with oysters, followed by smoked salmon, and then strawberries washed down with more champagne, served by pretty young girls in very short skirts. Finally, at about three in the afternoon, the cars, one by one, began to leave—until there were only herself and Benedict left.

'Shouldn't we be making a move also?' she asked nervously.

Although she was the one who was supposed to be pretending to forgive and forget, Benedict had done more than his share. He had shown her off, he had kept his arm about her waist, kissing her frequently, right there in front of the others, and he had given every impression that he wanted their friendship to redevelop also.

'There's no hurry,' he said and, taking her hand, he led her towards the house.

Tannice frowned. 'What are you doing?'

'The day is far from ended.'

'But——'

'But nothing, my dear Tannice. Come inside and let me show you around my home.'

'*Yours*?' she asked in surprise. This was the last thing she had expected.

'One of my homes,' he declared modestly. 'I have a flat in London and a villa in Italy.'

Tannice had no idea that he lived so close and she was not sure that she liked the thought. 'You've certainly come a long way,' she commented drily, and wondered if he would have done so well if he'd married. Maybe he had been right to concentrate on his career. She felt sure he hadn't been short of girlfriends—the best of both worlds, in fact.

The entrance hall was grand and imposing with its marble floor and panelled walls, an elegant, wide curving staircase leading from it. He showed her into each room in turn, proud but not boastful, and Tannice realised that he had lost some of his cocky arrogance of youth.

He was still undoubtedly an arrogant man but it was restrained now. He had made his mark and was content. He had achieved his ambition and could afford to sit back on his laurels. Or could he? Or did he indeed want to?

Tannice thought about the way his company had harassed her father and was now continuing to persecute her; she compared her continued loss of revenue with Benedict's riches, and anger filled her body. He made his living by feeding off people such as herself. If they stood in his way, he had no compunction about hounding them until he got what he wanted. She smiled grimly. It was most definitely time that someone took the wind out of his sails.

'I really think I ought to be getting back,' she said. 'You know what it's like in the hotel trade—there is precious little time off.'

'But you have excellent staff,' he reminded her, a faint frown carving his brow. 'I've seen that for myself.'

'And they're all worried about losing their jobs,' she retorted.

Benedict's brows rose. 'They need not be. We shall need more people when we open.'

'*If* you open, *if* I agree to sell,' she said, but she allowed a faint element of doubt to enter her voice.

He looked at her with a certain amount of speculation. 'I'm sure Simon will come up with a mutually acceptable figure.'

'Maybe,' she said. 'Why don't you take over the negotiations yourself, Benedict, if it's so important to you?'

His expression became enigmatic. 'Because that isn't the way we do things, and I haven't brought you here to talk about business.'

'Then why am I here?' she asked, disappointed he was changing the subject just as she was beginning to enjoy herself.

'Because I want the pleasure of your company.' It was a rough, low growl that unaccountably sent a tingle down her spine. They were standing at the bottom of the magnificent staircase and he touched his finger to her chin, tilting her head so that their eyes met.

Tannice found to her surprise that she could not pull away. Nothing was holding her, she was not playing a part, and yet her eyes looked into his, met the full danger of lethal darkness. His eyes had always had the power to disturb her, but never more so than in this moment.

Alarm bells rang in her head. This wasn't in her plan of things at all. Benedict was the one who had to fall, not herself. She must never give in to any sort of attraction, chemical or otherwise. Everything had to be pretence.

'I've thought of you often over the years, Tannice,' he muttered gruffly.

'Are you saying that you regret we ever parted?' If he had it would make her self-imposed task so much easier.

'No.' He shattered her delusion. 'I did the right thing. There was no place in my life for love. But now that we have met again I would like to see more of you.'

'I'm a very busy person,' she pointed out, panicking a little. Benedict was beginning to take over, whereas she had wanted to be the one in control.

'I thought you said trade was quiet?'

She clenched her teeth. Thanks to him! But she managed a faint smile. 'There are other things to do.'

'But none so demanding that you can't find time for me.' It was not a question but a statement.

She lifted her shoulders in an exaggerated shrug. 'I expect it could be managed.'

He looked pleased, and she thought she saw triumph gleaming in his eyes, though she couldn't be sure; and when his hand closed on her elbow it sent a further flurry of awareness through her limbs. 'Let's go upstairs,' he said.

Although the house was magnificently furnished, each room full of priceless antiques, it lacked the warmth of a family home and Tannice could not help wondering what a man alone wanted with such a place. His apartment in London would have surely been adequate. And a villa in Italy! Such extravagance.

It proved he had more money than he knew what to do with, and when she thought about how difficult and worrying life had become for herself Tannice's resentment boiled over.

Each bedroom had its own private bathroom, the whole house tastefully converted without losing any of its character. 'And this is my room,' he announced, when they came to the very last door.

He pushed it wide for Tannice to enter. The most dominant thing in the whole room was a four-poster bed. It was made from antique panelling and draped with fabric in reds, blues and russets. To her dismay, she could not take her eyes off it.

CHAPTER FOUR

'QUITE something, eh?' Benedict's hand touched Tannice's shoulder.

An electric shock ran through her and she spun round to meet the amusement in his eyes. 'It's big,' she said foolishly. She could think of nothing else to say. Her mind had run amok, transporting herself back to when she was seventeen and her heart belonged to Benedict, imagining the two of them making love beneath the heavy canopy. She grew hot at the very thought.

'And extremely comfortable,' he assured her, smiling slowly as though he knew exactly what was going on in her mind. 'And this is the bathroom.'

Tannice felt faintly embarrassed that he had guessed her thoughts, but when she saw the huge old-fashioned tub on gilded feet she was enraptured anew, able to forget the unwanted feelings that had surged through her body. The extravagant bath sat almost in the middle of the room, complemented with gold fittings, dark blue towels, and blue and russet floor-tiles. It was strong and masculine and suited Benedict to perfection.

'It's very impressive,' she said, turning to leave, alarmed to find him standing so close behind her that she could not move without brushing against that hard-muscled, dangerously virile body. She took a deep breath. 'Is the décor your own choice?'

'Interior designer's,' he acknowledged ruefully, and did not budge an inch.

'Shall we—er—go back downstairs?' she suggested, with a faint smile and the uncomfortable feeling that her heart was going to run riot.

'There's no hurry,' he muttered. 'What perfume is that you're wearing?'

Tannice frowned her surprise at the unexpected question. 'Obsession.'

'Aptly named,' he growled, adding beneath his breath, 'You could quite easily become an obsession with me,' although his tone was so quiet Tannice could not be sure she had heard him correctly. And then, before she could stop him, before she could even anticipate his movements, he pulled her hard against his body, his lips demanding and hungry on hers.

A rush of sensation sped its way through Tannice's veins but she allowed it no freedom. It was imperative that she keep a clear head—which wasn't too difficult in the circumstances. She only had to think of the callous way Benedict had treated her for the old bitterness and resentment to come surging back. His capitulation looked as though it was going to be easier than expected—so long as she kept control.

She wrenched her head away. 'What the devil do you think you're doing?' But she could not free herself from those arms of steel.

'What any man would do in the circumstances,' he muttered.

'Is that why you brought me up here?' she demanded. 'You can't get what you want by normal methods so you're trying emotional blackmail.'

Benedict's eyes narrowed. 'Is that what you think?'

'What do you expect?' she challenged. The trouble was that she had found his kiss exciting, had wanted more rather than less, and even now, as her lips were trembling with anger, her body was reacting treacherously to the perilous strength of him.

And when he kissed her again—even though it was more in the form of punishment for daring to question his motives, even though he ground her lips back against her teeth and his tongue deepened the kiss as it never had in the past—it was like an explosion of fireworks inside her head, an electric impulse that set every part of her body tingling with shock.

And nor could she pull away. It was Benedict himself who finally released her, who looked down with a smile of satisfaction on his face. 'Something tells me you enjoyed that, Tannice Muir, whatever harsh thoughts you might be harbouring.'

She flashed him a savage glance, her breast heaving. 'I saw no point in fighting. If you must know, I feel nothing but contempt for a man who forces a woman against her will.'

He gave a snort of anger and turned away, and they made their way downstairs. In the cool, ordered atmosphere of the drawing-room, where peach-coloured furnishings complemented Edwardian mahogany display cabinets, it was difficult to believe such a scene had taken place. Tannice perched primly on the edge of a rosewood sofa upholstered in silk, and looked down at her unsteady hands.

'I'll arrange for some tea,' said Benedict. 'Will you excuse me for a few minutes?' His voice was perfectly normal, as if nothing out of the ordinary had taken place.

Tannice inclined her head, glad of the respite, but he was back again before she even had time to gather her muddled thoughts, dropping on to the sofa beside her. 'Do you honestly believe that I'm trying to blackmail you?' His knees were almost touching hers.

'Isn't it a logical conclusion?' she asked, wanting desperately to edge away, forcing herself to remain still, feeling again, much to her dismay, a return of the stampeding emotions she had experienced upstairs. How was her plan ever going to work when she felt like this? It seemed to her that there was a very strong danger of her love returning and this was the last thing she wanted.

'I don't see you for over eleven years,' she said explosively, 'and then all of a sudden, when your plans for a new hotel complex reach an impasse, you turn up and try to turn back the clock. It's perfectly obvious to me what you're doing.'

He gave a sudden predatory grin. 'And it's perfectly obvious to me that you're not aware what an irresistibly attractive woman you've become.'

Tannice eyed him warily. It would certainly help her carry out her plan if this was what he really thought, but somehow she could not believe him. Nevertheless she forced a smile. 'If that's a compliment, I thank you.'

At that moment a beautiful blonde walked into the room, wheeling a trolley that held the most exquisite china and a mouth-watering assortment of fancy cakes. She glanced curiously at Tannice.

'This is Melanie, my housekeeper,' Benedict introduced her. 'Melanie, this is Tannice Muir, a very old friend of mine.'

His housekeeper! He had to be kidding. The girl was far too young and beautiful to lock herself away looking after someone's house.

The blonde's eyes were green and slanted like those of a tigress, and the smile she gave Tannice held more than a hint of hostility. Benedict's eyes followed her as she left the room, her bottom swaying seductively in the short black skirt. I'd have to be blind or a fool not to see what is going on here, thought Tannice in disgust.

'Melanie is the daughter of my old housekeeper, who unfortunately is in hospital,' Benedict informed her. 'I don't think Ellen will work again. However, Melanie is extremely efficient and I'd be a fool to get rid of her.'

'Of course,' said Tannice acidly. The girl was on to a good thing; and if she could cook and clean, if she made herself indispensable, then Benedict was hardly likely to let her go.

Tannice's mind flickered back to the four-poster bed and she could not help wondering whether Melanie shared this with him also. The thought surprisingly hurt, and she could not imagine why. What did it matter to her whom he bedded? She hated him, didn't she? Her only interest now was seeing him fall as hard as she had eleven years ago.

'Would you like to play mother?' Benedict's voice broke into her thoughts.

She nodded, admiring the elegantly styled tea-pot as she poured the golden liquid into wafer-thin cups. The cakes were home-made and delicious.

'Melanie has been taught well by her mother,' Benedict said, when she commented. 'In fact, she's good at everything.'

'You're very lucky to have someone like that to fall back on.' Tannice was unaware that acidity had crept into her voice.

A faint smile curved Benedict's lips, but Tannice was busy helping herself to an almond tart and did not notice.

'Extremely lucky,' he agreed. 'But enough about my housekeeper—I'm more interested in you. What do you do in your spare time?'

'What do you mean, spare time?' she enquired bitterly. 'I'm too busy trying to conjure up new business.'

'You know what they say about all work and no play.' Tannice shrugged.

'Or is it because there's no man in your life, no man to take you out and ensure that you have a good time?' He paused a moment for her reaction, but when none was forthcoming he went on, 'Rest assured, that is all a thing of the past. I have two tickets for the theatre tomorrow night. It's the premier performance of *Annie* and tickets are like gold-dust. I'll pick you up at seven-thirty.'

Tannice deeply resented the way he seemed to think she would drop everything in order to go out with him. On the other hand, he was making her plan so much easier. She swallowed hard, smiled faintly and tried to look pleased. 'I'd like that. I tried to get a ticket myself but I understand it's sold out for the whole run. How have you managed to get a spare one?' Or had this been planned all along as well?

'As a matter of fact I only got them yesterday,' he answered. 'A friend found at the last minute that he could not go and I thought——'

'That you could persuade me to go with you?' she cut in coolly. 'That was very presumptuous, Benedict. What if I'd said no?'

'I knew you wouldn't,' he said confidently.

Tannice flashed him an angry glance. 'What are your plans for the rest of the day? Another ride in your amazing car? A trip to the coast? Sunset over the sea?'

His lips quirked. 'Something far more prosaic, I think. We've stood around long enough—we need to use up some energy. Do you work out, Tannice?'

She looked at him warily, wondering exactly what he had in mind now. 'Occasionally,' she admitted. Certainly not on a regular basis, although she knew that Benedict had always been a fitness fanatic. 'What are you suggesting, a jog through the lanes?' She looked down at her high heels and silk two-piece, and then back at him speculatively.

He smiled mysteriously. 'There is something I haven't yet shown you.'

Her brows rose.

'Finish your tea and we'll take a look.'

When he finally escorted her down a flight of steps to what had once been the cellars, she was amazed to see a fully fitted gymnasium. 'You're impressed?' he asked, watching her face.

'I am, as a matter of fact,' she told him.

'Changing-rooms are over there,' he announced casually. 'Sauna and jacuzzi as well, if you're interested. Melanie usually leaves a few freshly laundered leotards at the ready, so I'm sure she won't mind you borrowing one.'

Tannice was not convinced; she had seen the speculative look in the girl's eye when Benedict had introduced them. On the other hand, it all looked very tempting, especially the swimming-pool just visible through a glass partition at the far end.

'Scared, Tannice?' he mocked, seeing her hesitation. 'Scared of revealing too much of your beautiful body?' His eyes boldly appraised her, lingering for far longer than was necessary on the pert thrust of her breasts. 'Don't forget I've seen it all before, my beautiful friend; you hold no secrets for me.'

Which was the awful part about it. This man knew her body almost as intimately as she did herself. She gave a quiet smile. 'Of course not,' and walked over to the changing-room.

Somehow, she thought, as she slipped out of her clothes, he was turning the tables. Instead of her doing all the running, subtly inviting him into her lair, he was taking charge. It made her wonder whether her plan would ever succeed; it also made her equally determined that it should, that it had to, that it would be the only way she would ever get peace of mind. All she had to do was turn everything to her advantage.

There were leotards in all colours, and she finally chose a burnt orange which suited her skin colouring and showed off her narrow waist and long legs to their best advantage. If her plan was to succeed, it was imperative that she looked her best for Benedict at all times.

When she emerged, he had just finished warming up and for a moment Tannice could not take her eyes off him. He had been fit as a young man of twenty-four but now, at thirty-five, he had broadened out and was in his prime. His body was finely honed, stomach hard and flat, legs lithe and muscular, chest powerful. He carried not one ounce of superfluous fat, and just from looking at him her body gave a surge of powerful emotion.

She was appalled that it was happening again and refused to believe that it was desire; it couldn't be, not after the way he had treated her. It wasn't even a chemical reaction; it was repulsion, that's what it was, a sense of loathing, and she had to overcome it; she had to be mistress of her feelings at all times.

His glance was frankly admiring, and when he instructed her on the various pieces of equipment, when he stood so close that they were almost touching—deliberately, she felt sure—she experienced again this same sense of repulsion and wanted to scream at him to get away from her.

Instead she forced herself to smile and respond and pretend that she was enjoying his nearness, though she knew that she must never appear blatantly sexy and inviting. She did not want the whole affair to end up with him simply desiring her; that would be her ultimate destruction. A very discreet approach was needed, and she was thankful now for the veneer of sophistication which running the hotel had given her.

They finished with an energetic swim in the heated pool, Tannice discarding the leotard for one of Melanie's somewhat revealing swimsuits, which was certainly not her own choice. And when Benedict eyed her almost insolently, she felt it proved her need to be ultra-discreet.

There was actually a whole cupboard full of sportswear, and Tannice did wonder whether it all belonged to Melanie or whether Benedict simply liked to be prepared for any eventuality. Perhaps he often brought girls here.

When the thought hurt, this time she dismissed it as pure cattiness. She didn't want him for herself, not as a permanent fixture in her life, so why concern herself about any other girlfriends he might have?

She came into her own where swimming was concerned. Her parents had taught her almost before she could walk. They used to call her their water-baby, and she was in her element now, racing Benedict the length of the pool, never winning but putting up a most creditable performance.

'I didn't know you could swim like that,' he remarked, as they paused for breath at the end of the pool.

'There's a lot you don't know about me,' she said. Their whirlwind affair had been more about physical emotions than anything else, a typical teenage romance—except that Benedict hadn't been a teenager. He had been very mature for his age—which had unfortunately been part of his attraction.

'I think that ought to be rectified,' he growled.

She wasn't looking at him as he spoke, but now she turned her head, her beautiful blue eyes echoing the colour of the tiles surrounding them. She surprised a look of intense desire, gone so immediately that she almost wondered whether she had imagined it, whether it was in her mind because of her earlier thoughts.

And then she recalled the kiss upstairs and his declaration that she could become an obsession with him, and knew that she hadn't. It would be up to her to let him see that a physical affair was not on the agenda, that she wanted a much more serious commitment from him; though how she was going to manage it she had no idea. It had to be done in such a way that he suspected nothing.

'I think,' he went on, and there was a challenge in his eye, 'that we should spend some time together just talking, finding out about each other.'

'You could be right,' she said, smiling with genuine pleasure. This was exactly what she wanted, the perfect start to his path to destruction. 'Our dates were always hurried affairs because you'd got somewhere else to go, someone to see about a job.' Unfortunately she could not stop a hint of criticism entering her voice.

'Things change,' he said dismissively.

'Yes, they do,' she acceded, and he looked at her quickly, surprised that she had for once agreed.

'Then I suggest we start right now.'

But Tannice shook her head and struck off for the other end of the pool.

He reached it before her. 'Why not?'

'Because as soon as I've finished my swim I want to go home. I think I've spent enough time with you today.' She gave him a tantalising smile as she spoke.

'The point is, have you enjoyed it, Tannice?' His eyes were intent on hers, as though her answer was important to him.

She lifted an eyebrow. 'As much as I can enjoy being with a man who's trying to wreck my life.' The words slipped out before she could stop them, and she cursed under her breath.

Benedict's jaw tensed. 'What happens between us business-wise has nothing to do with the private sides of our lives. Surely you're woman enough to separate the two?' His tone was distinctly sharp.

She looked at him coldly, all thoughts of revenge gone for the moment, intent only on fighting this man who was threatening her livelihood. 'You want to raze my hotel to the ground and build one of your featureless monstrosities and I'm supposed to have no feelings; is that what you're saying? I'm supposed to ignore that side of things and resume some sort of a relationship with you?'

A muscle clenched in his jaw. 'Of course you'll feel something, but I'm sure you'll agree that our offer is more than generous.' His eyes were hard on hers, and it was difficult to imagine that a few moments ago they had been filled with desire.

'I wouldn't say that,' she retorted crisply.

Benedict's brow slashed into a frown. 'Suppose you tell me exactly how much you are holding out for.'

She shrugged. 'When you hit the right price I'll tell you.'

A light gleamed in his eyes. 'So you do have a price, after all? All this talk of not selling under any circumstances was no more than a bluff?'

Tannice lifted her shoulders and grimaced. 'Maybe I've begun to see that I'm fighting a losing battle.' Let him think that there was light at the end of the tunnel.

'I'm glad you've come to your senses, Tannice.' His smile now was tinged with triumph. 'I shall make it my personal business to see that you do not lose out.'

Her brows rose dispassionately. 'I thought you never interfered in other people's decisions. I thought Simon Foxton was running this show.'

A flicker of something indiscernible crossed his face. 'If the situation warrants it, then I naturally take more than my usual interest.'

Tannice gave a cynical smile. 'In this instance, it's more than bricks and mortar that you're interested in—is that what you're saying?'

'We go back a long way,' he said, his dark eyes intent upon hers.

'We certainly do,' she agreed, 'but unfortunately all the memories are not happy ones, and I'm not entirely convinced that you'll stop Simon Foxton from harassing me. Business is business, as you once said yourself.' And with that she hauled herself out of the pool and headed for the shower.

Benedict was out in an instant, a heavy hand on her shoulder, spinning her to face him. 'Have you no faith in me, Tannice?' His face was all harsh angles, a fierce light in the blackness of his eyes.

'Faith? After what you did to me?' Her own eyes were openly hostile. 'I don't think I shall ever trust you again, Benedict Ryal.'

He let out a hiss of anger. 'You still think I'm using underhand methods to get what I want? You don't believe that I'm extending the hand of friendship for old times' sake?'

She gave a short laugh. 'Is that what you're doing?' But she also warned herself not to go too far. She could not afford to alienate him altogether.

With a growl of anger, and total unexpectedness, his mouth swooped down to claim hers. Sensation flooded through her limbs, all the old familiar feelings surfacing; but only momentarily. She squashed them immediately, and let all the loathing she felt for this man come to the fore, pummelling her fists against his chest, straining desperately to free herself. Tannice was aware that she could be jeopardising her chances of success, but her own sense of survival had automatically taken over.

When he finally let her go his face was suffused with raw emotion, his whole body rigid, fingers curled into fists at his sides. 'I think it's time I took you home,' he said grimly.

Tannice felt that he was over-reacting, that the occasion did not warrant such mighty anger. Nevertheless, she shot away from him and took a hurried shower. When they left the house, he showed her into a powerful BMW. Was he scorning the Sunbeam in order to accomplish the journey more quickly? she wondered.

He was still tight-lipped and formidable when he dropped her off, and he said nothing about the theatre, merely turning the car in the drive and roaring back the way he had come. Not a word had been spoken between them.

Tannice slept little that night, her mind tortured with thoughts of Benedict and what he was trying to do to her. She had no doubt that his main interest was the hotel, and she was a stepping-stone towards that goal. He probably thought that if he could get her interested in him again, if he could invade her defences, then he had a much greater chance of success. And the fact that she was not as easy to conquer as he had imagined was provoking his anger.

On Monday morning, almost before she had settled into her daily routine, she was surprised when Simon Foxton turned up with his revised offer. Annoyed that he had come to see her without an appointment, she took one look at the typewritten page and told him what he could do with it.

He frowned. 'You'll never get one better.'

'Then I won't sell,' she told him coolly.

His pale eyes narrowed suspiciously. 'Did you discuss this with Benedict Ryal?'

'Why should I,' she asked with some asperity, 'when you are the negotiator?' It crossed her mind that Simon Foxton could be here solely to question her about Benedict Ryal. There was no other reason for him to pay her a visit; he could quite easily have posted his amended offer.

'So what did he want to talk to you about?'

Tannice eyed him frostily. 'I think that is none of your business.'

'You didn't mention me?'

'Is there a reason why we should?' she asked, with raised eyebrows.

He shook his head, lips pursed. 'No particular one. It's just a little odd that he should stay behind like that. Out of character for Mr Ryal. He never mixes business with pleasure.'

'Who's saying it wasn't business?'

He looked startled. 'But you said that——'

'There are other types of business, Mr Foxton.' And let him make of that what he wanted.

'And this is your last word?' he asked. 'You are still refusing to sell?'

'Yes.'

'You'll be sorry.'

Tannice eyed him stonily. 'Is that a threat, Mr Foxton?'

He looked momentarily disconcerted. 'Of course not. But I can't keep upping my price. The way things are going, this place will be worthless before long. It would be in your best interests to accept this final offer.'

She shook her head. 'My answer is still no.'

'Then I'll bid you good-day, Miss Muir. I'm sorry you are refusing to co-operate.'

'Are you?' she asked bluntly. 'Somehow I don't believe that. I still don't think you'll give up.' But he would certainly be in for a shock when Benedict began to interfere—*if* he did! It could of course have been all talk, Benedict's way of trying to get round her. Otherwise, why hadn't he spoken to Simon first thing this morning? Her lips clamped grimly.

She heard nothing from Benedict all day and could not help wondering whether their theatre trip was still on, especially since she had turned down Simon's offer. She got ready just in case, choosing, after much deliberation, an elegant black silk and lace dress with a matching short-sleeved jacket. She did not want him to fault her appearance; she wanted him to be proud to be seen out with her, she wanted him to... A smile replaced her thoughts. Never before in her life had she been so devious, but then, no other man had broken her heart.

At seven-thirty precisely he knocked on the door, and this time Tannice was pleased to note that he entered through the hotel. He looked incredibly handsome in a dark suit and white shirt, and to her dismay she felt an instant, electric response.

She closed her eyes; it was all wrong. How could she possibly feel anything except loathing when he had hurt her so badly? She kept trying to convince herself that it was repulsion, but she knew it wasn't; it was too strong an emotion. What was she going to do?

Her chin lifted. 'So the date's still on?' she enquired coolly, pleased to note that there was no hint of disquiet in her voice.

Benedict's lips quirked as he slowly and insolently looked her up and down. He had evidently got over his anger of the day before. 'Something tells me that you wouldn't have been happy if I hadn't turned up after you'd made such an effort. May I say, my dear Tannice, how enchanting you look, how elegant. More than that— how utterly, utterly desirable.'

'I was simply being prepared,' she retorted, startled by the lavishness of his compliment.

He leaned closer towards her, his breath cool and fresh on her cheek. 'I'm glad to hear it.'

It was a low, nerve-tingling growl, and Tannice felt the heat of his body and an unexpected shudder ran through her. 'I'll get my bag and we'll go,' she said quickly and huskily.

She only had to walk a few steps to pick it up from the table and she didn't expect him to follow; but he did, and suddenly the whole apartment was filled with his presence. Tannice was furious, both with herself and him. She did not want him here, she wanted no reminders of her past to intrude on her present. He had never been in here and she wanted to keep it that way; he was far too dangerous a man. She snatched up her bag and headed back towards the door.

'What's the rush?' he asked, an amused smile on his lips, once again giving the impression that he knew exactly what thoughts were racing through her mind.

'I thought the show started at eight,' she reminded him crisply.

'So it does,' he agreed, 'but it's only a few minutes' drive.'

'And you thought you'd invite yourself into my home; is that it?' she taunted.

The smile disappeared, eyes narrowed. 'You're being particularly disagreeable this evening, Tannice, despite looking like an angel. Is anything wrong?'

'What do you expect,' she snapped, 'when you send your henchman with yet another ridiculous offer? I knew you were lying when you said you would make it your personal business to see that I got no more insults.'

Dark brows snapped together. 'Simon came to see you—today?'

'That's right,' she retorted crisply. 'I wasn't amused.'

'It was without my knowledge, Tannice,' he said harshly.

Her brows lifted. 'And I'm supposed to believe that, am I?'

'Yes.' His tone was resolute. 'I shall have a word with that young man.' He looked extremely fierce as he spoke, and it was with a visible effort that he smiled. 'Let us put this behind us; I want tonight to be an enjoyable occasion.'

I bet you do, thought Tannice, not believing for one minute that he would reprimand Simon Foxton. Hadn't he told her that he had every faith in this man? But she smiled also. 'I'd like to enjoy it too; why don't we—er—pretend that we've just met for the very first time?' Now, why had she suggested that? It could lead to all sorts of complications. But the words were out and it was too late to retract them; already Benedict was grinning wickedly.

'This evening promises to be a much greater success than I'd imagined.'

Don't get carried away, she wanted to tell him, remembering to her shame how eagerly she had revealed her feelings on their first date all those years ago. If he thought it was going to be a re-run, then he was very much mistaken.

His hand on her elbow was possessive as they walked through the hotel, and in his BMW outside sat a liveried chauffeur. 'Is this to impress—on our first date?' she teased, suddenly finding it easy to play the part.

Benedict inclined his head. 'A lady deserves the best treatment,' he said, as he helped her into the car and then slid into the back seat beside her.

The BMW moved silently and effortlessly forward and Tannice could not help thinking how nice it would be if this really was their first date, if he had not crushed and demoralised her, if he wasn't putting on a front just to get what he wanted.

Nevertheless, she was determined to put the past behind her—and lull Ryal into a false sense of security!

CHAPTER FIVE

THE show was every bit as enjoyable as Tannice had hoped, and when Benedict took her hand into his much larger, capable one she surprised herself by not objecting. It was all part and parcel of the game, of course, this pretence that she was renewing her interest in him, but it nevertheless concerned her that she did not have to act very hard.

In fact she found, to her consternation, that it was a pleasurable experience. It felt good after all these years to have a man at her side, and she began to think that it would be nice to have someone like Benedict whom she could depend on. Sometimes the burden of running the hotel single-handed, especially with the problems she was experiencing at the moment, almost became too much for her.

Benedict's dark eyes were on her often, more often than they were on the stage; and occasionally she looked back at him, and each time he enquired whether she was all right, treating her indeed as though she were a brand-new acquaintance.

During the interval they joined the rush for the bar, and then found a corner to sit and have their drinks. He put their glasses down, took her hands into his, and said, 'Now, tell me all about yourself, my new friend.'

Although they were surrounded by people, Tannice was aware of no one but Benedict. She had always found him compelling, but never more so than at that moment.

It both surprised and confused her that she should fall under his spell again when he had hurt her so badly.

She gave a weak smile, feeling the power of those dark eyes, the tingling pressure of his fingers. 'There's not much to tell.' Her voice sounded unnaturally husky. 'I'm twenty-eight, I have one unmarried brother who lives in Manchester and I've been running the family hotel ever since my father died a little over twelve months ago. I did want to be an artist, but when my mother had a fatal road accident my father needed my help. And that's about it. I'm not a very interesting person.'

'On the contrary,' he said. 'I find you most intriguing.' His grip on her hands tightened. 'Not many girls of your age own hotels. I bet you have a whole string of young men vying for your attention.' His powerful eyes held hers and it was impossible to look away.

'Hordes,' she agreed blithely.

'And is there anyone in particular?' He made the question sound as though her answer was important to him, though Tannice knew it was only because of the hotel. The fact that he was paying her so much attention was because of the hotel, the fact that he had asked her out tonight was because of the hotel—everything was primed in that one direction.

Nevertheless, she was suddenly enjoying this game, and mischief danced in her eyes. 'Would I be out with you if there was? Everyone else is after my money; I can see that you are different. As you're already rich, you must be interested in me for myself alone.'

A wolfish grin spread across his face. 'How easily you read me, my beautiful friend,' but his eyes were speculative as they rested on hers. 'Has there ever been anyone special?'

Tannice swallowed, not sure that she liked this un-expected twist. 'Once, yes. But he discarded me for purely mercenary reasons.'

Tension stilled him. 'Not a nice thing to do. Did you love him?'

She shrugged. 'I thought I did at the time. Afterwards I realised it was nothing more than infatuation. He was older than me and different from other boys, and I suppose I just lost my head. I'm wiser now. I would never make such a foolish mistake again.' She deliber-ately put a hard note into her voice.

'If he turned up, would you give him a second chance?'

Tannice shook her head determinedly. 'Absolutely not.'

'Maybe he has changed too?'

'A leopard never changes its spots,' she declared firmly, and at that moment came the announcement that the show would be resuming in five minutes. 'We'd better get back,' she said, finishing the last of her Martini, 'and later you can tell me about yourself. I've never been out with a millionaire before. I want to hear how you made your fortune.'

'It's very boring, really,' he declared, taking her arm so that they did not get separated in the crowd. 'I think you might be disappointed.'

'I'm sure not,' she responded, wondering if he felt this same electric current which attacked her every time he touched her. 'You must have a very exciting lifestyle.'

'A very busy one,' he affirmed, as they slid into their seats.

'No time for romance?'

'None at all.'

'Do you intend to get married one day?'

His eyes were suddenly unreadable. 'It all depends.'

'On what?' she asked, wondering suddenly whether there was anyone special in his life. If there was, it could ruin all her plans.

'On whether the girl I love will be agreeable.'

The girl he loved! So there was someone! And if that was the case, how was she going to persuade him to fall in love with her? All of a sudden, her revenge plan seemed doomed to failure.

She wondered who it was, and what the girl would say if she discovered that he had taken another woman out tonight? He would no doubt pass this evening off as business. Softening up a client in order to make his kill!

The blood froze in Tannice's veins and, as though he sensed her change of mood, he touched her chin with a firm finger and turned her face to his. 'Is something wrong?'

She shook her head and affected a smile. 'Just someone walking over my grave.'

He took her hand and did not let it go for the rest of the performance, his thumb stroking rhythmically and insistently. Confusion reigned in Tannice's mind—one half of her was involuntarily attracted to Benedict, the other more down-to-earth half knew exactly what he was trying to do and revolted at the very thought.

After the show, Benedict's chauffeur drove them home. Tannice had no intention of asking Benedict in but he, it seemed, had other ideas. 'No gentleman would drop a lady off without seeing her safely inside,' he announced firmly.

'You're not staying,' she insisted.

He simply smiled enigmatically and, once in her apartment, once the door had closed behind them, he took her into his arms. 'Do you realise you've been driving me crazy all evening?' he groaned, his mouth capturing hers.

Tannice's first instinct was to push him away, but she knew that to do so would ruin all her groundwork. And how could she, when his touch sparked an instant reaction? Her whole body had become throbbingly, vibrantly alive and, while she acknowledged that he was a bastard and the sooner she brought about his downfall the better, she still could not deny that the chemistry between them was stronger than ever.

His kiss deepened, his tongue exploring the soft moistness of her mouth, taunting and teasing, and his hands on her back urged their bodies together. Tannice felt the full impact of his arousal, and surprised herself with a quick picture image of his four-poster bed and the two of them making love on it. She banished the thought immediately. You hate Benedict, she reminded herself. Don't ever forget that. This is a game, a game of revenge; it must never end with him making love to you.

When one hand slid up from her waist to cup the swell of her breast, when the nub of his thumb stroked a surprisingly taut nipple, she wanted to scream at him to get away, to leave her alone, to stop tormenting her. Instead she allowed the pleasure of the moment to wash over her, even moved her body unconsciously against his.

He groaned and held her so tightly that Tannice felt there was a danger of her breaking in two, and it was many long minutes later before, with what looked like genuine reluctance, he let her go. 'I think we ought to call a halt before things get out of hand,' adding with a wry touch of humour, 'For a first date we've gone far enough.'

Tannice managed a smile, her chest heaving as she fought for control. The power of Benedict's kiss had taken her very much by surprise. 'I think so, too.'

'You're a surprising lady.'

'And you're quite a man.' She was back into her role.

'It's a shame the evening has to come to an end. I'll tell you what, we'll have supper sent up and then——'

'No!' cut in Tannice, alarm making her voice shrill. He was too easy a man to give in to. He had such a powerful, vibrant personality that it was difficult to deny him anything. If he stayed, then they would most definitely end up in bed together—and he would be the winner.

'Very well——' he held up his hand in mock surrender '—but I am most definitely going to take you out again.'

Tannice smiled faintly. 'I'll look forward to that,' she whispered, wondering whether he truly knew the reason for her panic.

It was such a relief when he went. The whole room had taken on a different feeling; she had found it difficult to breathe, to think, to do anything except wonder at this strong, animal response that he had somehow managed to evoke in her.

Now she dragged much-needed air into her tortured lungs, dropped down into a comfortable chair and closed her eyes. It was a mistake, because imprinted on the backs of her eyelids was a picture of Benedict. Tall, sexy, handsome Benedict, devastating Benedict, the first love of her life, the man who had made the biggest impact on her ever.

She had loved him unconditionally and then lost him; she had hated him passionately, and now she...? It surprised her to discover that all the old feelings were still there; all the desire, the excitement, the electric thrill—

but love? How about love? She shook her head. How could she ever love again a man who had dismissed her so casually?

Strangely, during the evening, she had gained the vague impression that Benedict wasn't pretending, that he wasn't trying to cultivate her purely for the sake of the hotel, that perhaps, against his will also, he was attracted to her.

Could it be? It was a totally bewildering situation and, if her suspicion was correct, then ought she to continue with her revenge plan? If the old attraction was still there—for both of them—would she want to hurt him in those circumstances? Would she be hurting herself even more? Her head spun and a very real headache threatened to develop.

It was time for bed, she decided, but even there, relaxing between the cool sheets, she could not stop her muddled thoughts, and she lay awake for long hour after long hour. Perhaps she ought to hold fire on her plan until she found out exactly what Benedict's feelings were? The trouble was, would she want him back even if her love did resurrect itself? Would she ever be able to trust him again?

The following day two dozen red roses arrived, and the same the next day, and the next, until her home began to look like a florist's shop. There was no card with any of them, but Tannice had no doubt they were from Benedict, and she wondered why he hadn't got in touch with her personally.

The hotel was, remarkably, fully booked for the following weekend, much as it had been in the past, and Tannice felt happier than she had for a long time—until, one by one, cancellations began to dribble in; until, in the end, they had no bookings at all.

Tannice was livid—she knew exactly who was to blame. It was clear now that Benedict had tried to lull her into a false sense of security—and he had almost succeeded. He had given her the impression that he had changed, whereas in fact he was still the same cold, unfeeling swine he had always been. Lord, how she loathed him. And she hated herself for weakening, for giving him the benefit of the doubt. How could she have been so foolish?

She tried to telephone him but there was no answer from his house, and KHG's head office told her that he was out of the country and wouldn't be back until the following Monday morning.

Tannice was on the telephone first thing.

'This is a surprise,' said Benedict, when the switchboard put her through, and it sounded like real pleasure in his voice. 'Did you get my flowers?'

'Surprise be damned,' Tannice cried, ignoring his question. 'Only the lowest of the low would kick a person when they're already down.'

A slight pause at the other end. 'Is that supposed to mean something?'

'Of course it damn well does,' she spat. 'You're a scheming, unscrupulous pig, and I——'

'Tannice,' he cut in abruptly, 'there's something very obviously wrong here and I don't know what it is. All I do know is that it cannot be discussed over the telephone. I'll be with you in half an hour.'

'It won't do any good,' she cried, but the line was already dead.

Tannice paced her office until he arrived. She was so uptight that she could not keep a limb still, and the second he walked in she went into the attack. 'If you think tricks like that will work, you're very much mistaken.'

'I have no idea what you're talking about, Tannice,' he said levelly, his dark eyes scouring her face, as if by so doing he could read the harsh thoughts in her mind. 'I would suggest, however, that you sit down and calm yourself and begin at the beginning.'

'The beginning?' she questioned derisively. 'Have you got a few hours to spare?'

He frowned harshly. 'What am I supposed to have done that is so awful?'

'As if you didn't know,' she flung furiously. 'Or is it your henchman who's to blame? Whoever, I hold you entirely responsible, and I shall be seeking compensation for my loss of revenue.'

'Loss of revenue?' There was a sudden stillness about him, his eyes narrowed and watchful. 'How the hell can I be responsible for that?'

'As if you didn't know,' she sneered. 'Every single booking for the weekend was cancelled. Do you think that is coincidence, or do you think someone's been spreading unhealthy lies?'

'And you're accusing me?' It was suddenly his turn to get angry. He seemed to grow in stature, dark eyes fierce on hers, jaw muscles clenched, and he took a step closer so that Tannice could feel the heat from his body. 'Don't you know me any better than that?'

'I think I don't know you at all,' she riposted. Somewhere in the back of her mind she knew that she ought to be afraid of him; there was an almost demonic look in his eyes that did not augur well. Nevertheless, she stood her ground and went on heedlessly, 'You were bad enough in the old days with your obsession for making money, but now you've turned into a monster. Don't you care who you hurt? Whose livelihood you take away?'

In the midst of their heated words, Tannice was appalled to discover that the sexual attraction was still there, the electrifying feeling that refused to go away. Her heart throbbed painfully and her mouth was dry as she stared into those dark, dark eyes.

'*All* of your bookings were cancelled?' he asked, his voice controlled and lethally calm.

She wondered whether he felt the sparks too. 'Every single one,' she told him coldly. 'I was left with an empty hotel. But if you think you're going to persuade me to sell that way, then——'

'Enough!' He held up his hand in an imperative gesture.

Her eyes flashed. 'What do you mean, enough? I'm not going to sit back and let you ruin me. It's unethical and unlawful and I intend seeing my solicitor.'

His eyes smouldered and his hands reached out and gripped her shoulders. 'You have proof that my company is responsible?'

Tannice did not allow her eyes to waver, even though he was hurting, even though she knew that she would have bruises tomorrow where his hard fingers dug into her sensitive skin. 'Not exactly,' she said tightly, 'but I can think of no other reason. It's not as though it's the first time it's happened. Bookings have been going down and down ever since your company first put in a bid, though I must confess I've never been left with a completely empty hotel before. You did well this time, Benedict Ryal, and I assume it was because I rejected your final offer. What's your next step going to be?'

There was such savagery in his face that Tannice almost felt afraid; she probably would have done if she hadn't been so fired up with anger. And then all of a sudden he thrust her from him, so fiercely that she almost lost her balance. 'There is no next step,' he rasped. 'It will never happen again, but I would like to take a look at your books.'

'So that you can check whether the same people have booked into your hotels?' she asked derisively. 'Drop dead, Benedict, they're none of your business.'

'There is obviously some dreadful mistake,' he said, 'and I don't think that losing your temper helps the matter.'

She snorted indelicately. 'I'm supposed to sit back and take it, am I? Let my business fall into the red and then beg you to take it off my hands?'

'Obviously, talking to you while you're in this mood will get me nowhere,' he said grimly. 'It's time I went. I'll see what I can find out and I'll be in touch.'

'In touch?' She almost screamed the words. 'Don't bother, I don't ever want to see you again.' And as for him saying he would see what he could find out, what the hell was that supposed to mean?

The days that followed were some of the most traumatic Tannice had ever spent—apart from the time Benedict had called a brutal end to their relationship. Nothing could ever surpass that. And again she was suffering at his hands! He really did deserve to be taken down a peg or two, made to see that he couldn't have everything he wanted. Was it still possible? Had she lost the chance of revenge by venting her wrath on him now?

Not expecting to see him again, not believing that he would dare show his face, she was taken very much by surprise when he turned up at the hotel a few evenings later.

She was working late in the office, as she had done every night all the week: studying accounts, juggling figures, hating the idea that she might have to get rid of some of her staff—something she was very reluctant to do—when a peremptory knock came on the door. 'Come in,' she called, her smile of welcome fading when she saw Benedict Ryal. 'What do you want?' she asked ungraciously.

As usual his dark eyes were intent upon hers, seeming to penetrate right through to the very core of her.

'If you've come to deny that your company had any part in what happened last weekend, then don't bother,' she told him. 'I wouldn't believe you if you swore on a Bible.'

'That's not why I'm here,' he said levelly.

'Then why?' she demanded.

He walked over to her desk and put his hands on it, leaning forward so that his face was inches from her own. 'We're going out, Tannice.'

He was unbelievable. Did he really intend having another go at winning her over? Did he think she was a fool? Did he think she wasn't aware what game he was playing? Her brows rose disdainfully even while she acknowledged the very essence of his manhood. It was unbelievable how it insisted on manifesting itself at times like this. Except that she knew now that it had nothing to do with love.

'It's not good for you to bury yourself in this office until nine and ten o'clock every night,' he announced.

Tannice frowned, pushing her chair back so that there was more breathing space between them. 'And how would you know that?'

He straightened. 'Your very loyal staff would never let me get past them, no matter how many times I tried. "Miss Muir is busy" was all I got.'

She felt surprise. No one had said anything to her about Benedict Ryal; she wondered why they had taken it upon themselves to keep him away. She had said nothing to them about it being his fault the hotel was virtually empty. Unless somehow they had found out? Whatever, it was credit to them, and would make it even more painful if it became necessary to terminate their employment. 'So how did you manage to get in this evening?' she asked coolly.

'I guess I had to use devious methods.'

She did not ask what they were; she was not interested. 'And what makes you think I'd even entertain going out with you again after what you have done?' Her blue eyes were bright with anger. She knew she was jeopardising any chances she had of getting her own back on him, but in her present mood she did not care.

An enigmatic smile curved the corners of his mouth. 'I'm under no delusion that it will be easy persuading you, but there are certain aspects of our relationship that surely even you cannot deny.' His voice had dropped to a low growl, and as he walked purposefully towards her desk Tannice knew exactly what he was talking about.

But if he thought sex was the answer to everything, then he had another think coming. She was ready for him. The instant he got close enough, her hand struck. And it was eminently satisfying to hear the sharp slap of her palm against his cheek.

CHAPTER SIX

To Tannice's amazement, Benedict gave a deep-throated chuckle. 'What a fiery little kitten you've become.' And it would not have surprised her had he turned the other cheek.

'With just cause,' she riposted.

'Physical contact was all you ever craved in the old days,' he pointed out, his lips quirking, his eyes challenging hers.

Tannice felt warm colour flood her cheeks. 'Thank goodness I've come to my senses.'

'But you cannot deny that there's still a spark of electricity between us?'

More than a spark, thought Tannice, a whole raging current. 'I guess so,' she admitted, 'but that doesn't mean to say that I don't still hate you. Sexual chemistry doesn't mean a thing.'

'How long will it take you to get ready?'

Tannice's chin lifted. The gall of the man! 'I've not said I'll go out with you.'

'But you will.'

His confidence was staggering. 'Do I have any choice?'

'None at all.'

'What had you in mind?' She was intrigued despite herself.

'I've a table booked at Staffords.'

The most expensive restaurant in town! That could do her good since she hadn't been eating properly lately. But...

'I suggest you go and get ready, because I have no intention of leaving this room until you agree.'

Tannice could tell by his tone of voice that Benedict meant what he said. She heaved a sigh and, getting up from her chair, began to cross the room. 'Very well,' she said stiffly. 'I'll try not to be long.'

To her annoyance Benedict followed, and she looked at him crossly over her shoulder. 'You can have a drink in the lounge while you're waiting.'

'And trust that you won't slip out the back way,' he growled.

'I have no intention of doing that,' she told him defensively.

'Even so,' he said with a faint smile, 'I think I'll join you,' and he continued up the stairs behind her.

Once inside her own quarters, Tannice wished she had been more insistent. She had forgotten how easily he filled the place with his presence, and she felt decidedly vulnerable as she stripped and showered, knowing that only a thin wall divided them, knowing that there were no locks on the doors and that if he chose to join her she could not stop him.

She remembered the last time he had been in her apartment, the way he had kissed her and she had responded; and the thought was enough to panic her and she was ready in no time at all.

'I'm impressed,' said Benedict when she re-entered the room. 'Most women I know take an age.'

'Perhaps I want to get the whole evening over quickly,' she retorted, resenting the way he was appraising her body. She wore a silky mauve dress that skimmed her curves and, though not blatantly sexy, was definitely provocative. Tannice herself was unaware of the impression it gave, seeing only that it was not too short or clingy.

'In that case, why did you agree?' he asked, dragging his eyes with reluctance from her high, rounded breasts to her face.

'It seemed easier than arguing,' she retorted.

'You certainly know how to make a man feel good,' he remarked shortly.

'What do you expect after you've virtually bankrupted me?' she flashed.

'Let's not talk about that,' he said.

'Why not?' she tossed back. 'It's a fact—why should we avoid it?'

'I didn't decide to take you out so that we could discuss business.'

'No?' she scoffed. 'What is your idea, then? Are you still trying to soften me up? Did you not get the reaction you expected?'

His lips compressed in obvious anger, his eyes darkly enigmatic. 'I'd prefer not to debate this.'

'Because it doesn't feel good not being top dog, is that it?'

'Tannice!' he declared warningly, his eyes murderously hard.

But she was not to be stopped. 'You still think that I'm fair game, that you only have to——' She was silenced when his mouth clamped hard and mercilessly upon hers, when his arms bound her in a grip of iron.

'That is enough, Tannice,' he muttered harshly against her mouth.

'How can it be enough when——' Again her mouth was imprisoned and this time the kiss went on for ever, his hands feeling the shape of her through the thin material of her dress, rising to her nape and hypnotically stroking.

Tannice felt a quiver of desire run down her spine. 'You're not playing fair,' she protested fiercely. He knew that making love to her like this would cloud her vision.

'Maybe I like playing dirty,' he growled.

'You can say that again,' she hissed.

Benedict stiffened momentarily. 'I'm not talking about the hotel.' And then his lips covered hers again.

It was an utterly irresistible, deeply erotic kiss, torturing every corner of her mouth, and before she knew it Tannice found herself urging her body against the intoxicating maleness of his. It occurred to her that it had never felt this good in the past.

He gave a shuddering groan that vibrated every bone in his body, sliding his mouth down her throat, nudging aside the soft material of her dress—and Tannice could not stop him. A heady, dangerous swirl of desire had taken over, all-powerful, all-consuming, pushing hatred and hostility into total oblivion.

At exactly what moment he slid the dress from her shoulders she had no idea, or when he disposed of her lacy white bra; she was aware only of teeth nibbling her breast, tongue rasping and arousing, of an ache that filled every fibre of her being.

That Benedict too was consumed by an equally potent hunger was very evident. His male arousal was complete, and somewhere in the recesses of Tannice's mind rang the warning bell that if they were not careful, things could really get out of hand.

When he lifted her in his arms and headed towards the bedroom her fear became reality. 'Benedict...' His name was a ragged cry. 'Don't do this.'

'You liked it enough in the past.' He laid her down on the bed, and ripped off his jacket, his powerful black eyes never leaving her face.

'I thought I loved you then.' Despite her protests, Tannice still felt as though she was melting. The hungry desire in his eyes was a dangerous reflection of her own, and it was impossible to think coherently.

'And now?' he asked gutturally, as he wrenched off his tie and tore open his shirt.

Tannice closed her eyes, unable to look at the savage masculinity of his body. She knew what she ought to be doing, she ought to be up off the bed and away, but somehow her limbs felt like lead. 'What do you think?' she asked hoarsely.

'I think that your protests are nothing more than a token.' His shoes, socks and trousers followed hurriedly, and he dropped heavily down beside her. 'The truth is that you cannot help yourself; that you want this as much as I do.' Expert fingers tormented the fullness of her breast. 'The time has come to stop pussy-footing around and give in to our very real needs.'

Her body screamed at him to get away. With space between them, she had begun to think more pragmatically. Would giving in to him help her plan for revenge? Could she revive it? The need to hurt this man as he had hurt her had never been deeper. She wondered if everyone felt like this about a first love who had let them down badly.

If it was pure lust that motivated Benedict, her plan wouldn't work, but if there was a more deep-seated emotion, maybe even the beginnings of love... But how could she tell? He was devious and cunning, and there was no way of knowing what thoughts ran through his mind. Nevertheless, she had to try; she owed it to herself.

Demanding lips claimed hers, and Tannice closed her eyes and let herself be swept along on a tide of desire, her soft, pliant body entwining with Benedict's lean strength.

'It does feel right, the two of us together, doesn't it, Tannice?' he growled roughly against her mouth.

Her throbbing heart felt fit to burst. 'Yes.' The admission was reluctant, dragged from the depths of her soul.

'It's been too long,' he muttered.

Her body ground against his.

'God help me, Tannice, I want you.'

Not, I love you. Not, I want you to love me. Just 'I want you'. Tannice stiffened. She had not realised exactly how much she wanted Benedict to admit that he loved her. Benedict frowned. 'I'm hurting you?'

She shook her head. 'I...' But no words came.

'You're overcome by the speed with which things are developing?'

She closed her eyes and curled into him. 'I want you, too,' she whispered hoarsely. And this, lord help her, was the truth; she wasn't acting, she wasn't lying; her whole body was filled with spiralling, burning desire.

Vaguely, as long seconds ticked away, it began to dawn on Tannice that some of the urgency had gone out of him. She looked across and he was watching her, his eyes hooded, any tell-tale emotion well hidden.

'What is it, Benedict?' Her voice was a husky whisper.

'I think I have my answer.'

She frowned. 'To what?'

'You don't hate me, Tannice.' Perspiration shone across his brow, and a shaking finger touched the outline of her mouth.

She cringed as if he had slapped her. 'So this was all an exercise, was it?' He was playing her at her own game!

'No,' he assured her instantly, gathering her to him yet again, clearly not expecting this reaction from her. 'None of it was planned. All I wanted was to enjoy a leisurely meal, to talk, confide, let you see that we could be friends if you'd learn to trust me.'

'So what happened?' she asked crisply, wanting to believe him, but how could she in the circumstances? Trust! He had one hell of a track record in that direction.

He grimaced. 'It's your own fault; you shouldn't have looked so beautiful, so utterly, utterly desirable. On the other hand, maybe you did me a favour. I suggest we get dressed and go for that meal, after all.'

But Tannice shook her head. 'I'd rather you went, Benedict. I'm not really very hungry.' For his body perhaps, but nothing more. She was tired and confused and wanted to be alone.

Dark brows rose. 'This is a dismissal?' And still his fingers traced the shape of her face, stroked back a strand of damp hair, emotion still shivering along his nerves.

She swallowed hard and nodded. How tempting it was to thrust herself hard against him, to beg him to make love to her. To ask him to stay the night! She was appalled by this last thought and rolled abruptly away from him, standing with her back to the bed, wishing he would move also so that she could grab a sheet and wrap it around her vulnerability.

It seemed an age before he finally got up and, as though he had read her thoughts, he yanked a sheet from the bed and tossed it across to her, pulling on his own clothes with far less haste than he had discarded them.

Not until he was completely dressed did he face her. Had he only known it, every nerve-end in her body was attuned to him. She was filled with raw hunger that would never go away while he was in the room.

'There *will* be a next time, Tannice.' The rasping softness of his tone added an extra edge to her desire.

'I'm not saying we shouldn't see each other again,' she whispered, 'just that I've had enough for tonight.' She needed to think things through. She still intended grasping the opportunity to hurt Benedict as soon as it presented itself; she was in no doubt whatsoever that he was playing games with her, despite the fact that her own feelings were undergoing a dramatic change.

Even business picked up a little, which surprised her, and she wondered whether Benedict had anything to do with it; whether he was having second thoughts about building a new hotel. Somehow she did not think so, and she took the precaution of gathering her staff around her and telling them exactly what the situation was.

'Isn't Benedict Ryal the man behind KHG?' asked Nick, her head waiter-cum-manager—when she wasn't there herself.

Tannice inclined her head. 'I'm afraid so. Was it you who kept him away from me?'

The young man nodded guiltily. 'I thought it was for the best. And I know I'm speaking out of turn, but do you really think you should be seeing so much of him? I don't honestly think he has your best interests at heart.'

'And nor do I have his,' she declared with an enigmatic smile. 'It's all right, Nick, I know what I'm doing.'

And with that he had to be satisfied.

And then suddenly, out of the blue, she had a telephone call. 'Jack Sommerby of Sommerby Developments,' announced a hearty voice. 'I expect you've heard of us.'

'Indeed I have,' she said. They were one of KHG's biggest competitors. 'What can I do for you?'

He came straight to the point. 'I believe your hotel is up for sale. I'd like to make an offer; can I come and see you?'

Tannice hid her shock. 'I'm afraid someone's been feeding you the wrong information, Mr Sommerby. The Grange is not on the market.'

There was a pause at the other end before he went on. 'KHG have made you an offer—isn't that right?'

'Actually, yes,' she admitted, 'but I've told them the same thing. I'm not interested in selling.'

'Which puts them in an unfortunate position, Miss Muir.'

'That's not my problem,' she told him haughtily. 'And I see no point in continuing this conversation.'

'Every one has their price,' he declared. 'I'd like to come and talk it over with you.'

Tannice had taken an instant dislike to Jack Sommerby and had no intention of agreeing to his request. 'I don't think any good would be served by it; my mind is made up. Goodbye, Mr Sommerby,' and she put down the phone.

Ten minutes later it rang again. 'Let's not be hasty, Miss Muir,' came the over-effusive voice. 'Let's meet and discuss this matter in a civilised way.'

Tannice did not feel very civilised where this man was concerned; on the other hand, maybe no harm would be done by speaking to him. He had aroused her curiosity, if nothing else, and it would be interesting to see what sort of a figure he came up with. She might even be able to use it against Benedict. 'I might agree to that,' she said, 'though I'm still determined not to sell; you'd be wasting your time.'

'That's my worry,' he said. 'I could be there for twelve. Will that suit you?'

'I'm afraid not,' she answered, knowing that it might prove difficult to get rid of him. 'How about one, in the new bistro by the theatre?'

'I'll be there,' he answered.

Jack Sommerby was every bit as detestable as Tannice had imagined. Short, tubby, red-faced, beady-eyed, a sweaty handshake—in fact, everything she abominated in a man. He made Benedict look a perfect gentleman.

'I understand you run a very successful business, Miss Muir.'

'Do I?' she asked, with a faint lift of her brows.

'You inherited from your father, is that not right?'

She frowned, not liking the way this man had dug into her private affairs. 'I think that has nothing to do with it.'

'Of course, I apologise.' A few beads of perspiration appeared on his brow. 'I just wanted you to know that I am aware that it is a long-established family business, and as such has a great deal of value to you.'

'More than it's actually worth, is that what you're saying?' she asked sharply.

'Not at all,' he blustered. 'I simply appreciate how you feel.'

'I'm glad to hear it,' she said crisply. 'Tell me, Mr Sommerby, what are your plans for my hotel?'

He looked surprised by her bluntness. 'Plans? What do you mean?'

'I believe KHG are competitors of yours. Would it be in your mind to use the hotel as bargaining power? Perhaps re-selling to them at a much higher price than you hope to pay me? Would you be trying to use me, by any chance?'

'Miss Muir!' he exclaimed, with a great show of indignation. 'I——'

'Or,' she cut in shortly, 'were you thinking about forcing them to sell the rest of their newly acquired properties to you, so that *you* will be the one developing the whole complex? I'm well aware that it will be a very profitable investment, and I'm well aware that I, at the moment, hold the ace card.'

'I didn't realise how astute you were,' he said, mopping his brow with his handkerchief. 'Goodness, it's hot in here.'

'So now you do,' she said sweetly, finishing the last of her soup.

Jack Sommerby had hardly touched his, but he waved the waiter to take it away. 'Not that it matters, of course,' he said.

'You mean you weren't thinking of trying to take advantage of me?' Her blue eyes were alight with devilment.

'Not at all, Miss Muir.' He strove to look offended. 'I intend making you a very fair offer.'

'And that is?' she asked coolly.

The figure he gave her was a little over Simon Foxton's last offer, and it surprised Tannice that he was offering such a good price to begin with. Perhaps, somehow, he had knowledge of what KHG had quoted; perhaps he knew someone within the company. Perhaps they had a mole! Not that it mattered; she still had no intention of selling.

'You've gone very quiet,' he said.

'It's a most generous offer.'

He looked pleased. 'Then we're in business.'

They had both ordered lamb, and it was now placed in front of them and he attacked his meal with relish. She could see the light of success in his beady little eyes.

'Not exactly, Mr Sommerby.'

His mouth fell as he put down his knife and fork. 'But you said that——'

'I know what I said,' she interjected, 'but that doesn't mean to say that I'm willing to sell.'

'You're standing out for more?' For the first time a harsh note crept into his voice.

'No.' Tannice shook her head firmly. 'As I said on the telephone, The Grange is not for sale, not at any price. I did say you'd be wasting your time. Nevertheless, it's been a most interesting few minutes, most interesting.' She paused for effect before adding, 'And now I think I will leave. I've just discovered I'm not really hungry.' With that she picked up her bag and walked out.

But if she thought that was the end of it, she was mistaken. When she left the hairdresser's the next day, Jack Sommerby was outside. 'Miss Muir,' he said, dropping into step beside her. 'I realised the moment you departed that I shouldn't have insulted you with such a price. I hadn't taken into account the intrinsic value of The Grange.'

'Really?' she asked coolly, wishing it wasn't such a long walk to her car.

He took her elbow in a familiar gesture and, because she did not want to cause a scene in the busy street, Tannice said nothing, merely hurrying her steps. Jack Sommerby hurried with her. 'Therefore I am willing to add a further ten thousand to my offer. How does that strike you?' He sounded confident, as though expecting her to jump at it, as though she would be a fool not to.

Tannice waited until they reached the car park before answering. She actually had her key in the lock when she said, 'I'm sorry, Mr Sommerby, my answer is still no, and I'd appreciate it if you'd take that as final.'

Swiftly she slid into her car, slammed the door, pressed the central locking button—just in case—and drove away. She caught a glimpse of him through her mirror, looking red-faced and furious. Maybe, Tannice thought, she should never have agreed to see him in the first place.

That evening Benedict rang and declared that he wanted to see her, and she was surprised when he took her back to his own house. It was the first time Tannice had been there since the day of the rally, and she could not help feeling faintly apprehensive, especially when she discovered that it was Melanie's night off.

And the fact that Benedict was in a foul mood added to her sense of unease. Was he still angry because she had sent him away the other night? Had he brought her here so that there could be no recurrence, so that she would be completely at his mercy?

'A drink, Tannice?' he asked abruptly, his eyes ice-cold on hers.

'I'd rather know what's troubling you,' she said.

'Would you, now?' He folded his arms across his powerful chest, feet slightly apart, and Tannice did not have to wait long to find out.

'How long have you known Jack Sommerby?'

Tannice's blue eyes widened; this was the last thing she had expected. 'I don't really know him at all.'

'Of course not,' he snarled, white teeth gnashing, his whole bearing one of total disbelief. 'It's pure business between you and him, isn't it? You're selling out to him, aren't you?' He bounced forward and shook her violently. 'Dammit, Tannice, if you've dared to strike a deal with him behind my back, I won't be responsible for my actions.'

CHAPTER SEVEN

'BENEDICT, that's not the way of things at all,' protested Tannice, trying unsuccessfully to shake herself free from his bruising fingers.

'Are you saying he's not interested in The Grange?' Dark eyes glittered dangerously, his body tense.

'No, that's not exactly true, but——'

'Of course it's damn well not true,' he growled. 'I know Jack Sommerby, I know the tactics he uses—and I saw him holding your arm. But if you're thinking of letting that slimy bastard into your bed, then let me give you a word of warning. Jack——'

'I don't need your advice,' she interjected fiercely. 'I'll do whatever I think I have to do, and if that's why you've brought me here than you can jolly well take me straight back home again.'

'Not until you promise that you won't sign any deal without talking it over with me first,' he rasped.

'So that you can increase your offer?' she taunted, hating to acknowledge that her hotel was still of more importance to him than she was.

He abruptly let her go. 'That's unfair.' His eyes were unreadable, no expression at all on his handsome face. It was like a mask, cold and hard and unfeeling.

'Isn't that why you want to know what his figure is?' she asked, chin high, eyes provoking.

'Hell, Tannice, you should know better than that.'

'I'm afraid I don't know better,' she said.

371

'He's an unscrupulous bastard and I should hate you to get tangled with him.'

'Aren't you a teeny bit unscrupulous too?' she enquired.

Benedict shook his head. 'I might be a bastard and I might be ruthless, but unscrupulous—never! I believe in fair deals.'

Tannice felt indignant; *she* certainly hadn't been treated fairly.

'I would never intentionally hurt you, Tannice.'

'You hurt me eleven years ago,' she pointed out.

His mouth twisted wryly. 'My whole attitude to life has changed.'

'Really?'

'Yes, Tannice, really.'

'So what's the current position between you and me?' She kept her blue eyes cool, not letting him see by the merest flicker of an eyelash that—even in the midst of her anguish—all sorts of indecent thoughts were tormenting her mind and body.

Benedict gave a groan that was almost a cry of pain, and in a couple of strides he closed the gap between them and gathered her into his arms. 'I should never have let you go, Tannice,' he muttered hoarsely. 'I was a young, irresponsible fool and I've paid dearly for my foolishness.'

Tannice could not believe what she was hearing. Was he apologising? Did it mean that he had begun to care for her? Was success in her grasp? Was sweet revenge just a hair's breadth away? She was in no doubt that her own feelings were still nothing more than physical desire. There was no chance that she would ever fall in love with him again; he had hurt her once too often.

His mouth came down upon hers, long fingers stroked the soft curve of her breast, and her heart hammered at an alarming rate. 'My love, my beautiful Tannice,' he muttered thickly, 'why have we wasted all this time? Why did I let you go? What an idiot I was. But no more,' he declared hoarsely, 'no more. I love you.' He stunned her with his words. 'I love you from the bottom of my heart. Tannice, my darling, I want you to marry me.'

There was a loud silence between them. This was her big moment, the moment she had rehearsed over and over in her mind; she knew exactly what she was going to say. And even though something in the back of her mind told her that she was making a big mistake, that it would be in her best interests to hold her tongue, she still felt the need to hurt Benedict as cruelly as he had hurt her. She still felt that she could not entirely trust him. It was too much of a coincidence that this declaration of love had come after he had seen her with Jack Sommerby.

She wrenched herself from him and let all her pent-up fury of the last eleven years come to the surface. 'I'm sorry, Benedict,' she stated, chin high, eyes bright, 'but I'm more interested in making money than making love.' They were out, the famous words that she had waited all these years to fling back in his face. Why didn't it feel as good as it should have done? Why did it feel as though she was drowning in an ice-cold lake?

Benedict frowned, the colour draining from his face. 'Tannice, I——'

But she would not listen; she had started this and needed to go on while her nerve still held. 'If you really think I could ever fall back in love with a swine like you, you're a fool,' she thrust coldly. 'It's over between us, Benedict; it's been over for eleven years, and nothing you can say or do will make any difference. This is the end, the very, very end, and I hope you suffer as much as I did. I hope you lie awake at night in misery and despair. I hope you feel wretched for the rest of your life.'

She turned and walked out of the room, slamming the door behind her, tears stinging her eyes. Outside, she leaned against the wall and drew in a ravaged breath, but it was several more long seconds before the truth hit her, before she knew why revenge was not all she had imagined.

She loved Benedict! Despite everything, despite all he had done, despite the way he had treated her, despite him wanting the hotel from her—she loved him. She shook her head; it could not be true. But it was. What she had thought was hatred and bitterness, what she had thought was pure sexual chemistry, was love—pure, unadulterated love. She loved him despite his faults, despite the fact that he had tried to ruin her. She loved him unreservedly.

When the door was abruptly and unexpectedly wrenched open, she spun round to face him. He frowned when he saw the tears. 'What's this?' he asked fiercely.

Tannice swallowed hard and rubbed the tears away with the backs of her hands. 'Nothing.'

'Throwing my love back in my face wasn't as pleasurable as you thought, is that it?' he growled.

'It's not that at all,' she replied, chin jutting; and because she felt the need to defend herself in some way she added, 'I'm just disappointed that you had to resort to a proposal of marriage to get your hands on my hotel.'

He gave a roar of mighty anger. 'Is that what you think it was?'

Tannice hesitated.

'Dammit, woman,' he rasped, 'I'm not in the habit of proposing marriage simply to get my hands on someone's assets. I do have scruples. What I cannot believe is that you had this moment planned all along. Maybe it is I who should be questioning *your* motives. You let me believe that you still felt something for me, that——'

'No, I didn't,' defended Tannice heatedly. 'I've never let you believe that my feelings were anything other than physical.'

'And are you sure now that's all they are?' The question was loaded and the air between them heavy with tension. Tannice knew that if she did not tell him the truth, this really would be the end. Benedict had been her first love, still was, and if the truth were known she wanted him to be her last and only love. She swallowed a lump which felt as big as a golf-ball in her throat, and closed her eyes.

'Well, Tannice, I'm waiting.'

It took her several more seconds to pluck up the courage to answer. 'No, they're more than that. I—I love you, Benedict.' It was the lowest of whispers and he did not hear—either that or he pretended not to.

'I beg your pardon?'

She licked her parched lips. 'I said, I love you.' It was still only a whisper and floated across the silent hallway like a wisp of smoke.

Benedict remained motionless. He certainly did not react as she had expected, and she closed her eyes. She ought never to have said anything. He was trying to humiliate her.

'Do you mean that?'

'Yes,' she said huskily, somehow unable to hide the truth.

'And yet you threw my declaration of love back in my face,' he barked. 'What am I supposed to make of that?'

She grimaced. 'I didn't know I loved you then. I thought it had been killed all those years ago. You hurt me too, Benedict, remember?'

His lips twisted too, and his face went ashen again. 'Only too well,' he groaned, 'but I never thought you would turn the tables as you did. You've grown bitter, Tannice.'

'With just cause, don't you think?'

He took her hands. 'Let us sit down, Tannice. There are things you ought to know.'

She allowed him to lead her back into the sitting-room.

'It was Simon Foxton who tried to put you out of business,' he declared, once they were settled together on one of the over-stuffed sofas. 'I had nothing to do with it.'

'Simon Foxton is your employee,' she pointed out. 'He's surely only following instructions. You cannot make him a scapegoat.'

'I'm not doing that, Tannice, it is the truth,' he said gravely. 'I'd had my suspicions for some time that he wasn't playing exactly by the book, that his working methods weren't entirely honourable. I saw how he was harassing you, and I thought if I gave him enough rope he would hang himself, which he did. I'm sorry if you got hurt in the process, but it was something I had to do.'

'What's happened to him now?' she asked.

'He's left the company,' Benedict announced tersely. 'Gone to join his uncle—Jack Sommerby.'

Tannice gasped. 'So that's how Jack knew how much you were offering me.' And she shook her head in bewilderment. 'They make a good team. Jack Sommerby's a hateful, creepy bastard; he made my skin crawl.'

'So you didn't accept his offer?'

She flung him an offended look. 'What do you think? I told him what he could do with it.'

'And you didn't let him . . . touch you?'

Tannice shuddered. 'Hell, no.'

'Lord, I was jealous, Tannice, when I saw you with him. I almost came and knocked him down right there in the street.'

'I wish you had done,' she said, 'and I also wish you'd let me in on what was going on.'

Benedict grimaced. 'I couldn't afford to take the risk.'

'My father died because of Simon,' she reminded him, her tone acid for a second.

'That's not strictly true, Tannice,' he said, looking sad for a moment.

She frowned. 'What the hell would you know about that?'

'Your father had a serious heart problem,' he told her, taking her hands into his. 'He hid it because he didn't want you to worry.' His dark eyes were sympathetic.

'You're lying.' But it did cross her mind that her father hadn't looked well on several occasions, and he had often had a severe shortage of breath, though she had put that down to the extra weight he was carrying. Whenever she had questioned him about it, he had always said she was imagining things. 'You couldn't possibly know that when I didn't,' she told Benedict now.

'I'm afraid I did,' he said quietly. 'He had a close friend, Phyllis Short—do you remember her?'

'Phyllis? Of course I remember,' she said. She had been delighted that her father had found someone else, had even hoped they might get married. The woman had been distraught when he had died, and had since gone to live with her sister in Cornwall.

'Ellen, Melanie's mother, and Phyllis Short are cousins,' Benedict informed her. 'Both great talkers. Ellen used to tell me all sorts of things.'

Tannice shook her head; did everyone know her father had been ill except herself? 'I still wish he had told me.'

'Darling Tannice.' Benedict took her into his arms. 'I'm here to take care of you now. I love you. I should never have let you go.'

'Have you loved me all these years?' she asked wonderingly.

He grimaced and looked decidedly guilty. 'Maybe I have, but I didn't know it—not until recently. I have to be totally honest—I did try to seduce you simply to get my hands on the hotel. I soon realised it wasn't working, however, that you meant more to me than——'

'Bricks and mortar,' she finished with a smile. 'It's all right, Benedict. I guess we were both devious, and both unsure of our feelings. I'm still not prepared to sell, however. I love The Grange; it's always been a part of my life.'

'I think that's the least important item on the agenda at the moment,' he growled, as he urged her against him. 'Do you honestly and truly love me, Tannice?'

She nodded.

'Unreservedly?'

'Yes,' she whispered.

He groaned and his arms tightened. 'No more harsh thoughts?'

'None.'

'No recriminations?'

'No.'

'Then I will ask you again, my sweet one; will you marry me?'

There was one last question Tannice needed to ask him. 'You mentioned once that there was some other woman you loved, some other woman you intended asking to marry you. What's happened to her?'

Benedict looked confused for a moment and then laughed. 'I was talking about you, my silly idiot. That was the moment I knew that I was in love with you. *Will* you marry me?' His tone grew urgent.

Tannice felt a faint, niggling suspicion that they ought to discuss the question of the hotel first, but she just as quickly thrust it out of her mind. What did it matter so long as she had Benedict? And if he wanted to build his precious hotel complex, was it really such a terrible thing? It was like a ghost street these days, with all the empty buildings on either side of The Grange. The day would come sooner or later when she would have to close down.

'Yes, Benedict, I will marry you,' she said finally.

He let out his breath sharply. Tannice had not even realised he was holding it. And his arms about her tightened. 'I want no regrets, Tannice.'

'There will be none,' she assured him.

His kiss was more powerful, more draining than any he had yet given her. Their first kiss in true love, she thought, and responded with utter abandonment, her body melting into his.

'I don't want to wait,' he said at length, 'not now I've found you again. By the way, who *was* that good-looking guy I saw you with all those years ago?'

Tannice grinned. 'Still jealous? It was my cousin, actually, up on holiday. I was showing him the sights.'

Benedict groaned. 'Your cousin! Why couldn't you have told me?'

'Why couldn't you have believed me when I said I wasn't two-timing you?'

He shook his head. 'Youth hurts, doesn't it? Is everything forgiven now?'

'Absolutely,' she told him. 'And do you forgive me?'

'Unreservedly.'

There was a long silence as they sealed their promise. There was still a lot they had to talk over, Tannice knew, but for the moment this was enough. In Benedict's arms she felt that she had come full circle at last, that this was where she belonged. Forever and ever and ever.

A years supply of Mills & Boon romances — absolutely free!

Would you like to win a years supply of heartwarming and passionate romances? Well, you can and they're FREE! All you have to do is complete the word puzzle below and send it to us by 29th February 1996. The first 5 correct entries picked out of the bag after that date will win a years supply of Mills & Boon romances (six books every month—worth over £100). What could be easier?

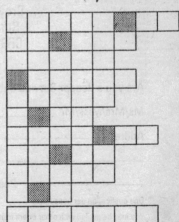

GMWIMSIN

NNSAUT

ACEHB

EMSMUR

ANCOE

DNSA

RTOISTU

THEOL

ATYCH

NSU

MYSTERY DESTINATION

Please turn over for details on how to enter

How to enter

Simply sort out the jumbled letters to make ten words all to do with being on holiday. Enter your answers in the grid, then unscramble the letters in the shaded squares to find out our mystery holiday destination.

After you have completed the word puzzle and found our mystery destination, don't forget to fill in your name and address in the space provided below and return this page in an envelope (you don't need a stamp). Competition ends 29th February 1996.

Mills & Boon Romance Holiday Competition
FREEPOST
P.O. Box 344
Croydon
Surrey
CR9 9EL

Are you a Reader Service Subscriber?   Yes ❏   No ❏

Ms/Mrs/Miss/Mr _____

Address _____

_____

_____ Postcode _____

One application per household.

COMP495
B